Into The

Mystic

**An inescapable passion, a world in chaos...
Their destiny carried them from the ports of Boston
to the warm turquoise waters of the Bahamas**

Amal Guevin

Amal Guevin

Into The Mystic

Daniel Devereaux was the successful, rich, and handsome owner of the Devereaux Fishing fleets in Boston, Massachusetts, with the world at his fingertips... but he was a man drowning in pain. Seduced into marrying the wrong woman, his life was a nightmare until the miraculous day a gentle smile from a beautiful stranger made him want to live again. From that moment, he could not rest until she was his.

Alea Gabrielle was a brilliant orthopedic surgeon from Chicago, dedicated to her work, with no time for love. She never expected to feel the flames of passion that were lit the day she met Daniel Devereaux. But she hid a painful secret, a secret she was too ashamed to reveal, until Daniel.

From childhood Daniel had learned to fish, dive, and surf the sparkling turquoise waters of Spanish Wells, Eleuthera as well as any native Bahamian. He longed to share the wonders of the islands with Alea and took her on an adventure that would ultimately change their lives forever.

While on their honeymoon on his private cruiser, Into The Mystic, the most destructive solar flare in earth's history obliterates electrical power worldwide, flinging life for mankind 40,000 years backwards. Still afloat but powerless on the Atlantic ocean with a hurricane approaching, Into The Mystic drifts to a stunning but curiously uninhabited island where Daniel and Alea must struggle to survive, marooned and alone, until the world of men finds them once more. Little do they know the important role they will play in re-shaping the cruel new age in which they find themselves.

Will the island people of Spanish Wells and Eleuthera be able to adapt to the perilous world threatening not only their lives, but the future of their children as well? Can man's true source of power defeat the forces of evil and oppression?

A Novel of Survival, Hope, and the Power of Love

Amal Guevin

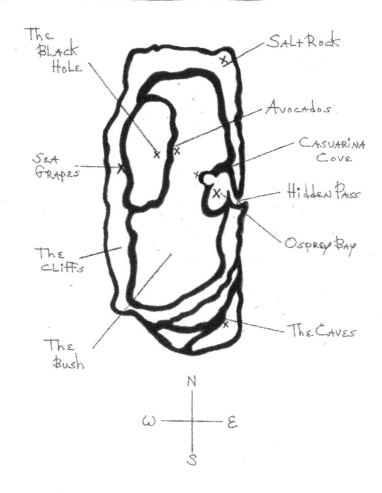

Amal Guevin

Into The Mystic

Copyright © 2020 Amal Guevin

A Speculative Fiction, Romantic, Action & Adventure Novel

Cover Art by Patricia L. Parhad

ISBN: 978-1-0770-4702-0

Amal Guevin

For my husband Dennis,

My Daniel

The definition of strength, patience, tenderness, and understanding, but beyond all... Love.

Come with me now, Into The Mystic!

Table Of Contents

Amal Guevin

Prologue

The sun was dying.

It had been dying since the day it was born, four and a half billion years ago. But the sun still had a long life to live until that time, in another ten billion years, when it would first expand into a glowing planet-engulfing red giant, and finally flicker out as a cold black nebula. Any life that depended on it for survival would disappear forever into the icy void of space. For now, however, the sun was offering a miraculous gift to planet Earth.

Fortunate Earth had been chosen for this gift out of a score of possible celestial candidates. This perfect and delicate balance of distance from the sun, with steady light and heat, enabled the mystery of life to grip and cling to the sea and soil, rising and reproducing in countless forms. The sun's bubbling cauldron of powerful forces governed the patterns of wind and rain, growth and decay, calm and storm, even pulling violently on the planets very core.

For eons, Earth had been constantly bombarded by millions of exploding solar flares of varying strengths and sizes. These erupting flares burst out from the sun's densely packed center of gases and subatomic particles and were released along the strongest magnetic lines at the surface. It remains unclear if the resultant showers of electromagnetic radiation actually affected the development of life on earth itself. That intriguing question may never be answered.

But the spectacular lights of the Aurora Borealis must have given prehistoric man pause for thought, amazement, and a glimmer of divine mysteries as he struggled for survival in the wilderness. They were the only symptom he would ever see of the restless and violent thrashings of the slowly dying sun until the 20th century, when science was surprised to discover that modern man's ultimate destruction had always been right above him... hidden in every sunrise.

From his earliest beginnings, man had relied on the strength and size of his body and his remarkable opposing thumb, coupled with the one other strength that separated him from all other lifeforms.

The power of Abstract Thought.

No matter the highly debated origin, this thought process was a universe-shaking ability. To think about the concept of all trees, not just one tree. To recognize cause and effect. To plan a task. To adapt behavior. To strategize. To create. To problem solve. To form a judgement.

Combined with reason, controlled emotion, and the unique capability to love, a dynamic evolutionary cocktail had been mixed. No other creature on land or sea could boast of this combination of abilities or use them in the myriad of ways man would ultimately achieve.

Fire, stone tools, weapons, the flesh and skins of animals, primitive shelters... these were the methods early man used to translate his mysteriously attained powers into the physical world around him. Survival also hinged on the grace of the sun, the weather, plant and animal food sources, availability of fresh water, the movements and powerful effects of the vast oceans, and the size of man's own population, whether too large or too small.

Failure meant disaster and death. Control meant success of the species. At the very least, control meant the success of a small bonded group. But despite many challenges, man seized the opportunities of his environment to thrive and grow for many hundreds of thousands of years.

It was not until the known calendar time of the early 1800's that the discovery of electricity gradually lured man into a sybaritic lifestyle far removed from anything he had ever before experienced. It was a phenomenal 200-year bonus in the rich 800,000-year history of Homo Sapiens, a bonus that the arrogant human race now took for granted, assuming the world was his to manipulate in whatever manner he desired. His humble beginnings were forgotten or ridiculed.

Television, cell phones, stereos, computers, manufacturing, appliances, utilities, automobiles, boats, airplanes, weapons, medical devices... all electrically-based products and services that, in the year 2019, sustained a weakening and dependent population who bowed down in artificial worship, and was no longer able to care for itself without extensive support from its own creations.

That was all about to change.

On a particularly lovely morning on the Caribbean waters of the Bahamas, the blazing sun was not yet ready to descend into its final death throes. But an unsuspecting, blind-sided, and completely unprepared human race would taste some of the pain of that epic future event they would never live to see.

The destruction that had hidden in every sunrise since the dawn of time was about to reveal to modern man that the control he so egotistically sought could be taken away in an instant of time.

Amal Guevin

Chapter 1   Daniel

Diamond flashes of sunlight danced off the turquoise-blue waves rushing past the bow of the cruiser as it leisurely cut through the serene waters off the west coast of Eleuthera.

Studying the vista ahead, the searching brown eyes of Daniel Devereaux narrowed slightly as he stood at the helm on the flybridge, his dark hair rippling in the light southern breeze. The noonday Bahamian sun radiated with a deep penetrating heat, tempered only by the salty sea air, as he studied the surface waters ahead. He was on casual alert for jagged reef tops that could appear unexpectedly from the 30-foot depths of the sandy bottom of the Bight channel. Even with state-of-the-art navigation systems, Daniel knew that nothing could truly replace the sharp eye and senses of a seasoned sailor.

These were the same hidden coral reef formations that had devastated a thousand ships since Columbus first sailed west to land on San Salvador Island in 1492. As the son of the owner of Devereaux Fishing Incorporated, based in New Bedford and Boston, Massachusetts, Daniel had spent most of his twenty-eight years on the sea. He was well-aware of the potential dangers of even the most beautiful bodies of water from the North Atlantic to the Caribbean.

Fortunately for Daniel, these reefs often concealed their true bounty from the inexperienced. The Caribbean spiny lobster bred in the deep rocky holes and flat ledges of these coral condominiums, seeking shelter from foraging nurse sharks, grouper, and octopus, and feeding on mollusks and bottom vegetation. If a diver was incredibly lucky, dozens of lobsters could on occasion be spotted marching in single file from reef to reef, in response to an ancient and mysterious urge of nature. These forays not only gave Daniel an opportunity to free-dive down to spear an easy dinner, but also allowed him to photograph the remarkable military-style procession that never failed to remind him of the mysteries and wonder of the restless and beautiful ocean he'd loved since he was a child.

Today he was scanning for just such a reef, and for a very special reason. Suddenly, his eyes lit up and he smiled with satisfaction. Powering down the twin inboard diesel engines, he decided to anchor. He had found what he was looking for.

For the last five years, the cold northern winter months of February through April were spent cruising and exploring the Bahamian waters of 700 islands with his childhood friends, Ronny Robello and Matt Kennedy. But this year, Daniel was cruising in the hot summer month of July, which he had only done a few times in his life. And the reason was unbelievably joyful for him. He was filled with feelings of quiet peace and happiness as the boat began to slow.

The beauty of the brilliant blue sky and the scattered white billowing clouds only added to his feelings of happiness when he heard a soft step coming up the stairs behind him from the lower deck. A light lily-scented perfume drifted on the breeze as two slender strong arms circled around his trim waist from behind, pulling him close.

He closed his eyes and smiled. Alea, his new bride, his love, his joy. His miracle.

"Husband," she whispered, turning him halfway around and kissing the corner of his mouth. Not enough, Daniel thought, as he continued the turn and wrapped his arms around her, his hands drifting down to her firm round bottom. He pulled her in tight and claimed her moist pink lips, as his tongue re-discovered her warm and ready mouth.

She gently held the sides of his face as the kiss deepened, their lips tasting each other with an aching hunger that the heat of their honeymoon had not yet been able to satisfy. Her hands dropped slowly to slide along his wide shoulders and strong arms, reveling in his lean but muscular body. She tilted her head up to gaze into his eyes, and they smiled broadly at the same time, as if aware of some delicious secret only the two of them knew.

"That was nice," she whispered. "I thought perhaps you were already getting tired of me." Alea deliberately stepped back and let her white beach robe fall open to reveal a black bikini low on her hips and barely covering her breasts. Her warm hazel eyes flashed, her lips curving into that certain tempting smile he knew only too well. "And we've only been out here on our honeymoon for a week."

"I think I've already shown you quite a few times that I'm definitely not tired of you, wife," he said, pulling her back to his broad chest, then flipping her around and slapping her rear playfully. That'll never happen, he knew. "But if I pass on this very promising dive spot, there'll be no lobster tonight."

"Well, if you put it that way, I'm pretty sure I can wait long enough for something as good as fresh lobster," she quipped, as she peered into the water. "Where's the reef? Can I come along? Haven't had a chance to use my new mask and fins for a few days." She peeked at him from under long dark lashes. "You've kept me rather busy," she said softly, with a shy grin. "I'll get ready and wait for you."

Alea walked back downstairs, letting her white robe fall to the deck and kicking off her flip-flops as Daniel dropped anchor, waiting to make sure the 52-foot cruiser would securely settle with its bow into the breeze. Only then could he relinquish the flybridge and join his new bride down below to prepare for the dive. He peeled his t-shirt over his shoulders and arms, already wearing his favorite blue and white surf trunks, and pulled on a blue long-sleeved rash guard. No need for the warmth of a wetsuit in 88-degree July water. He was confident he could locate at least two lobster in no time. With ten pounds of dive weight, mask, fins, and a 3-pronged pole spear, it was a sure thing. As long as the bugs were there, he knew he would have them.

Alea loved to snorkel, occasionally donning a weight belt to go deeper. But she usually preferred to enjoy the silent film of Daniel slowly sinking below the surface and transitioning from air-breathing man into stealthy ocean hunter, becoming one with the very creatures he sought. Once the wary citizens of the reef began to relax with his suspicious and invasive underwater presence, he was able to target his unfortunate prey, come up for a quick breath, and return to the bottom, almost motionless, to approach and shoot. He did not miss very often.

"Ready babe?" Daniel looked her over to make sure she was safely geared but couldn't help wondering if the lobster was worth it right now. Alea had pulled her dark wavy mass of waist-length hair into a high ponytail and slipped a tight black rash guard over her bikini. Black mask and fins gave her a sleek and slightly dangerous appearance, but her wide and beautiful smile was anything but.

"I'll go first!" she squealed and fell back over the edge of the dive platform.

****

Daniel paused on the platform, surrendering once more to the fascination her smile never failed to elicit. He had fallen in love instantly with that smile almost a year ago. But after that life-altering and landmark day, it took several months before he was able to act on the bewildering realization that he was in love with a woman he had never really met. He was still sorting through the confusing maelstrom of his battered emotions and the ongoing legal actions of his divorce, which prevented him from doing what his heart demanded.

Three years. Three years of his young life beaten down and trampled by a woman who had first lured him as a tantalizing siren, a lovely mermaid, entangling him in her spell, only to finally shed her outer skin and reveal the nightmare inside.

Karen. His ex-wife.

He shuddered involuntarily and pulled his mask over his eyes. That was all in the past, he reminded himself, as he jumped over the edge to follow Alea into the water.

****

Daniel's destiny changed forever on what was undeniably the worst day of his life.

He was alone, walking dejectedly along an empty corridor of Boston Hospital, his thoughts as hopeless and agonized as his heart. The doctor had just updated him on Karen's condition and the police finally concluded their investigation. He felt dead inside. The last few days of turmoil and distress had stretched out until he lost track of time. He could not eat. He could not rest. His parents spent the afternoon with him at the hospital, reluctant to leave, only agreeing when he insisted that he would be okay. But Daniel wasn't certain he would ever be okay. He could never live with Karen again. Not after this.

With his head hanging down and not caring where he was going, Daniel listlessly made his way toward the hospital parking garage. Lost in a dull hazy fog of his own painful thoughts, he was only vaguely aware of the soft hiss of an elevator door sliding open somewhere ahead.

The light fragrant scent of lilies filled the air. Like a sleeper first waking, he lifted his head to see a lone woman walking towards him. A lovely woman. No, he corrected himself, a very beautiful woman. A flowing waterfall of silky dark hair blew behind her as she approached. Her face was fine-boned and delicate, with clear sparkling hazel eyes that had an exotic tilt.

As they drew closer together, their eyes met and locked. She slowed slightly, appearing unsure whether she should stop, as if she thought she recognized him. Unexpectedly, a somewhat quizzical but gentle smile lit her face. Daniel somehow knew she could sense his inner pain, feel his devastated emotions, his bruised and wounded soul as clear to her as through a window of glass. He felt uncomfortably exposed, naked and vulnerable, until an unspoken message of compassion, of solace, of hope, flowed from her beautiful eyes straight into his tortured soul. His heart clutched in his chest.

She shyly ducked her head, uneasy with the intensity of their connection, and continued walking.

He pivoted around to watch her, the back of her white lab coat moving further away from him, her long slim legs with low heels tapping lightly on the bare tile floor. She turned to enter the keycode for a side exit and glanced at him, hesitating once more, perhaps deciding whether to speak. She finally seemed to change her mind but lifted her lovely hazel eyes to meet his own with daring directness. A pulse of powerful energy surged between them, strong and palpable, pulling like an inexorable magnet.

Daniel froze in place, stunned, as her beautiful lush pink lips curved upwards in an uninhibited smile that penetrated his worn and weary heart like a bolt of lightning.

He was reborn in that instant!

His heart picked up its rhythm again, steady and pounding. He wanted this woman. He could not conceive of ever wanting another. He wanted to laugh, to cry, to hold her, to take her in his arms and never let her go. He had to speak!

She startled slightly at his expression and blushed deeply. Looking away from him, their connection broke. She quickly entered the key code, pushed open the door, and was gone.

He stood like a statue in the deserted hallway and blew out a long deep breath he hadn't realized he was holding in. As air returned to his lungs, he felt a wave of wild joy course through his body, struck by an unaccountable burst of belief that his life was no longer hopeless. How had a smile and unspoken message from a lovely stranger done that? He could not lose her. Should he follow? He broke out of his frozen stance and walked over to the door she had entered, but it was locked. He knocked and waited, but no one came. There was no sign that identified where she had gone.

Daniel, he said to himself, what are you doing? He backed away from the door. I'm not sure what just happened here, but I will find her. I must! And I don't even know who she is.

But someday, she will be mine.

His certainty and resolve were ironclad. The strong sense of hope continued to flow through him, as if the brief but intense moment they shared had injected him with a healing serum. All at once, Daniel understood why he was looking forward to the future.

Holding his head high and squaring his shoulders, he strode from the hospital with renewed purpose. As he climbed into his pick-up truck, he understood exactly what he had to do. He started the engine and pulled out of the parking lot. It was time to end his personal nightmare.

****

The memory of her radiant smile returned often over the next few months, as the wheels of his life began to slowly and deliberately roll forward. Before Daniel went back to find her there was still much for him to accomplish and he needed to re-group... and emotionally, he just needed to breathe.

He returned to his work enthusiastically and re-connected with his concerned family, uncloaking the outgoing and happy Daniel they loved and sorely missed. One night at dinner with his friends, he laughed out loud for the first time in three years. Ronny and Matt looked at each other in disbelief, hit a high five, and ordered another round. Daniel was back!

It didn't take very long to get some information about her after several of his business contacts made discreet inquiries. But Daniel continued to bide his time. He was in no hurry. He was a patient man. His complicated life affairs were being handled quickly and quietly by his attorneys and the divorce would be final in four months.

When he was free, he would devote his complete attention, with no distractions, to the dream that was keeping his heart alive. The day he would finally begin the pursuit of a woman he did not even know, but would spend the rest of his life loving.

Chapter 2   Spanish Wells, Eleuthera

Devereaux Fishing Incorporated was able to boast a proud history of over 65 years. Now a multi-million-dollar company, many jobs had been created and tremendous wealth poured into the local economies of Boston and New Bedford. The French-Canadian, Portuguese, Finnish, Scottish, Irish, and Italian fishermen that the company employed were more than able to support their families from the harvest brought in by the boats. Cod, haddock, pollock, flounder, crab, and lobster were the target piscatory populations and continued to be the most popular consumption for many decades, but the longline and net boats also sought the fine dining favorites of tuna and salmon.

Daniel's family could trace their roots back to Quebec and even further back in time to distant relatives from the French provinces of Normandy and Brittany. His grandfather, Lucien Devereaux, started fishing in the 1950's out of New Bedford on Four Winds, a 100-foot side trawler that combed the North Atlantic.

Lucien and his wife Jeanne, who was a seamstress for a small dress shop that catered to the wealthy socialites of New Bedford, worked hard for ten years and painstakingly saved enough to purchase the trawler from the owner when he decided to retire. Lucien became captain of Four Winds and brought on two of his much younger but very good friends to add to the original crew of six.

George Robello was an experienced Portuguese fisherman with a reputation for steady hands and a cool head on the long haul. Shawn Patrick Kennedy was a hard-drinking Irishman with a good heart and the uncanny ability to pilot any boat, anywhere, and in any ocean conditions. With a crew of eight that Lucien trusted, Four Winds became the most productive single side trawler in New Bedford for years. Even bycatch was kept and sold to specialty markets.

James Lucien Devereaux was born on Lucien and Jeanne's third wedding anniversary. His dark brown hair stuck up in tufts and his eyes matched his hair perfectly. His earliest memories were of his father being absent for long periods of time when Four Winds was at sea, but his mother was patient and loving and they formed a close bond. Jeanne made sure he was well-versed in both English and French before he reluctantly started attending St. Joseph's Catholic school.

Each time Lucien came home, James pleaded with him to be allowed to go out on the boat and join the crew. Lucien finally agreed to take James out for a two-week trip when he was nine years old. Although life onboard was coarse, brutal, and cold, James loved it. The crusty but kind crew enjoyed his energy and enthusiasm, which inspired them to see just what he was capable of learning. They were not disappointed. He fought with his parents when the trip was over but they both insisted he continue his studies. He suffered through parochial school until age seventeen, threw his books away, and never looked back. He was promoted to 1st mate on his father's boat by the time he was nineteen.

Devereaux Fishing continued to be successful, a small but growing enterprise. James encouraged his father to expand, and over the course of the next several years they purchased four additional stern trawlers and two lobster boats, hiring experienced local crews, as well as eventually branching out with a second fleet and office in Boston.

As the years passed, the company became the first on the New England coast to begin researching the fledgling science of sustainable fishing, spearheaded by James, who predicted the inevitable future of the industry. The transition would be difficult, but was politically popular with the outspoken and environmentally conscious crowd of the 1980's and 90's.

George Robello and Shawn Kennedy remained with James and the company when Lucien eventually retired many years later, not only as respected employees, but as confidants and friends. George married a local Portuguese girl and she bore him one son, Ronaldo. Shawn's longtime girlfriend, Bridgette Flanagan, gave birth to a son Matthew and two daughters. They never married but stubbornly remained together despite regular and uncomfortable lectures from Father Carmichael, the local parish priest.

James was happy for his friends and their growing families but was completely invested in developing the company with his father. He resigned himself to the fact there never seemed to be time to pursue his own personal happiness.

His loneliness disappeared in an instant on his 25th birthday. James returned to New Bedford just before Christmas after a long, cold, and grueling trip and met Dolores Bouvier. He was captivated by her cascades of black curly hair, mischievous black eyes, pale white skin, and full red lips as she served him cocoa at the church bazaar. Despite heavy resistance from her family that James would never be able to meet their high society standards, Dolores refused to consider any other man, and the wedding took place on her parent's large estate six months after they met.

Daniel Dominic Devereaux was born the only son of James and Dolores. During the first year of their marriage, while pregnant with Daniel, his parents went on vacation and discovered the islands of the Bahamas for warm weather getaways. They fell in love with the people and the location, which was ideal for the family's yearly sailing adventure to escape the cold Massachusetts winter. From the age of one, Daniel, his grandparents, George, Shawn, and their families, spent the months of February through April on the island of Spanish Wells, Eleuthera.

The small island was a short ferry ride from the main island of Eleuthera and boasted famous historical freshwater wells and a bustling winter tourist season. Most importantly, it was the epicenter of a thriving Bahamian lobster industry, a fact that immediately caught James' attention.

But it was the incredibly beautiful white sand beaches along the entire north side of the island that won their hearts. The water remained shallow for a quarter mile out from the beach, blue-green and sparkling against an impossibly brilliant sky filled with pillow white clouds. They would wade out in thigh-deep water in complete safety and watch as schools of small bait fish and large silvery-white bonefish swam the flats, close enough to touch.

Spanish Wells and Russell Island were in close proximity, both stretching east to west off the north tip of Eleuthera, with a deep channel running in between. A 100-foot bridge over the channel connected the two islands, with Spanish Wells sitting north of the larger, less developed Russell Island.

The mile-long channel boasted a bustling harbor front lined with both private and commercial docks, as well as stores and restaurants. Double-decker ferry boats picked up passengers bound for Nassau and dropped off returning residents. Freighters from the U.S. and Nassau delivered goods that were transported over to Eleuthera by ferry, the busy Customs office located directly in front of the freight dock.

Charter boats were readily available for tourists to fish the shallow grassy flats nearby for bonefish. The charters were also within a mile or two of deep-water fishing grounds where marlin, tuna, mahi-mahi, and wahoo could be caught.

Private boat owners tied off their craft to use when they were able. Sailboats and catamarans filled the channel moorings.

Spanish Wells belonged to the sea, depended on the sea.

The lobster boats returned after a week or two hunting the Caribbean waters and the crews offloaded large bags of lobster for shipment all around the world. A food source once largely ignored until the late 1800's, lobster was now the undisputed king of the seafood market, and Spanish Wells was rich from the demand for the succulent and delicate meat.

Colonial-style cottages and homes lined the docks and were situated closely side by side along the narrow streets of the island. Sky blue, pearl pink, lemon yellow; the cottages were proudly painted with the colorful and vibrant hues of the islands. Precious land to build on was at a premium, the neighborhoods tight near the waters of the channel and along the north beaches.

But the people were close as well, everyone knowing their neighbors, with a friendly wave and acknowledgement of each person polite and expected. If a person needed a hand, it was always offered with a smile and perhaps an invite to come over for dinner. With a population of no more than 2000 people between the two islands, it was important for the residents to know who they lived with, who they could trust, who they could rely on.

That's just the way it was done and had been done for over three hundred years. The people were hard-working and industrious, and the lovely island displayed the results of their efforts. Spanish Wells was a jewel of the Caribbean.

There was open acreage on both islands where homes were built in the 1950's on larger plots of land by wealthy investors. Daniel's parents had been interested in buying a home that could house their family and many friends and were fortunate to be offered a rarity. Bonefish Bay was an open, breezy, eight-bedroom beachfront estate nestled on four acres on the north side of the island.

The property uniquely offered a small protected cove facing the sea, deep enough to anchor James' 60-foot sailboat Red Cloud. When not on the island, Red Cloud was kept moored and tended by his good friend Benjamin Knowles, the owner of Knowles Marina, Boat Repair, and Storage, ready for use whenever they came down to Spanish Wells. They also owned an 18-foot center console Boston Whaler for fishing and dive adventures to shallow offshore reefs and some of the cays nearby. The Devil's Backbone and East Egg Reef were two favorite dive sites, rocky graveyards for many ships through the centuries as they approached the island.

From his earliest memories, Daniel's two best friends were Ronny Robello and Matt Kennedy, Daniel being the youngest of the trio. Special arrangements were made with their schools so the boys could accompany the families each winter to the Bahamas. They made up their studies with home schooling and summer school in the states.

They learned to fish, free-dive, and surf the crystal waters of the calm Caribbean and the wilder Atlantic side. James often bragged to friends and clients that his son Daniel was more at home in the ocean than on land and most likely hid gills that appeared as soon as he dove in.

They had full access to any kind of boat they wanted to use, courtesy of his father's friend Ben, and his two sons Gilbert and William, who ran the fish, dive, and sight-seeing charter side of the business. The three boys were almost daily visitors to the marina and repair shop. It didn't take much begging for Gil and Will to start including them as unpaid but enthusiastic deckhands on some of their charter trips for seasonal visitors, where the boys learned tropical inshore and offshore boating and fishing skills.

Gil was the older boy at twenty-one; quiet, serious, tall and lanky, with kind black eyes, black curly hair, and dark cocoa skin, a replica of his father Ben. Will, at nineteen, was more like his English mother, Vernita, with sandy red hair, bright blue eyes, and dusky tan skin. The more adventurous of the two brothers and with the humorous good nature of his mother, he kept everyone around him laughing.

With Ben, Gil, and Will as their guides, the boys learned more about the Bahamas than any tourist would ever know. They traveled between islands, exploring the isolated beaches and small sleepy towns of Exuma, Cat Island, Abaco, Long Island, San Salvador, and the Berries, as well as many of the smaller uninhabited islands like Finley Cay near Nassau and Pimlico Island off Eleuthera. Within just a few years there was no boat, large or small, that all three boys could not run, sail, or repair.

The underwater world became not only their playground, but a school that taught them invaluable lessons about nature and survival. The ocean was a strict and serious instructor, it's beauty often disguising danger. Daniel, Matt, and Ronny were willing students and had the intelligence to accept the risks and rewards along with the adventurous spirit to enjoy every exciting moment. Most important was the lesson of reliance and trust. No one survived the ocean proud and alone. Bonded with each other and with the support of their Bahamian companions, there was no challenge, exploration, or daring escapade they were afraid to attempt.

They hunted for large hogfish which hovered sideways in the bottom grasses, camouflaged by sea fans undulating lazily in the current. Using single or 3-pronged pole spears, they dove for grouper, mutton snapper, and lobster, perfecting the important skills of confident breath control and use of dive weights. They lost their fear of sharks once they discovered that the toothy predators usually only wanted their fish. But they remained watchful and cautious of any shark, especially of the aggressive and unpredictable bull shark. By holding a speared fish out of the water as they swam back to the boat, most of the incentive for a shark to approach a diver was eliminated. The sinister barracuda tailed a diver ominously, hoping for an easy fish dinner, but were usually no problem. They were only a threat when attracted by fast movement or shiny objects.

They learned to spot the large, moss-covered pink shells of conch that blended into the grassy sea floor and to free-dive straight down to pick them up by hand. A few well-placed hits with a machete and some minor surgery with a filet knife would free the rubbery conch from its shell. The meat could then be cleaned, chopped, and mixed with salt, onion, green pepper, and lime juice for a delicious conch salad. Ben would often treat the boys to fresh conch salad made right on the boat.

Gil showed them how to handline from rocky shorelines using pieces of squid or bits of cut-up fish that would lure the local favorites of margate, parrot fish, coneys, and trigger fish. Their palms toughened as they pulled in the thick line with a heavy, struggling fish on the hook. They learned how to scale, gut, clean, and fillet their catch using only seawater as a rinse to maintain firm texture and freshness. The Bahamians loved to eat their fish cooked whole, devouring every meaty tidbit and leaving nothing but a small pile of white bones. Even the head and cheeks were considered a delicacy.

On many of the islands, limestone rock boulders littered the sandy bottom near the shoreline. Some of these rocks were quite tall, having been sheared off the sides of twenty to forty-foot cliff walls by waves and storms over many centuries. Corals took up residence on these huge structures, creating reefs that were endlessly fascinating and full of life, rising from the sea floor like silent sentinels. Schools of black and yellow-striped sergeant majors and colorful angelfish floated in and out of the coral and rock formations. Covered in algae and short grasses, they were the main source of nourishment for the many creatures that depended on the reefs for food and safe haven.

Thousands of small silvery baitfish clouded around the divers underwater, blocking their vision even a few inches ahead. Daniel's arm would stretch to touch, but the restless cloud darted away, just out of reach, before turning back to tantalize again. Large schools of cero mackerel, adolescent jacks, and yellowtail snapper skirted the reef on their quest to spawn, fast enough to avoid even a well-aimed spear.

They learned to understand the power of wind, to observe the pattern and flow of clouds, to calculate the movements of the tide, and to be aware of the phases of the moon and its pull and changeable effects on the inhabitants of the sea. They could predict shifts in the weather and knew when to seek a wind-protected cove or harbor.

Their first surf lesson came from a friendly, middle-aged, bearded local who was sitting in the shade of a large sea grape bush at Surfers Beach, smoking a joint and weary from an early morning surf session. In exchange for a couple of their sandwiches and a coke, he initiated each of them on how to catch and ride a wave on his old Jerry Lopez 6'8" Lightning Bolt thruster. After that day, Ben kept the surfboards the boys brought back from the states on display in his office, ready for their next trip.

The months spent every year in the Bahama Islands were a formative time in their young lives and would mold each of them into unique and special men. They could never guess how important these years would ultimately prove to be.

Ronny Robello was a free spirit, friendly and talkative with a mildly sarcastic but nevertheless hilarious sense of humor. He never hesitated to say exactly what he thought, and was usually right, which only served to inflate his already ample ego. He was tall and slim, with the long lean muscles of an Olympic swimmer. Dark of hair and eyes, with the olive skin of his Portuguese ancestors, he was a fearless thrill-seeker, always the first to suggest pranks or impossible stunts. A born lady's man, he favored girls with blonde hair, long legs, and ample bosoms, but traded them in every few weeks, once his fickle attention had faded.

Matt Kennedy was Ronny's complete opposite in every way. He never spoke much, but when he did, it was with a wry Irish humor that slayed Daniel and Ronny. His deep blue eyes, long red hair, and firm model-toned physique always captured the initial interest of the girls, but he never seemed to keep one for long. Matt's lack of conversational skills eventually drove women away. Daniel was sad that his friend saw no need to be more outgoing, since he knew Matt was very intelligent. But as Matt told him after each break-up, when it was right, it would be forever, and he was willing to wait.

Throughout high school, the boys all worked part-time with James, George, and Shawn at Devereaux Fishing, where they were taught the commercial fishing business, from deck hand to management. Ronny and Matt began fishing full-time after graduation, with Daniel just starting his junior year.

Daniel's grandfather, Lucien, passed away just before he graduated high school and his grandmother Jeanne was in a nursing center battling end stage cancer. James asked if Daniel would work with him for a few years before starting college. As the eventual owner of the company, it would give Daniel the chance to immerse himself in the trade and begin to develop his own ideas for the business in the future. There was no better university than on the job, out on the boats with the crews, and at his father's side for training and experience, which he did for three years.

Impatient to move Devereaux Fishing into the 21st century, he finally decided to attend Boston University and complete a Master's in Business. He met Karen there his senior year. By the time he was twenty-eight his marriage was in shambles, but he was prepared to assume complete control of Devereaux Fishing when his father was ready to retire.

Alea Gabrielle was about to step into his life.

Chapter 3 Alea

On a cold January morning just after New Year's Day, three months after he first saw the lovely dark-haired stranger in the corridor, he unexpectedly found himself back at Boston Hospital.

Matt Kennedy had been airlifted that morning from one of the Devereaux lobster boats at sea in the Atlantic. Massive swells had caused a large lobster trap to break loose, ramming into his left lower leg with a resulting loud snap, the fall causing his head to slam the deck. It took the Coast Guard forty-five minutes in high winds to reach the boat and he was flown immediately to Boston Hospital, where an orthopedic surgeon was waiting on stand-by. Matt's father Shawn, his mother Bridgette, and Daniel sped to the emergency room entrance, arriving just as the helicopter touched down on the rooftop landing pad.

For the next several hours they waited anxiously. A steady stream of family, friends, and Devereaux staff came and went, offering words of comfort. There was much discussion of how the accident had occurred, a rarity for the attentive and safety-conscious company. Daniel's parents, James and Dolores, sat with Matt's family to offer their support and groups of people were scattered around the room waiting for news of his condition. He had been in surgery for several hours and concern was growing. Radio reports from the captain revealed that white bones had been seen protruding out of the severely fractured leg as the coast guard prepared Matt for departure. They prayed he would not lose his leg.

Daniel sat somewhat apart from the others with his eyes closed, in anguish. Matt may not have been very talkative, but he'd been a solid and faithful friend since childhood. There was no need for him to go out with the crew on that trip. Although he handled most of the radio communication and computer data between the main office in Boston and the boats at sea, he loved the thrill of danger, the hard work, and hanging out with his friends. The ocean was his real home and he lived in Boston Harbor on an old, re-fitted 45-foot trawler, alone and content. He had gladly volunteered to take the place of a crewman who was ill and was now suffering for a careless accident that never should have happened. As one of the owners of Devereaux Fishing, Daniel was responsible for the safety of the men and the boats. He was angry that someone had obviously not done their job and he would investigate this one personally.

But he couldn't help remembering the last time he was at Boston Hospital and the miserable events of his life he was still doggedly trying to put behind him. Unhappy memories flooded him and threatened to overcome, until the doors to the waiting room swept apart. The delicate fragrance of lilies filled the room.

Daniel's eyes startled open. A bolt of electricity shot through him and he quickly turned his head toward the flowery scent. Standing in the doorway was the raven-haired beauty who had so mysteriously touched his heart, then quietly disappeared. She was looking at him too, with a slightly puzzled expression. A moment later, recognition lit her face and she dazzled Daniel with a slow smile. He immediately stood up, his eyes never leaving her, blood pounding like a hammer in his ears. He noticed her blue scrubs and name tag before she turned to the rest of the room. His decision was instant and his personal timetable to meet her jumped forward by a month.

"I'm Dr. Alea Gabrielle, the surgeon who operated on Matt Kennedy. Are you all family members?" she asked softly, glancing around the room at each person. Everyone in the waiting room stood up.

Shawn Kennedy extended his hand. "Sure, I'm Matt's dad and, yes, everyone here is considered his family. How is my son, doctor?" They crowded around her, not only anxious for news about Matt, but amazed that such a beautiful young woman was the instrument of his healing. Dr. Gabrielle laughed and stepped in closer to the group. She placed a gentle hand on Shawn's arm. It was obvious that Matt was his son, with their matching dark red hair and blue eyes.

"The operation went quite well, Mr. Kennedy. He sustained complete but clean breaks of both his left tibia and fibula in the lower leg, which have been set and pinned, and internal bleeding has been stopped. I have Matt on medications to prevent infection, as well as for pain. The fall also caused a concussion, which Dr. Sudbury will discuss with you next, as his neurologist. He's in the recovery room but you can see him soon," she said, with a smile and an amused glance at all the people in the room, "but perhaps just one or two of you for now. Tomorrow might be better for more visitors when he is fully awake. It will take some time before he can walk without aides, but he's young and should return to normal activities eventually."

Shawn breathed a sigh of relief and Bridgette grasped the doctor's hand in silent thanks, tears flowing down her cheeks. Voices began to fill the room as friends and family said their relieved goodbyes for the night. Dr. Gabrielle continued to speak quietly to Bridgette, glancing over at Daniel who was still standing near his chair, his eyes never leaving her. As the waiting room began to clear, for some reason she couldn't bring herself to move on, even with the dozens of things she needed to handle.

I remember him well, she thought, that heartbreakingly sad man in the hallway looking so lost. I could feel his pain. There had been something about him... She felt herself blush as she remembered the surprising rush of attraction that caught her off-guard. She'd been so cautious for over three years, never allowing herself to get too close to any man again. Not after Chicago. She just wanted to work and forget everything in the operating room, her ultimate comfort zone. She first saw this man several months ago for less than five minutes. How could she feel drawn to a stranger? Impossible. But it was hard to deny the pull she felt. She thought about him for days until she firmly steeled herself to stop, never imagining she would ever see him again. But there he was, standing a few feet away.

She studied him out of the corner of her eye even as she spoke with the others. Yes, very handsome. He was tall, well over six feet. His thick mane of dark brown hair was wavy, parted on one side and brushed back, trimmed to his ears and the nape of his neck. His eyes matched his hair, glowing with warm caramel highlights. His skin was a ruddy tan, obviously from outdoor exposure, and his body was perfectly muscled, not too heavy and not too lean. He reminded her of a majestic young lion. His shoulders were broad with strongly defined arms and forearms. She shivered as she imagined those powerful arms around her. What? Where did that come from?

But it was his face that fascinated her. Not just the chiseled jaw, wide mouth with generous firm lips, aristocratic nose, brooding brows, and high cheekbones. It was his eyes, she pondered, amazed at her own growing responses to his steady gaze, which radiated with the intensity of a laser of light straight into her soul. The protective emotional shell she had so studiously built cracked like an egg. His dark eyes held her spellbound. She could not look away.

There was satisfaction on his face, as if he had finally found a long lost and valuable treasure. He stood quietly, his arms crossed but with one hand to his chin, index finger running back and forth across his lips. A hint of a smile curved his mouth, inviting her, beckoning her to come to him. The magnetism was undeniable. She couldn't help wondering how kissing those incredible lips would feel.

Suddenly unsure of herself, Alea looked away. I'm not being very professional, she thought, I don't even know this man. He must be someone from Matt Kennedy's family. But she could not ignore the sweet burst of heat that permeated her body, unwanted as it was, and long unfamiliar. Her legs began to tremble. Flustered, she forced her attention back to Matt's parents.

"Here is my card. Please feel free to call my office if you have any further questions and I will get back to you. Matt should do well and either I or my physician assistant, Joe Delaney, will always be available to you at any time."

She started to leave, but stopped. He made no overt move, but willed her to turn back to him, his silent call echoing in her heart, and as their eyes met, the flame ignited between them.

She sensed a vibration around her, as if the air itself was dancing in the space between them. She gasped slightly, her moist pink lips opening in surprise. He smiled, one side of his mouth cocking upwards, his gaze daring her closer.

The room began to spin. She felt faint and was afraid she would fall to the floor right there in front of him. It was then he moved quickly to her side. How did he know? She felt a firm hand under her elbow, his warm breath in her ear.

"Come with me."

****

Ignoring the startled look from his parents, Daniel led her out of the waiting room. With one hand supporting her elbow and the other possessively placed at the small of her back, he guided her down the hall until he spotted a small conference room and led her inside.

Alea followed as if floating on a cloud. What am I doing? She allowed him to propel her as if she were a puppet as the door closed behind them, muffling all sound from the hallway. The spinning sensation began to subside. She gathered herself and turned to face him, wondering at her own lack of fear and again astonished by the molten heat in her core. She was close enough to breath his intoxicating warm male scent.

He stood quietly, releasing his arm from around her waist, but left his hand supporting her elbow. He made no gesture that gave her cause for alarm but remained near.

"Who are you?" she whispered. She did not pull away.

Marveling at her beauty, Daniel touched her cheek, then lifted both of her hands in his own.

"You know me, don't you, Alea Gabrielle?" He drew her closer and his arms reached around to encircle her waist gently.

"I'm the man you're going to marry."

He didn't give her time to protest as he quickly pulled her tight against him, slowly and deliberately lowering his lips to hers. He reveled in her sweet delicate taste as he deepened his kiss and heard the sharp intake of her breath under his mouth, as Alea finally understood she was being passionately kissed by a man she barely knew but did not fear. She was instantly stricken by the truth. She wanted this man's kiss! She wanted this man! She could feel his desire, the firmness of his chest against her breasts, the heat of his thighs, his arms capturing her. Throwing reason and common sense to the wind, she threw her arms around his neck and pressed her body into him with a fierce passion she thought had been burned out of her long ago.

His kiss seared her, marking her, claiming her. His tongue leisurely sought her depths and she opened for him willingly. This stranger was reaching deep inside, re-igniting the very desires she had fought for years to suppress, disintegrating hard-won emotional boundaries, pulling them down one by one with passionate intensity and primal male heat. In his arms she was no longer only a surgeon. She was his woman. He was her man.

She knew instinctively she could trust him. How this was possible she was unable to dissect or logically explain, but she knew it would forever be the truth of her life.

Daniel lifted his lips from hers, her cheek resting against his, his voice in her ear.

"My name is Daniel Devereaux and I'm in love with you."

****

Alea walked into Café Francais at eight that evening. The lighting was dim and the subdued hum of the restaurant was relaxing. Decorated in luxuriant hues of burgundy, gold, and warm chocolate brown, the well-appointed room suited the high-end clientele who dined late. The tantalizing aroma of fresh baguettes, aromatic pates, garlic escargot, and pungent cheeses filled the air, a soothing retreat to conclude stress-filled days of high finance, politics, and legal intrigue.

Alea had never been here.

She had agreed to meet Daniel after her surgeries and duties at the hospital were done. She finished discussing her patients with her physician assistant, Joe Delaney, when she casually mentioned she had a dinner date that evening. His expression of unbelief told her everything she suspected, and if she'd been wavering about going, Joe's expression ended her debate. It was Friday night and she was not on call for the weekend. The memory of Daniel's kiss still burned her lips. She needed to know if what she felt was real or not.

He had held her quietly as their breathing slowed, his heart-stopping words filling her with overwhelming joy. But there were patients waiting, orders to be signed. Alea didn't want to leave him but knew she must, and slowly stepped back out of his embrace. He instantly released her.

"Alea, can you meet me for dinner tonight? We need to talk. Café Francais? Eight o'clock?" He didn't push. He was moving much faster than his self-imposed timeframe, unable to wait even a moment longer when he saw her that morning. It was now her choice.

"I can be there. I do want to talk. This is almost too much for me," she said, her hands trembling. "I would like to know more about you, Daniel Devereaux." She laughed shyly. "It's not as if something like this happens to me every day."

He covered her delicate trembling hands with his own and her shaking instantly subsided.

"All I can say is this. I have felt deeply for you since the first day I saw you. I can't explain it, Alea. I planned on introducing myself to you at some point soon, but the moment I saw you today, I couldn't help myself." He smiled and gently drew her back to him.

"You know, there are mysteries that defy explanation and I think this qualifies." He lifted her hands to his lips and kissed them almost reverently.

"You do need to know I am in the process of a divorce that should be final in one month. If this is an issue for you, I will walk away right now. But please know this." He pulled her in close and tipped her lovely face up to look at him.

"I will love you forever, no matter what you choose."

****

Alea slipped off her black cashmere coat and let it fall behind her shoulders as Daniel appreciated the enchanting vision before him. She preferred not to check her coat. Café Francais was pleasant, but January in Boston chilled her to the bone.

She had gone home to shower and change before leaving to meet him, the steaming water clearing her head and calming her nerves. She washed her hair and allowed it to air-dry as she worked it into a cascade of flowing waves with her fingers. Liking the effect, she decided to wear her hair down, held off her face with two gold clips.

Alea stared at her naked body in the full-length mirror of her bathroom suite. What would he be expecting? She hadn't been in a relationship with a man for three years and that one time, her only time, ended as a dreadful disaster. Would a man like Daniel understand? Or perhaps he'd prefer a more worldly and experienced woman? The thought made her cringe and her confidence fell. How could she tell him what happened? If they ever made it that far...

She applied her make-up carefully, enhancing her cat-like hazel eyes with dark liner and mascara. She chose a deeper rose lipstick than she was usually comfortable wearing and went into her bedroom to decide on her clothing.

After much consideration, she selected a black form-fitting dress that ended just above her knees, with a sweetheart neckline and cap sleeves. Her large high breasts would not need a bra. She pulled on black lace panties and sheer black stockings with a garter belt. She kept her favorite signature diamond stud earrings but added a gold necklace with a teardrop diamond that her parents gifted her with when she left Chicago. The gold and diamond tennis bracelet she had bought for herself on a whim. Black silk pumps with 3-inch heels completed her ensemble.

She hadn't been this dressed up since high school prom.

Daniel's eyebrows lifted when he saw her arrive and pause at the entrance to the restaurant, where he was waiting. She was stunning! He approached at once and took her hands, struggling to conceal his desire.

He chose to greet her with just a light kiss on the cheek, but his eyes flashed with emotion. Alea returned his kiss and waited. They did not speak as they stood face to face. He encircled her waist with his arm possessively as he guided her to their cozy corner table. Her understated elegance and dark beauty drew the immediate attention of every man in the room, conversations pausing briefly, appreciative male eyes following them as he pulled out her chair to seat her.

She watched as he sat down across from her. He looked incredibly handsome in tailored light-grey dress slacks with leather dress shoes, a pale-blue button shirt with a midnight blue and silver tie, and medium grey jacket. His hair was still slightly damp from his shower and he brushed a stray lock off his forehead. It was difficult not to stare, but he was gorgeous! Was she feeling simple animal attraction? Or was there more to this?

The candle in the crystal table sconce flickered softly, casting shadows that emphasized his strong chiseled jaw and high cheekbones. The caramel highlights in his expressive brown eyes danced, a private secret pleasure obviously on his mind.

"You look so lovely, Alea." He leaned towards her, stretching out his hand between them, and waited.

Alea looked at his hand, palm up and relaxed against the white linen tablecloth, his expression calm and accepting of any way she would go. What was her heart telling her? That impetuous organ had fooled her once before and there had been plenty of time to think, to choose, before starting that doomed relationship. She silently contemplated his face, accepting the glass of ruby red cabernet the waiter placed in front of her. His hand remained waiting, his face patient, his eyes lit with a fire from within. She tapped her finger on the table as she made her decision.

It just felt right, he felt so right. She breathed a silent prayer as she took his hand in hers.

"You know, Daniel, there are mysteries that defy explanation and I think this qualifies."

They burst out laughing at the same time.

****

The delicate wine, the thick filets with a buttery sauce, and the velvety chocolate mousse were delicious. Alea sat back in her comfortable chair, more relaxed than she had been in years, taking a final sip of her after-dinner liqueur. She glanced around the room and noticed that the wait staff was cleaning and preparing to close for the night. How late was it? She had completely lost track of time, captivated by Daniel's wonderfully entertaining conversation. She'd laughed more this evening than she could remember since leaving Chicago, catching herself drifting off into pleasant fantasies that had nothing to do with dinner, as the deep rich timber of his voice lulled her. Whenever they were not eating, he kept her hand tucked firmly in his own. She felt incredibly cherished.

He was delightful. Warm and intelligent with a great sense of humor, he told her enough about his life to enable Alea to piece together a picture of his personality and character. He even shared the much abbreviated, he said, story of his first marriage. There are always two sides, she reminded herself, but at one point excused herself to recover in the restroom. Her heart swelled with sorrow and she now understood the broken man she passed in that empty hospital corridor. Her instincts had been correct. Perhaps, she thought, she should be paying closer attention to those instincts tonight. It was becoming unbearable to think of never seeing him again.

Daniel paid the check and helped her into her coat. He took his time; draping it around her shoulders, helping her arms to slip into the long sleeves, lifting her silky hair to waterfall out onto the soft black cashmere. She could smell his enticing subtle male spice, feel his breath on her cheek. She quivered when his hand inadvertently brushed the side of her breast as he buttoned her coat against the cold winter night.

When done, he lowered his arms to his side and waited, his eyes telegraphing all she needed to see, what she longed for him to ask. A wave of uncertainty threatened, but she choked it back. She was done with the past. This man was her future. She believed that now.

She nodded; her answer clear.

He reached out to pull her close, touching his lips to her hair. There was no turning back. He took her hand and led her into the night.

Chapter 4   The Five Senses

Daniel followed her black Mercedes in his gray Toyota pick-up as they drove to Alea's downtown condominium. The gated underground parking garage was considerably warmer than the freezing Boston night. Alea tapped in her private code for the elevator and they walked inside to begin the ride up to the top floor of the 12-story building. Unable to wait any longer, he turned her around to face him and pulled her close.

Pressing her gently against the glass elevator wall, he melted her with a soft lingering kiss that did not end until the elevator doors hissed quietly open. Her lips parted in surrender and she sweetly returned his embrace. Reluctantly parting, they stepped out into the two-story garden solarium that separated Alea's unit from her only other neighbor. Daniel was briefly distracted by what he saw.

Despite brisk winter winds, snow, and thick ice covering the buildings outside, the solarium was warm, filled with tropical plants and flowers. Small birds darted among the trees, having access points to the outside if they chose, but much preferring the green environment within. The garden was serene, with cushioned benches and low wooden tables for sitting, reading, or quiet contemplation. Alea often came out with a cup of coffee to enjoy the solitude and privacy of her oasis in the city. Floor to ceiling windows bordered the glass roof of the solarium on the north and south sides of the building, with the glass elevator positioned in the center of the north wall. Alea's condominium took up the entire east side, with her neighbor to the west.

She keyed in her front door entry code, finding it difficult to concentrate as Daniel lightly kissed the back of her neck. The dark mahogany double doors swung wide automatically.

He escorted her inside, pausing momentarily in the foyer to absorb the simple grandeur of Alea's home.

An expansive and open living, dining, and kitchen area was centered on the main floor, with an office and powder room off to the right and a library on the left. Patio doors from the kitchen opened out to an inviting summer deck and gazebo. A graceful curved staircase led to a spacious master bedroom suite over the library, with a wide balcony that overlooked the living room. A second staircase on the opposite side led to a guest bedroom suite. Towering glass windows reached up to the second level, allowing an unobstructed view of downtown Boston and out towards the Cape.

She had decorated in a clean modern theme but included large comfortable soft suede couches and carefully selected eclectic furniture pieces that gave warm character to the rooms. She chose a unique and tasteful color palette of golden amber, salmon pink, shades of brown, and pale celery green. Impressive artwork accented the ivory textured walls and the mahogany floors reflected a soft sheen.

Daniel walked over to the tall natural rock gas fireplace in the living room, kneeled down, and ignited the flames. Timed evening lights were already glowing on low and the room was cozy and inviting.

Alea stood hesitantly in the middle of the foyer. The firelight began to flicker and dance as he stood and turned, instantly noting her discomfort.

"Do you need some time to freshen up, Alea? I can wait for you here in the living room," he suggested. Daniel didn't want her to feel pressured. They were here, they were together. He would have been content to just hold her, but he was hoping for so much more.

"I think I'd like that. I won't be long. The bar is over there, if you'd like a cocktail." She walked to the staircase, taking off her coat as she went. He watched her slim shapely legs ascend to her bedroom and disappear.

He removed his coat and suit jacket, loosened his tie, and unbuttoned his shirt collar. Stepping over to the well-stocked bar, he poured two vodkas straight, found the mini-fridge, and added ice and a twist of lime. He set them on the coffee table in front of the fireplace and relaxed back on the couch. It was only a few minutes before Alea rejoined him, still in her black dress and heels from dinner.

She sat down next to him on the couch, looking anxious, her fingers clasping and unclasping nervously. He captured one hand and held it tenderly. She picked up her drink and took a sip. He leaned in to kiss her, but she shook her head.

"Daniel, I haven't been completely honest with you."

"In what way?" he asked casually. He was very curious but refused to allow her hand to escape his warm grasp.

"I've never made love to a man before."

****

At twenty-eight years old, Daniel was no stranger to women. His first sexual encounter was at age fifteen, a girl he met on the beach in Exuma. Since that time, he'd dated many women, with one disastrous marriage. But he never expected a woman in her twenties, beautiful, intelligent, and a doctor, to tell him she'd never been with a man. Certainly not his lovely Alea.

He said nothing but would not release her as he realized how her revelation made him feel.

He was delighted!

She sat frozen, staring down at the floor, her face a bright pink. Why was he still sitting next to her? Shouldn't he be walking out the door, on his way to find a partner who could claim normal sexual experiences, a partner who at least knew what to do? Although logically she knew there was nothing to be embarrassed about, she couldn't help feeling ashamed and self-conscious. Intellectually she could quote textbooks about sex, but as a woman, she wouldn't even know where to start.

Daniel slid closer and put his arm reassuringly around her shoulders. She inhaled his warm clean scent, his dark chest hair visible at the top of his unbuttoned shirt. She fell into his strong embrace, unable to prevent the tears from slipping down her cheeks. He stroked her hair lightly, as if comforting a child. There was nothing that would ever keep him from wanting her in his life.

"Alea, my sweet darling, I would be honored, if tonight, you would allow me to be the fortunate man who makes love to you for your first time."

****

They sat on the thick soft carpet in front of the fire nursing their aperitif as she grew quiet, the secret of her past finally told, the burden lifted from her heart. She softly blew out a sigh of relief as Daniel gazed thoughtfully into the flames of the fire. She laid her head on his firm thigh, emotionally spent, as he caressed her shoulder.

He hurt for her. Hot anger filled him for the fool who had put her through such torment, pain, and humiliation, who almost ruined her promising career as a surgeon. But tonight, he would not allow her past to come between him and the woman he treasured. Not after she had chosen to bare her soul, risking her heart and her self-esteem to share the long-hidden story. His love flared to even deeper depths and he would have done anything to protect her from harm.

Daniel wanted to be her refuge, her solace, her comfort. He wanted her to feel free to safely abandon herself with him and never fear again. She had been violated once, but she did not yet know the joy of being loved by someone who really cared.

She would know tonight. But he needed to carefully woo her, or she might frighten too easily. He considered his possible approach and smiled at the idea that came to him.

"Alea, you're a doctor. Tell me, what are the five basic human senses?"

She sat up with a puzzled expression. "Well, taste, touch, sound, smell, and vision. What an odd question."

"I think it's time for you to go back to school."

She laughed, tilting her head questioningly.

"Are you willing to do whatever I suggest?" He smiled at her raised eyebrow. "I can promise you will enjoy it," he teased, his voice dropping low.

Alea was intrigued. This wonderful and sensitive man drew her like no other. It wasn't just his looks, although for the life of her she'd never seen anyone more attractive. No, it was his spirit that spoke directly to her spirit in a mystical way she couldn't comprehend. It was as if God had designed a man just for her, the perfect complement to all she was, a man that made her feel safe, whole, accepted, and loved. Was he what people called a soulmate?

"Alright, Daniel. I will. I will because I feel I can trust you."

"Most important question then..." He watched her closely.

"Do you want me to make love to you?"

She was taken aback but liked his approach. Direct, honest. He'd been nothing but totally real with her, shockingly so, but real. He deserved the same honesty and forthrightness from her. She'd never met anyone who was so unafraid to risk. Alea took his hand and held it to her cheek.

"You turned my world upside down today, Daniel. I can't explain any of this rationally, but there is one thing I am quite sure of. I want you to make love to me. I need you to make love to me."

Daniel silently stood up and pulled her to her feet, vowing that this astonishing woman would finally learn tonight what it was to be wanted, to be loved, to be fulfilled. He kissed her upturned lips tenderly and stepped back.

"In that case, I'd like to start your first lesson with the basic human sense of ... vision."

He smiled widely and lifted his arms out to the side.

"Undress me."

Alea blinked. "You... you want me to undress you?"

"Take all the time you want, sweetheart. Do whatever feels natural."

Alea needed no more encouragement. She wanted this too. She reached up and began to unbutton his shirt. As it parted, she could see more of the mass of curled hairs that stretched wide across his chest and narrowed to a point heading into his belt. He was broad and muscular, his washboard abdomen hard and ridged. She couldn't stop herself from running her hands down his body from neck to waist. Was it permitted to enjoy touch at the same time?

She pushed his shirt back, letting it fall to the floor as she caressed him from the top of his shoulders down along the length of his powerful arms. When she reached his fingertips, he captured her own and raised them to his smooth lips for a kiss. Then he turned his back to her.

She stared in amazement at the sculptured V-shape from shoulder to waist, his ripped muscles impossibly defined and cut. Stroking his chiseled body was irresistible and she soon recognized a wet warmth between her legs. She ran her hands up to his neck and into his thick hair, kneading and combing, enjoying the feel of his luxuriant dark mane. Was the blazing fireplace overheating the room?

"Enjoying your visual sense? Keep going, Alea. We are far from through."

She turned him to face her and reached for his belt. It was awkward for her to unclasp but once she did, she froze. The large bulge straining beneath made her hesitate, but she fought back her apprehension and continued. Unzipping his pants carefully, she had just started to lower the waistband when his engorged organ sprang into view.

She startled and her eyes grew wide. He was magnificent! If the average size organ that deflowered her had hurt so much, what would this do to her? She decided to stop thinking and allow herself to simply experience.

Alea loved the look of his massive manhood, the ridges, the smooth head, and the very appealing dark hair at his groin. It had a unique scent of its own and she decided she liked that too. She chose to ignore his obviously happy condition to explore further. He did say she could take her time...

She dropped his trousers all the way to the floor. His thighs and calves were stone pillars of muscle. She longed to explore the moist and mysterious hidden area between his thighs but was utterly enjoying her commanded adventure to undress him. She would move on.

Well, this was awkward. She would have to remove his shoes and socks first. He saved her the embarrassing decision and kicked his own shoes away. She then slipped each sock off, one at a time, followed by his trousers.

Looking up from her kneeling position, Daniel stood naked above her, a classic marble statue come to life. As she reached out to touch him, he slowly rotated in place so she could see every part of him. How could she have missed his firm athletic rear? She caressed each massive globe in awe, his powerful leg muscles rhythmically flexing as he moved, so mesmerized she almost did not hear him speak.

"Now, it's my turn to undress you."

She quivered with anticipation as he helped her up from her knees and reached for the hem of her skirt. He gently pulled the dress up over her hips, her arms raising overhead as the soft silky material peeled away. He tossed it to one side and stepped back to look at her. A jolt of passion rocked him and his knees almost buckled.

Alea's back was to the fireplace, it's warm flickering light a halo behind her. Her hair was wild as it fell in dark unruly disarray over her shoulders and down to her waist. Her large breasts were bare, the nipples rosy and hard, and she shyly tried to cover them with crossed arms. Black lace panties stretched low and enticingly across narrow hips. A garter belt held up sheer stockings that traveled all the way down the length of her long slender legs, feet still arched in high-heeled black silk pumps.

For Daniel, the lesson was over.

He lifted her in his arms, and she wrapped her legs tightly around his waist, his hard, thick organ throbbing and bucking against the fold of her buttocks, her lips crashing into his. She was consumed by an uncontrollable need and raging desire for him, almost savage in its intensity.

Dropping ravenous kisses along her neck to each lush breast, he carried her to the couch and lowered her into the cushions, continuing his passionate assault of her firm twin mounds. He cupped each one, sucking her aroused nipples into his mouth, his tongue circling and licking as she moaned beneath him. He feasted until her breasts were swollen, her nipples red. She cried out in loss when he left that sweet pleasure to search for new discoveries below, her arms frantically trying to pull him back.

He followed the curve of her waist down to her belly as he kissed her hungrily, leaving a damp trail with his lips. Pulling the garter belt down, he unclipped the stockings, the silky skin of her inner thighs gleaming in the warm firelight. He pulled off each shoe and stocking until she lay in nothing but the black lace panties, her eyes glowing with sultry intensity.

"You are the most beautiful woman I have ever seen, Alea," he whispered, as he drank in the sight of her perfect creamy skin and elegant curves.

Alea melted back on the couch, her sleek legs stretched out on either side of his waist. Daniel gripped the black panties and considered what to do. Dipping his head, he placed his mouth over the delicate lace between her legs and blew out a long, hot breath. Alea gasped as the heat permeated through the flimsy material, making her writhe with an unfamiliar wanting. He closed his eyes and inhaled the musky scent of her female essence, and for a few moments, allowed himself the luxury of thoroughly enjoying, for the very first time, the tantalizing bouquet of his woman.

Once replete, he raised his head. He wanted so much more. And she absolutely deserved more. He gripped the interfering black lace and tore it off her hips, tossing the shreds away. Raising her thighs with his arms, he gazed at her soft dark curls and luscious pink folds glistening with moisture. She was ready. Before she could protest, he buried his eager face between her legs and took a deep, wet lap.

She screamed with pleasure.

Her hips trembled and rose, seeking him, demanding his intimate attentions. He began a leisurely exploration of each rosy crevice, his mouth moving lazily but deliberately to target her source. Once found, the tiny sensitive pearl of flesh began to swell as his tongue flicked back and forth quickly, then slowed to circle and tease.

She was mad with sensation. Nothing in her past had ever prepared her for this onslaught of primal need that only this man could fulfill, his roughened warm tongue licking, kissing, nipping, massaging, creating a passion in her never before experienced. She startled when his finger slipped inside her, her own soaking juices allowing it to slide in and out easily. When he added a second finger she began to moan, and he re-applied his hot tongue to her delicate bud.

She could feel it building... building. Suddenly, Alea's breath caught as the vibrations began to flutter deep inside, steadily fluttering faster and faster until rippling waves of exquisite throbbing pulsations tore through her, her cries of pleasure echoing repeatedly in Daniel's ears. The brush of his tongue became featherlight as she eased down from her powerful orgasm, her swollen and sensitive bud finally coming to rest. He kissed her mound of dark curls and lifted his head to look at her.

Her hair was disheveled and fanned out across the back of the couch, her arms overhead, her eyes closed. Her breasts rose and fell as she panted, a sheen of moisture covering her entire body. She was delectable.

Daniel climbed off the floor and lay next to her. He flipped her over on top of him, her cheek resting on his chest, and could feel wet tears slipping down his side.

"Daniel," she whispered, "I don't know how to tell you what I'm feeling." Her body was shaking, as if cold. "I've never felt anything like that before, or even believed it was possible."

Pride filled him, and a deep sense of satisfaction that had nothing to do with his own pleasure. It had all been for her. For his delicious Alea.

"Darling, you don't have to say anything. This is what you should be receiving every single day from a man who loves you." He lifted her chin and kissed her lightly. "Like me."

She brightened despite her tears. She could taste her own musky essence on his lips. "I want to please you too! But I honestly don't know where to start."

He mocked a serious expression and tapped his chin.

"You know, officially, you are still my virgin. But I think I can suggest a way out of your terrible dilemma." He took her hand and placed it on his still engorged member, showing her how to grip his girth, how to slide up and down. He was thoroughly enjoying her lessons.

Alea loved the feel of him. She stroked gently at first, trying different tensions and speeds as she observed his reactions. This seemed quite promising. He was growing even harder and his back arched in pleasure. His hands roamed her body as she stroked him, and he groaned whenever her soft palm skimmed over his sensitive damp head. He wouldn't be able to take much more.

He flipped her over on her back and rolled on top, the weight of his body causing a burst of heat in her core. He lifted her legs to encircle his waist and positioned his throbbing organ at her damp opening. He had never wanted a woman as much as he wanted her. She was a breathtaking vision, her flashing eyes inviting him to take her.

Their eyes locked as he pushed carefully inside. He lowered his head to kiss her as he continued his deliberate thrust. She whimpered slightly under his mouth, but he did not stop until he was seated inside her as far as he could go. She was his virgin, and although he needed to be gentle, there was no way around this.

Alea clung to him, fearful at first. There was discomfort as her wet canal adjusted to his imposing size, but no real pain. As he penetrated to fill her, she felt incredibly vulnerable, helpless against his powerful maleness that made her weak and dizzy with desire. But it also made her understand what it meant to be a woman. Daniel's woman.

He pulled back, almost to his tip, then pushed inside again. With each rhythmic thrust she gradually relaxed until she was riding easily with him on each stroke, raising her hips to meet his heated lunges. Holding his face in her hands, she kissed him. He felt himself nearing the edge and began to thrust with a stronger, quicker tempo. The tightness of her smooth wet depths was astounding and the realization that he was her first real lover hit him hard.

Her expression suddenly changed to one of surprise as she called out his name, the intense orgasm causing her to clench down on him even tighter. He began pounding into her with abandon, the hair of his groin grinding into her softness as he drove in to the hilt. All she could do was cling to him, moaning wordlessly in pleasure.

"Alea!" he roared, as he came in volcanic surges of release, his male essence spurting deep, his passion further enflamed by the vision of her head tossed back in ecstasy, reddened lips parted, and tangled dark hair spread beneath her. His eyes closed as he slowed his thrusts, their bodies slick with sweat and ripe with the smell of their lovemaking. He sank down on top of her and they rolled to one side, still linked.

"Now you are mine alone, Alea," he whispered in her ear. "I am so in love with you."

Her eyes glistened with tears. It was now crystal clear this was the man she had been waiting for, the dream she had longed for all her life.

"I love you too, Daniel Devereaux," her soft voice cracking with emotion. She kissed him tenderly. "And I'm all yours."

Lifting her easily, he carried her up the curved staircase and laid her gently on the king-size bed. He nestled up behind her and pulled her in tight. They fell asleep instantly. By the time they woke up late the next morning, they celebrated their 24-hour anniversary, and Daniel selected one more of the five human senses to thoroughly explore.

****

It was all rather backwards, wasn't it? Alea actually found her situation quite amusing. Shouldn't you fall in love after you know someone, after you've spent enough time together to see how you fit, to know how you really feel?

But she realized she was deeply in love with Daniel and had been since yesterday at the hospital. Or perhaps it really began three months before, after seeing him in the hospital corridor. It didn't matter. They were two people who met and somehow knew it was right, mystically understanding that they alone could never have planned such a circumstance.

They spent the rest of the weekend indoors, seeing no one. Alea was not on call but checked in with Joe briefly and was able to assure Daniel that Matt was doing quite well and visiting with his family. He called Matt later and they spoke until the nurse arrived with much needed pain medication. Daniel promised to see him soon. But he refrained from telling him about Alea. This was Daniel's time to savor. The rest of the world would remain a dim and distant memory until the dawn of Monday morning would call them back to reality.

They talked for hours, curled around each other in front of the warm crackling fireplace. He couldn't believe how smart, strong, savvy, and confident she was, but tender and sensitive as well. She wanted to discover who he was, what made him tick. No judgements. No secret agenda. She just loved him.

He encouraged her to tell him about her life in Chicago. Her work as an orthopedic surgeon was important to her and when she discussed a particularly difficult case she glowed with excitement. Alea had intently focused on her medical career to the exclusion of all else in her personal life, and Daniel's captivating stories of the Bahama Islands were fascinating, transporting her to an exotic world she could only imagine. Her genuine enthusiasm and curiosity revealed a latent spirit of adventure that matched his own, the same adventurous spirit he had temporarily lost during the painful years of his marriage.

They drank hot cups of coffee laced with Irish Crème liqueur and ate fresh croissants steaming with dripping butter and orange marmalade. Daniel opened dusty bottles of fine wine and they ordered home delivery for every meal, discovering a mutual passion for fresh sushi and crispy thin-crust sausage, gorgonzola, and basil pizza.

His desire and hunger for her was never-ending and they made passionate love for hours. Afterwards, he would watch her emerge from a refreshing shower, standing naked with her towel, and innocently drying her hair. He couldn't prevent himself from seizing her and tossing her, laughing, back into the bed for more detailed and exhaustive lessons of love. She was a willing and apt pupil.

Daniel chastised himself for not using a condom during her first time with him. He didn't regret that mistake too much, however, as she'd been wonderfully tight, warm, and moist. But he did make sure he used them thereafter.

Alea kept a small supply of morning-after pills on hand, not for herself, but for the occasional panicked request from one of her girlfriends after a night gone wild. Today, she was the one grateful to have them. She knew she would now have to consider some method of birth control. Her relationship with Daniel was too new to do otherwise.

They walked together in the quiet, flower-scented solarium, holding hands like teenagers. A sense of peace flowed around them as they meandered the cobble-stoned pathways. There was no need to speak. They rested on one of the cushioned benches, simply to breathe in the existence of each other and to revel in the power of their love.

Alea had captured his heart from the first day he saw her, and he was simply not sure how she had done it. Their love was a mystery, but he decided not to question this amazing gift from God. They had healed each other, and they could now travel together into the future, into the unknown, into the mystic.

Chapter 5   Karen

Karen Sullivan was manic-depressive, but he didn't know it when he met her. On a crisp October morning at breakfast in the cafeteria during his senior year at Boston University, a voluptuous redhead sat down next to him at the table and promptly spilled her coffee down the front of his jeans.

In later years he considered it may have been deliberate.

He jumped up and began to drop his pants until he caught himself. He was in a public place and chose to dab at the hot liquid with paper napkins instead. The redhead began to giggle, then put on a serious expression and tried to help. They ended up laughing together and Daniel found himself rather captivated by her pale but sharp blue eyes.

She was not tall, but more than made up for lack of height with an impressive 40c chest size that caught the wide eyes of most guys on campus. Her chin-length flaming red hair was natural and although not Daniel's usual type of woman, her wit engaged him, and she made him laugh.

In bed she was a wildcat, leaving him panting with exertion as she rode him to fiery orgasm. She liked it rough, fast, and loud. There was no reason not to enjoy her. They seemed to get along well and he was ready to settle down anyway.

He introduced her to his parents, who were polite but reserved. Karen hadn't spoken to her parents in years and was uncomfortable around Daniel's family after realizing they disapproved. Ronny told him outright he didn't like her, as Matt quietly nodded his head in agreement.

Despite his friend's warnings, they were married one month later in a small civil ceremony, with no one in attendance. She told him she wanted him all to herself on their special day.

For their honeymoon she wanted to go to New York, saying she loved the cacophony of noise, the constant movement of people, the stimulation of shops, theater, restaurants. She was never still, ever-restless, always needing to travel somewhere, anywhere.

She gave up her plans to become an attorney after three failed attempts to pass the Massachusetts bar exam. It was the essay section, she reasoned, they hadn't liked her unique and progressive theories. She refused to spout back the usual pap they wanted to hear. "I'd rather stay home and be a good wife," she said, with a shrug.

The nightmare had just begun.

In bed she was insatiable. His eyes would be closing to sleep until she abruptly rolled on top of him, biting and kissing as he laughingly pleaded with her to stop. If he was able, he'd try to satisfy her. Then it began again. What man could complain? he told himself.

By their one-year anniversary Karen was sleeping only two hours a night, which usually meant Daniel didn't get much sleep either. Close neighbors in their Boston condo complex were complaining when she repeatedly woke up screaming. There were ghosts, she insisted, behind the shower curtain in their bathroom.

She began eating large amounts of candy and baked sweets, suggesting casually to Daniel that she might be pregnant, and her weight began to balloon rapidly. She alternated between hysterical fits of crying one day, the next she would calmly report she was starting a strict diet and began exercising for hours at a time.

She had no friends. Anyone she met always seemed to do or say something to upset and anger her, causing outbursts of creatively foul language that Daniel had never even heard at the Devereaux fishing docks. He was desperate about what to do. The first time he suggested a psychiatrist, she refused with a stormy expression, informing him that doctors were all charlatans and quacks and that a person knew what was best for themselves. When he tried to apologize, she pushed him away from her so forcefully he almost fell backwards.

"Man, you have got to get her to a shrink," declared Ronny, as they sat together in their favorite Boston bar, The Rusty Scupper. "Pearl may get mad at me and the kids now and then, but this sounds way beyond normal," he said, and knocked back a shot of tequila and salt. Daniel knew that Ronny never withheld his honest opinions. He was always well-intentioned but painfully blunt when he critiqued even the most delicate situation. Unfortunately, he was also annoyingly accurate in his assessments most of the time.

Daniel took a sip of his cold Guinness and solemnly nodded in agreement. "Ron, now she wants a baby. I just can't do it. I mean, I really want kids but I'm afraid to try with her. I can't bring a son or daughter into a world with a mother who might be unstable. Do you know how I would worry if I'm out on one of the trawlers? Or traveling on business?"

"Do you even know what's wrong? Can't fix what you haven't checked out. We run tight ships, don't we? Make her go to a doctor." Ronny put an arm around Daniel's shoulders and gave a quick squeeze. "We'll keep this between us, Danny, but you are aware that everyone's talking, aren't you? Your mom and dad know better than to push you, but they're ready to crack at this point."

Daniel's voice lowered, as he looked around to see who was near. "Ronny, this might sound strange to a guy, but she wants sex constantly when she's happy and high. I use a condom every time, which really ticks her off. But I keep noticing something unusual." His voice dropped even further. "I think she's taking the used condoms into the bathroom and trying to get herself pregnant."

Ronny slammed the shot glass down on the bar. He said nothing. His angry look told Daniel all he needed to know.

He made the appointment the very next day. Karen was thankfully in her "good place" when he told her and easily agreed to attend the appointment, set for the following week. He prayed she would actually go when the time came.

Dr. Duncan Forsythe, a top psychiatrist at Boston Medical Center, met with them for an hour, then ordered a complete physical evaluation of Karen, as well as scheduling regular sessions with her. He did ask if she wanted Daniel to attend with her, for support. After a few moments of consideration, she agreed to accept treatment, but preferred not to have her husband present.

The final diagnosis: Manic-Depressive Disorder. Bi-Polar. Karen went silent when the doctor told her the results of the tests and his evaluation, explaining the diagnosis in detail. Dr. Forsythe wanted to order medication he was positive would help her, but she hesitated as she pondered his words. She enjoyed her times of hyperactivity. It was during those times she felt strong, powerful, godlike, as if there was nothing she couldn't do. Her weight even dropped. And sex was a burning need, if she could shame Daniel into sleeping with her, which was becoming less frequent day by day.

It was the other times, when she felt sad and grew unhappy and depressed with how everyone she knew constantly hurt and disappointed her, misunderstanding her completely. She would eat to numb the terrible pain and emptiness. If the medication could help those times, she told the doctor, she'd agree to try it. But when Dr. Forsythe explained that she would generally become leveled out in every area of her life, without the extreme emotional highs and lows, Karen quietly decided that medication was not for her. However, she smiled sweetly and agreed to fill the prescription. Once she got home, she put the package in her bottom dresser drawer and covered it with her underwear. She never took a single pill.

She laughed when she told Daniel the ridiculous diagnosis. The doctor was obviously off base, she claimed, waving her hand dismissively. But for Daniel's sake, she assured him, she had agreed to take the pills. He breathed a tentative sigh of relief, but his instincts were warning him otherwise.

She developed ingenious methods to keep Daniel in the dark, going to great lengths to plan her words and actions to prevent him from discovering she was not really accepting treatment. Refusing to allow him to discuss her progress with her psychiatrist made it easy. He couldn't understand why the medication appeared to have no effect.

For the next two years Daniel lived on the edge of a knife, learning to maneuver, to defuse, to please, to sacrifice his own happiness and needs to maintain some measure of peace. He became self-protective, only speaking when required. The one act he quietly took for himself was to stop having sex with Karen. He didn't trust her and certainly no longer desired her. She raged, accusing him of having affairs. He didn't bother to argue. He would not sleep with her.

He spent long hours at Devereaux Fishing. He took on most of the duties for the buying, repair, and selling of the trawlers, planning trip schedules, dealing with the crews, and taking necessary business trips around the northeast. He was heavily invested in moving the growing company completely into the new world of sustainable fishing and seeking new types of catch that were marketable. He also added a fish processing branch to enable the catch to move quickly from ocean to customer. His father allowed him to take on more and more responsibility, as it was clear how desperately Daniel needed the escape. He was making millions for Devereaux Fishing, but he was drowning in pain.

However, he never skipped his winter trip every year to the Bahama Islands with Ronny and Matt, no matter how much Karen screamed. He kept his 40-foot cruiser, Seahorse, safely berthed in Spanish Wells at Ben's marina. It eased Daniel's mind to remember she would be ready for him whenever he chose to go down. It was the only thing keeping him sane.

He thought about divorce, but Karen hadn't given him any obvious cause to pursue that course... yet. She was still in psychotherapy and he felt morally bound to allow her time to improve. Besides, he was simply too tired and disheartened to think about it.

On that bright September Sunday morning, he sat dejectedly at the kitchen table. He'd made a pot of coffee and was waiting for Karen to come downstairs to breakfast. How would he get through an entire day with her? Other than a planned visit to his parent's home by himself later that evening, he had no justifiable excuse to leave. His gut clenched in misery as she breezed in, refusing her usual cup of strongly brewed coffee with a meaningful glance. Grabbing his hand, she announced with a flourish, "It's finally happened!"

Daniel waited quietly with no expression, not sure how to proceed. He had learned the hard way, many times, not to say or do anything that might set off a violent reaction and to give himself time to think and respond.

"Well, aren't you interested?" she growled.

He sighed to himself and plastered a tense smile on his face. "Of course, Karen, what's your news?"

"I'm pregnant!" she shouted and started to laugh with glee. "Maybe now you'll stay home more often, give up going to sea or traveling. You're an owner and really don't have to work. We have lots of money, more than enough for whatever we need! We could be together all day, all the time!"

Daniel's face blanched and he swallowed back the rising nausea in his throat. No. No. No. He stood from the table, trying to control his shaking hands. She can't possibly be pregnant, he reasoned, unless it isn't my child. He remained completely still, his mind a morass of emotions. He was at a loss for words, unable to speak, and was paralyzed with fear, his mouth dry and his heart racing.

Karen stared at him, her pale blue eyes cold as ice, her face twisting with rage. "You don't want a baby? Our baby? Or is it that you don't want MY baby?" she screamed.

"Karen," he finally choked out, "you know it can't be our child... and you know why."

Racing around the table, she flew at him with arms flailing, fingernails aiming for his eyes. He was easily able to stop her, restraining both arms before she could harm him.

"You're not well, Karen. I'm calling Dr. Forsythe and having you admitted to the hospital."

She kicked up with one knee hard into his groin and he let her go with a grunt of pain, dropping to the floor. "I'm not going anywhere!" she screamed. "You hate me, they all do!" She ran to the kitchen drawer and pulled out a long fillet knife. Before he had any time to react, she slashed his arm viciously with the blade, blood immediately oozing, staining his sleeve red.

"Who will believe you now, asshole," she said, all of a sudden eerily calm. "It was self-defense. I had to protect myself." Her lips curled upwards into a smile, but the look in her eyes chilled his blood. "You're going to jail."

Turning the knife towards herself, she drove it deep into her abdomen.

****

The paramedics arrived within minutes of his phone call and transported her immediately to the nearest emergency room. After initial questioning, the police escorted Daniel to

Boston Hospital, where he received treatment for the knife wound, which had been bloody, but relatively superficial. Afterwards, detectives questioned him further as they waited for news of Karen's condition.

She barely survived the six-hour surgery. When she awoke late that afternoon, her surgeon informed her gently that she had not been pregnant, but she would never be able to bear children because of her injuries and the subsequent surgery. Even in her semi-drowsy condition she contemptuously spit in his face, refusing to believe his ugly lies. Dr. Forsythe was called for confirmation that Karen was under his care and Daniel gave permission for her transfer to a psychiatric facility when she was recovered enough to be moved.

The day after surgery, her physicians notified Daniel that her bloodwork revealed she had never taken the medication that would have given her a stable life. Multiple packages were later found stashed in her bedroom closet.

The police interviewed him extensively several more times over the course of the next few days, but he was cleared of any potential charges. Her fingerprints alone were on the knife. There were no bruises or other injuries, no history of violence or abuse for Daniel. Their condominium neighbors testified about her disturbing behaviors. Interviews with his family and friends only confirmed Karen's mental condition.

He went to visit for the fourth day in a row after her surgery. She was lightly restrained and on suicide watch. As usual, she berated him with foul language, screaming and crying the entire time he was in the room. There was no way to speak with her rationally. His brief visit was token. He was never going back. He left her room for the last time in hopeless depression and began to head out to the parking garage.

By the time Daniel reached his truck, his life was forever changed. He had been visited by a fragrant dark-haired angel in the corridor.

He drove away from hospital determined never to see Karen again. She would get the care and attention she so desperately needed, but he was done. All communication and financial arrangements were handled by his attorneys.

The divorce was final four months later.

Chapter 6   Beginning of the End

The core of the sun was changing. The magnetic stew of the interior was moving and shifting for unknowable reasons. Perhaps the cause was the pull of a huge lone asteroid, or the cosmic slam of radiation from a dying star millions of light years away from earth. Who could know, who could control? The constantly aging and fluid skin of the sun only reflected the heartbeat and flow deep within.

But today, along the magnetic lines at the surface, a force was gathering unequaled to any that had ever gone before. A volcanic and monstrous solar flare was preparing to unleash itself on an unsuspecting and oblivious planet.

Politics, persons, cultures, and religions could continue their endless battles for power and supremacy. This flare would be the common denominator.

And it would not care who or what lay in its path.

Chapter 7   The Perfect Wedding

They were in no hurry as their new 52-foot cruiser traveled south along the west Eleutheran coast, anchoring for the first three nights in remote isolated coves, protected from the predominant east winds and the stronger pounding waves of the Atlantic ocean. Eventually moving past Eleuthera, they continued heading south.

Daniel turned east into the Atlantic after leaving Cat Island, then turned southeast past San Salvador, heading towards their final destination of the Turks and Caicos. They'd been cruising for six days and decided to anchor that night in the Atlantic on a high sea mount. The ocean swell was low and gently rolling, but Daniel was keeping track of a low-pressure area in the east that appeared to have the potential to develop into a storm, possibly even a hurricane.

It was a magical honeymoon. Safe on their seaworthy boat, there was nothing to distract them from days and nights of the almost unbearable pleasure of each other.

Traveling only by day, Daniel pointed out the beaches, reefs, cliffs, and waterfront towns of each island. They swam nude in the luxuriantly warm Bahamian waters, climbing back up the dive platform to make love wherever they happened to drop. At times, they dove together simply to photograph the spectacular undersea world. For one whole day they wore no clothes at all. They lay on thick mats on the sunny deck to soak in the hot sun, their skin glowing with a golden richness. They watched small private planes flying low overhead as they made their way to sleepy island airports. Often, the pilot and passengers waved as they passed by. They spoke to no one. Nothing mattered but to be together, inseparable.

Daniel liked to stop and anchor in the late afternoon to spear a fresh seafood dinner. They celebrated with glasses of chilled champagne in crystal flutes as Alea prepared either lobster, grouper, or hogfish for dinner. Sometimes, he fed her small bits by hand, and she would pull the morsel and his finger into her mouth with gentle suction, an unmistakable invitation in her eyes. Dinner often grew cold.

Daniel had never known such happiness. She was the exotic beauty he dreamt of, but never believed he would really find. Her mother was Egyptian and her father French. Long waves of fine dark hair fell to her waist, her almond-shaped eyes a bewitching hazel with soft gold highlights and fringed with thick lashes, her lips a pale natural pink.

Daniel was tall, well over six feet, and her head grazed just under his chin. She had the lean graceful muscles of a dancer, with narrow hips, but her breasts were large and firm. Her high cheekbones and oval face were strikingly beautiful and gradually tapered into a slightly heart-shaped chin line. His French-Canadian roots, with the rumor of a possible distant American Indian ancestor, had inclined him to the exotic, and in his late teens and early twenties he'd dated some very sexy women in New York, Boston, and the Bahamas. But none of them could compare with Alea.

All in the past, he thought, taking a sip of his champagne. He gazed out over the sun-dappled water, allowing his mind to wander. I couldn't have prayed for more than I have in this exact moment in time. Perhaps that's the secret, he mused. The past is gone, untouchable and unchangeable. The future unknown and unknowable. All we can really take hold of is the present, and even that rushes by every second. He felt a brief shiver of fear.

The sparkle of the champagne bubbles caught his attention as the last rays of the setting sun reflected into his glass. Learn from the past, take hold of the present, and trust for the future. Suddenly, he had a strong sense that God was smiling at him and that nothing that happened in his life was by chance. Or a mistake. All was as it should be. His fear melted away.

He realized that for many years his life had been fulfilling and busy, but perhaps a bit shallow. He cared deeply for his parents and friends, traveled the islands, breezed through college near the top of his class, and was very involved with Devereaux Fishing. He lacked for nothing financially. Women were drawn to his extraordinary good looks and he'd never been turned down when he desired a woman. But his deeper emotions remained untouched until his marriage to Karen.

Those years of uncertainty and turmoil began carving out superficial character traits, replacing the carefree, wild, and sometimes reckless boy of his youth with a man of more quiet strength and thoughtfulness, assessing situations, and people, more carefully before jumping in headfirst.

He started looking at everyone around him with a more sensitive inner eye. He saw he was not the only one whose heart was empty and wounded, realizing that most people were hurting in some deeply personal way. He learned just how important it was for a person to feel they were not alone, that someone cared.

As hard as he tried for three years, he'd already known, deep inside, that Karen was not the one to fill his empty heart. He had lingered, in foggy limbo, until he caught a brief glimpse of hope in that long, empty, hospital corridor.

Alea changed everything from the first moment he saw her. He could finally allow his heart to rest and begin to live again with her as his first true love and wife.

He allowed his mind to drift to the happy memories of their wedding, as he took another sip of champagne.

****

The new cruiser was his pride, having purchased her as a surprise wedding gift for Alea a month before their wedding, a style not yet available for public sale. The boat was an Ocean Queen, one of the top brands of motor yachts in the world. She boasted an enclosed flybridge lounge, golden teak decks, and cream, white, and blue accents throughout, sleeping six with a king master suite, two guest cabins, a full galley, and 3 heads with showers. With a beam of 18 feet, a hull draft of only 3 feet, top speed of 30 knots, and cruising speed of 27 knots, the cruiser was more than ideal for traveling and living aboard in comparative luxury. Her twin Volvo diesel engines ensured power and speed whenever needed. A 12-foot hard-bottomed inflatable tender with a 15 hp outboard was secured on davits at the stern.

When he saw the spectacular prototype in a brochure during a random visit to a boat dealer in Newport, he knew he had to have her. He couldn't help it. The boat's name came alive to him immediately, symbolizing his new life with Alea.

Into The Mystic had to be his!

He sold his older cruiser, Sea Horse, the following week. Prolonged negotiations with Ocean Queen, as well as a hefty check, secured the deal. Ocean Queen decided it would be good business to have a model on the water in advance of public sales, in exchange for Daniel's expert assessment. A few minimal cosmetic preferences aside, his personal survey evaluation and photographs gave the cruiser an A+ rating. Ronny and Matt were highly impressed with the quality of workmanship and all the amenities and couldn't wait to run her down to the Bahamas.

Daniel brought aboard his extensive fishing gear and tackle for both trolling and casting, and dive gear that included two powerful blue water spearguns, as well as pole spears. He was a certified scuba diver but preferred to free-dive, which he considered more intimate and demanding.

Once she arrived in Spanish Wells, Ben looked her over and gave his full approval. The wedding was still a week away and Daniel was due to arrive soon. Ben knew instinctively what his gift would be. He set about creating a custom-crafted storage locker filled with items that, he cryptically told Ronny and Matt, would be essential for safety, if ever needed. He placed the key in a small box and asked his wife Vernita to wrap it up. He would give it to Daniel and Alea after the ceremony.

Into The Mystic was not only Daniel's surprise wedding gift to Alea but would serve as their honeymoon getaway while cruising the Bahamas, showing her the islands he grew up exploring, the people he cared for, and the ocean he loved.

****

The wedding had taken place the week before in Spanish Wells, the most daring idea Daniel had ever conceived. His mother was not completely sure it was even sane. Six months after he and Alea met, Daniel decided it was more than time. He planned the wedding, set the date, invited the guests, and made all the preparations.

He hadn't even asked her to marry him yet.

He would propose to her on the deck of Mystic while in the Bahamas, surrounded by family and friends, presenting her with a custom created 3-carat diamond engagement ring. The wedding ceremony would immediately follow, as soon as she took enough time to prepare herself and put on the designer wedding gown Daniel had personally selected.

Everyone knew Alea was getting married. Except Alea.

****

The July sun rose hot in the eastern sky on the day of the wedding. It was officially hurricane season. Daniel would be watching the forecast closely, but he deliberately chose the month of July, knowing Alea would love the warm summer waters that were as sensuous as a hot bath.

Into The Mystic was moored dockside in the harbor with a wide sturdy ramp joining boat to shore. Native decorations of palm fronds, pink conch shells, and tropical flowers filled every crevice and spilled over the decks and railings, luring guests up to the flybridge lounge. Colorful lights were strung overhead and all along the rails.

Dockside, near Ben's office, an expansive white wedding tent had been erected and the concrete dock area beneath painted white. Strings of gold and white lights lined the tent rafters like stars and large fans were positioned to provide cool air. Buffet serving tables were positioned in all four corners of the tent. A raised dance floor in the center was surrounded by round dining tables, to be set with fine, pale pink bone china rimmed in tiny rosebuds, intricately carved gleaming silver cutlery, and crisp white linen tablecloths and napkins. Floral bouquets of light pink hibiscus, white madonna lilies, violet orchids, and dark pink roses would bloom in the center of each table, with chilled bottles of fine champagne peeking out from silver buckets of ice, and Swarovski crystal champagne flutes sparkling at each place setting. The waiters were hired locally and would wear custom-fitted white tuxedos with black tie.

A famous New York television chef was flown down to join local chefs in preparing a sumptuous buffet of Bahamian and French cuisine. Daniel was allowing the wedding feast to be featured for an hour-long episode on Food Network TV. The food was being prepared in the kitchen of a popular Spanish Wells restaurant, with a film crew recording each step and irritating the local chefs with their invasion of the limited cooking space. But with volatile temperaments kept in check, everyone seemed to be enjoying the creative chaos. A steady flow of rum cocktails helped lubricate and soothe any tensions and soon the preparations themselves became a party.

Close family and intimate friends would first board the boat to witness Daniel's proposal to Alea. Afterwards, all invited guests would then be escorted onboard to enjoy silver trays of avocado crab hors d'oeuvres, miniature pecorino crostini with heirloom tomato, and a choice of cocktail, with lively island music playing low in the background. The wedding ceremony would take place on the bow of Mystic, officiated by Pastor Higgs from The Gospel Church.

At dusk, the gourmet wedding feast would be offered buffet- style under the tent on the dock, with the famous chef and his assistants presiding. The kitchen and wait staff were invited eat and join the party, once in progress, with two men of the film crew serving as the official wedding videographer and photographer. It was rumored that Lenny Kravitz might show up to join the popular local band, The Beach Buoys, to play and sing for the reception.

The buffet was planned by Daniel and the chef to reflect both he and Alea's heritages, as well as honoring the Bahamas. The offerings would include Lobster Thermidor, boneless duck stuffed with veal, beef, and truffles in a light French pastry shell, battered and grilled cracked conch, mango-glazed fresh tuna, prime rib au jus, asparagus with Hollandaise sauce, new potatoes with creamy garlic-butter sauce, Dijon mustard and mushroom potato salad, arugula and butter lettuce salad with goat cheese and balsamic honey vinaigrette, fried plantains, classic Bahamian peas and rice, tropical fruit salad, conch chowder, and a wide selection of specialty breads and cheeses. Daniel made sure that one of

Alea's favorite dishes, pistachio-stuffed leg of lamb, was also featured.

Dessert would be a highlight of the evening, with slices of pineapple rum upside-down cake, golden French custard, guava duff, mango cheesecake, and chocolate mousse with heavy whipped cream. Daniel requested a childhood favorite of chocolate chip pecan cookies, to be served with white chocolate ice cream.

The wedding cake was a simple rich vanilla with three tiers, white buttercream frosting, and a thick layer filling of fresh strawberries blended with vanilla custard, decorated lavishly with sweet white and blush pink rosebuds and white orchids. Sitting on the very top of the cake, in a sea of frosting, was a tiny replica of Into The Mystic, with small figures of the couple standing together at the bow, gazing out ahead as they began their journey of life together.

They would be cruising for one month. He secretly made all the arrangements for her absence with her surgical group, and many of the physicians and staff would be attending the wedding as well. Daniel paid for each person's travel expenses, family, friends, and coworkers. Accommodations were set-up for guests to stay at either the Bonefish Bay house, with close friends, or at local hotels. Golf carts for transportation were made available day and night. He missed no detail and didn't care what it cost. Alea would be his wife tomorrow and he wanted this to be an event in her life she would never forget.

To get her to the island, Daniel was finally able to convince her she needed time away from her busy orthopedic surgery practice. They had taken only short weekend trips together during their six-month romance and he told her he wanted to take a longer vacation with her, in the Bahamas, for their first time. He would travel to Spanish Wells before her, with

Alea to follow several days later, in order to complete her scheduled surgeries and follow-up care.

When she arrived, he would propose on Mystic, with the wedding to follow immediately. This was how he did business. This was how much he wanted her.

He had no doubts about Alea's answer.

****

She flew in to North Eleuthera Airport early that morning and Daniel was waiting while she cleared Customs. As soon as she emerged from the door, he caught her in his arms and they hungrily kissed, eliciting cheers from the porters holding her luggage. They slipped into the air-conditioned cab that would speed them to the dock at Jeans Bay, where they would board the government ferry to Spanish Wells.

Inside the taxi, he released her from his embrace only to produce a large bouquet of her favorite madonna lilies, the scent of her perfume that he loved.

"Oh Daniel, you're so sweet! I love them," as she inhaled deeply. "What a nice start to our first real vacation together."

She kissed him tenderly and took his hand as the cab pulled out on Queens Highway. She was fascinated with the vast expanses of greenery and trees that contrasted with the bright blue sky. They passed a stand displaying fresh red tomatoes, squash, and limes, the woman sitting inside raising her hand in greeting. The small towns were a bit shabby and run down, but friendly waves and smiles acknowledged them the entire way to the dock where the ferry waited.

"Daniel, it's so unbelievably beautiful here!" Alea exclaimed, as they boarded the small government ferry for the short ride to Spanish Wells. The day was bright with sunshine and a soft warm breeze, the light turquoise water of the bay shimmering. Casey, the ferry captain, was entertaining them with island trivia as they pulled away from the dock.

"I hope you like Bonefish Bay, honey. We can freshen up and have some lunch, but later I have somewhere I'd like to take you."

"Sounds good. I had to make two connections and I could use a break. My goodness, but this bay is just incredible! The water here is nothing like Boston. It makes me want to jump in and cool off." She stood up and looked towards the rapidly approaching long stretch of harbor docks.

"Wow, someone's having quite a party, it would seem. Look at that motor yacht near the white tent at the dock!" She gaped in amazement at the graceful lines of the splendid cruiser and the festive white tent right next to it.

Daniel grinned mischievously. "Yes, and we are invited to the party. That's where I wanted to take you later. Did you bring anything a bit dressy?"

"Oh, yes, I have something nice but not too fancy. It's quite hot here, isn't it? Glad I brought several swimsuits and cover-ups."

"I'm sure they'll come in very handy, my sweet."

He glanced over at his boat again, pleased with what he saw. Preparations were going well. It wouldn't be long now.

****

"You look lovely, Alea!"

She twirled around happily in a circle to show off her dress. With spaghetti straps and a tight V-neck bodice to her waist, the pale peach chiffon skirt flared out dramatically, then fluttered lightly down to mid-calf length. Her hair was pulled back into a high ponytail and her diamond stud earrings were her only jewelry. She wore white sandals and carried a small clutch purse.

She eyed him appreciatively. "You too, Mr. Hot Stuff."

Daniel wore a Caribbean-themed short sleeve shirt featuring palm trees and white orchids, white linen slacks, and sandals. He was classy, casual, sexy, and handsome and Alea thought twice about going out this afternoon. She decided to bide her time until later. She was always proud to be seen with him.

He escorted her to the golf cart and helped her in. As they drove to the dock, Alea enjoyed looking at the colorful homes set close together, a warm community feel to the entire island. She could glimpse the blue-green ocean peeking between properties and the people passing in other golf carts waved. She waved back, learning from Daniel that even if you didn't know who they were, it was considered polite to wave anyway. She made sure to greet every cart as they went by.

He pulled up to a designated parking area near the yacht and helped her off the golf cart. She was curious. Was it really permitted to go onboard? There was no one around. She turned quizzically to Daniel, but he just smiled and took her arm, escorting her up the gangway.

The lounge was fabulous! Spacious, open, and bright, with four full-sized soft beige leather couches, royal blue cloth upholstered chairs, and mahogany coffee tables, the room invited conversation. Tiny outdoor lights glowed around the room and along the deck rails. Cocktail tables with beautiful flower arrangements were scattered all over the boat. But the lounge was empty.

"Daniel, are we too early? There's no one here," she asked anxiously.

"Why don't we go upstairs?" he suggested. "Perhaps the captain can tell us what's going on." He took her arm and led her to the stairwell. They ascended to the enclosed flybridge and Daniel opened the door to allow her to enter first.

"Surprise!" Three dozen people stood around the edges of the flybridge, holding glasses of champagne raised to her in greeting.

Was she dreaming? Wasn't that her father and mother? And her brother Roger? Daniel's parents? Ronny and Matt? What, their families too? Her partners? Who were the others? What was going on?

She turned to Daniel and was shocked to see him down on one knee, reaching for her hand. She froze in bewilderment.

"Alea, my love, my life, my heart. I love you so completely and could not imagine this world without you."

His other hand reached into his pocket and he gazed at her, all his love in his eyes.

"My sweet darling, I would be honored, if you would allow me the incredible privilege, of agreeing to become my wife."

He extended the sparkling 3-carat gold and diamond ring and waited. The room filled with people grew silent.

Joy lit her face and her smile made Daniel weak. "You were the husband of my heart from the first day we met." She touched his cheek softly, her eyes glistening.

"Yes, Daniel, I will marry you."

He slid the diamond on her finger and the room exploded with cheers.

****

The flybridge rang with congratulations, hugs, and tears of joy. Alea's mother Nadia clung to her and Daniel talked with her father Armand off to one side. The happiness of their family and intimate friends for the couple was quite evident and the party began in earnest. The crowd began to filter downstairs to enjoy the hors d'oeuvres and cocktails before the ceremony, as other guests began to arrive.

Ronny and Matt decided to slip off to find a cold beer, after an obligatory sip of champagne. Matt stopped at the stairs and turned, his tortured eyes seeking Alea one more time. Sighing in resignation, he slowly followed Ronny down below.

After accepting the congratulations of each person, Alea finally tugged Daniel over to a corner of the room.

"Daniel, you're so wonderful, my darling! I love you!" She pulled him close, kissing him softly. "But what about all our families and friends? It must have cost them a small fortune to fly to the Bahamas, with hotels, food, and other expenses, just to see us get engaged? And we haven't even talked about a wedding!"

Daniel enfolded her in his arms and laughed.

"My love, we're getting married in one hour. And you're the only one here who didn't know."

****

Alea stood in front of the full-length mirror and stared in disbelief at the image reflected back to her. She was getting married in less than an hour. To Daniel. He had done all this for her, because he loved her. She would never deserve this man if she lived a thousand years.

As soon as they had left Bonefish Bay, the housekeeper re-packed all her clothes and delivered them to the boat. When she walked into the master cabin, her personal belongings were neatly folded, and an unfamiliar gold case lay on the bed. But something else had been placed in the room as well.

A long plastic garment bag hung on a hook near the closet.

Her wedding gown.

Daniel had personally engaged a designer to help him create the dress he longed to see her wear for their wedding. He knew her so well she was certain she could trust his choice. But whatever was revealed when she opened that bag, she would wear anyway, for his pleasure.

Nadia slid the zipper down the front of the garment bag and lifted out a cloud of lace as Alea emerged from the bathroom, make-up and hair complete. She had chosen to wear her long hair down, like a veil. She couldn't wait to see her dress.

Eyes wide, she touched the breathtaking garment in awe. Her mother helped her slip it on, the zipper disappearing into a slim crease. It was a perfect fit, with a soft white lining that caressed her skin. Alea turned to face the mirror again.

The dress was pure white, with a delicate lily flower lace pattern over the soft white lining. The neckline was a wide deep sweetheart extending out to her shoulders, with unlined lace sleeves ending just below her elbows. The body of the dress was simple, contouring her sleek figure until reaching her thighs, where the skirt flared out into a flowing cascade of lace that sparkled with hundreds of tiny melee diamonds.

She loved it! She loved that Daniel had envisioned her in this elegant and beautiful gown. She would have chosen this dress herself. Her eyes glistened with tears of joy.

Nadia opened the gold case on the bed and gasped. Diamond earrings sat on a bed of black velvet, with a 1-carat round diamond at the ear and a 2-carat pear-shaped diamond hanging just below. A wide diamond crusted bracelet lay next to them. They were the only jewels she would wear, other than her engagement ring.

Her mother lifted a sparkling headpiece from the case and held it up to admire. A mother-of-pearl hair comb was woven with small diamonds, pearls, sequins, and fresh lilies, with long tendrils cascading down one side, crusted with white silk flowers and tiny seed pearls. Alea felt faint. Daniel had done too much.

"Alea, my daughter," her mother called softly, "this man is certainly in love with you. You will make Daniel very happy today."

She hugged her mother tight.

"I pray I will always be worthy of him, Mom. He's all I will ever want."

Chapter 8   Honeymoon

"Daniel?" Her soft voice drew him back into the present. Alea reached over and covered his hand with her own. "I didn't want to disturb you, sweetheart, but I'm curious what you were daydreaming about. You were so quiet."

He turned her palm up and kissed it. "I was thinking about you. About our wedding. About how much I love you." He slid her deck chair closer to him and wrapped an arm around her shoulders as he kissed her cheek.

"I'm so happy," she sighed. "I never expected any of this. It's a dream for me, Daniel. You are my dream come true, even if that sounds like it's right out of some medieval romance novel." She laughed and raised another bottle of champagne. "Please pop!" as she handed it to him.

"With pleasure!" Daniel responded, with a wry smile.

The sun was just starting to touch the horizon to the west, almost too glaringly bright as the reddish-yellow disk began to sink lower in the sky. In fact, Daniel thought, he couldn't remember such an intense color to the sun. He stood up to drop a shade to shield their eyes before opening the bottle.

"We've already talked about it so much, but everyone really seemed to enjoy our wedding," she beamed, "but not as much as I did. It was all so amazing! I can't believe everything you accomplished. And what you assumed, my love."

She watched his face with anticipation as she sipped her cold champagne. "What would have happened if I had said no?"

He smiled confidently as he poured himself a glass. "Not even a possibility and you know it."

She grinned. So right. But why tell him that? She knew he was a proactive man who wasted no time in wondering about what if's. But neither was she.

Recognized as gifted by age four, she graduated high school at fourteen with top grades, although it wasn't just top grades that took her through college, medical school, internship, and residency in the highly competitive medical community of Chicago. Alea had resolutely persevered, winning the respect of each of her teachers, one by one, who were impressed with her intelligence and drive, despite her youth. She overcame the prejudices that almost prevented her from becoming an orthopedic surgeon, a male-dominated surgical specialty, by sheer will, fortitude, and her innate talent.

Alea quietly but insistently rose to the top of her chosen field, learning not only the art of professional diplomacy, but how to butt a head or two when called for. She discovered the invaluable secret of how to ultimately turn a foe into a friend, without compromising her values or goals. Be as wise as the serpent but as harmless as the dove, her father would say.

Leaning back in her chair, she closed her eyes. Chicago had been difficult for many reasons, but only one of them was the real reason she decided to move to Boston. She shuddered involuntarily and turned to enjoy the last rays of sun.

Alea Rose Gabrielle was the daughter of the noted cardiac surgeon Dr. Armand Gabrielle, who re-located from Paris to Chicago to accept the highly coveted position as Director of Cardiothoracic Surgery at Northwestern Memorial Hospital. Her mother, Nadia Soliman, was an Egyptian beauty who chose to leave the Middle East to escape the repressive society and extreme prejudices, especially involving women. She was a highly skilled nurse specializing in cardiac care when she met Armand. They fell in love during a quadruple bypass surgery and were married two months later. Roger was born first, with Alea following several years later. Armand and Nadia kept a large apartment near the hospital during the work week, but on weekends they traveled northwest to the small town of Barrington, where they had purchased a home on the lakefront with ten acres of property.

Between the city and the lake, Alea and Roger experienced their childhood with the best of both worlds, and with a happy and loving family. Education, literature, open expression, courtesy, honesty, faith in God, and love were important to her parents. Respect for each person's humanity, choices, and beliefs were ingrained in the children. Awareness of evil and discernment between right and wrong were also explored. Armand and Nadia were patient and gentle teachers, doing their best to mold the young minds and spirits they'd been given in a healthy, well-balanced manner. Although they were encouraged to follow their heart, Alea and Roger chose to become doctors. The whole family had been in medicine for over three centuries, and their many relatives practiced in Chicago, New York, and Paris in a variety of specialties.

With medicine in their blood, Roger and Alea were excited to follow family tradition. They graduated with honors from high school and attended the University of Chicago for pre-med and medical school. Roger selected neurosurgery and planned to remain in Chicago. Alea chose orthopedic surgery but emotionally felt it was better for her to relocate. After her final year of residency in Chicago, she joined a surgical practice in Boston. For the last three years she'd been quite happy with her work, her partners, and with Boston Hospital. Her career was everything she'd ever wanted.

Until Daniel.

She gazed at her handsome husband with desire in her eyes. She knew exactly what she wanted at this moment. It was her honeymoon, after all. Carefully setting her champagne glass down, she took his hand.

"Come with me."

Chapter 9   The Flare

The boat rocked lazily on the gently rolling Atlantic swell in the dim light of dawn. The wind had laid down during the quiet lull between cool night and warm light. Just after dawn, Daniel made his way to the galley to brew the obligatory pot of coffee that was always required to start his day.

He noticed a pink glow rising in the east.

"Red sky at night, sailors delight, red sky at morn, sailor be warned," he mumbled, as he turned the handle for the water faucet. Opening the upper cabinet door, he noticed the galley was rapidly filling with a pale red light. That's unusual, he said to himself. Finishing coffee prep, he turned the pot on to brew.

He walked back to the bedroom to check on Alea, who was already emerging through the cabin door, dressed in white shorts and a yellow tank top, her hair pulled into a low knot.

"Honey, have you looked outside?" she said, with some alarm. They walked to the stern and stood on the deck, looking to the east. Daniel was immediately concerned. He pulled Alea to his side, wrapping both arms around her protectively. He had never seen anything like this!

Streaks of angry multicolored light danced across a solid red horizon that stretched from the ocean to the heavens, rapidly spreading in all directions in a fast-moving arc that began to fill the entire sky. Daniel had marveled at the lights of the Aurora Borealis many times, but it was rarely seen this far south in the northern hemisphere, and never in daylight. The frightening phenomena mutating before him now was on a scale a thousand times greater. Crackles of what sounded like lightning could be heard off in the distance. The atmosphere radiated an intense dry heat, the rising sun glowing like a superheated giant coal, the sharp pungent odor of chlorine stinging their throats and nostrils as it filled the air.

They heard the hum of a small plane engine as it started to pass overhead about 500 yards in front of the bow, seemingly unaffected by the supermassive light show.

"Daniel, what is going on?" Alea gripped his waist as Daniel stood silently. "Should we be worried?"

Before he could answer, a brilliant flash of piercing white light erupted from above. Alea screamed. Instantly blinded, they dropped to the deck, still holding each other. Even with their eyes slammed shut, the superlight penetrated painfully behind their eyelids.

Suddenly, there was nothing but deep silence, except for the lapping of the waves against the hull. No sound came from the boat. The coffee pot was mute. The hum of the plane engine was gone.

"Oh my God, what happened?" Alea cried out. "Daniel, are you okay?" White light throbbed behind her eyelids.

"I'm here Alea! I think I'm alright, but I can't see anything. What about you?"

"I can't see either! Oh God, please let this be temporary," she said, then went still. She sat up and clutched his arm, tilting her head as if to hear better.

"Wait," Alea whispered, "I hear something, but I'm not sure what it is... like a rushing wind?" Daniel raised himself up slightly to listen as well.

Seconds later, a loud explosion hit the water ahead of the boat, causing them both to cringe and fall back down to the deck. A woman's scream of painful agony cut through the air. Alea wept in Daniel's arms, fear coursing through her. There was nothing they could see, nothing they could do. They lay huddled together, entangled around each other, blinded and helpless.

"Just stay down, Alea," he ordered. "I'm almost positive the plane we heard flying over just crashed somewhere ahead of the bow. If it's on fire, I think it's far enough off that it won't come near us. But if you feel heat or hear any unusual sounds, tell me right away. Until we can see something again, just hold on tight to me, sweetheart."

Fifteen minutes later, their vision started to return. The burning wreckage was the first thing they saw. The plane had crashed into the ocean just ahead of the boat, missing them by only two hundred feet. There were no survivors.

The sun slowly returned to its usual brilliant and glowing yellow hue, with only a tinge of pink remaining in the sky, as though nothing untoward had even happened.

As they stood somberly surveying the debris and death in the water, they did not yet understand that mankind had just been flung 40,000 years backwards.

And it had only taken twenty minutes.

****

The silence was broken only by the whisper of the wind when they finally turned away from the smoking wreckage of the plane. Their vision almost clear, Daniel guided Alea over to a deck chair. He wanted to make sure she was unharmed before making any decisions. He sat down next to her and took a deep breath to focus.

Into The Mystic was still afloat, apparently undamaged from either the superflash or from the plane, but he was anxious for his sight to come back fully before proceeding with a more detailed inspection.

Debris was scattered in the water around the boat, already spreading out and being pulled away by the current. He could not determine the actual size or make of the plane from the metal chunks bobbing on the surface, but the sight of charred human remains impaled on some of it was sobering. The rest of the aircraft had sunken out of sight.

Alea's eyes were red from tears and her body shook.

"There was nothing I could do!" she cried. "Someone was still alive for a few minutes but there was nothing I could do!" She clutched his hands as she struggled to compose herself. "Daniel, I know there was no way to help or save them. I really thought we might die too. What do you think happened?"

He paused for a moment. "I have an idea but let me check the boat's power before I answer. Wait here for me, Alea." He stood and leaned down to kiss her, then carefully made his way up the stairs to the flybridge. Complete silence greeted him there as well.

The instrument control panel was black, with no sign of power. However, the magnetic compass still displayed true north. No electricity needed for that compass, he realized. He flipped the switches for the ventilation fan and fuel pump. The indicators did not light up. Not looking good. He decided to try starting the engines anyway. With a fervent prayer, his hand reached forward and turned the key.

The engines cranked but would not start. Daniel thought the problem could be either fuel supply or ignition, which were both electronic systems on Mystic. But he was starting to form a theory.

He stared at the cluster of useless instruments that had cost him thousands of dollars. Might as well have a couple of sturdy wooden oars, he wryly chuckled to himself. He recalled many of the books he had read growing up, stories of the sea, of ships, and of the men that sailed them. Books that taught how to use the stars for navigation, how to ride the winds, and steer with the currents. Stories that also told of the disasters at sea. A man needed to learn that the ocean was ultimately in control when you chose to ride it's back.

We've gotten very spoiled, he realized, as he turned to head below to the engine compartment. His jaw clenched with determination. There'll be no disasters for us, if I can help it. It was time to check the batteries.

Once inside the compartment, he went straight over to the heavy metal shelves that supported six large marine batteries. The connections looked solid and unharmed but there was a slightly sulfurous odor in the air. Pulling out his toolbox, he retrieved a simple battery tester, a style that didn't use an electronic circuit. Starting with the first battery, he touched the probes to the positive and negative terminals. Drops of sweat beaded his forehead. The battery correctly registered 24 volts and each of the other batteries showed the same. Relief flooded him. It was not the batteries.

But his worst suspicions were now confirmed. Every single electronic system on Mystic was dead.

They had experienced a massive solar flare.

****

"I'm sure you're right, Daniel. After what we saw, it must have been a solar flare." Alea walked to the deck table with bread, a plate of cheese, and glasses of apple juice. No coffee. Nothing in the galley was working.

"I don't know much about them, but I once read there was a big one in the eighteen hundred's that destroyed telegraph lines. It was called the Carrington Effect, a solar flare that emitted a strong EMP, short for electromagnetic pulse. I'm not sure what else was electric back then. After that event, the use of electricity morphed for decades until it's now part of our daily lives."

"Yes," he replied, "and because there was so little electricity in use back then, it wasn't felt to the extent we would today. There have been smaller solar flare EMP's since then that affected some services briefly. But the sky-consuming "Aurora Borealis" we saw before the superflash has never happened in recorded history. We're positioned more than a thousand miles south of where the Aurora is usually seen, and never that extreme. That alone tells me this Flare was something quite different. That's why that plane went down, Alea. The EMP killed it's engine, and the pilot was certainly blinded as well." He reached over and took her hand, as her eyes misted.

"I wonder if the effects of this solar flare are worldwide?" he pondered. "If that's true, airplanes everywhere dropped out of the sky. I know the U.S. military can shield their strategic equipment from nuclear or solar-produced EMP's using metal shielding called Faraday cages. Keeps electronics and circuits from being destroyed by the pulse."

The impact of the morning suddenly struck Daniel and he fought back a wave of fear. But she needed to hear the truth.

"Alea, if we eventually learn that this was indeed a planet-wide solar flare, life will never again be business as usual. Any electronic device that was not shielded from the Flare and EMP is gone and will never come back. Any device that uses certain forms of electricity are toast. Newer cars and boat engines with electronic circuits can't run. Our battery bank seems exempt from the effect, thank God. Batteries don't use electronic circuits. My immediate concern is how to survive out here on the Atlantic with no power and how to get back to shore. Without the VHF and satellite phone we can't call for help. And if the power is out everywhere, no one will hear us anyway."

Daniel sat straight up in his chair. "The anchor winch is electric too." They were still anchored on a high sea mount in the Atlantic, where they had overnighted on their way to the Turks and Caicos.

"Oh yeah, I can release the electric drive and crank it up by hand, using the manual windlass," he said, relaxing somewhat with that realization.

"Can you actually manage that heavy anchor by yourself? Would I be able to do it or help you with it?"

"Anchoring is going to become serious business at this point, but I can lift it. It's geared to a 10 to 1 ratio, but it'll take time to raise it."

"But without power, how will we move the boat?"

"I'm thinking the only way we can move is to drift. The main current here is from the southeast moving to the northwest, so we'll drift into the islands. There was a forecast of a possible storm or hurricane coming from the east and that would be a big problem for us," he admitted. "Hopefully we'll drift close enough to a populated island where we can signal for help and perhaps get towed into a harbor. Even if we have to anchor her offshore, we can row the skiff to land."

Daniel considered his next words carefully.

"Alea, I can't predict how people will handle this disaster. Hopefully, we will actually get help when we ask for it. If the Bahama islands and any other countries affected by the Flare are without power, it's going to be chaos. People are going to suffer. Many could die. Some things we took for granted aren't going to be there anymore."

He took her hand and looked her straight in the eye.

"We could be in danger from anyone we encounter, wanting what we have and being in competition for resources like food and water."

"I understand, Daniel." she said. "You know, I took an oath to care for people and here I am, on my honeymoon, on a boat with no power, in the middle of the Atlantic. We can't move anywhere quickly, and even if we could, how would we get back to Boston at this point if airplanes can't fly? So, I simply need to accept what has happened and do whatever I need to do for our survival." She paused thoughtfully.

"I've also been considering how a hospital would handle this emergency." She winced. "Without back-up generators there won't be much they can do to help people."

She squared her shoulders. "Daniel, there must be a reason why God is allowing this to happen. We often aren't given the why of a situation, but I've believed that all my life. I love you so much, my darling. I'm here for you and I know you love me too. With God's help, we'll get through this together."

Alea walked behind his chair and wrapped her arms around his neck. They stayed close, not speaking for several minutes, absorbing strength from each other and praying for protection and guidance. After a few moments, Alea stood up and walked over to the siderail, gazing into the deep blue water. She paled and turned to Daniel in alarm.

"Both of our parents were planning to stay over in Spanish Wells at the Bonefish Bay house for a week after the wedding. My brother Roger. Ronny and his family too. Do you think there is any chance they were on an airplane flying home when this happened? Oh Daniel..."

He sighed, a stab of pain shooting through him.

"I'm really not sure what date they all planned to leave. They hadn't bought return flight tickets yet." He walked over and gathered her to him. "All the other guests flew out a couple days after the wedding. The only way to know for sure is if we can get back to Spanish Wells."

"Is there any way to contact Ben? I need to know if they are safe," Alea insisted.

"The VHF, the satphone, our cell phones, and laptops are all down. The World Wide Web most likely down too."

The serious implications of their situation were sinking in for them both. Without power to operate modern machinery, the ability to manufacture replacement parts or essential goods on any large scale would be impossible. With no way to re-establish electrical services, grow and distribute food, or utilize even basic computer technology, mankind would be prevented from progressing any further for potentially over 100 years.

"We've got to make a plan, Alea." He scanned the skies as he assessed the weather conditions. "It's clear now, but we might get a sprinkle later, if those clouds keep coming. There's a low southeast swell, about a foot and a half. Why don't we get some rest, then decide what to do later?"

"Sounds good. I'm exhausted. Before we lay down, I'd like to check the refrigerator and see if we need to take care of any food. The fridge should stay cold enough if we keep the door shut. And water. I'll check on how much drinking water we have, since we don't know when we can get more."

She started to walk inside, but Daniel stopped her.

"Stay with me for a moment," he whispered, pulling her back and breathing in the soft scent of her hair. It was going to be a long day.

It was only ten o'clock in the morning.

Chapter 10   Facing Reality

The cabin was getting warm as the sun rose higher, heading towards noon. With no air conditioning, Daniel opened all the windows and the overhead skylight for air as they laid down to rest. He curled around Alea and pulled her in. The silence was lulling, and they fell asleep instantly with a breath of cooling breeze circulating in the cabin.

A splash echoed from outside and he awoke with a start. The blazing sun was directly above the skylight and for a moment he was blinded again. He rolled on his back, pulling gently away from the still sleeping Alea. The air was heavy with humidity and he was perspiring. Stretching his arms overhead and closing his eyes, he began to form a plan.

There was no point raising the anchor, he thought. It would be best to stay where they were and spend the rest of the day taking inventory of supplies. Try to save as much food as possible. Identify what might help them survive. That was the logical first step.

Second, how to get to land. No matter how he played it, the drift was the only way. With the prevailing north-flowing currents of the Atlantic and the Gulfstream, that also diverted west into the calmer Caribbean waters, he was sure Mystic would drift close to one of the larger islands. Especially if the winds were favorable. He'd have no issue with anchoring offshore and rowing the tender to land. What they would find was anyone's guess, but he would protect Alea with his life, if that's what it came down to.

There were no military-type weapons on board. He had his father's ten-year old Glock 9 mm semi-automatic pistol for general protection, the two blue water spear guns, his pole spears, and a selection of knives. He'd never envied Matt's gun collection before but would have given much to have even one more weapon in his possession right now.

The fishing fleet in Boston and New Bedford! Many of the boats and crews must have been at sea when the EMP struck. Those men were his friends too. Matt was flying home three days after the wedding. Did he go out with one of the boats or did he stay in port? Daniel willed himself to stop worrying. There was nothing he could do for them with his own tentative situation. It was his immediate responsibility to protect his wife and get her to safety, especially with a possible hurricane brewing in the Atlantic, a hurricane he was anticipating based on his observations of the swells, sky, and winds.

They would start the drift in the morning, he decided. After that, it was all in the hands of God.

****

After a quick lunch of sandwiches and a soft drink, Alea began to open cabinets and drawers in the galley. She wrote down everything she saw on a pad of paper to show Daniel. Plates, cups, glasses, utensils, pots and pans, kitchen towels in one column, food listed on the next. They had brought a lot of the wedding feast leftovers to enjoy, along with sour cream, butter, milk, and potatoes, planning to shop for necessities at local island stores.

She noted several click-on firelighters as well as two large boxes of stick matches. Wasn't it just a few nights ago they'd anchored in that small quiet cove at Cat Island and made love on the beach next to a roaring driftwood fire? She shook her head to clear that wonderful memory. It felt like a lifetime ago. Focus, Alea, she reminded herself.

She located a medium bag of rice, a few cans of soup, several boxes of crackers, and numerous small plastic bottles of salt, pepper, garlic salt, smoked paprika, parsley, cumin, sage, and cayenne pepper. She also found a bag of flour, sugar, a jar of honey, two containers of ground coffee, a selection of teas, a bottle each of olive oil and vegetable oil, balsamic vinegar, two bottles of lime juice, several bottles of hot sauce, one jar of molasses, and jars of peanut butter and strawberry jam. These were all the dry goods on the boat.

The contents of the galley had been enough to help create delicious meals along with the lobster, crab, fish, or conch Daniel harvested fresh each day. Would it be enough to feed them until they reached shore? Her next priority was checking their water supply.

Five-gallon bottles of pure drinking water were stored in a galley pantry. She counted eleven remaining full bottles and two empties. The one they were currently using was loaded into an electric dispenser that could provide hot, cold, or room temperature water with the press of a button. That obviously won't be working anymore, she realized. Those big bottles are heavy, but Daniel can lift and pour into pitchers. We can jump in the ocean to bathe and can then rinse off with at least some fresh water. I need to ask Daniel about the water source on this boat for the bathrooms, she decided, and headed down to where he was working below deck.

Daniel was able to locate the manual crank handle for the anchor windlass in one of the storage lockers. When the time came to start the drift, he would disengage the electric motor from the mechanical drive of the windlass, enabling him to manually retrieve the anchor off the sea floor, hopefully with no difficulty. It had been calm when they dropped anchor the night before. Perhaps it was merely resting on the rocky sea mount and not dug in by the tines. He'd have to wait and find out in the morning.

He re-confirmed that the anchor locker contained a second auxiliary anchor with 300 feet of line and pulled out his heavy toolbox to check its contents. Hearing steps behind him, he turned around to see Alea's lovely face peering down into the dim interior, which reminded him to locate the flashlights and some candles for the night.

"How are you doing down there?" she questioned, looking at the array of tools and gear spread out on the lower deck, and the mechanical maze of pumps, lines, and tubes crowding the small space, foreign and unfamiliar.

"The hull of the boat is intact, no damage from the airplane debris," he confirmed. "I'm pretty much just re-familiarizing myself with all of our equipment. In a pinch, I want to know I have what's needed."

Alea glanced around the hold. "Daniel, what does Mystic use as a freshwater source? We have more than enough drinking water for the present time, but where do the three bathrooms and the galley get supplied from?"

Daniel walked her around the corner to a large rectangular white container with an electric pump, lines sprouting up and to the sides of the hull. "This is the 500-gallon freshwater tank we've been using so far." He checked the gauge on the side. "There's 350-gallons left in there, but without power I'll have to pull water out of the inspection hatch with my manual bilge pump to fill a bucket. The hatch is only one foot in diameter." He gave a short laugh. "That's quite a few runs up and down for water. At least we'll stay in shape."

"Good to know," she chuckled. "Now, for the million-dollar prize, how do the toilets operate?" It wasn't particularly a laughing matter, but she grinned sheepishly anyway.

God, he loved her smile. Made him melt all the way down deep. The planet had just gone to hell but all he could think about was taking her back to the bedroom and making love until morning. Her soft skin. Her hair draped over his chest. Oh well, toilets first.

They made their way up to the main deck. Daniel took Alea into the master head and pointed out a feature they didn't have the time or the inclination to discuss while on their honeymoon. He pointed out the grey metal handle on the side of the stainless-steel tank.

"This is a manual purge, sweetheart. No power needed. Into The Mystic is set-up with a system that uses seawater for the commodes. So, there's never been a waste of freshwater," he told her, with no small sense of pride. "And I can switch the system from dumping waste into the boat's septic tank to a direct drop into the ocean. In port, though, it's usually not a great idea to dump waste in the water right next to the docks. That's being a very bad neighbor."

She laughed outright, the musical sound making his heart leap. "That's a lesson I never thought I would need."

They'd been working the entire afternoon. All the portholes, doors, and windows were open for circulation, but it remained stuffy inside, with the early evening breeze just starting to pick up. The flybridge was the coolest interior spot on the boat. They climbed topside to watch the sun begin its descent to the watery horizon, their dinner plates loaded with wedding leftovers. The food would be impossible to preserve much longer, the contents of the refrigerator unable to be eaten beyond a couple more days, despite having been transferred into a large cooler filled with the last of their ice.

"Husband." She loved being able to call him that.

His strong jaw was in profile to her, his face lit by the evening sun. A surge of love for him melted her heart, disintegrating any fears she had kept to herself during the challenging and difficult day. Suddenly, a flow of warm assurance swept over her. Despite the horrific and terrifying events of the morning, Alea was surprisingly filled with a spirit of hope. Their destiny was now carrying them into a new life, a life she could never have predicted.

Daniel looked at her, feeling her love. Not needing to speak, they both turned to say goodnight to the sun.

It had only been fourteen hours since the massive solar flare produced the electromagnetic pulse that would dramatically alter the course of human history forever. A man and a woman sat together with hands entwined, facing their glowing enemy and marveling at its beauty, as it slowly sank below the horizon. Their eyes locked as the sun disappeared and twilight darkened the silent evening sky. No matter what lay ahead, no matter the danger, soul to soul, they were one.

Tomorrow morning, the unexpected adventure of their lives would begin, a journey that would last however long they were given. Daniel and Alea would begin that journey together, in love... into the mystic.

Chapter 11 The Drift

Daniel stood in the bow with the manual windlass crank in hand, his brow scrunched in concern, as the very scene he fervently hoped would not happen began to take shape. The morning sun gave no further sign of the prior day's rebellious destruction but rose above the eastern horizon in ominous reddish tones, which indicated rain in the distance. Billowing clouds were gathering on the horizon and a larger ocean swell was rolling the boat. He remembered that a low-pressure area had been spotted on the doppler just coming off the African coast before they left Spanish Wells, but he hoped they'd be closer to a major harbor if a storm developed.

I need to get this anchor up as quickly as possible before the tines imbed into rock, he realized. The increasing swell was making that a real danger as it pushed the boat away from the anchor, tightening the line. He leaned over to disengage the power drive and inserted the crank into the receiver.

"Alea!" he called. "I'm starting the drift and I need you up at the bow." He startled when her hand touched his shoulder. She was already standing right behind him.

"I'm here, baby. What do you want me to do?"

"One of us needs to be on deck at all times," he said. "As we drift, be on the lookout for shallow areas, rock reef, anything that might damage the hull. I can manually lower the tender to evacuate if we're in real trouble, but I'm hoping the current will keep us in deeper water." There were so many potential dangers, but he didn't want to worry her unnecessarily.

"It will take me about fifteen minutes to bring the anchor up by hand, Alea. Once it's off the bottom, Into The Mystic will start to drift. So, if you feel the boat starting to move and

I'm still cranking, don't be concerned. Just let me know if you hear or see anything that looks suspicious."

Daniel considered her, his loving and beautiful woman, her ponytail blowing in the wind. She wore a tangerine swimsuit, gray shorts, and white boat shoes, her golden tan setting off sparkling hazel eyes that were full of confidence in him. No fear. He really wanted to live up to that confidence, even if he wasn't quite feeling it at the moment.

"I'm ready," she said. "Let's do this!"

He pushed the handle in firmly and began to turn. It wasn't too heavy at first, but when the anchor chain began to lift off the bottom, the weight increased. Turning the handle became more difficult as he felt the chain lift completely off the rock and the anchor itself began to rise.

It must have just been laying on the rock, he thought with relief. With low swell and light winds, the tines must not have dug in. This was good! Drag disappeared. Yes! The tines were free! Mystic began to drift slowly with the current. He was about to tell Alea their efforts were a success when he felt the anchor stutter against more rock.

He doubled his efforts, perspiration dripping from his chin, and was finally rewarded when the anchor popped free and began to rise unrestricted up towards the boat.

"I got it!" he cried out. Alea moved to his side and patted his back, still scanning the surface waters as instructed.

Ten minutes later the anchor locked into place. He stood up, exhausted, letting the ocean breeze cool his heated skin. Into The Mystic was floating free and drifting sideways with the current towards the west. There were no islands in sight, but Daniel determined to bring a pair of binoculars out to the deck and search as they drifted.

"Great job!" Alea handed him a bottle of water, which he guzzled down thirstily. She tossed him a hand towel to dry off his dripping face and neck, and they walked inside to find the binoculars and have a cup of coffee. Daniel had remembered that by manually lighting the propane stove in the galley with a firelighter, they could boil water in the tea kettle, and then use the glass French Press to brew a pot of coffee. When the remaining two cans were empty, he would seriously miss his usual morning caffeine wake-up.

Heading back outside, Daniel noted the wind was gradually increasing, the ocean swell was growing, and the skies were turning partly cloudy. He lifted his binoculars to scan the horizon on all sides of the boat. No land in sight. He was really missing the VHF marine forecast, but his many years spent in the North Atlantic and the islands had taught him how to read the telltale signs of deteriorating weather accurately. And he knew there would be trouble coming soon.

Alea brought out two plates with sandwiches made with rich multigrain bread and thick slices of lamb with marinated onion and tomato, along with a small salad for each of them. Setting the plates down, she disappeared again and came out a few moments later. Daniel's eyebrow raised when he saw her carry out two glasses of red wine.

She laughed as she handed him one of the glasses.

"If we're not sure what the rest of day will bring, let's at least celebrate being together and safe for right now, even if it's only eight o'clock in the morning." She gazed out over the water as the boat drifted steadily on the current, the wind also pushing her along with invisible arms.

"It's really quite lovely out here, so quiet and serene. Time almost has no meaning for me, after everything we've been through," she said, feeling a little sad. A disturbance next to the boat caught her attention and she resolutely set aside her melancholy.

"Daniel, look, dolphins!" She ran to the portside railing and leaned over. He joined her to see a pod of five or six dolphins swimming alongside the boat, casually breeching and diving twenty feet away. With no loud engines running or propellers spinning to frighten them, the pod appeared curious about the large white hull floating above them.

Alea was thrilled and watched the dolphins dance and dive for some minutes before they disappeared beneath the water. Daniel had introduced her to an exciting and exotic world she never would have discovered for herself. Her surgical practice and patients had been the only priorities of her life for many years. Daniel not only offered her all of himself and his love, but also shared remarkable stories of his experiences with the ocean and the islands. She was completely fascinated with his world, and with Daniel.

Before the Flare, she was just starting to enjoy a whole new side of herself, a simpler and more natural Alea, in tune with the rhythms of the earth, the vistas of the sky, and the restless sea, content, and at peace. It was exhilarating to immerse her body in the warm Bahamian waters, swimming straight into massive schools of bait that first parted to accept her, then returned to surround her completely, so immense she was lost to view. The purple and black lace of sea fans waved at her from their tethers on coral reef formations and fish of many colors and sizes swam unconcerned below her, disappearing into and emerging out of a maze of rocky holes and crevices. Nature's underwater world danced with vibrant life, a silent spectacle of unbelievable beauty.

She was surprisingly good at spotting the long antennae of lobster poking out from under the safety of flat bottom rocks. Daniel taught her a hand signal to let him know where the bug was hiding and he'd dive down with spear in hand, shoot, and retrieve their meal for the evening. Alea felt quite proud of her contribution to the dinner table.

She learned to avoid skin contact with painful fire coral that grew in large colonies on submerged rock. The pale yellow, antler-like projections were actually the protective homes of a type of jellyfish or stinging anemone. The creatures secreted a milky liquid that hardened into their distinctive coral shape, with small openings for their multiple hair-like stingers. Daniel cautioned her that contacted areas of skin would light up red and burning for days. Even the covering of a rash guard did not completely protect from the toxins injected. Rinsing with vinegar or alcohol eased some of the discomfort.

She was already a good swimmer, exercising three times a week by lap swimming at the hospital rehab facility pool. Snorkeling and diving with Daniel felt quite natural. Learning to cast a fishing lure from a pole was still somewhat of a challenge. But Alea loved the excitement of hooking up a fish and reeling the hard-fighting mutton snapper, grouper, or cero mackerel to the boat, where Daniel landed it either by net or pulling it up by line. She was happy to let him gut, clean, and fillet the fish, however. He'd laugh at her, saying she was a surgeon, for heaven's sake, and ought to at least give it a try. Nevertheless, she decided to leave the messy prep in his very capable and experienced hands.

She gladly took over cooking duties in the galley. Alea had spent many pleasant hours with her mother learning how to prepare a variety of American, French, and Mediterranean dishes and she enjoyed cooking and baking. It was relaxing for her and Daniel loved her delicious creations.

She loved watching Daniel surf! Surfing was a completely unfamiliar sport for her that she had never paid attention to. He seemed so fearless and took off on powerful waves that frightened her at first until she saw his skill and the joy surfing brought him. Alea much preferred a soft boogie board that propelled her at what felt like amazing speed as she picked up a smaller wave heading towards the beach.

Unless he swam right next to her, she was leery of deeper water, having spotted several big sharks during one dive with Daniel the week before. She chose to re-board the boat rather quickly, but he remained in the water to finish spearing a big lobster. After climbing back onboard, he told her they were probably more interested in a fish than in her, but she firmly decided that she'd rather not be the main course on the shark's menu that day, thank-you.

Alea turned away from the disappearing pod of dolphins and slipped her arms around Daniel's waist. This would now be her life, her world too. As long as Daniel was with her, she was ready.

****

Into The Mystic continued to drift with the current for the next several hours. They were helpless to control where the boat was heading, and the current had so far kept them in relatively deep water. With a draft of three feet it was unlikely they'd run aground, but Daniel kept a sharp eye out for any potential problems.

The wind was gradually rising, about ten miles per hour, he figured. It was one or two o'clock in the afternoon and the swell was growing, the clouds were building.

I need to find somewhere safe to anchor up for tonight, he realized. I think the predicted storm is definitely heading our way. Standing on the bow, he re-focused the binoculars and scanned the sea in a slow circle. We were already well south of San Salvador when we first started the drift, he reminded himself, checking the horizon to the west. Startled, he lowered the binoculars and rubbed his eyes, then looked again. There was a dark spot on the horizon! He raced up to the flybridge to look at the compass and re-checked. The dark spot was still there... and it wasn't moving.

Land!

Daniel bounded down the stairs to the main deck where Alea was dumping a small bucket overboard. She wrinkled her nose as he came near.

"Some of the refrigerator food is going bad. I'm dumping it," she told him. "It's from the wedding, over a week old, and without any more ice, I'm worried about keeping it around."

"Honey, that's fine, whatever you decide. You're the doctor. But I have news! We're drifting towards an island! I can't tell which one it might be or how large it is, but so far the boat is heading in that direction."

"What?" she exclaimed. She set the empty bucket down and wiped her hands on a towel. "Oh, that's wonderful! Can you show me?" He handed her the binoculars and turned her shoulders in the direction of the possible island.

"Yes, I see something! And it does look like land!"

Daniel took back the binoculars. "I'll be keeping track every fifteen minutes from this point on," he assured her. "When we get closer, I can decide what to do. I'm worried about the weather and I'd really like to be in a harbor or away from the wind. With no power or ability to steer the boat, this will be getting rather interesting."

He turned to go, but she pulled him back and slid her arms around his waist. Tilting her face up, she parted her lips, the invitation unmistakable. His arms encircled her waist and his mouth captured hers. They kissed tenderly, lost in the warmth of each other, until Alea drew her lips away and buried her head against his strong shoulder.

"I love you, husband. I never fear when you're with me," she whispered. He held her tight.

"I'd die before any harm comes to you, my love. Trust me."

She raised her head and gazed solemnly into his intense dark eyes. That's how it would be for her too.

****

The late afternoon sun cut through brief holidays in the billowing cloud bank. The southeast wind was playing in their favor and the small dark spot on the west horizon was rapidly becoming larger. It was definitely an island, but difficult to estimate its actual size. They were about five nautical miles away. Daniel believed they'd be drifting to the windward side, with the current sweeping to the north. He had no doubts that a storm was approaching. All the natural signs he grew up watching were clearly evident. They needed to find safe harbor soon if Mystic was not steered by the Gulfstream current to the more protected western leeward side.

From his distant vantage point, it appeared that the eastern side had rock cliffs varying in height from about ten to thirty feet. The swell was crashing against the cliffs, sending showers of white spray high into the air. He couldn't see any sandy beaches or any obvious coves or inlets. Not good. To anchor on that side would mean a storm from the east would dash Mystic into the rocky cliffs and leave them no safe egress. And he really did not want to be exposed on open water in what was looking like a developing hurricane. His jaw clenched and his brow furrowed with worry.

Alea also spent the afternoon out on deck, watching Daniel as he ran between the flybridge and the main deck, constantly checking their path on the drift and keeping tabs on the approaching island. With nothing much to do beyond making sure Daniel drank some water and ate a bit of food, she was free to observe her ever-changing surroundings.

She saw several frigate birds diving down to strike the frantic bait pod that a school of medium-sized tuna were feasting on, a splashy and spectacular show of predator and prey. As the pod dove to escape from danger, the leaping torpedo-shaped hunters suddenly disappeared under the churning waters in hot pursuit, re-emerging several hundred feet away as they drove the panic-stricken pod back to the surface, the massacre beginning all over again. So interdependent, she mused. One life to continue from the death of others. Their only goals; to eat and to reproduce endlessly. But from that timeless cycle, the ocean and each one of its many inhabitants had survived for millions of years, ultimately nurturing and sustaining the life of mankind, and of the earth itself.

These fish and birds don't care about an EMP, she thought. They don't even understand that our world has been changed forever. But only our human world, she corrected herself. Alea considered that for eons of time, plant, animal, and human life had progressively evolved without any reliance on electricity. For that matter, it was only a very recent part of mankind's total existence.

We've grown soft and deadly vulnerable. I wouldn't be much different now than a 19th century civil war surgeon, operating with a hacksaw and knives, sealing wounds with hot irons. She shivered, contemplating the vast and devastating changes to modern medicine that would have to be accepted. No cardiac surgeries. No orthopedic or neurosurgeries. Certainly nothing oral or cosmetic. Patients with a pacemaker will be doomed, she realized. The small implanted electrical devices would fail instantly after a major EMP. And once the existing stores of medications are exhausted, we will once again have to rely on leaves, roots, bark, sap, and berries. But the pharmaceuticals I used every day evolved from those very ingredients, did they not?

The entire scenario and its future implications overwhelmed her with sadness, especially when she wondered about her parents and brother Roger. What were they going through? Did they remain on Spanish Wells? Were they on a plane to Chicago that crashed when the Flare struck? Had they made it home safely, only to be endangered by violence and chaos? What about my patients? Our friends? She wiped away the tears that were sliding down her cheeks.

She took a deep breath and chided herself. I need to pull myself together and focus on what's in front of me. Daniel doesn't need a sobbing, overly emotional woman when every decision we make, every action we take, means life or death. She chose to table these troubling thoughts until they had time to discuss the likely problems of a powerless world, which was their working assumption at the moment. They hadn't seen any settlement lights, boats, or airplanes so far, which seemed to confirm their suspicions.

A splash and movement in the water caught her attention. A giant brown and black whale shark was leisurely cruising at the surface about fifty feet off the port side. The shark looked to be well over twenty-five feet in length and was feeding through the black filter pads in its mouth that took the place of teeth. Daniel told her the whale shark ate ocean plankton, krill, squid, and clouds of spawned fish eggs, and she was quite relieved to hear him say that the behemoth was uninterested in humans. As the enormous whale shark swam slowly off to the west, Alea was humbled and grateful she'd been permitted to see the majesty of such a creature.

Her friends, the dolphins, did not re-surface all afternoon, but in their place a sea turtle popped its rounded head above the waves for a breath of air. She could see the mossy green high top of a broad shell just before it sank back down. She waited for the turtle to come up again for air, but the quiet creature had already faded away into the silent depths to feed on grasses and seaweed floating in the current.

The boat was drifting quickly in the increasing wind and Daniel was sure they'd be passing along the east side of the island. Projecting their possible path, he realized the water might be deep enough for Mystic, as the current was strongest in depths over fifteen feet. That was good, as he did not want to run aground. But there was always the danger of barely visible rocks that could severely damage the hull and wouldn't be seen until the last moment.

He decided to prepare for any eventuality. He brought up the sea anchor duffel from below, ready to toss off the bow if he needed to slow Mystic down for any reason. The sea anchor was a water parachute that ran off a long rope and would deploy as water filled it, slowing the speed of the drift and keeping the bow into the wind.

The main anchor was set to drop with the pull of a lever. He might not be able to completely avoid a coral head or crash into the cliffs if the current was so inclined, but any control he could manage over the direction of the boat he would doggedly pursue. He also made sure the electric drive to lower the twelve-foot tender was disengaged so he could manually lower it to the surface, in case they needed to abandon ship. The tender was already outfitted with oars and PFD's. He removed the 15 hp outboard engine and tied it down to the deck. The electronic ignition had been rendered useless after the EMP and he did not want to deal with dead weight on the tender.

With the depth sounder also useless, Daniel had to watch for bottom structure to show itself visually. Into The Mystic had drifted into shallower water of perhaps twenty feet, as the southern tip of the island loomed a half mile off. With all equipment in a state of readiness, he turned to Alea.

"We need to talk." He sat down at the deck table as she joined him. He reached over and took her hand.

"The current and wind are taking us close to the east side of the island we've been watching. At this point I'm not sure how this will go, but I'll be needing your help."

"Of course, Daniel. Tell me what I can do." She gripped his hand firmly, determined and ready.

"I want you at the anchor, Alea. If I tell you to pull the lever to drop, please do it immediately. I'll be trying to avoid a crash into the rocks. I have to decide if we should anchor on the east side of the island or if we should just keep drifting. The storm does look like it's coming our way."

He hesitated thoughtfully before continuing. "I'd rather not drift at night. If we get into trouble on the open ocean, in the dark, it would be very dangerous to abandon ship."

She laughed to lighten his intensity. "Yeah, I'd rather not be on the Titanic at night. At least the waters nice and warm here and I'd let you get up on the raft with me."

He couldn't help but laugh with her. This was his wonderful woman, brave and supportive no matter what. The Flare had ruined the remainder of their honeymoon, and possibly the future of mankind, but he would never permit Alea to be in harm's way. Not while there was breath in his body.

****

The sun could no longer be seen behind the heavy bank of clouds. Alea took up her post at the anchor as Daniel watched the distance between Mystic and the island grow smaller. With dusk soon approaching, it was time to act. He decided to deploy the sea anchor just as the current began to veer the boat north from the southern tip of the island. He tied the end of the line to a secure deck cleat, lifted the tightly pre-folded package over the bow rail, said a quick prayer, and dropped it.

The 75-foot line began to run out as the parachute spread to catch water, like wind in a sail. Into The Mystic began a slow turn, with her bow pointing into the southeast wind and with the stern now leading their way. Speed soon reduced in half and Daniel blew out a sigh of relief.

Mystic silently drifted along the cliff, about two hundred feet offshore. Thick gnarled brush grew on the clifftop, with the occasional palm, coconut, or casuarina tree standing tall, sometimes overhanging the rock edge and stretching towards the water. Multitudes of birds darted in and out of weather-hewn holes, where safe shelter beckoned, and nests had been precariously woven.

The limestone cliffs were engraved and etched from the pounding elements of wind and water over millennia. They had been formed at the bottom of the ocean from layer upon layer of crushed shell, small dead sea creatures, and minerals, filtering down into the depths. The debris gradually grew into mountainous peaks, ultimately compressed into stone under its own weight.

These peaks stood high during the ages when colossal sheets of ice covered most of the northern hemisphere and lowered sea levels significantly. When the mighty glaciers melted, rivers of imprisoned water were freed to return to the oceans. The towering limestone mountains were all but submerged, with only a small percentage of their actual height visible and inhabitable.

The 700 Bahama Islands were born.

An artistic fascia of crags, holes, and ridges covered the cliff walls in muted tones of white, grey, sandy beige, and black. To the imaginative eye, pictures and sculptures emerged of lions, horses, wings, and faces. Trees and brush bravely attempted to take hold on the edge of the cliff walls, ultimately doomed after being drenched in heavy salt spray, bleached and twisted limbs silhouetted against the rocks.

His attention was drawn to a pair of osprey flying inland from the ocean, their wings graceful curves against the clouds. One of the osprey suddenly looked down and caught Daniel's eye. To his utter amazement, the bird broke away from his mate and swooped down towards the boat, circling lazily right over Daniel's head. Unlike its mate, his all-white body feathers were not the typical mix of white, brown, and grey Daniel was familiar with. The bird's head was pure white, a black bandit mask covering black eyes rimmed in white. His widespread wings were also white, the leading edge with a wide streak of dark charcoal grey. The osprey gave him a long searching look before screeching loudly. Then, with a strong beat of its wings, the bird flew back into the sky and headed north well ahead of the boat, soon passing over the edge of the cliff and rejoining its mate. That's when Daniel saw the white osprey tuck both wings, beak down, and dive.

He was instantly alert. Osprey would dive underwater to catch fish swimming near the surface. He knew they also liked to hunt lagoons and coves, and the way they were circling inside the cliff line told him the pair might be flying over an inland body of water.

Moments later, he rose back into the air, holding a good-sized fish in his talons. Together, both birds continued their journey west until they were out of sight. They must have a nest on the island, he thought.

His hopes soared. There was water inside those cliffs! Deep enough for the birds to strike. But was there a way in? He had to think fast. With dusk coming up quickly there were only two options. Either continue a risky drift into the night or anchor. The osprey made up his mind for him.

"Alea, drop anchor now!"

She gripped the release lever immediately and pulled. The anchor splashed into the water and line began to run out quickly. Daniel rushed to replace her at the anchor controls and gradually engaged the brake as the boat slowed towards a full stop. He wanted to make sure the Danforth dug deep and held in the sand and grass bottom.

He selected two landmarks that were about fifty feet apart so he could judge distance, to determine if the anchor was holding bottom. The first was a palm tree at the top of the cliff right in front of him and the other was a leaning coconut tree further down the cliff from the palm. These landmarks would allow him to tell when the boat was finally stationary. If the anchor was dragging along the bottom, he would have to start all over again.

Daniel waited until he finally felt confident that Mystic was holding position. She had settled in nicely with her bow facing southeast, at a 30-degree angle from the cliff line and about a hundred feet out.

"Yes!" Alea gave a little jump and pumped both arms into the air, her victory dance amusing Daniel, who could do no more at that moment than stand and watch her happy celebration. She ran over to him and threw her arms around his neck in excitement. He held her, all the while watching the ominous sky over her shoulder.

"Not to be a spoilsport, honey, but we're not done yet," he cautioned. Releasing her gently, he reached over the bow and began reeling in the parachute, which had deflated as soon as the boat stopped, the sandy bottom allowing him to retrieve without any damage. He dropped the wet mass on the deck, knowing he would spread it later to dry, and pulled Alea back to him. Before he made another move, he wanted to explain the reasoning for his actions, worried that his decisions may have appeared erratic.

"I decided to anchor because there may be an inlet up ahead. I saw an osprey dive inside the cliff line, and he caught a good-sized fish before flying west. If we had kept drifting, and there actually is an entry to a protected area inside the cliff, there wouldn't have been enough time for us to stop the boat. And it's going to be dark soon. With the weather getting worse, I'd prefer to overnight here and check out our possibilities in the morning."

"That sounds like a good idea," she replied. Alea trusted Daniel's judgement completely. "What's next?"

"There's no way around it, honey. We'll have to stand watch all night and sleep on deck, in case the anchor breaks loose from the bottom, which can happen with changes in the wind or swell. In the morning, I'll paddle one of my surfboards north along the cliff and see what I can spot."

Daniel remembered the dark searching gaze of the unusual osprey and its dive for fish that guided his decision to stop the drift. Had the bird given him a message, a sign? It could just be an inland pond, he argued to himself, but I have a strong feeling... no, it's more than a feeling, he concluded. It wouldn't have been the first time that he sensed a mysterious presence, calling, urging, speaking straight to his heart and soul, filling him with strength, reassurance, and hope.

Daniel had experienced that mystery once before, when he and Alea first met and fell in love. It had been their destiny. He believed that with all his heart. Now it was flooding him again and he knew that his life, Alea's life, fit into some greater purpose he could not see, but believed was coming. He was glad he had heeded the osprey.

He and Alea would meet whatever tomorrow brought with strength and humble faith, together. With a silent prayer of thanks, he pulled her even closer and touched her fragrant hair with his lips.

"Tomorrow," he murmured under his breath, "Tomorrow."

Chapter 12   The Island

Daniel lifted the water bottle and drank as much as he could before recapping it and setting it down. The morning sun that had unleashed such fury two days before was mostly hidden behind an angry bank of distant dark clouds on the horizon. The wind direction was changing to straight east at almost twenty miles per hour.

It was time to go. Wearing surf trunks, a long-sleeved rash guard, and reef shoes, he picked up his big wave surfboard and carried it to the dive platform at the stern of the boat. Into The Mystic was rolling in the swell and the backwash off the cliffs, but handling it well.

"I'm going in and will paddle north," he told Alea. "Not sure what I'll find, sweetheart, but if we can't safely ride out this storm that's approaching fast, we'll have to continue drifting, get past this island, and back into open water before it hits. The last thing I want is for Mystic to crash into the rocks. If she sinks and we have nowhere to go but into the tender... well, I know you understand."

Alea nodded solemnly, their predicament extremely clear. And her own, as well. She had no survival skills or training, no life experience with boats or the ocean. If something tragic were to happen to Daniel, she would never be able to survive alone. She wouldn't want to. She lifted her chin.

"I'm sure you'll do what's best for us, Daniel."

He encircled her waist with his free arm and pulled her in, kissing her hard. "I'll be back for you soon." He smiled at her brave expression that he knew was trying to mask concern and gave her a confident little shake. "Stay right here and wait for me, my darling."

He stepped down onto the dive platform, watching the roll of the waves. As a larger wave approached, he launched off the boat, holding the surfboard away from his chest, then lowered himself down in one smooth motion as he hit the water. He pushed backwards to sit up.

"I love you, Alea!" he called out over the wind. Laying out on the board, he turned the nose north and started to paddle.

The July water was warm but felt refreshingly cool against his hot skin. The increasing waves and the repeated slap of their length against the rocks filled the air with clouds of spray and mist. Daniel's powerful arms pommeled the water in a regular rhythm as he paddled along the cliff line. He fought to keep from being swept into small caves as the wind and waves joined forces to push his surfboard towards them.

He could see the high tide line a few feet up the side of the cliff. So, it's probably low tide and perhaps still going out, he reasoned. He was in about fifteen feet of water and was being swept forward by the current. So far, he had seen nothing but solid rock face as he paddled, tempting him to lose hope for an inlet. He buoyed himself by remembering the white osprey. The bird had not been that far away when he first saw it dive and made the decision to drop anchor.

He paddled a short distance further when his head turned sharply to the left. Daniel gasped in surprise, almost choking as a wave broke over the tip of his board and hit him squarely in the face. He could now see the end of the cliff wall, and beyond the edge, an unexpected expanse of blue-green water. He couldn't believe it! He quickly nosed his surfboard left to glide into what looked like a small cove.

It appeared to be about thirty-five feet wide. At the far end of the cove opening, the cliff wall was set back deeper into the island by well over twenty feet, creating a northeast face. Impossible to spot until he was right at the cove entry.

But how far in did this go?

Looking towards the back, his heart sank to see a rear rock wall about seventy-five feet from the cove front, apparently a dead end. The cove could offer some protection, but not from an Atlantic storm or hurricane, especially for a boat as large as Into The Mystic. The rock walls would simply be too close to the hull for comfort in rough seas, and only if the anchor would hold. Swallowing his initial disappointment, he decided to paddle in anyway.

Daniel looked down into the water under his surfboard. The bottom looked sandy, with boulders scattered randomly, most of them near the base of the cliff walls where they had tumbled in over time. The depth of the water was getting increasingly shallow. Fifteen feet... twelve feet... ten feet. As he neared the rear rock wall, he was puzzled by light streaming in from the right side, the light growing brighter the deeper he paddled in.

Astounded, Daniel sat straight up, mouth open, eyes wide, unable to utter a sound.

A channel opened to the right of the rear cliff wall, a channel he would never have seen from Into The Mystic if they had continued their drift. A channel that angled to the right in a graceful arc that opened into...

A bay! The most beautiful bay Daniel had ever seen in all his years in the Bahamas! A push of the swell lifting his board forward nudged him from his stunned silence.

Oh Lord, what have you done? Yes! The shout of joy from his mouth echoed off the walls of the channel. It was the miracle he'd been praying for! He closed his eyes and bowed his head, tears running down his face. When he finally looked up, he thanked his new friend the osprey as well. Then, laying out on his board, he resumed his paddle.

The channel at low tide was about six feet deep and Daniel estimated it was thirty feet wide. At high tide the depth could increase from one to three more feet, depending on the moon phase. More than enough depth for Mystic's 3-foot draft, he thought. But he didn't want to make any hasty decisions until he'd investigated the bay itself.

Osprey Bay. His heart named it instantly as soon as he saw the calm turquoise waters.

The bay was not large, only the size of two football stadiums. But what it lacked in size did not matter. An uninterrupted half circle of sparkling sand beach was laid out along the west shoreline. Beyond the long stretch of beach was a tropical forest of trees. He saw coconut branches dancing in the wind. Casuarina trees carpeted the sand with soft evergreen-like branches, as well as their prickly seed pods. The pale silver-grey trunks of buttonwood stood out from the thick green bushes and lush foliage beneath.

Birds twittered, swooped, and darted among the treetops. A wasp landed on his arm briefly and flew harmlessly away. The deep silence around him was comforting and reassuring. The east wind was cut-off abruptly by the high cliffs and although Daniel could still feel a strong breeze, it was nowhere near the increasing windspeeds at the cove entry.

He could see the trees ascending gradually behind the beach, which told him the island increased in elevation at least in that direction. Good, he thought. That meant any rain would drain downhill, increasing the odds for a freshwater pond or stream. His hopes rose immediately.

A loud screech drew his attention. The white osprey flew low over his head, heading back out to sea. The bird interrupted its journey to circle Daniel, dark eyes peering down at him, and screeched again, as if to say, "I told you it was here."

Daniel smiled and raised a hand to wave as the bird turned off and curiously dipped a wing before continuing its flight. Was the bird greeting him too? He felt certain the osprey had been sent to guide him to this very place and he was speechless with gratitude.

He floated motionless, allowing the serene and quiet beauty of the bay to wash over him. He felt his fears melting away, calm flowing through his mind, tense muscles relaxing from the strain he didn't know he carried. With his decision made, he swung the nose of the surfboard around and began to paddle firmly back to the channel, back towards the woman who meant more to him than his own life.

****

He glided through the channel and back into the entry cove. Needle-like biting spray whipped his face as he pumped his arms harder against the turbulent surf. At the right cliff wall, he turned to head back to Mystic. He saw the cruiser in the distance and roughly estimated how far he needed to go, about a thousand feet. Daniel groaned, arm muscles screaming with his efforts. He paced himself with a regular breathing rhythm like a long-distance runner. He was fighting the current, the wind, and the waves, but could see the tide was still going out, perfect for the plan he was devising.

Alea waited anxiously on deck, watching him struggle to approach the boat. She grabbed a lifebuoy with a length of line attached and held it in readiness to throw to him in the water, if needed.

"Daniel, over here!" she called out, hoping he would hear her voice over the wind. She stood where he could easily see her, waving her arms.

He maneuvered alongside the dive platform and rolled off the surfboard. It was attached to his ankle with a leash, which freed him to climb the ladder. He pulled the board up next to him and released the Velcro strap. Alea lifted the surfboard and carried it to the deck, then returned to where Daniel was sitting, catching his breath.

She wrapped her arms around his shoulders, his chest still heaving as he recovered. Alea felt him starting to shiver and ran into the master cabin where she grabbed a blanket. She covered his shoulders and upper body for warmth and began to dry his hair with a towel. He reached up to stop her hand, holding it in his own, and kissed her palm. Tossing the wet towel over his shoulder, he got up and they walked inside to the main lounge.

She brought him a bottle of water that he drained thirstily. He peeled off his dripping rash guard and trunks, standing naked in the warmth of the room. She gazed at him, desire rising and curling inside her, surprising her with its intensity. He was simply magnificent, with powerful arm and thigh muscles clearly defined from his exertions in the water. His hard-cut abdomen rippled as he dried himself, his tanned skin glistening. Dark hairs curled around his impressive maleness. She never tired of looking at him, wanting him, even now with their lives in jeopardy. She marveled again at the miracle of having him in her life.

They sat close together on the leather couch, holding hands. For some time, neither one spoke.

****

Alea was disturbed. Daniel told her everything about his discovery of the hidden pass and the bay. It sounded like a dream come true. If nothing else, they might make it through the storm. As much as she longed for a feeling of security, she had many questions that worried her tremendously.

"Why are you frowning, sweetheart?" he asked. "There are still a few obstacles I need to figure out real quick before the tide turns, but I think this is our best bet with the storm almost on us. For all we know, this could turn out to be a very strong hurricane."

"I completely understand, Daniel. I'm not saying we don't try. I think we should too, for our own sake. But I'm so afraid this will mean we might never see people again. Our families. Our friends. If the Flare has affected the entire planet, we may be marooned here forever. How would we ever get Mystic out of that bay, once she's inside? You say she'll never run again. How can we survive? If something happened to me, you would be alone. And vice versa." She paused, with a sigh.

"And my next biggest concern. I'm a doctor, Daniel. People will be needing medical care and attention more than ever. And there's nothing I can do from a deserted island."

She fought back her tears. What was she doing? This wasn't helping him at all, even if she felt better for expressing her thoughts. It was time to face the reality of the situation, no matter how unpleasant.

"I'm so sorry, honey," she apologized. "The truth is, I won't, I can't, be anywhere but here with you, right now." Resolved, she took a deep breath. "So, I say let's do this and let God take care of the future." She slipped her arms around him gently. "I did say for better or for worse, right?"

Daniel was relieved. Her concerns were quite valid, but he needed her onboard with his plan. And he always wanted her to express herself sincerely. He had grown up with people who encouraged others to be themselves and to discuss ideas or differences openly and respectfully. That's how Devereaux Fishing had prospered under the guidance of his grandfather and father. That's how he, Ronny, and Matt treated each other. Often, the creative thinking of others turned out to be much better than his own thoughts and he harbored no false ego to prevent him from trying new or unusual things. He valued openness and honesty. The subterfuge and lies from Karen almost destroyed him. But Alea was never afraid to gently share her real feelings about anything and work out their issues calmly. He loved her so much for that.

He pulled her into his arms and rested her head under his chin. "Thank-you, Alea. We need to get Mystic to safety, but I promise to do whatever I can to get us back to our families. And in the future, I know your medical skills will be invaluable to those who need you."

She leaned against his shoulder and sighed, his deep voice rumbling in her ear. It would have to be enough for now.

****

They had to work fast. The tide was starting to turn. Daniel would need the strong flush of the incoming if his crazy idea was to succeed. He'd never attempted a maneuver like this, but strange times called for new ways of thinking.

They stood at the bow as Daniel released the anchor lock and began to retrieve with all his might. He didn't need it to come all the way up, just enough to clear the sandy bottom. As the Danforth and chain lifted off, he could feel Mystic begin her drift again, stern leading the way. He cranked a bit more, then stopped the anchor at ten feet off the bottom, letting it hang in the water and trail along with the boat. He engaged the lock lever and Alea stepped in to take his place. He would tell her when to drop anchor again.

He ran over to the starboard side. Mystic was drifting along the cliff line at a steady pace, gravitating a little closer than her starting point of one hundred feet off. That's good, he thought. The current is directing us towards the entry to the cove. He tensed with expectation as they approached.

"Alea, get ready!" he shouted. The stern began to pass the first cove wall.

"Wait for it, wait for it," he muttered to himself.

Just as the stern reached the center of the cove opening, he shouted to Alea. "Drop the anchor!"

She pulled to release, and the anchor dropped straight to the bottom, laid down, and dug in. Daniel hurried over to her side, re-locked, and they waited to see if the Danforth would grip and stop the drift.

"It's holding!" she yelled in excitement. The stern began a leisurely swing towards the cove opening, although still about forty feet away.

"The plot thickens," he chuckled, congratulating himself. He waited a moment to feel confident the anchor was holding well. Then, gripping the brake handle, he gradually released the anchor line, which allowed the boat to begin backing down towards the cove. He watched intently, ready to stop the backwards drift at any sign of danger. The incoming tide and the east wind were now aiding Mystic's retreat.

As the stern entered the cove proper, Daniel kept releasing more line. Alea positioned herself at the rail to warn him if they wandered too close to the rock walls. The tide was sweeping the boat deeper into the cove and heading straight back to the rear wall. Daniel increased tension on the brake to slow the drift and inwardly cringed. The portside hull had to hit the right rock wall or Mystic's 52-foot length would never pivot into the 30-foot wide channel, the rock wall serving as a fulcrum. There would be damage to the hull, but it couldn't be helped.

Alea stood with him at the bow. Into The Mystic was about to crash into the edge of the cliff and that was just what Daniel wanted. He held his breath as the stern reached the channel entry and continued to float straight back. Would his timing be correct? He began to tighten the brake on the anchor line. He only wanted twenty-five feet of the boat to pass the channel entry.

He took a deep breath as the critical moment approached and stopped the anchor line completely. Mystic stuttered and hit the channel wall exactly at the pivot point he needed to turn her. Daniel's heart sank when he heard the fiberglass crunch but kept the line firm and uttered a fervent prayer.

Pushed by the incoming tide, the wind, and the current, the boat bounced once off the wall and the stern turned neatly into the channel. Holding back a cry of joy, he released the brake, allowing the boat to continue its moonwalk, line running out as she floated slowly backwards.

Into The Mystic slid out of the hidden channel and into the turquoise beauty of Osprey Bay's inviting arms.

Chapter 13   Osprey Bay

The softening of the wind was the first memory Alea would carry of Osprey Bay for the rest of her life. It was a dream-like memory, warm and tranquil, with swaying and whispering coconut branches, the singing of small birds, the golden expanse of beach, and turquoise waters shimmering under dappled rays of sunlight that pierced through swirling dark clouds. It took her breath away. She walked to the stern and stood silently. It felt as if they had come home.

Mystic glided further into the bay as Daniel released more anchor line in an effort to get her as close to shore as possible without grounding. The bay was deep enough for the shallow draft of the boat and she lazily floated towards the north end of the beach. The tide was still coming in. He thought they were in about six feet of water depth and he knew it would get even deeper with the incoming tide.

He looked around for Alea and saw her quietly looking out over the wind-rippled water. He wanted to go to her, but there was one more important task he needed to complete before the storm hit, and it was coming on quickly.

He ran down below and pulled out the auxiliary anchor with several hundred feet of line. Hauling it up to the bow, he secured the end of the line to a cleat. With Mystic still slowly drifting towards shore, he dropped the second anchor off the bow. When he felt it bite into the sand, he permitted fifty feet of line to run out before tying off. He then locked down the main anchor and retrieved any extra line until both anchors were holding fast. Mystic finally stopped one hundred feet from the beach, just as the first light raindrops started to fall.

"Alea?"

Turning and running to him, she pressed against his chest, his strong beating heart pounding in her ear as she wrapped her arms tightly around him. He was her home, wherever that happened to be. Nothing else mattered.

She didn't need to speak. Daniel understood.

"This bay should be safe, my darling," he said. "We can ride out the storm on the boat. She should hold in place, even with the main anchor outside the cove entry. I'll have to think about that problem another day." The rain was falling harder and Mystic was rolling slightly in the roughened water.

"I feel so odd," she told him. "The beauty here is astonishing. It looks untouched. How could there be no one here?" She looked up at him in wonder. "But somehow it feels right, Daniel, like this has always been waiting for us."

He raised an eyebrow. He would tell her later about the white osprey and the bird's mystical message.

"That's how I feel too. As if we were supposed to have found this island."

There was much to think about. He had no clue what was happening on the other Bahamian islands or in the states since the solar flare. Or the rest of the world, for that matter. He was sure there had been a powerful EMP, but there was no real way to confirm his fears. If only he could contact Ben on Spanish Wells. For now, he had to focus. First things first.

"Okay, let's look at this logically. There are no boats in here, but you can see why. The entry cove hid this bay extremely well and only certain types of boats could make it in without damage. And I haven't seen many bays on the Atlantic side in the Bahamas. This is quite rare. No obvious signs of people on this beach and no homes visible. Perhaps there's a town over on the west side? This island doesn't look very big, but it's large enough it will take some time and effort to explore."

She nodded. "Yes, I agree with all of that and I do want to explore, especially for a fresh water source. Rain is good but unreliable, and how would we capture and store quantities of it? After that, finding food." She laughed for the first time that day. "I'm certain we'll never lack for seafood."

Daniel grinned. "Speaking of food, why don't we get out of this rain and get something to eat? I'm starving and I want a Guinness, even if it's a warm Guinness. After that, I need to dive down and tie off a couple more lines to the bottom to help hold us. Hopefully there'll be a few big boulders or something solid down there. And I want to look at the port side of the hull. I heard a pretty good crunch when we made the turn. I expected that to happen, yes, but I should check it out."

"So, we ride out the storm on Mystic."

"Safest place for us to be," he assured her. "Let's see what our brand new two-million-dollar boat can really do."

The rain was beginning to pelt their faces with piercing, cold wet beads. The skies had darkened, and even in the protected bay, the winds were howling. The storm had arrived. They had made it to safety with only moments to spare.

It was eleven o'clock in the morning.

****

If a person is safely tucked away in a solidly roofed concrete house with expensively shielded windows, a supply of candles, water, food, and in particular, a variety of adult beverages, a minor hurricane might not be too bad. More like a temporary reprieve from daily life and job, with an extra-added dose of danger and excitement thrown in for good measure. Daniel had experienced that scenario a couple of times.

Relying on their tentatively anchored 52-foot yacht, rolling in angry waves and swept by at least seventy-five mile per hour winds and sheets of driving rain, promised to be quite a different experience. Daniel was extremely interested in how Mystic would handle. She was the cradle of life for them this night and the cradle was rocking.

Hours earlier, he had added two extra lines from the boat to the bay floor, ensuring Mystic was facing into the oncoming winds. She was holding well, and while he was in the water securing the lines, Daniel checked the port side of the boat. Damage to the fiberglass was something he expected might occur and he was happy it was not worse. At least the crushed section was above the waterline and basically repairable with the tools and supplies he carried on board.

They felt the frantic roll of the disturbed bay all through the night. It was the first time Alea had ever been seasick and he cared for her best he could, making her drink water to stay hydrated and giving her a seasickness pill. He held her and tried to comfort her until she weakly requested that he leave her alone in her misery. She vomited any food she tried to eat and remained nauseous until the next day. The raging storm crossed over the island just before dawn and she finally began to recover as noon approached.

Daniel remained awake all night, listening to the storm and walking the rain-lashed decks of the boat when not with Alea. He observed and analyzed her reactions to the waves and wind, on alert for any emergency he might have to deal with. By morning he was impressed and satisfied. He would never know the true strength of this hurricane, but Into The Mystic had been worth every penny.

They were alive.

Chapter 14 New World

With only a few hours of restless sleep near dawn, the sun was already peeping through brief gaps in the passing cloud bands when he awoke in the late morning. Alea was already out of bed and in the bathroom. He could hear the splashing of water but was relieved not to hear the sounds of nausea. When the door slid open, he saw that she was still pale but steady, with her hair tied in a loose knot and wearing a fresh pair of tan shorts and a lacey white tank top. Daniel jumped up to meet her at the door.

"Feeling better?" he asked gently, supporting her with an arm around her waist as he led her back to sit on the bed. They sat with hands clasped.

"I feel so embarrassed." She couldn't meet his eye and kept staring at the floor. "I've never been seasick before and you had to see all that."

"Honey, you don't get on any boat without eventually going through it at least once," he chuckled. "You should've seen Matt's projectile vomit. I think it's a permanent part of the wall décor in the galley of North Wind. Looks like a Picasso. The crews of South Wind, West Wind, and East Wind all want him to decorate their boat too."

Alea had to laugh. "Well, I'm no artist like Matt so I made sure I cleaned up all my "paint", so to speak." It felt so good to feel better. She sighed and leaned into him.

"Did you get any sleep?"

"A few hours. I can't wait to get over to the island and start exploring. Still too rough to row over today and the rain is on and off. I think maybe tomorrow. You need to recover, and we need to take stock of our food. The cooler is empty. I had to pitch everything in there. We'll have to restrict ourselves until I can get back in the water. And I want to see what's available on the island."

"How's our water situation? she asked. "At last count we had eleven full 5-gallon bottles left. We used two before the Flare and we finished the partial in the dispenser afterwards."

"Down to ten since yesterday," he told her. "We need to stay hydrated and still be conservative. I'm hoping to find fresh water here but it's always a question mark on any Bahamian island. Spanish Wells fortunately has a massive underground reservoir. Eleuthera itself has only a few deep wells, which were inadequate for their growing population of 11,000. They tried desalinization of seawater, but it turned out to be very expensive for questionable results. They won't be able to use that system anyway if the EMP killed the electrical systems that run it. Businesses and homes won't be able to use electric well pumps either."

His heart sank. Daniel anticipated there would be extremely painful times ahead. Life was so dependent on power in the modern age. There would be hoarding, robbery, killings. The immoral and the strongest would be the first to take resources by force. The days ahead would define each person and what they were willing to do to stay alive. He and Alea needed to be alert and aware of the many potential dangers they could be facing.

"The Bahamas have a rainy season mostly in the summer, from July to October," he explained. "For all other months of the year, rain can be sporadic to non-existent. Wells need to be replenished by the seasonal summer rains. The problem is the limestone base rock of the undersea mountains that form the Bahama Islands. It's very porous and allows rainwater to drain down deep where it can't be accessed. The best wells are found in more solid types of rock. Spanish Wells is lucky that their deep and solid granite rock reservoirs have retained and provided fresh water for centuries."

Daniel quickly assessed their supply status. "We have a total of fourteen 5-gallon water bottles, so we can easily collect rain with tarps and store it. But a consistent source would be ideal. We should still boil it to drink, don't you agree?"

"Yes, boiling any drinking water first is the safest thing to do. We don't have purification tablets, but I did read that you can fill plastic bottles with water, cap them, and set them out in direct hot sun for a day. Supposedly, this kills the bacteria and makes it safe to drink, but still quite warm. Maybe the water could be cooled off by setting the bottles in a shallow pool or in a shady location."

Alea was finding herself challenged by the problems they would be facing. She was not one of those "preppers" she had heard about, often disparagingly from her fellow colleagues at fundraisers or cocktail parties. There was never any reason or need to pursue the topic beyond superficial internet searches for her own amusement. Under the present circumstances, however, she could see their logic and wisdom. They needed to learn as much as possible about the environment in which they found themselves. Basic needs had to be met and there was no infrastructure to support them.

Preppers at least had the advantages of time and plenty of well-stocked stores to choose from as they established their base of operations for an anticipated negative future scenario. But there were no grocery or home repair stores here. She and Daniel would be limited to the supplies on Mystic, whatever the island provided, and their own innate human abilities to adapt, learn, and create in order to survive.

She was aware Daniel had spent many years in the islands, with intimate knowledge not only of the ocean, but also of the trees, plants, birds, and animals that called the Bahamas home. She was suddenly very grateful for his invaluable skills, abilities, and experience, understanding that he would be the deciding factor in whether they would ultimately live or die on this island.

But Alea was determined to help him and understood her own value as a physician and surgeon. Although the practice of surgery as she knew it could never again take place under these current conditions, there was still so much for her to contribute. She was instantly inspired to use the island as her own personal survival university and start from scratch. No degree or certification was going to help her now. She'd have to become a tropical prepper and bush medicine woman! She looked over at the island, examining it with new eyes, and a thrill ran up her spine.

"Your water idea is terrific, honey, and sounds like it might work. I've never heard of that technique before," Daniel said.

Alea felt relieved he approved.

"Well, it may all be a moot point if we find a community on this island."

"Maybe," he said, keeping his face expressionless. Daniel did not want to reveal his fears to a hopeful Alea. As reassuring as locating a community sounded, it was now an unpredictable and uncertain world.

The Flare had made finding other people the deadliest thing that could ever happen to them.

Chapter 15   Exploration

The tender cut the water neatly as Daniel and Alea rowed towards the beach. The sun had risen quietly that morning with the full heat of a late July Bahamian summer day already bearing down. Humidity hung in the air, wet and palpable, and the wind switched to a light northwest. The hurricane had roared past to devastate others.

Alea wore a light blue swimsuit and a wide-brimmed straw hat. She was perspiring heavily as she dipped her oar into the water and pulled back firmly. She glanced over at Daniel. He was rowing in tandem with her, attempting to steer the tender to an area of the beach that had caught his attention earlier. His rash guard and surf trunks protected his skin from the sun, and he wore a favorite old beat-up fishing hat.

The tender approached the beach and skidded up with a sandpaper rasp as the water shallowed to a few inches. The boat stopped and began to turn sideways with a gentle rocking motion. They were finally ashore! Daniel jumped out first and dropped the mushroom anchor, then pulled the boat further up on the beach. Alea stepped off and into the warm bottom sand, happy to be back on land. Hand in hand, they surveyed the terrain before them.

The curved shoreline was white sand beach with only a few scattered rocky areas. The hurricane had brought down many trees and pushed seaweed in from the Atlantic, tangled in brown snakelike masses all along the high tide line. They followed the beach a short distance to investigate a small cove, about thirty feet inland from the bay and just as wide.

"I think there's a stream of water flowing in at the back!"

Daniel stepped into the shallow, knee-deep cove and sloshed towards what looked like the source of the incoming water. His initial high hopes were somewhat dashed. It was a barely usable stream, running out into the cove through a gulley that cut through the topsoil, a foot wide and just a few inches deep. Over time, he thought, the stream must have been created by rain running down the sloped hill to meet with the saltwater of the bay, causing much of the sand to erode out and form the cove. Earthy debris flowed down the hill with the stream. It was a source of fresh water, yes, but not as clean, plentiful, or reliable as he would have liked and would need to be filtered. Daniel wondered if the stream disappeared entirely during the dry season.

But he was quite pleased with the cove for another reason. A grove of casuarina trees grew close to the shoreline, branching their evergreen-like boughs halfway out over the water. This area was sure to become cool and shady after the sun passed noon. There were several trees a past storm had likely toppled over, exposing tangled root balls. Their trunks would provide natural seating and the dead branches would make excellent firewood. Casuarina logs imparted a unique smoky flavor to seafood and meat as well. One large tree had fallen into the water, creating a solid surface to scale and clean fish. They could continue to live on Mystic, but he was already picturing the beach hut he would build here in the future.

"What are you thinking about?" Alea was curious why he was studying the area so closely. She was hot and took a long drink from her water bottle.

"This is where we'll land when we come over. What do you say to calling it Casuarina Cove? This spot has a freshwater stream we can work with and we'll have shade most of the day. We can keep tabs on the boat from here. Do you see all the baitfish swimming around us? Places where fresh water and sea water meet are natural habitats. I bet this bay has a lot of fish and maybe conch too! There could be crab along the rock walls to the east. I know there has to be lobster near the channel and outside at the cliffs."

He felt a rush of excitement and renewed hope. "Alea, I can feed us here!"

He tallied the blessings of the last few days. The drift had brought Mystic into the safety of Osprey Bay. The boat was sheltered from storms, the island was lush with vegetation, there was some source of fresh water, and always the mainstay of seafood. It was a very good start and relief flooded him.

He turned and ran towards her, lifting Alea high into the air and twirled her around in a circle.

"I love you, woman!"

She slid slowly down his body until her lips met his, as he growled in anticipation. The stress of the past several days drained away as she pressed her nipples into his chest and felt him harden and rise against her. She broke away from their kiss and whispered suggestively in his ear. She was ready to play.

Daniel threw his head back, laughing, and took off running with her in his arms out to deeper water. With Alea shrieking in mock horror, they plunged in together.

She sputtered as she came up for a breath of air, trying to stop laughing, her long hair spreading out on the surface like a mermaid. Daniel peeled her blue swimsuit off her body and down her legs until she was naked, floating easily on her back. He yanked off his wet rash guard and ripped off his trunks. Flinging them away, he began a slow deliberate stalk towards her, his eyes dark with desire.

Alea squealed and tried to swim away as fast as she could, but a hand capturing her hair stopped her escape. He held her wavy, waist-length locks like the reins of a horse and pulled her to him until her white buttock cheeks were firm against his throbbing member.

With one hand reining her hair and his other arm wrapped around her hips, he plunged inside as she arched and cried out. He began a steady pumping, hammering hard, again and again. The turquoise water splashed out in rhythmic waves as Daniel drove into her relentlessly.

"Is this what you wanted, woman? You wanted me to ride you?"

He let go of her hair and began to stroke her sensitive bud, never slowing his driving thrusts. Her breath paused for a long moment before she exploded in a wild throbbing orgasm. He plunged once more, planting himself in her depths as he held her trembling hips tight against him, and released in pulse after pulse of overpowering pleasure.

He pulled out slowly and sank to his knees in the soft bottom sand. He drew Alea to him, as he wrapped his arms around her waist and dropped his head to rest on her back. Osprey Bay bathed them in salty warmth.

They had officially made the island their home.

****

She brought out a small cooler and they sat close together on one of the fallen casuarina logs, eating slices of bread, cheese, and a couple of apples with hungry relish. Alea popped open a can of ginger ale and handed it to Daniel before opening a pre-sealed bottle of apple juice for herself. Neither spoke as they ate, mesmerized by the tropical beauty surrounding them. Her hand caressed his thigh lightly and she sighed softly with contentment.

Alea never realized how noisy the old world had been. The ever-present roar of traffic, the blare of radios and stereos, repetitive mall background music, the thunder of airplanes flying overhead; the myriad cacophony of sounds that modern society no longer consciously paid any attention to. It was just always there... abrasive, grating on the brain, making sure adrenaline kept the body in constant low-level stress. People couldn't seem to function without it, to the point of wearing earbuds and headphones all day to keep themselves soothed and stimulus medicated. There was no real peace anywhere.

Except here. She lifted her face to the azure sky and closed her eyes, absorbing the quiet. She did not often allow herself the luxury to simply sit and just be. It felt odd. It soothed her, but at the same time left her feeling somewhat anxious, as if something was missing, something left undone. Are we all so empty that it takes constant stimulus to make us feel that we even exist? she wondered.

Do we always have to fill ourselves up artificially to make our lives feel worthwhile? Stuffing the empty voids inside with money, drugs, sex, food, or careers to find comfort, to feel a semblance of peace, security, stability, and belonging? None of those fillers can be taken with us when the end of life finally comes, she realized.

I did the same thing, she admitted to herself. I filled myself deliberately with work and ignored so much of what I really needed. Love. I feared love, I see that now. I just didn't want to hurt again. I made sure there was no time to think about the past, allowing the demands of work to consume my mind every hour, day and night. My patients, the staff, my partners, and the planning and decisions for each surgery left me no time, opportunity, or desire, for that matter, for any kind of satisfying personal life. Was I deluding myself that I was content? Even my short vacation to visit my parents wasn't very pleasant. It took three days just to detox and clear my head. But that's when the memories returned... and I left immediately to go back to Boston. So I could forget.

Alea's eyes shot open as the unhappy memories flooded her once again and she slammed them down deliberately and hard. Those days were the worst of her life and she hated it when the thoughts came unbidden to her mind.

But that was all before Daniel. Her lips curved in a Mona Lisa smile. She could rest with him and felt a deep serenity, a completeness she had never known before. Her empty spaces no longer existed. The power of Daniel's love had filled her and made her whole.

The breathtaking beauty and tranquility of the island was seductive. The sounds of light wind rustling the trees and brush. The gentle pat of small waves rushing the sand and retreating with a hushed whisper. The animated flicker of dancing sunlight threading through the lacey branches of the treetops. The call of seabirds winging against the blue sky. An occasional disturbance out in the bay; the splash of a fishtail or the head of a turtle poking up cautiously for a breath of air. She was entranced.

She glanced at Daniel. He was crunching the last bite of his apple, deep in thought, but looking relaxed. She envied his ability to meld wherever he was and with whomever he found himself. She was thoughtful and reserved. He was more open, pleasantly approachable, and drew people to him naturally. He lived his life with the same proactive forward drive she did but emanated an inner peace, strength, and dependability. He "surfed the wave" of life, taking on each day as it came, making decisions based not only on the circumstances around him, but trusting his own intuitions as well, quickly, and with no regrets. He planned ahead with incredible foresight but could adapt to the unexpected as easily as a surfer reacting to the capricious wave beneath him.

The wonder and amazement at how they met never dulled. It was still a miracle for her. Alea no longer tried to dissect why she had responded so strongly and immediately to Daniel. It was inevitable, fated, irresistible. She had been waiting for him all her life, their souls drawn together like two powerful magnets, once in close proximity. She trusted him completely at the deepest level she was capable of, surprising herself with that realization.

Something she now realized she could never have done with Brad Brockdorff. Shivering as if a cold winter wind had caught her off guard, she slammed the memories back again.

****

Daniel stood up and stretched, tossed the apple core into the bush, and reached out his hand.

"It's time to explore."

Alea nodded and took his hand. Although she was enjoying her quiet time of reflection, she was also anxious to see what the island had to offer. They returned to the tender and pulled out their backpacks.

Daniel insisted that they both change into long pants, long-sleeved shirts, and sturdy shoes. He wasn't sure if poisonwood trees were on this island, but he couldn't take that chance. The trunks were identified by a light tan color with irregular black splotches and peeling bark. The wood, bark, sap, and leaves were much worse than poison ivy or poison oak. Once even lightly contacted by skin, red irritated bumps were produced that soon developed into wet pustules, leaking toxins all over the body until they were widespread and unrelentingly itchy. If one were to give in to the natural inclination to scratch, the inflamed pustules would worsen, scab over, and permanently scar. Poisonwood was also very communicable. The infections took months to disappear on their own and there was no real natural antidote. A specialized prescription from a physician was the only known cure. He would prevent Alea from having to endure that misery at any cost.

Once dressed, they each tucked a plastic water bottle into a side pocket of their backpacks and slung them on. With Daniel carefully leading the way, they headed inland.

He decided to explore the entire island over the course of the next week, mentally dividing the land into four sections from their campsite: south, southwest, northwest, and north. Each day they planned to walk as much of one section as possible. Locating a source of fresh water was absolutely imperative. Once back at the beach, Daniel would dive for their dinner before they retired to Mystic for the night.

From his perspective on the boat while in the Atlantic, the island appeared to be an oval shape, running north to south, with the cove and channel into Osprey Bay approximately center along the eastern shore. He loosely estimated the island was about six miles long, width to be determined during their exploratory walks.

The incline of the land gradually rose in the direction of the western perimeter. The island somewhat resembled an extinct volcanic caldera, even though he knew the Bahamas did not have any seismic history or origin. But it encouraged him that perhaps he might locate an inland pool or lake of fresh water. For today, he selected the northwest section to begin their explorations, as it was the most convenient to Casuarina Cove and the day was already half gone.

Daniel moved carefully through the thick bush and trees. He held a sharp machete in his right hand, which would serve to clear smaller tree trunks and brush out of their path.

The machete, or cutlass, was the main cutting tool of many islands in the Caribbean. No electric power was required other than the power of a strong arm and careful eye. The African slaves first brought over by British and French planters were issued this vital tool during the day to chop and clear the fields for planting, but at night they were held accountable to turn them back in until the next morning.

Tobacco was the first crop of any worth to landowners, but the thin and rocky island soil was soon stripped of nutrients by the heavy demands of each plant. Repetitive crop failures caused many to depart for the richer, more productive fields in the Americas. Many island-born slaves were permitted to stay behind and remained to populate the Bahamas under British rule. Although officially freed in the 1800's, the islands did not become independent until the 1970's. The machete continued to be used preferentially by private landowners, farmers, and landscapers.

Daniel was quite comfortable with a machete, having used one many times before, not only for clearing landscape, but to crack the thick shell of conch to get to the meat inside. Keeping Alea comfortably behind him, he swung at the thick bush with a regular sweeping rhythm as they headed west-northwest. He kept track of the progress of the sun and its arc across the sky. The walk was becoming more difficult as the land rose in a gradual incline and they both began to pant in the heat of the afternoon.

They struggled for over an hour, swatting at mosquitos as he chopped. Daniel estimated they'd only walked about a mile and a half. He was relieved when the bush and trees began to thin out and a cool westerly breeze unexpectedly picked up in front of them. A quarter mile further and the trees abruptly disappeared.

Surprised, they stood facing a sweeping flat plain of waving grasses and small shrubs. Another quarter mile away was the rise of the western cliffs and Daniel could see they were almost to the calm Caribbean side. They hadn't encountered a single human being. There was no town, and more importantly, no lake or pool of fresh water.

****

Alea stepped out onto the grassy plain. She was happy to be out of the bush and even happier when the mosquitoes and other hungry insects seemed to vanish once they moved away from the tree line. Daniel was already walking forward to cross the plain and she jogged to catch up.

"Those bushes growing on the side of the cliff ahead, isn't that sea grape?" she called out to him. "I remember seeing them at the beaches on Eleuthera."

Daniel removed his sunglasses and squinted.

"I believe you're right!" he exclaimed. Early summer was the season for the tart and juicy reddish grapes to ripen. He had often satisfied his appetite with clusters of the delicious fruit straight from the bush after a morning surf. He'd suck the soft flesh off the core of small seeds in the center and spit them back to the ground to root and spread. Did they have a bag to carry some back?

Alea was curious about the plain. The acres of treeless land were so different from the bush and she couldn't remember seeing a similar piece of land since she first arrived in the Bahamas. She shook her head in amazement. Wasn't it just a week ago she had flown in for vacation?

The plain was not completely flat. The land rose gently as they approached the cliffs where sea grape thickly occupied the slopes. She observed reddish-colored soil under her feet, mixed with black dirt and sand, with short grasses growing in scattered clumps. Limestone rocks littered the landscape. It looked like photographs of the Mars surface, except for the grass. Small scrub bushes gripped the surface, no more than a foot tall. A variety of low plants snaked their vine-like tendrils through the grass. Nothing looked edible.

"Why is the ground so red?" she asked. He kept walking but reached down to pick up a handful.

"Red dust from Africa blows from east to west on the trade winds and during hurricanes. The dust has landed here in the Bahamas for thousands of years and creates this red soil. In some wetter locations it becomes hard and clay-like, not great for plants unless mixed well with good black dirt. Pineapple thrives quite well in it, though."

"Daniel, can we stop? I want to try something. Can you bring your machete over here?"

"I won't let you use this until you've had some practice, Alea. What do you want to do?" as he came back to her side.

"Let's see how deep it goes."

"Why?"

"Well, it's unusual terrain, the most usable land we've seen so far, and I'm wondering how to take advantage of it, maybe growing food of some kind. Not sure, just curious."

"Alea, there's no water in sight. Even if we did have water, hauling it here for crops would be very difficult."

But the discussion started him wondering about what to eat other than seafood. He knew they would slowly starve on an exclusive protein diet. He was eager to reach the cliffs but saw no reason not to do as she requested. Daniel shrugged off his backpack, gripped the machete with both hands, and began to chop into the ground. He decided to open a short trench and loosen the topsoil before going deeper. After digging for ten minutes, with Alea using both hands and a stone to remove loose debris out of the trench, the machete finally struck solid rock about a foot and a half down.

"Not bad," Daniel conceded, "but we can't be sure the whole plain is even this deep. And what would you plant? We have no seeds." He loved her genuine enthusiasm and certainly did not want to squelch any helpful idea she came up with, but he doubted this one would ever take place.

"I got that, but I'm trying to keep an open mind and look at the long-term picture. It's important for us to think creatively and I really want to find ways to grow food, if we'll be here for a long time." Had she angered him?

He tossed the machete aside and scooped her up. "I'm sorry, Alea," silencing her relieved laugh with a kiss. "Keep those ideas coming. Now, let's go get some sea grapes."

The sea grape bushes covering the cliffs were heavy with fruit. They picked and ate until they were stuffed and Alea placed several bunches into the top of their backpacks. They'd return in a few days with bags to collect much more. The fruit was ripening rapidly and would soon be devoured by the many birds nesting on the island. They needed to take their share while it was still available.

The steep climb from the plain to the top of the cliff made their leg muscles and lungs burn. Once standing high above the Caribbean sea, they gazed silently out over the edge. The cliffs continued to the north and south at a height of almost forty feet from the water. There were no homes. Scanning to the west, there was no other island visible from their vantage point, and no boats in sight.

Daniel turned to look at her, his expression neutral, and she gave him a resigned smile.

They were truly alone.

Chapter 16   Miracle Island

The island continued to amaze them every day and Daniel was astounded at their good fortune. Except for the nagging problem of fresh water, the island was a Garden of Eden in the middle of the ocean that held almost everything he and Alea needed to survive.

They found fruit trees everywhere. Coconut trees sprang up along the beach as well as inland, their rustling long-limbed branches swaying lazily in the hot midday breezes. Clusters of coconut grew below the branch stems and the fallen nuts were easy to collect. Daniel used his machete to crack younger nuts open for coconut pulp or for the tasty water. Mature coconuts absorbed their water but instead offered dense white coconut meat they could chop or shred.

In close proximity to camp, they found several large groves of heavily laden papaya trees and quite a few mature mango trees, some already bearing dozens of their ripe yellow fruit. Alea brought reusable canvas grocery sacks from the boat to carry back anything they gathered.

A particularly special find for Daniel were the sour orange trees. The bittersweet juice was excellent for preserving fish, lobster, and conch, essentially "cooking" the meat without requiring heat. Seafood soaked in sour orange juice could remain edible for almost a week.

On one hike, Alea spotted a group of trees with elongated oval-shaped leaves that looked somewhat familiar. Daniel was excited to discover they were banana trees, with numerous bunches of still green fruit. But a lingering question that had been troubling him often during their days of exploration re-surfaced as they walked.

Banana trees should not have been here. They were not a seed-based fruit tree. In fact, he wondered how some of the tree varieties they were seeing had even gotten to the island, as they were not native to the Bahamas, and required a cutting or root to propagate. He was puzzled they were here at all. The miracles were stacking up in his mind.

****

The sun was low in the west as they boarded the tender to row back out to Mystic. They off-loaded four bags of bananas, sea grape, papaya, mango, and sour oranges before Daniel donned his dive gear to hunt for the evening meal.

For the present time, the propane for the stove and oven could be lit by hand. Once depleted, however, they would have to grill over an open fire on the exposed beach. Daniel collected large rocks to form a campfire circle at Casuarina Cove and Alea stored deadfall logs, branches, and twigs under a small tarp to keep the wood dry. They were using the butane firelighters and matches for now but planned on attempting to start a fire the ancient Cro-Magnon way, with wooden stick and platform. Daniel also knew how to use a magnifying glass in the hot sun to ignite tinder.

Food choices were becoming limited as the basic supplies on Mystic rapidly dwindled. Fish, lobster, crab, and conch were their staple proteins, with fruit as the only side-dish. Alea was sorely missing bread. Their one bag of rice was long gone. She was concerned there was no source of necessary fats other than the cholesterol in lobster. Nuts are a good source, she thought. I need to ask Daniel what kind of nuts grow in the Bahamas. She could probably recognize a tropical almond tree, but not much else.

Alea decided it was time to become a medicine woman, as in some of the popular books she had read, and her backpack served perfectly for that purpose. She pulled out a dozen plastic zip bags and a black marker to keep with her during explorations, as she began collecting small amounts of leaves, roots, and bark to test as food or for medicinal value. She was going Stone Age and wondered what her medical colleagues would think about that. They would eventually have to do the same, if they were even alive.

Daniel drew a rough map of the island, noting Hidden Pass cove and channel, Osprey Bay, Casuarina Cove, the cliffs, and the plain. He made a second copy for Alea, and at the end of each day of exploration they would pencil in new discoveries. Alea marked the location of any fruit trees and bushes on her copy. The map was a simple method to remind herself where she had collected her trial foliage.

They sampled a palatable hot tea she brewed from the shiny green leaves of a dark-red trunked tree. Daniel thought he recalled older Bahamians saying it was gala-something, but he couldn't recall the name of the tree. He desperately missed coffee, the last cup savored the week before, but drank Alea's tea politely.

Daniel soaked whatever seafood they did not immediately eat in plastic containers with lids, soaking in sour orange juice as a preservative. Fish bones and other remains were tossed overboard, and on several evenings they were entertained by a pair of reef sharks coming in for a free meal near the boat. Alea finally asked Daniel to dump the bones inland and not in the bay. She enjoyed a cleansing swim off Mystic after dinner and was not keen to face a hungry shark.

They watched the sunset each night from the stern deck. The dwindling bottles of wine did not prevent them from enjoying a glass as they recovered from their exertions of the day. It would be gone soon enough, leaving behind pensive memories of easier times. The pair of osprey were usually seen heading back to their inland nest with a fish or two tightly clenched in their talons. Daniel always gave them a nod and a wave, and the white osprey would dip a wing in reply. He often circled the boat, his dark masked eyes meeting Daniel's, and gave a screech in greeting before flying on. Daniel was glad the bird didn't mind sharing the island with he and Alea.

They formed the habit of going to bed right after sunset. The few candles on the boat had been used up weeks before and the quiet dark made sleep feel natural. They often made love at twilight, then jumped into the bay to cool off and rinse. Once in bed, one or the other would tell a story from their life until fatigue overcame them. Mystic rocked gently and silence enveloped them in a quiet cocoon. As they drifted off, Alea drowsily wondered why she had ever owned a television as she snuggled close to Daniel's warm skin.

The humidity of late August became stifling, with daytime temperatures over one hundred degrees. The bay waters were almost too warm. Heavy rains poured down every afternoon, spiking the muggy humidity to unbearable levels. The Atlantic hurricane season was still a threat and would not end for three more months. Daniel anxiously watched the skies daily for any sign of trouble.

"We're down to two of the bottles of water we brought from Spanish Wells," she reported one morning. Drinking water on the boat was getting seriously low. Bathing and personal care was done exclusively in the salty bay and Alea longed for the luxury of a fresh hot shower.

"We only have the one stream," Daniel reminded her. "I feel lucky to have it, as time-consuming and difficult as it is to funnel water into the bucket." He greatly feared the dry season after November.

It took several hours each morning to direct water from the stream into a bucket, then strain it through a piece of kitchen cheesecloth before pouring the semi-pure water into a five-gallon bottle. Daniel would re-seal with the plastic cap and set the bottle on a rock in the blazing hot sun for most of the day. The heat purified the water as much as possible but Alea still preferred to boil it before they drank, for safety's sake. They would soon have to do that in a pot over an open fire on the beach when the propane ran out on Mystic.

To supplement the stream water, they draped tarps on the exposed boat decks to catch rainfall, guiding the flow into plastic tote containers. This water was used to rinse after a saltwater bath and was a successful technique in this rainy season, but even so, they were just getting by.

Her shoulders sank. They discussed this problem every day but could no longer ignore the harsh reality coming with the winter season. They would never survive without a reliable source of fresh drinking water.

She understood why ancient man lived near lakes or rivers. It made perfect sense; to ensure a steady supply of life-giving water. Modern times had allowed people to range out and live in any dry location, with water pumped in. The Flare had most likely turned those areas into dead zones. If she and Daniel, only two people, were straining their environment, how would millions of unprepared men, women, and children compete and survive in a powerless world? Her fears took hold of her emotions, fears she had quietly held inside for weeks.

"Daniel, please tell me, what are we going to do?" she cried out in frustration, her shoulders slumping in despair. "I'm completely at a loss how to find enough water to keep us alive. I've simply run out of ideas. It takes all my energy, for half a day, every day, to strain and boil our drinking water. And let's not forget to include harvesting fruit, diving, fishing, and exploring every inch of this island for whatever we can find. Daniel, I love you so much, but I'm wearing out. You lived in these islands all your life. I did not. I'm exhausted."

Feeling defeated, Alea dropped her head in her hands and began to sob.

Daniel didn't know what to say. Her tears were devastating, and he was paralyzed with uncertainty of how to comfort her. He felt the same way more often than he cared to admit and realized he simply had no words to give her at this moment. All he could do was pull her shaking shoulders to him and hold her close, his love for her flaring in his heart.

Without conscious effort, his mind slowly drifted over the life-changing events of the six months since he met Alea, and of the last incredibly stressful four weeks they had spent on the island. Almost imperceptibly at first, he felt a gentle nudge deep inside, heard a quiet whisper in his ear, and the answer seemed completely clear. He closed his eyes and prayed.

As they clung to each other, neither were aware of the soft glow of light that haloed around them briefly, then faded away like mist in the morning sun.

All at once, an inexplicable wave of peace flowed over them like a warm shower. They both opened their eyes, blinking as if awakening from a deep sleep. Something had changed. They were no longer afraid. They looked at each other with a silent question, then instantly accepted that something beyond their understanding had just taken place. It would not have been the first time for them. It would not be the last.

They glanced up as the osprey unexpectedly appeared in the sky overhead and glided down to the boat, peering at them intently. The cool early morning breeze held him aloft as the hawk uncharacteristically hovered right over Daniel's head. He slowly floated to the stern deck, landed, and calmly folded his wings. Daniel looked at Alea in amazement.

The bird began to strut unswervingly towards Daniel, then suddenly launched itself at him. He thrust Alea behind him and extended an arm forward to protect himself, but the osprey only fluttered his wings and gently landed on Daniel's forearm, talons lightly clutching without harm. The eyes of man and bird locked for a silent moment before the osprey bobbed its head once, spread it's grey and white wings, and lifted back into the sky.

Something was coming. Daniel believed that his prayer had been heard. The feathered messenger circled one more time and dipped a wing as he headed out to sea.

****

They both had an overpowering urge to sleep and did not stir for hours until the sun crossed its zenith. Refreshed, Daniel rolled away from Alea's back, where he loved to nestle as they slept. He turned her to face him and caressed her cheek. She looked relaxed and beautiful, with long tangled hair, no make-up, and a deepening tan. He loved her body and was glad she enjoyed sleeping in the nude.

"Why don't we harvest the last of the sea grapes today," he suggested. "Then we'll take a couple days off." Alea could use some non-survival time. They'd been working too hard and there was enough food and water to last a while.

Alea grinned, hazel eyes sparkling with delight. "Maybe we could camp onshore?" She was re-energized and intrigued at the idea of sleeping on land for a change. "We can set-up the tent and make a bonfire. I'll bring a tarp for extra protection in case it rains."

Daniel was relieved to see her excited again and would have agreed to swim to Bimini if she'd asked.

"Absolutely. Why don't we pack the camping gear and bring it with us? We'll go pick the sea grapes first. Their season is almost over, and I'd like to get as many as possible."

Alea leaped up naked and began grabbing clothes and towels in a wild, exuberant frenzy and Daniel laughed out loud. "Honey, slow down! An hour of good planning please or I'll make you row back to Mystic if we need something." She ran over and kissed him swiftly before dashing to the closet to dress and pack. He headed below to find the tent.

They stashed the gear under a favorite casuarina tree and covered it with a blue tarp held down by heavy rocks before shouldering their backpacks and turning inland. Alea made sure to pack the grocery bags to carry the sea grapes back to camp. The path to the west cliff was well-trodden over the last few weeks so they could easily follow their own footsteps. It enabled them to make the journey in half the time and as they walked, Alea enjoyed the tropical foliage and trees in glorious full summer splendor.

The orange-red flowers of the poinciana tree bloomed boldly against fans of lace-patterned green leaves. The black-trunked beauties were scattered across the landscape, never grouping, always solitary, the strong vibrant color standing out vividly against the background of the verdant bush.

The delicate flowers of the yellow elder danced in the slight breeze; each tree heavy with hundreds of sunny blooms. As the national tree of the Bahamas, they stood in golden groves, with a multitude of darting hummingbirds feasting on the delicious nectar.

Daniel pointed to a dreaded poisonwood tree. He'd found one within the first few days on the island and she memorized its identifying characteristics quickly, avoiding contact at all times. It was similar to her gala-tea tree, but she knew the differences and hadn't been fooled so far.

Morning glory vines covered tall treetops, spreading in what looked like a tangled effort to suffocate each one. But their bell-shaped purple and white flowers were dazzling, and she forgave them their quest for survival after Daniel told her the vines politely retreated in the winter season.

The plant that Alea detested the most were sandspurs. With the appearance of a harmless clump of grass, round spikey spurs grew at the top of long stalks that emerged from the center. As she walked through grassy areas, the spurs would attach to her shoes, socks, and pant legs. She would painfully discover multiple sharp burrs uncomfortably pricking into her skin. She spent a lot of time gingerly handpicking them off daily. A spikey needle from a spur could easily penetrate her fingertip if she squeezed too hard, and she ended up plucking out quite a few with tweezers.

Approaching the plain, they stopped for a drink of water and a short rest. It took only a little longer to reach the sea grape bushes on the cliffs and they harvested what was left of the reddish berries. The birds had apparently fed well. Alea loved the distinctive round leaves that were the size of sandwich plates, the grapes hanging in clusters all over the large bush, which could grow as tall as fifteen feet.

Heading back to the beach, Daniel led the way single file. He always carried his machete as they walked, ready to chop and clear. He planned on instructing Alea how to safely use the second machete soon. They kept up a casual verbal patter as they walked, so he wouldn't have to turn around repeatedly to keep track of her whereabouts.

They were approaching the bush forest when Alea called for Daniel to stop. She pointed to a group of trees at the edge of the plain, well off their usual path.

"Honey, what kind of tree is that? I think I see green fruit on it from here."

Daniel pulled the binoculars up and focused. Grinning, he lowered them quickly and turned back to her.

"Alea, you may have spotted an avocado tree! Let's go see!"

What a remarkable discovery if it is avocado, he thought, as he altered their course over the plain. They were not only delicious and one of his favorite foods but were also one of the most nutritious fruits on the planet. Loaded with healthy fat, seventy-seven percent worth, avocado could be the source of fat and vitamins they were sorely missing. Daniel often ate an avocado for a light lunch before a dive or surf and the energy it provided lasted hours. Another miracle to check off for the island, as far as he was concerned.

Daniel was explaining this to Alea as they veered towards the tree, and he resumed the lead as they neared. Suddenly, he realized she was not answering. Turning around, he froze.

Alea was gone.

Throwing his backpack and carry bags down, he bolted back in the direction they had come from. He skidded to a halt just in time as a black hole in the earth gaped in his path.

"Alea!" he shouted. "Where are you?"

From deep in the hole he could hear her. "Daniel! I'm down here!" And the sound of splashing. What?

He dropped to the ground and looked over the edge of the hole. He could see the rapid movement of water, and as his eyes adjusted to the blackness, he saw Alea's face. Her arms were moving back and forth to keep her afloat. Afloat?

"I'm here," he called out. "Can you see me? Are you alright?"

"I'm okay!" Her voice echoed underground. "Yes, I can see you, Daniel. I'm treading water. What is this? Can you get me out?" She was a good swimmer but this black hole she did not like. With the little light that filtered down she couldn't judge the size of the pool at all, but she sensed it was big.

Daniel's mind raced. How to extract her? Her face was ten feet down from the entrance of the hole and he had no rope. That would change as of today, he vowed. He needed to be prepared for anything. He must get her out soon, before dark, and before she tired.

He looked up at the trees and bush. An idea sparked.

"Hang on, Alea, I'll be right back."

He jumped up and ran to his scattered belongings on the ground. Grabbing the machete, he darted over to the tree line. There were no vines that could hold her weight, he realized, but the trees gave him another idea. Locating a young sapling about the thickness of his wrist and over fifteen feet long, he began to chop at the base with the machete. He dripped sweat, his heart pounding. He could not lose his Alea. The sapling fell as he gave a final chop with all his strength. He made short work of clearing the smaller branches but left the stubs of the thicker branches to serve as ladder rungs for her feet.

He ran back to the hole. "Alea, are you there?" Relief poured over him as he heard her voice. She seemed calmer, no panic.

"I'm still here, Daniel. I'm trying to stay right under the light. I don't feel a current, so it's not too hard to stay in place."

"I've got a tree trunk I'm going to push down to you. I'm holding one end up here. Get a good grip and start to climb." He placed the thicker base of the young tree into the hole and lowered it carefully. He could hear the trunk splash the water. "It'll be just like climbing a ladder, sweetheart. Put your feet on the branches and push yourself up."

"I got it!" she called out, and he felt her pull down. He took a firm hold on his end and leaned it against the edge of the hole for support. But as soon as he did, the weight of the trunk cracked off more rock and soil, which fell into the water below. He almost lost his grip and jumped backwards as he saw the perimeter of the hole crumble.

He blanched with the horrible realization that if he fell in too... they would both die.

"Let go and swim away, Alea! I need to find a solid edge." He waited until she was clear of the opening, then jammed the trunk harder against the crumbling rock. The hole grew wider but finally stopped after opening two more feet. A soil layer of one foot lay on top of a dark rock base, which seemed thin at about eight inches thick. Was this what they'd been walking on each time they crossed the plain? A thin fragile rock layer over an underground lake?

"Go ahead and climb now. I won't let go." He gripped the green sapling and held on with all his might. The tree pulled down and angled directly beneath him with her first tentative step. The trunk swayed back and forth as she continued to find footholds and pull herself up. Daniel watched as the top of her head appeared at the edge of the hole. Her hand reached out and searched for something to grab.

"Take hold of my leg! I've got the tree and I'm standing on solid ground."

Locating his shoe, Alea pushed herself higher on the tree ladder with her legs and grabbed his ankle. It didn't take any convincing for her to scramble up and out quickly and she lay sprawled on the dirt, wet and gasping for air.

Daniel pulled the sapling out of the hole and tossed it aside. He was still unsure about the stability of the ground beneath them. Lifting her like a feather, he carried her towards the tree line and lowered her gently against a wide trunk.

He dropped down to the ground next to her, breathing hard, and brushed aside a scorpion aiming for her leg. They were stunned by what happened! This was no game. One of them could be lost at any time, leaving the other alone, stranded, and heart-broken in a post-Flare world.

"Daniel," she gasped, "I think I just got my wish."

"What do you mean, sweetheart?"

"Remember when I told you I would give anything for a nice salt-free shower?"

He nodded.

"That water was not salty. And I feel really clean."

An underground reservoir of fresh water was right under their feet. And they never even knew it was there...

His prayer was answered! A tremendous sense of reverence and awe enveloped his heart. There was no doubt this island had been given to them, a gift of survival and of hope for their future. There was great power surrounding them, protecting them, guiding them, loving them. Power that had nothing to do with electricity. He could feel it intensely, even if he could not see it. It was nothing short of miraculous!

Alea looked at him, the wonder and joy on his face mirroring her own. Daniel took both her hands in his and pulled her close, knowing she would understand his next words.

"We have been gifted, my love, with a Miracle Island."

Chapter 17   The Black Hole

Avocados and camping would have to wait. They rowed out to Mystic, physically exhausted by Alea's rescue. She dropped the sea grapes as she fell into the underground reservoir, but her backpack remained secure. She was a strong swimmer and kept it on her back as she treaded water. Its loss would have been sorely missed. The trek back to the beach gave them both time to reflect on what the discovery of fresh water meant for their survival and for their future. It would enable living on Miracle Island to become a long-term reality!

Daniel leaned back on the couch and thoughtfully lifted the precious item he was holding. The last bottle of Guinness. He sighed, popped the cap, and gulped down some of the warm liquid. No more, he quietly mourned. He'd miss the relaxation one beer allowed him after a long day in the heat, but with their discovery of unlimited fresh water, he could finally stop worrying. It was an evening to celebrate!

Over at the bar, Alea cut the foil on the last bottle of cabernet sauvignon, uncorked it expertly, and set it down to breathe. She retrieved a wineglass from the cabinet and poured a half glass for herself, breathing in the fruity aroma as she swirled the dark red liquid around the crystal rim. The last of our adult beverages, she mused. Wine had been a pleasant indulgence during their romance, wedding, and honeymoon cruise. But a responsible surgeon needed to maintain a sober self and she generally allowed herself a cocktail only a few times a year on special occasions, preferring water and juices anyway. She took her wine and sat next to Daniel on the leather couch, putting both feet up on the built-in coffee table.

"A toast?" she asked, as she extended her glass.

"Absolutely!" He grinned and touched the tip of his bottle to the edge of her wine glass. He hesitated thoughtfully, and then continued.

"I have no words to explain or understand everything that has been allowed to happen; to our planet, to others, and to us. But I will forever be grateful for the love, guidance, and protection we have been given by God... and for the love of my wonderful wife."

"I too am so very thankful, Lord, and for the gift of your love as well, Daniel," she said reverently. Alea clinked with him again for good measure and they both took a sip. It was time to get some questions answered.

"Okay, Daniel, tell me anything you know about the Black Hole I "found" today, ha-ha." She was feeling a bit like Lara Croft, an explorer and adventurer. The frightening collapse of the ground beneath her and her plunge into darkness had been more than worth it. She hadn't felt this clean in weeks.

"I'm no geologist, but I have been interested in the Bahamas since I was a kid, and there's quite a bit of information on the internet. I've looked up different subjects as they came up over the years and I do remember reading an article about this water feature, because many islands have them. Indonesia, Hawaii, the South Pacific. It's called a water lens."

"You mean like a contact lens for a human eye?"

"Sort of. The shape is the same. Here, I'll draw one for you." He pulled over his notebook and started to sketch with Alea looking over his arm to follow along.

"The islands are formed from limestone, with solid granite base rock even deeper down below. Limestone, as you know, is quite porous and will hold rainwater, but it will slowly soak in over time. The limestone core of the island is saturated with seawater as well. Anyway, there must be a bowl or lens-shaped depression that gradually filled with rainwater over centuries of time. That water will eventually fill the bowl and soak down to meet with the infiltrated seawater in the limestone. They will blend a bit, but seasonal rains continue to build up on top until the lens becomes a lake."

"Then how did it get covered with the flat rock of the plain, where we couldn't see the lake?"

"Not positive about that. But it's possible that as the island first began to form, there was always a cap layer of denser rock over an initial shallow depression. As rainwater filtered down on the edges, where the rock seems thinner than in the center, the underground limestone may have dissolved over a long period of time. I really don't know for sure, my sweet, I'm just happy it's there for us."

He finished off the last sip of Guinness and set the bottle down. "The other possibility is that the lake is enclosed in a natural granite cistern, with rain keeping it topped up, just like the reservoir on Spanish Wells. Either one would be fine. We won't know much more until I get in."

"What, you're going to dive down there, Daniel? Why?" She remembered her fall into the eerie and watery tomb, the one lone ray of sunlight keeping her panic at bay.

"I want to get a feel for the size and depth of the lake. It will have to sustain us for a long time. And you know what?" His eyes flashed with anticipation. "I can't wait to explore!"

There was nothing more to say. That was her Daniel.

****

He stood at the edge of the hole and peered in. Blackness stared back at him, a bright beam of midday sunlight shining straight down into an abyss of darkness, an alien portal he was anxious to explore. Daniel did not fear water. He reveled in the weightlessness, the encompassing pressure, the cool or warmth enveloping his body as he swam through it, a liquid astronaut.

They used heavy branches to pound the surface surrounding the original hole. Not much more rock and soil broke off and Daniel was more confident in the supporting thickness at the edges, which ended up as a circle of six feet in diameter. This time he came well-prepared, with two hundred feet of rope, knotted at intervals for handholds. His heart was hammering with excitement. How big would it be? Would he be able to see with only the small amount of sunlight?

To ensure safety and egress, he tied one end of the rope to a large tree at the edge of the bush, about one hundred feet from the Black Hole. He walked the rope from the tree to the hole and attached a five-pound dive weight to the end. Tossing the weighted rope into the water, it dropped quickly and soon struck what felt like a flat rock bottom. Daniel pulled up the extra line and measured.

"Alea, the depth is twenty feet here at the outer perimeter of the plain. And this could be the shallow section of the lens. Do you understand what this means?"

She surveyed the plain and could only imagine how big the reservoir might be, the gallons of water impossible to figure. An underground lake of this magnitude could support a small town for years, especially if regularly replenished by seasonal rains.

"It should do," she deadpanned.

"Should do?!" he exclaimed. He threw her over his shoulder and they laughed, rolling to the ground together. He stopped on top of her and held both her arms over her head, kissing her neck, her chin, her eyes, her lips. She didn't struggle and wrapped her legs around his waist.

"Oh no woman! None of that. Diving before love." He kissed her one more time and disentangled from her warm thighs. It was time to prepare. He helped her up and she dusted the grass and dirt from her clothes.

"You're no fun at all, husband." She stuck out her tongue.

"I bet you'll be much nicer to me after you get another bath, wife."

"Oh, in that case, off you go!" and she swatted his rear end. "What will I be doing while you're in there?"

"Stand where I can see you from the water, near the rope. I may need you to call out to me. Even in the dark I will hear sound. The sun is in our favor, shining straight down."

Now that he had a feel for the depth, he wanted to fan out and locate the end of the lens near the bush. Would he find a wall or an incline? Did anything live in the water? He put on his fins and weight belt with ten pounds. Wetting his mask and snorkel with bottled water, he pulled the mask onto his forehead. He would secure it completely once in the water. He paused for a moment at the edge, took a breath, and jumped in feet first.

It was like landing in a bottle of black ink. He rose to the surface and allowed his eyes to adjust to the dim cavern.

The sun was a piercing spotlight into the murky depths. Looking up, he could see Alea's anxious face peering over the edge. He pulled his mask down over his eyes and nose, checked for tight suction, and tucked the snorkel into his mouth. Giving her a thumbs up, he took a deep breath, jack-knifed, and descended completely into the dark.

He followed the rope straight down, the sunlight dwindling rapidly as he descended. The cold water was pure and clear, with almost no particulates reflecting in the light. Reaching the bottom, he noticed the dive weights were resting on white limestone base rock before allowing his lungs to slowly float him back to the surface for a breath.

Re-orienting himself to Alea and the rope, he swam towards the tree line, which he knew was one hundred feet away. The darkness made him blind in the water and he held both arms out in front to prevent hitting the edge. The bottom began to incline upwards rapidly as he swam. He did not have far to go when his hands contacted a smooth white rock wall. He raised his head. There was plenty of air space between the water and the rock roof. Turning away from the wall and with his arms extended, he ducked and dove, the bottom gradually sloping down as he propelled out and away. No need to theorize any further. He was absolutely certain the underground lake was a limestone water lens.

The immense reservoir was clean and fresh, replenished by rain over thousands of years. Judging from the size of the plain, it was a vast storehouse never before tapped by man.

He turned himself in a circle until he saw the beam of light at the hole streaming down and began to swim back towards the opening. His anxieties vanished. They would never run out of fresh water!

Miracle Island could now become their permanent home.

Chapter 18   Island Life

Right before the wedding, Daniel hung a favorite Bahamian-themed calendar in the master cabin and Alea was marking off each day since the wedding and start of their honeymoon. They'd been living on the island since late July. It was early October, with two months of the tropical hurricane season left to go. They considered themselves quite fortunate, with only one minor storm that bore down in mid-September.

The weather was still hot, but Alea could feel a slight change. The humidity was not quite so oppressive, the afternoon rains were less frequent, and nights were cooler. She was enjoying the minor seasonal differences of the sub-tropics.

Since finding the Black Hole they had relaxed emotionally, confident in having enough water to live. Alea found herself willing to try different activities that Daniel suggested, more for the adventure and enjoyment than strictly for survival, although she never lost that frame of mind. She assessed every aspect of island life from a survival viewpoint.

It was always exciting to find a unique way of performing a necessary task or discovering a new food source. Her previous successes in cooking were challenged with so few ingredients, but she tried to create unusual and tasty combinations for every meal. But there was only so much you could do with a papaya, she sighed.

They ran out of their one container of table salt after the first month. It was critically important to replace this essential mineral that they sweat out in buckets every day. The problem was solved in early September on an exploration to the north end of the island. Sea spray from past storms had accumulated in rock crevices on top of a high northeast-facing cliff, sun-drying into piles of sparkling white sea salt crystals. They gleefully harvested handfuls and trekked back for more when needed. Toothpaste was long gone, and they used the gritty crystals to brush and clean their teeth.

The three saltwater flushing toilets on Mystic were a luxury when they slept on the boat, but they were spending their days, and frequently nights, on land. In order to meet Alea's requested privacy and sanitation needs, Daniel scouted two deep limestone holes on opposite sides of Casuarina Cove to create an outhouse for each of them. Secluded enough for personal comfort and with the pathway leveled and cleared, the walk was less than a minute.

He cut slender trees to lay across the hole in a crisscrossed pattern, leaving an opening in the very center. The trunks were secured using homemade rope created by braiding sinewy vines together, an idea Alea devised. Over the center opening, he created a raised commode using large pieces of driftwood. The new toilets were functional and quite artistic. Alea loved her outhouse and wove a coconut frond basket for each of them to keep by the commodes, filled with bunches of thick grass and soft leaves to use as toilet paper. She also asked Daniel to eventually build semi-enclosed huts over each outhouse for cover on rainy days, as he had already done for their cooking firepit.

Each seasonal change brought out new growths of fruit. The avocados finally ripened from the hard, green knobs they first discovered, and the added fat content and rich flavor were a welcome pleasure. Daniel found several key lime trees, the juice adding a sharp zest to grilled fish and lobster.

She longed for potatoes, rice, carrots, tomatoes, and lettuce. She dreamt of onions, could smell them, and would have petted a shark for a few cloves of garlic. She was still trying to figure out how to make a basic flatbread. The surgeon had become a farmer, but she blossomed in her new life.

Alea was a willing sponge for anything Daniel could teach her. His years of knowledge and experience fishing the North Atlantic and the islands were her Wikipedia of survival. She ingrained his demonstrations and listened intently to his explanations, occasionally questioning the reasons why he did things a certain way and offering suggestions that seemed reasonable to her. He would sometimes chuckle when she first described an alternative idea, but often discovered that her input proved valid and helped create a useful technique. They spent hours at twilight around the campfire and into the night talking about their day, brainstorming how to solve a problem or need, and planning future explorations.

They grew closer in a deeper, primordial way, respecting and appreciating each other even more than if they were living a comfortable pre-Flare existence. This was human life the way it had been done for millennia, with cooperation, trust, and innovation the keys to survival.

He instructed her how to safely use a machete and she kept her own well-sharpened blade tucked into a leather sheath on her belt. She used her machete daily for bush clearing, wood chopping, digging, and conch and coconut cracking. They had not encountered any indigenous small animals and Daniel assured her there were no poisonous snakes in the Bahamas, but she simply felt safer with a means for her own protection in hand.

He taught her how to scale, gut, and clean smaller fish to roast whole on the camp grill over an open fire. Daniel left fish prep to her once he saw she was a natural, and this time she accepted the task, filleting only the bigger fish that couldn't be eaten in one meal. The fillets were prepared as either a ceviche with sour orange and lime juice, or salt-cured and dried. She could crack open a conch shell like a pro with her machete. Trimming and cleaning the tough conch meat was a tedious chore, but even without the traditional ingredients of onion and green pepper, he loved the fresh tangy taste she achieved with salt and sours. But she left the catching and cracking of lobster and crab for Daniel.

She learned how to tie a variety of nautical knots and began to experiment with her initial idea of making cordage from braided vines, creating coils of rope with the same techniques she often used on her own long dark hair. They had a limited amount of real rope, with most of it already in use on the boat and at the Black Hole. Daniel relied on her homemade vine-braided lengths for his building projects.

The recently completed lean-to beach hut served many purposes. Daniel used small tree trunks for framing, making it tall enough to stand under, as well as wide and roomy. Coconut palm fronds covered the walls and Daniel laid down rubber mats borrowed from Mystic for a floor. The beach hut offered shade and a protected dry area to store the fruits, nuts, and other produce they collected daily. Fish were cleaned on flat rocks near the edge of Casuarina Cove or on the fallen tree trunk over the water. Those not immediately eaten or filleted were salted and strung nearby on lines in the sun to dry and cure. The hut was also a comfortable place for their heat-inspired midday nap. The glaring sun was merciless from noon to late afternoon, and they soon learned to rest for an hour or two until the sun passed its zenith before continuing to work or explore.

Scorpions and centipedes were always a painful possibility when camping on the ground and mosquitoes by the dozen swarmed relentlessly at dusk. The camp tent was a protected sleeping enclosure, but once damaged beyond repair, there was nothing to replace it. Alea loved his solution.

Daniel decided to build a treehouse. Utilizing the large trees behind the cove as the main supports, he planned a rain and wind-resistant shelter as high off the ground as possible. A shelter they could sleep in, dry, with minimal bug intrusion. He knew it would never be completely bugproof, but enough to keep Alea happy. Although he still found it rather funny, he preferred to keep her startled shrieks at the appearance of a multi-legged biting centipede to a minimum.

On nights when the skies were clear, Daniel gave her lessons in stellar navigation. The constellations and the North Star were viewed differently from their position in the sky from the latitude of the Bahamas compared to the latitude of the northeast coast of the United States. Without the advantage of satellite systems for navigation, they would now depend on an art thousands of years old to guide them across the ocean, using only their knowledge, a compass, nautical charts, and a sextant.

They devised a makeshift backpack arrangement with straps to enable Daniel to carry a five-gallon water bottle to the Black Hole for refills. Alea was not able to make the walk with the topped-up weight of 45 pounds, so it was Daniel's job to travel once a day to fill a bottle and bring it back to camp. With the bush path so frequently used and beaten down, the walk was only twenty minutes each way.

They decided on the safest and easiest method to pull water up from the Black Hole. After making sure the surrounding surface cap rock was solid enough, a 20-foot tree was chopped down and laid across the 6-foot wide hole. Daniel rigged a pulley and rope on the tree trunk, with a bucket attached. This allowed him to lower the bucket down to fill with water and retrieve the load easily. Once at the surface, he tied the rope off. Just a short reach in to grab and the precious water was carefully poured into the empty 5-gallon bottle, with three buckets more than enough to fill it. He'd then leave the bucket securely tied to the trunk, ready for the next day's visit. Alea often accompanied him if there was something she wanted to harvest. For safety purposes, Daniel kept a heavy-duty rope, knotted at intervals, hanging in the Black Hole just above the waterline. If one of them should ever fall in again, there would always be a way to escape back to the surface.

They kept half of the water bottles on Mystic, with the others stored in the shaded beach hut. It took quite a while for them to get used to drinking warm water with no ice. A nice perk of the electric age, Alea bemoaned, but nothing she couldn't live without.

On this night, Alea lay awake as she considered that exact aspect of the life she and Daniel were trying to build. There was so much they were living without, and yet they were prospering, in the same manner as the men and women that lived in ancient times. Fire was warmth, light, and fuel for cooking food. Fresh water was the blood of life itself. Their intelligence and adaptability allowed them to make the most of what mother nature offered. And if mother nature was not respected, she would no longer provide.

Electric and nuclear power played no role in their current daily life. Mankind had long forgotten that the essence of his survival was independent from manufactured power sources. It had enabled many useful advances, yes, but also produced resultant declines. Cities with unrestrained population growth burdened available limited resources and the environment. The explosion of technology had slowly weakened mankind as much as it had moved them forward. But it was technological movement that gave a false sense of security, because without its support, man was even more vulnerable than ever before. The Flare would leave billions of people unprepared to survive a world without the crutch of manmade energy sources.

Alea was intelligent enough to know these may have seemed like simple statements to the lettered and powerful, but she could not deny their truth. If only mankind had accepted the frailty of what they believed was progress, when it was all really shifting quicksand beneath their feet, easily destroyed by the ever-changing forces that drove the universe. She was living that truth right now.

She wondered how the rest of the world was coping. If the entire planet was shattered by the Flare, perhaps the distances between nations, especially if separated by oceans, would keep aggression to a minimum. Her most urgent fears were about their family and friends possibly caught by the solar flare while still on Spanish Wells. But perhaps it was for the best. Living conditions on the U.S. mainland must have degenerated rapidly. It was painful to think about millions of people searching for food that would inevitably vanish within weeks, the misery that would follow, the many deaths, and the deaths of humans... by humans.

She knew their families would have the Spanish Wells house for shelter, but was there food and water? Were medications available? Were people cooperating and helping each other or had the island fallen into anarchy? There was no way to find out and she missed them so much. Closing her eyes, she rolled on her side and curled up against Daniel's warm back. His steady breathing was calming and sleep finally quieted the ever-present worry in her heart.

****

Daniel admired Alea as she stood in the bow of the tender, holding the anchor in hand, prepared to drop at his command. He was so proud. She looked like an Amazon warrior in her black swim tank top and bikini brief, her hair in a single long braid trailing down her back, her lean body silhouetted against the sun. Their daily diet of seafood, fruits, natural greens, and nuts, as well as the hard work of living on Miracle Island, had toned and molded her body to perfection. Alea's ample breasts had not suffered, he noted with pleasure.

Her golden tan gleamed from the coconut oil she made from boiled and reduced coconut pulp. She'd also found numerous prickly aloe plants scattered across the island, using the clear cooling gel to soothe cuts, sunburns, and to moisturize skin. But she preferred not to damage the giant aloe-like century plants. Some of these ancient plants stood fifteen feet tall and took many years to mature. He enjoyed watching her island medicinal skills continue to grow.

Daniel's appearance was also changed. His hair was longer, kept under control by Alea with a pair of kitchen shears. He kept his beard trimmed with a combination of small scissors and the final few razors, a dark stubble now Daniel's new post-apocalyptic look. His trace of American Indian heritage gave him a reddish tan, his dark hair displaying sun streaks from constant immersion in saltwater. He'd never been so fit and strong, and he was very glad for it. Their survival depended on his ability to dive and fish and for any task that required brute strength. Alea called him her Tarzan.

They often rowed the tender out to Hidden Pass, the name they had christened the entry cove and channel into Osprey Bay, and tied up to the buoy floating not far from the mouth of the cove to fish or dive. Two months before, Daniel decided to leave Mystic's main anchor and chain in place where they first dropped it. He dove down with a short rope attached to a buoy and secured it to the anchor, detaching the several hundred feet of rope still running back to Mystic. Alea then retrieved the entire length as he rowed back to shore. He spread the rope out to dry, hanging like a thick spiderweb on tree branches, before coiling it neatly and storing it for future use. If they ever needed to pull Mystic back out to sea, the rope would be invaluable.

Today, Daniel planned to dive an outer reef on the Atlantic for lobster and fish, and he liked the tender anchored close to his dive site for safety. That way he wouldn't have to swim back too far to offload his catch into the boat. He did not want to attract a hungry bull, reef, or tiger shark, drawn by the audible signals emitted from a struggling fish or by blood from a spear wound.

He also kept watch for passing schools of tuna, wahoo, and mahi-mahi moving in from deeper waters. These fish could frequently reach weights of over 40 pounds and one kill would feed them for several days. He always brought his blue water spear gun just in case. If Daniel managed to impale one of the giants and land it, they could call it a day and go back to camp. There was no point in taking more than they could handle.

They often fished using rod and reel. Daniel set Alea up with a rod to cast lures, as well as a pole for using cut-bait. She was already skilled at tying knots, as a surgeon, and was well-able to change out lures, hooks, weights, and leader on her own. He enjoyed watching her excitement when the tip of her pole began to bounce. She would yell "Fish On!" and start talking to the highly reluctant creature as she reeled it in. Then he sat back for the show.

"Come on, baby, come to momma! That's it, no, no, I got you. There's no going back down there. Let me see you smile! Yeah, I got him! It's a big one. Oh, he's trying to run... Wow, he's strong. Line running out. Yes, Daniel, the drag is tight. Let me stop you right there, boy! Come to the boat, come on. It's a tuna! Where's the net? Okay, he's up and... he's in the boat! Let me get that hook out of his mouth!"

Daniel was always amused.

He could not have wished for a woman more perfect for him than Alea. With no prior survival training, she had rapidly adjusted, adapted, learned, and grown in all the skills needed for their life on the island. She added important and useful information derived from using her intelligence to assess a situation and choose a plan of action. Even with her education and medical background, she supported him unconditionally as the leader of their little island Tribe and gave him the final say in every important decision. She trusted him. They were partners, friends, lovers, and soulmates. He vowed to respect their rare and wonderful relationship every day.

—

Chapter 19   Alea's Secret

"I'd love another piece of lobster."

Daniel leaned forward from his beach chair and gingerly plucked a wooden skewer of slightly charred lobster chunks from the campfire grate.

"Enjoy," as he passed the steaming skewer over to Alea and selected another for his own plate.

"This is delicious," he said. "Your crushed mango and sour orange marinade gives the lobster a very different flavor. And the sea salt makes it taste even better."

A comfortable silence fell over the campsite as they relished the feast, their feet overlapping. A customary routine had been established each evening as light waned for the day. Daniel would get a fire started and heat up the steel grill top. Earlier, while the sun was still bright, they'd select the makings for the evening's dinner and marinate, chop, and otherwise prepare to cook the catch of the day, supplemented with fruit or greens that Alea had harvested that morning.

She was researching the use of the many vines, flowers, leaves, and grasses she found during forays into the bush, in order to safely add vegetables to their daily diet, but was also interested in any medicinal applications. When she saw a new plant, she would harvest one to take back to camp, the leaves, stems, and roots, and document the plants location on her map of Miracle Island. She could then experiment in leisure over several days, chewing small bits and waiting for her body's reaction; noting taste, whether sweet, sour, bitter, or salty, and the smell. Positive effects, such as pain relief, were a plus but special attention was paid to negative physical side effects. Nausea, pain, cramping, indigestion, diarrhea, skin rash, itching, or blurry vision were all charted in detail using a hardcovered notebook she found in a drawer, that quickly became one of her most treasured possession. She kept it dry in a plastic zip bag that almost never left her backpack unless she was recording her findings. It was no secret she loved it when Daniel called her "His Medicine Woman."

But there was a secret she had yet to share with him, a secret she held to herself for weeks as she weighed and pondered the implications of her discovery. A blissful secret that filled her with complete joy. And absolute fear.

She was pregnant.

****

They sat back in the beach chairs after dinner, content and full, twilight slowly fading into night. The flames crackled and popped, dancing shadows cast into the trees and reflecting on the still water of Casuarina Cove.

Daniel loved these moments of quiet contentment. The busy day was done, the wind whispered through the casuarina tree boughs, and his love was right next to him. The anxieties and questions of the day would just have to wait.

With no artificial entertainment, they enjoyed spending the early part of each evening in front of the fire telling stories. One night, Alea would tell a story from her life, the next night would be Daniel's turn. Since discovering Miracle Island, they were growing intimately closer as they divulged more of their past personal lives to each other.

They laughed and cried together, revealing the adversities that had caused them pain, what gave them happiness, the disappointments, the amazing successes. There was no fear in sharing their deepest feelings. They were in love, hearts safe in each other's care. She was totally aware of his misery and anguish with Karen, but Daniel re-lived those years over

184

again with Alea, in the flickering light of many evening fires. Her arms held him as he told her details he preferred to forget, and she suffered with him. He felt her love enfold him protectively and any remaining poison, uncertainty, or regrets drained away from his grateful soul. The jagged wounds, briefly and deliberately re-opened and examined, closed permanently.

There were nights when all they needed was to make love hard and fast, falling asleep holding each other, exhausted from the day. But on other nights, Daniel would sensuously stalk her like a hungry lion, taking her leisurely, drawing out her pleasure as she cried out again and again.

Alea was in no hurry to break the peaceful serenity of the moment. She pulled his hand to her lips and kissed it. How she loved this man! Her husband. She had never felt so cared for, so fulfilled, so treasured. Feeling strong, she leaned back, holding Daniel's hand, closed her eyes, and let the old painful memories flood back in.

****

"Damn it, Alea, get moving! I don't want this guy to bleed out!" Dr. Brad Brockdorff barked out loudly. The chill in the operating room got even colder as the rest of the team stared her down. No one said a word. None of the other final year residents wanted the critical eye of Brockdorff to fall on them.

Alea silently completed the closing stitches as the operation came to an end. Once Brockdorff called it, she stepped back from the table and walked out to begin her own clean-up. Her hands were shaking in anger, her lips clamped down, eyes blazing. She angrily peeled off her gloves and mask and began washing. Her final year of residency at Chicago General was certainly not the rewarding experience she had anticipated. She finished washing and left the prep area through the automatic doors, heading to the female locker room to change into her clothes and lab coat. She couldn't stop shaking and did not hear the door open quietly behind her.

She startled as two arms encircled her from behind and kept her from moving. She closed her eyes and sighed. Turning her quickly, Brockdorff crashed his lips down to hers, her own opening for him despite her anger. She raised her arms around his neck and pulled him in, deepening her kiss as the flame rose again. This is pointless, her mind told her, even as she crushed herself to his chest. As their lips parted, he kept his face close to hers and held her gaze.

"It's for your own good, Alea," he breathed. "I can't have anyone thinking I favor you in any way." He glanced around the locker room and pulled her into a private cubicle.

"You don't speak to any of the other residents the way you speak to me, Brad. It's demeaning and rude. And you leave me no choice but to say nothing and look like a wimp, or to go after you verbally. You're my supervisor. I lose either way." Alea tried to push him away, but he was too strong.

"I cannot lose face here, Alea. Even for you. You know I love you." He grinned down at her and moved one hand to cup her breast, leaning forward to nuzzle her neck.

She rolled her eyes. He'd been telling her that for months now but wasn't any closer to leaving the wife he claimed he no longer loved, even though Magda was pregnant with their first child.

Alea wasn't proud of the fact that she was in love with her supervisor... and that he was married. Her parents had taught her to pursue healthy relationships, nevertheless, she could not deny the strong attraction that blossomed between them just before her final year of residency. She resisted the urge to date after graduation from high school, completely focused on college, pre-med, medical school, and internship. She had never been in love before, and she was a virgin, a fact she did not reveal even to her closest friends. Men were great, yes, but her goal of being a great surgeon took precedence. Until she met Brad.

She was starry-eyed at first, enthralled by his attentions, a well-respected orthopedic surgeon and teacher. He was about her height, not tall for a man, but with a stocky build and piercing blue eyes. He was ten years older than Alea, wore glasses, was not particularly good-looking, and was losing his hair, a non-descript brown. However, he emanated a cocky confidence and sureness that she surprisingly enjoyed. His voice was commanding, and he was an excellent teacher the residents respected. After a long, searching look into her eyes the day they were introduced, he singled her out quickly, for reasons she would not comprehend until much later.

For the first time in her life, Alea felt sexually attracted to a man. It was all new and thrilling for her; the heated glances, the seemingly accidental brushes against each other. When he asked her to meet him for a cocktail, she accepted, but with reservations. After all, Dr. Brockdorff was her supervisor and it could be awkward. He gradually swept away her concerns after several wonderful hours of engaging conversation that grew more intimate as the evening wore on. When he kissed her, she thought she was in love.

The next few months were both heaven and hell.

They met almost every evening for dinner at tucked away bars or restaurants far from the hospital, talking, kissing, laughing. But he would always depart to go home to his wife, leaving Alea heavy with unfulfillment and wondering if she had done something wrong or was lacking in some way. When would he finally decide to end his miserable marriage and be only with her?

He firmly refused to make love to her or to let her touch him intimately, telling her his religion did not allow him to take their relationship to that point. Not until he could leave his wife and marry Alea. Then they could be together. Yet he pursued her ardently, telling her he loved her, how beautiful and sexy she was, making her feel wanted and desired.

She was completely confused. Her girlfriends were having terrific sex with their boyfriends and two were dating married men. She'd been told many times before how attractive she was. What was wrong?

He was a difficult taskmaster in surgery and during rounds, often using her bluntly as a negative foil to teach the others, as he put it, what not to do. It took all her strength to remind herself that he loved her, and it was just as he said, he was only trying to make her better by his actions. But she was wearing out emotionally. Month after month of his demeaning public treatment was draining her spirit.

It had been a long tough day in the operating room and Alea was exhausted. The cases went well but her ears rang from the reproofs she suffered. Nothing she did was good enough for Dr. Brockdorff and the other residents snickered behind their masks frequently, not bothering to hide their growing disdain.

She washed her hands quietly, still smarting from a parting caustic comment, and went to the small unit supply room to locate some special bandages. He followed her inside and closed the door.

"Are we okay?" he asked, his arms surrounding her.

"Yes, I suppose. I can't take much more, Brad. You have to lighten up on me. The others do not respect me, and you are making me look incompetent. This cannot go on any longer." She pulled away from him and turned her back. "I'm a damn good surgeon and you know it."

"You are, my dear. The best so far. And improving rapidly all the time. One of the reasons I love you so much."

He turned her around and smiled. She wearily envisioned another night of misery, frustration, longing, and excuses.

Enough was enough. Alea's patience ran out.

Did he want her or not?

She pulled his hands up and placed them on her breasts. His smile widened and he leaned in to kiss her. She lowered her arms, took hold of the waistband of his scrubs, and pulled down. His slowly rising organ dropped out and she quickly wrapped her hands around him clumsily, beginning a rough, unpracticed stroking. He was not large, which surprised her, but he had never permitted her to touch him before. She really didn't care, she just wanted him to make love to her. He closed his eyes and sighed, only making a feeble effort to stop her. She kept stroking as she kissed him, and his breathing grew harsh. Was she doing this right?

He broke their kiss and pulled her scrub pants down to her ankles. Spinning her so her back was to him, he shoved her forward from the waist onto a small steel table, exposing her buttocks and pink folds. What? Alea tried to turn to face him but one of his arms kept her pinned down as his other hand swept between her legs, grazing the wet that started to flow when she first kissed him.

Without another word, he jammed himself deep inside her. The unexpected assault and intense stabbing pain brought an anguished cry. Was this what she had longed for? For her first time? Hot tears of shame filled her eyes.

Ignoring her obvious distress, he pulled out just once, then slammed back in, abruptly stopping. He quivered, his mouth a silent gaping oval as he pulsed and spurted, falling forward over her back. She trembled with pain.

It had taken no more than 15 seconds.

Breathing heavily, his flaccid organ slipped out. He wiped it off on her scrub top before pulling his pants back up. He stood looking down at her with a cold blank expression, heedless of her tears, wild hair, and the streaks of blood and semen now painted haphazardly on her top and running down her inner thighs.

"If you say a word of this to anyone, I will destroy you." He opened the door and walked out.

****

Two weeks later, Alea Gabrielle was back in the operating room, tackling a complicated multiple spinal fracture case. Watching the operation proceed with an approving smile was her new supervisor, Dr. Bennett Nelson. He'd never seen such skill, such confidence, such precision!

He still couldn't fathom why she'd been transferred to him from Brockdorff. The prick wouldn't even discuss her work, walking off and dismissively waving him away. The Dean gave him no reason either, her face calm and unreadable, but insisted that Bennett assume responsibility for supervising the remainder of Dr. Gabrielle's final year of residency. But it really didn't matter. It was clearly evident she was something extraordinary and would excel as an orthopedic surgeon.

Alea finished the difficult case, more than satisfied with the results. The patient, a 40-year old man seriously injured in a car accident, was stable and Alea would follow him closely. She confidently and respectfully directed the nurses and the surgical assistants in the closing procedures before leaving the operating theater, on her way to see the man's family, who were anxiously pacing in the waiting room.

"Dr. Gabrielle, may I speak with you for a moment?" The voice came from an open door to a nearby conference room.

Dr. Marjory Lane, the Dean of Chicago General Hospital, beckoned with a slight wave to come in. Alea did not hesitate, closing the door behind her. Ignoring the conference table, they sat down together on the leather couch and Dr. Lane handed her a paper cup of foamy hot chocolate.

At age 50, her short, perfectly styled, dark red hair framed a plain and serious face. She wore very little make-up and sported sparkling two-carat diamond earrings and a glittering diamond wedding band. A smartly tailored black pantsuit, crisp white blouse, and sensible two-inch heeled black pumps gave her a classy, professional appearance. Dr. Lane was approachable and warmly polite, but also straightforward and firm. The administration took her opinions and directives seriously and Chicago General won numerous awards under her guidance. The doctors knew she was dispassionately fair but would hold them expressly accountable for poor decisions and negative outcomes. Excellent patient care demanded no less.

"How are you doing, Alea? she asked quietly. Dr. Lane took a sip of her own cup of hot chocolate and sat back to wait for her reply.

"I'm so much better, Marjory. It's like night and day working with Dr. Nelson." She grasped Marjory's hand with a grateful squeeze. "Thank-you for hearing me out and not condemning me for what I allowed to happen. I can do this now." Her eyes glistened with tears.

"Did you see your gynecologist, as I recommended?"

Alea sat up straighter. "Yes. I'm good. She saw me in her office the same day, gave me the morning-after pill, and took blood. Nothing noteworthy to report."

Dr. Lane nodded in approval. "I am so glad you came to me. Your father and I are good friends, as you know, and, poor judgement aside, I would never allow something like this to affect your future." She leaned in closer. "There's nothing I can do to him officially, you understand, but I'll be damned if I'll let that pompous fool ruin you. And, after our recent private chat, I believe Dr. Brockdorff understands I'll be keeping a much closer eye on him in the future."

Marjory chuckled. "Apparently, his inflated ego has always been much bigger than certain other, ahem, parts... Shall we nickname him Quickdraw, just between you and me?"

They both burst out laughing, wiping the tears from their eyes as they looked at each other, then laughed again. Alea was thankful she did the very thing she had counseled others to do many times before. Tell someone.

Setting down their cups, they stood up from the couch. Dr. Lane reached out and pulled Alea in for a quick warm hug.

"You have a great career ahead of you, my dear, and you can be assured there will always be a place for you here at Chicago General, if you choose."

Alea was pleased and hugged her again. No way.

"I so appreciate all you've done, Marjory. But thanks to your glowing letter of recommendation, I'll be moving right after graduation. I've been offered a position when I finish here. In Massachusetts. At Boston Hospital."

"Wonderful! And by the way, Alea, my recommendation letter aside, your work speaks for itself."

Alea smiled. She couldn't wait to leave Chicago.

Chapter 20 Surprises

Strong east winds began to pick up the next morning, giving Daniel some difficulty getting the fire started to brew their morning tea. But he managed to have a hot cup ready for Alea by the time she emerged from the tent, rubbing her eyes and combing her long hair straight back with both hands. She wove a quick braid and gave Daniel a warm good morning kiss as she accepted her tea.

As they sipped, they walked over to the partially completed treehouse. Daniel had selected a grouping of eight large-trunked trees as the vertical posts for a raised floor and walls. The roughly octagon-shaped area was a good size of twenty by twenty feet, with the biggest tree right in the center. He was currently working on building the floor, which would be three feet off the ground. Using lengths of Alea's sturdy vine rope, he was lashing smaller tree trunks horizontally between the posts and across for support. This would provide an almost solid floor of wood, with the crevices to be stuffed and padded later with coconut branches and grasses and topped with thick woven mats. They rolled over a large boulder with a somewhat flattened side to be used as a temporary stairstep from ground level.

Having Mystic to live in for the present time, Daniel was in no hurry to complete the treehouse. He wanted it strong and able to resist heavy winds and rain up to at least Category One. Beyond that strength, there was no shelter alternative and the problem was preying on him.

"What do you have in mind for the roof?" Alea asked.

"Well, the original Taino tribes in the Bahamas, the Arawaks and the Lucayans, used a steeply-sloped A-frame roof. Rain ran right off, and the open ends allowed air to flow through. I like that idea, but I need to modify their plan because of the irregular tree patterns here. So, a sort-of octagon shape works for us because of where the main tree trunks are located. Then I'll slope the roof out from the center tree. I'd like to leave the top of the walls open at least a foot for air circulation. Maybe you can weave some mats as screens to prevent bigger bugs from entering."

"I really like your ideas! We have the beach hut if we need to work outside. I'd prefer the treehouse to be more of a sleep-relax place." She looked around their campsite. "This whole area is our home, really. Just not under a single roof."

"We're Robinson Crusoe and Swiss Family Robinson all in one," he joked. "I loved those movies!"

"We're going to be here for the rest of our lives, aren't we, Daniel?" she asked sadly. Sighing, he took her hand. Walking back to the fire, they sat down and stared somberly into the smoking flames.

"Alea, we still don't know what actually happened. My best educated guess, however, after seeing the superflash, the engines of both Mystic and the tender dead, and the falling airplane... is that a massive solar flare caused an EMP. If that's true, we're not alone. This could be worldwide. We might not be with other people, but they'll be going through the same problems we are. But worse, much worse."

"Huge population numbers with no food," he continued. "No water. Death and violence rampant. It makes me sick." He paused to check her reaction. She sat stone-still, listening to him intently.

"I'd rather be stranded here, my darling. We do not have to cope with the violence of others. We have no competition for food. You're safe and that's all I care about."

He looked up into the sky, asking for the right words to say.

"It's a miracle we were together on Mystic when it happened, and that you were not still in Boston. It's a miracle the airplane just missed crashing into us. It's a miracle we drifted to this island and found Osprey Bay. It's a miracle we have seafood and plants. And it's a complete miracle we found the Black Hole. We're both still young, strong, and have no physical ailments. We can survive here. And there may not be a choice to leave."

She looked up at him through her long dark lashes, with a shy tilt of her chin and a slight smile. "There is one miracle that hasn't been mentioned."

He gazed at her, relieved she wasn't upset. "What's that, sweetheart?"

"I'm going to have your baby."

****

He just couldn't help it. A split-second stomach-churning memory of Karen... and then it was gone. This was Alea, his true love, and she was having a child. Their child! Joy shot through him like a bolt of lightning. He pulled her up and into his arms, covering her face with kisses.

"Oh my God, I'm so happy! I swear to care for you both with my life." He couldn't believe it. He was going to be a father. And this woman he adored would be the best mother.

Her tension and anxiety washed away, and relief melted her fears. "I was so worried about telling you, Daniel. Having a baby here on Miracle Island, all the problems that could arise, the extra responsibility for us both when we are just trying to survive. What kind of life would our child have? What if something happened to both of us?"

"Alea, don't think about anything except I love you and we'll take each day as it comes. Again, remember, miracles?" He quirked an eyebrow and grinned down at her. Her spirits lifted immediately, and a wave of optimism flooded her. She raised her lips for another kiss.

She was three weeks overdue and guessed immediately but decided to wait before telling Daniel. Not expecting a planet-altering solar flare, she brought only enough birth control pills for what she initially anticipated would be a relaxing Bahamas vacation, only to find out she was getting married and going on a month-long honeymoon cruise. The pills might last the month, but she started to worry a few weeks after the Flare. Daniel made sure there were quite a few packs of condoms on board, but eventually everything ran out. They hadn't always remembered to be careful in the wee hours of the morning, when he awakened her slowly with his warm gentle hands and hot sensuous mouth.

They finished their tea and headed to the tender. Today he planned another Atlantic dive at the entry to Hidden Pass for lobster and fish. Conditions appeared to be developing for a storm, maybe even a hurricane, and they needed to bring in as much catch as possible. Late season systems were still rolling sporadically across the Atlantic from the volatile west African coast. If the storm hit soon, another productive dive day was highly unlikely.

They rowed out and tied up to the buoy. Daniel geared up and dove in. The waves were about two feet, the east wind was picking up. He was anxious to finish and return to camp. Alea remained on the tender and secured each fish, crab, or lobster into the cooler. They had no ice, but the cooler prevented fins, claws, or sharp shell from injuring either of them or poking a hole in the inflatable tender.

Alea sat on the boat seat, enjoying the breeze and casually scanning the cliffs and open ocean as she waited for Daniel to surface. She loved the peace and quiet, the sounds of the sea, the chatter of birds. So many different birds, she wondered. Miracle Island was a refuge for them, some using high caves scored into the cliffs to shelter their eggs and young, others nesting in the trees. Splotches of white guano refuse decorated the sides of the cliffs, creating interesting and artful patterns.

Over the past three months she had enjoyed watching a variety of bird species; cormorants, pelicans, herons, sea gulls, owls, hummingbirds, sandpipers, egrets, frigate birds, doves, pigeons, cuckoos, mockingbirds, and sparrows. She had even spotted a pair of pink flamingos. And of course, the antics of their beloved osprey. Daniel rejected killing most of these birds for food. Too lean, he complained. But doves and pigeons would still be on the menu, if times got tough.

The birds held a special place for Alea. They were her friends from afar and she envied their abilities. They flew high and free on the winds, traveling wherever they chose to go, able to rise above any danger and not caring a fig that a cellphone or television didn't work. In her daydreams, she often wished she and Daniel could do the same. But their ability to soar to great heights encouraged her to believe that mankind could also rise above the challenges of these problematic times and be the better for it, perhaps without repeating the same mistakes that weakened them before the Flare. Was it possible for people to really change for the better?

Her chin was slowly dropping to her chest when a loose oar startled her awake. Where was Daniel? She turned her head in all directions as she searched the waters around the tender. She spotted him with a large mutton snapper pushed up and into the air on his spear as he swam back to the boat. A flash of white further out caught her attention. Her eyes squinted and strained. Was it only a whitecapped wave?

Daniel reached the tender and yanked the fish against the rim of the bucket, disengaging it from his spear. The snapper dropped, slapping the sides frantically to find escape.

He quickly pulled his snorkel out of his mouth. "Alea, what's wrong?" he gasped. He could see her agitation clearly as he approached the tender.

"Daniel, I think I see a boat!"

****

Daniel handed his spear to Alea, pushed up with both arms, and hauled himself out of the water. He yanked off his dive gear and grabbed the binoculars, slamming them up to his face. His body went still as he adjusted focus. It was definitely a boat. A white catamaran. Sailing north.

He was not pleased.

Who was traveling out in the Atlantic in a sailboat during prime hurricane season? He scanned the boat carefully from bow to stern to find a body in view, but there was no one in sight. He suddenly tensed, his hands clenching the binoculars. The catamaran had changed direction and was sailing straight towards them. He lowered his arms slowly, every muscle taut, his face grim. Alea remained silent until he finally spoke.

"It looks like we're going to have company." He cocked his blue water spear gun and clipped his dive knife to his trunks.

"Daniel, what are you going to do?" Her face was pale as she watched him prepare.

"They've spotted us. They'll see the cove, but I don't want them to see the channel into the bay. We'll wait here until they pull up. No matter what, let me do the talking."

He was unhappy that Alea was even present. He knew he would do whatever it took to keep Alea and his unborn child safe, and Miracle Island needed to be kept their secret. Daniel was content with isolation, even with its inherent dangers. He harbored no illusions about what men were capable of. They had found a haven here and the safety of his wife and baby were his primary concern. He was prepared to kill to protect them, without any hesitation.

The catamaran continued to sail towards their tender. As it neared the cove entry, about two hundred feet out, the boat came about, and the headsail started flapping in the breeze. A lone figure raced to the bow. Daniel heard the anchor drop and the catamaran began to back down slowly, finally halting a short distance away. The name Barefootin' out of Boston, Massachusetts could be clearly read on the stern.

The figure appeared on deck again. It was a man, tall and gaunt, rail thin and obviously emaciated, with light brown hair and a worn and weathered face. He called out a questioning hello and stood waiting for a reaction, smiling nervously and watching Daniel closely. He held nothing in his hands. Then he called out again, and this time Daniel could hear the fear and anguish in his trembling voice.

"Please, we are in trouble and really need help."

****

With the tender pulled up alongside and secured, Daniel climbed to the deck of the catamaran, his knife hidden under his rash guard. A hand reached out to help him up and Daniel accepted, his cautious eyes locked onto the man's face and outstretched arm.

Once he was on deck, the man began to weep and threw both arms around Daniel's shoulders. Daniel was startled but did not move away. The thin shoulders shaking against him felt fragile, the body emaciated and boney. He was wracked with sobs and almost fell to his knees. Daniel quickly supported him and realized something was very wrong. It took a few moments, but he regained control of himself and released Daniel, wiping his tears with his hand.

"Thank-you, thank-you! I didn't know what to do, where to go. It's been a living nightmare," he croaked hoarsely, through dry and cracked lips.

Alea boarded quietly and approached Daniel's side. When she saw the man, she stopped and stared in disbelief.

"John? John Garner?"

The man's eyes met hers with a shocked expression. "Alea Gabrielle? This is not possible!"

They moved towards each other and the man enveloped her in a tight bearhug as they simultaneously burst into tears. Daniel was shocked. They knew each other? But his initial caution began to subside. He glanced around the deck of the catamaran, taking note of its deteriorated condition, as their emotional reunion continued.

"I can't believe this! Alea, how are you here? How have you survived?"

"There's so much to tell you, John! But let me first introduce you to my husband, Daniel Devereaux."

The men shook hands in a more formal introduction. "My name is John Garner, Daniel. I'm a general practitioner who met Alea at Boston Hospital. We both worked there, and I was also her primary care physician. I simply can't believe this!"

"Where are Josey and the kids?" Alea asked.

"They're together in the master cabin. Josey is unconscious and the boys are in and out. We've had nothing to eat for days except raw fish and very little water."

"Oh no!" she exclaimed, immediately concerned. "We have plenty of food and water in camp. We can take good care of them once your boat is safe and secure."

He looked at the tender, then at the island. "Where do you live? What are you doing out here in a small inflatable on the Atlantic? Are you even aware of what's happened?"

Daniel smiled for the first time and clasped a hand to John's shoulder. "Trust me, John, we'll have plenty of time to catch up. But first, we need to get your boat into Osprey Bay."

****

Barefootin' was much easier to ease into Hidden Pass than Mystic. With the boat's minimal two-foot draft and a reefed, or partially furled, mainsail to catch the increasing east wind, Daniel and Alea were able to use the tender and a rope to tow the catamaran into Hidden Pass and through the channel. As much as Daniel loved Into The Mystic, he could not ignore the possibilities that a sailcat would bring to their lives.

John was speechless as the 45-foot Barefootin' slipped into sunny Osprey Bay. He turned to Daniel, a million questions in his eyes. But he felt hope returning, hope he had lost while he and his family were trapped, kidnapped essentially, on St. Thomas. His wife Josey and their two sons, Sam and Noah, were too weak with hunger and dehydration to come out on deck. He planned to go to them as soon as the boat was safely anchored in the bay and tell them he had found help.

Daniel assured him there was plenty of food and water, and John knew that the best treatment he could administer to his family was nourishment. He couldn't wait to see Josey's face when she heard the news. Josey knew Alea from social events in Boston and they were good friends. The boys loved her too. She was the cool "auntie" who played with them whenever she was able to visit.

John was relieved the events in St. Thomas were behind them. He wasn't sure if his wife could have taken another day. She was eight months pregnant.

Chapter 21 John's Nightmare

John sat back in the comfortable beach chair, his appetite satisfied after a plate of fruit, grilled hogfish, and greens. The cup of fresh coconut water tasted like a fine wine. He hadn't eaten this well in months but could only tolerate very small portions. His shrunken stomach needed to re-adjust to food of any reasonable volume. He gratefully accepted a bottle of water from Alea as if it were a precious jewel.

He and Alea had awakened Josey and the boys right away, offering Daniel and Alea's intended lunch of lemongrass tea, water, and fruit. Clumps of the long-bladed lemongrass plant grew everywhere on the island and Alea remembered it was useful for fever and infection, as well as delicious for hot tea or a cold drink.

Josey's eyes widened in surprised recognition when she saw Alea hovering over her. She tried to speak but was too weak, falling back asleep after eating a few bites of food and drinking some tea. Her body was rail-thin, the child swollen within her. Alea prayed the newborn would be healthy after assessing her friend's condition.

Sam and Noah roused more quickly, and after seeing their father with food and water, sat up and ate ravenously before they too fell back to sleep. John was content. At least they'd eaten. He would awaken and feed them every few hours. With Barefootin' safely moored and his family asleep, John and Alea rowed his tender to shore to meet Daniel at the campsite. He couldn't wait to hear how they had found Miracle Island. It was now his family's miracle too.

He was frankly awestruck by the spectacular paradise before him. After seeing the secret channel into Osprey Bay, the surrounding protective cliffs, and how the winds lightened considerably once inside, he instinctively knew Barefootin' would be safe here. He was highly impressed that

Daniel had maneuvered his cruiser through that channel and was glad to see the boat was afloat with insignificant hull damage. And if any hurricane had come through, Mystic had obviously been well-protected in the bay.

He and Josey were not able to attend the surprise wedding in mid-July. He couldn't arrange for time off from his busy practice until the week after, and their own family Caribbean cruise was already planned, a sailing adventure from Boston south to the U.S. Virgin Islands of St. Thomas and St. John on their sailing catamaran, Barefootin'. Not wanting to reveal the secret wedding plans to Alea, they sent their gift along with another physician who planned to attend. Josey was only four months pregnant and they wanted to sail well before the baby was due. The boys were out of school and it seemed to be the ideal family getaway.

In some ways, he believed they'd been lucky. In other ways, the trip had been a disaster.

"Incredible, just incredible," he commented in awe, after Daniel finished telling him the story of their adventures since the wedding, with Alea jumping in occasionally to add her comments and perspective. The sun dropped behind the trees to the west and a contemplative silence fell between the three of them as they sipped cups of hot lemongrass tea.

"You two have been unbelievably fortunate, more so than almost everyone else out there since the solar flare."

Daniel's ears perked. "Yes, that's what we've been wanting to know, John. We could only evaluate based on what we saw. Can you tell us, was it really a solar flare with resulting EMP? Or was it an electromagnetic pulse from nuclear detonations? Is the world at war?"

John sighed and looked solemnly at Daniel and Alea, his expression grim.

"It was the biggest solar flare ever recorded. The entire world has been affected, with none spared. War, nuclear bombs; all pointless. No one can invade anyone else. No one can cross the oceans in large numbers. Millions are already dead from starvation and disease. Humans preying on humans. There is little or no government. Society has regressed thousands of years. We're on our own."

His eyes grew sad as he thought about his children.

"Our planet will never be the same again."

****

"Josey loves to sail. She saw Barefootin' at a boat show in Boston Harbor after lunch with her girlfriends. She was only a year old and in excellent condition, but the owner suffered with a back problem and was reluctantly selling. She toured the boat and took the owner's card. We returned together the next day and I wrote the check. Fantastic boat! Took her out for a sea trial and I was hooked. We loved the name and left it intact. There was more than enough room for the four of us, and for one or two more in the future, if we chose.

"We sailed her together for the next year, whenever I could find time, and kept her in Boston Harbor. I'm pretty sure the baby is the result of some very good times we had on that boat! We took Sam and Noah out with us often and were teaching them to sail. They love to be on the water, and even as young as they are, they're decent little sailors. So, when we decided to take a month off in late July to sail to St. Thomas, we felt ready. We were invited to the wedding with many of your friends from the hospital, Alea, but I couldn't get away yet, and we never seemed to find time for you to introduce me to Daniel. I sent the gift with Bob Hollings. Did you open it? Well, if it's here on your boat, still wrapped, maybe we can have a little party to open some of your gifts.

"Anyway, we set sail towards the Virgin Islands. It was still early hurricane season, usually not a problem, and we'd been sailing about ten days. Wouldn't you know it, got a report on the radio of a possible storm brewing in the Atlantic. We were about five days out from St. Thomas and there was still time to make it there before bad weather. But the EMP struck the next day.

"I had anchored near a small uninhabited island the night before. We enjoyed a terrific evening swimming in the warm water and the kids explored the beach. I caught a big grouper that Josey grilled with a pineapple relish and spices. We were nicely worn-out and full by bedtime.

"I was out on deck at dawn when it happened. First the blood red sky, then the flash. It was so bright my first thought was that an atomic bomb had detonated high overhead, but there was no sound. I was completely blind and shouted for Josey. She came racing out and grabbed me, in a panic. She and the boys had been in the cabin, which offered some eye protection. She could still see but her vision was blurry at best. She helped me inside and we waited... For a tsunami wave. For the sound of an explosion. Anything. But it was completely silent, except for the whisper of the breeze.

"It gradually dawned on me. There was absolutely no sound. Nothing was running. No pumps. No fans. No sound from the refrigerator. No hum of any device using power. How can you have a power out in the middle of the Atlantic? That's when I began to worry about my twin 100 hp outboard engines and their batteries, as well as the back-up batteries and generator.

"Josey called the boys over and we huddled together as our vision began to improve. Sam was chattering, asking question after question. Noah was quiet. Josey shook off her concerns and made us eat some breakfast, which helped calm everyone down. When I was finally able to see clearly, I went to start the outboards, and inserted the key.

"The engines turned over but wouldn't fire. After trying one more time, I decided to check the batteries and pulled out my voltmeter. I touched the probes to one of the 12-volt battery terminals. There was no reading. Was the battery dead or was the voltmeter broken? Then I remembered my voltmeter used an electronic control unit. Perhaps the flash had affected it somehow and I didn't carry an alternative. What else did I have?

"My test light! That device didn't use an electronic circuit. Locating it from another toolbox, I touched the probes to the terminals again. The bulb lit up! The batteries were okay. So why were the engines not starting?

"I see you nodding, Daniel. This happened to you too? Yes, that's when I got it. A solar flare. Batteries won't be affected, just electronics, unless protected by a metal Faraday cage. The electronic ignition module was the problem. But at least I knew the batteries were functional, until they lost charge. I foolishly chose not to install solar power on Barefootin' and would now pay the price.

"The only highlight of that frightening day was our sail. We were positioned much closer to St. Thomas than the U.S. and could thankfully continue on to our destination using only the wind as power. We'd have to manually operate the sails and anchor, but that was not a problem for us. Even Sam and Noah knew how to handle that.

"So, we kept sailing towards St. Thomas. I used my nautical charts as a reference, but to determine our course during the day, I had only a magnetic compass and the sun as my guide. Ironic, isn't it? A few days later, Josey spotted St. Thomas with the binoculars and we steered towards port.

"As we approached the capitol city of Charlotte Amalie, the beautiful sight of white homes scattered on the hills around Magen's Bay was blotted by plumes of dark smoke. Instead of the usual array of yachts, cruise ships, and sailboats anchored peacefully, every boat was tied up at the public or cruise docks and along the shoreline, one right next to the other, almost touching. The bay itself was empty. Cars were scattered in random locations, not moving. Groups of men stood around in the streets. I was very concerned, but with a storm looming, we needed a safe harbor.

"I dropped anchor out in the bay. Almost immediately, four men jumped on a skiff tied up at the main dock and began to row out towards me. It wasn't until they were twenty feet away that I saw that each of them was holding a gun. I don't know weapons, but they looked like shotguns or rifles. I told Josey and the boys to go inside and I waited anxiously as the men climbed onboard.

"Two of the men were white and two were black. One of the black men announced himself as Mr. Collins of the St. Thomas Post-Power Emergency Collective Government. None of the four men wore a uniform. He asked how many persons were onboard and I told him myself, my pregnant wife, and two sons. His face displayed no emotion. I was informed that my boat was forfeit to the Collective and we were to be escorted to a secure location for our own safety. When I protested, he shoved his weapon in my face. I was forced to comply.

"I called Josey, Sam, and Noah to the deck and told them to pack their suitcases. Mr. Collins barked at them to stop. Only their essential personals and a change of clothing was allowed. Everything else was now Collective property.

"We were only given a short time, then hustled into the skiff. Once on shore, we were directed to walk up a steep hill road for half a mile, in terrible heat, then ordered to stop at an old school building. We were unceremoniously escorted inside to an auditorium packed with hundreds of frightened tourists, probably the owners or passengers of the many boats tied-up to the docks and shore, I figured, just like us.

"Everyone was speaking in hushed tones and did not make eye contact. People sat or lay around the room in a random manner, clutching their few belongings. There were no chairs. Standing guard at the perimeter were men holding weapons. No one wore a uniform or displayed insignia of any kind. It looked like a concentration camp.

"I found an area to lead my family, a relatively clean location next to a pillar. We were ignored, except for the closest guard, who studied each of us intently before turning away to scan the crowd. I noticed a long line of men and women leading to a back room and guessed it led to the bathrooms but decided to confirm that later.

"After several hours of sitting on the coarse concrete floor, hot, thirsty, and exhausted, the double doors in front burst open. A procession of armed men entered, surrounding an unsmiling, older man with pale white skin and a shock of white hair. He was formally dressed in a tailored gray suit, impeccable white shirt, peacock blue patterned tie, and black crocodile shoes, with a large gold and diamond ring on his right hand and a thick gold chain around his neck. He walked straight to a wooden podium and addressed the crowd, his expression cold and unemotional."

"Good afternoon ladies and gentlemen. My name is Calvin Rutledge, St. Thomas Police Commissioner. As of three days ago, I have assumed control over the island of St. Thomas and have declared Marshall Law, due to the unprecedented event of the solar flare and resultant electromagnetic pulse. These events have essentially shut down all usual operations on St. Thomas, and from information I have gathered, has done the same worldwide. To prevent conditions from deteriorating, my police forces and new military recruits will be directing everyone, citizens or foreigners, in any manner I choose to protect this island and its inhabitants.

"None of you in this room are local residents of St. Thomas. Some of you are American citizens, but I no longer recognize the authority of the United States over this island."

He stopped as a wave of angry voices rose in the room, and held up one hand, palm forward.

"This island stands alone, is alone. You can be certain there will be no assistance or help coming from anywhere and it is up to me to ensure the survival of St. Thomas."

No one said a word.

"As of this moment, each of you will be expected to serve in whatever manner I determine. Your boats are forfeit to the Collective. The powerboats are of no use, except what we can glean off them. However, all sailboats are commandeered to provide food by fishing daily with crews of my selection. If you wish to eat, you will serve. If you want your children to eat, they will serve as well."

He surveyed the room slowly, with no expression.

"Welcome to the sovereign nation of St. Thomas."

****

"Josey was assigned to work in the kitchen near the docks. There were at least ten kitchen facilities scattered around the island that served two meals a day to workers. Sam and Noah, despite their young ages, were assigned to the gardens. Every morning they were sent with a group of other children to one of numerous homes or lots that had open land for planting crops, tilling, weeding, and trimming until dusk. A supervisor with a weapon directed them.

"We were quartered in a dilapidated apartment complex of six units. There were eighty people assigned to those six units. Conditions were abysmal; crowded, no privacy, thin mats as beds on the floor. We used a hastily dug backyard hole as the only latrine. Wealthy tourists who could have paid for the finest accommodations now battled over a scrap of blanket or a torn and filthy pillow.

"I was required to take Barefootin' out every morning to fish the waters surrounding St. Thomas and St. John. I was given a crew of eight fishermen and divers and we were expected to bring home a large catch. We did everything; handlining, netting, diving, and bait fishing with poles. There was always an armed guard, who did nothing but watch the rest of us work. A couple of the divers were native to St. Thomas. All the others were forced tourist labor. The punishment for not meeting our quota... half rations for dinner. We were allowed one day a week off, but if I took the day, someone else was assigned to captain Barefootin'. I didn't want my boat handled by anyone else, so I went out daily.

"Each of us were given one 8-oz plastic water bottle but no food while we worked. We ate in the morning before leaving, then dinner at night. There was severe discipline if you took extra food or stole it from someone else. I saw many examples of what happened to those folks.

"Water came from private wells, ponds, and the downpours of daily rain. There was plenty of water on St. Thomas. But it was guarded by Rutledge's men 24/7 and divvied out sparsely to the foreign workers. The only bathing allowed was in the ocean, if you had the strength or time. Diseases were killing hundreds of people and the sewage situation wasn't helping. Homes were required to dig a hole for waste and in town near the common latrines, well, let me just say it didn't smell very good. Flies and rats were the new citizens. We stopped trying to figure out what type of meat we were given, if any. Fish wasn't filling, but at least I knew what it was.

"Even though Josey worked in the kitchen, she was only given as much food as the rest of the workers, which wasn't much at all. The fishermen and gardeners received somewhat larger portions, but the police and military goon squads ate well. Josey was losing weight, and no one cared that she was pregnant. Rutledge didn't care. I think he was planning for certain groups of his people to ultimately survive, the rest of us considered disposable and replaceable.

"Many people died. If they didn't already have a medication necessary for their disease or disorder, it wasn't long before another poor soul was being tossed into the Pit of Death, as it became infamously known. The Pit was a deep chasm between two distant inland hills. I was very glad not to be assigned to the death detail.

"Men and women who couldn't work, whatever the reason, simply disappeared. Nothing was ever said or done to find them, and it wasn't a very good idea to enquire. If they'd left children behind and no one accepted their care, the children eventually disappeared too. Yes, Alea, really."

All of a sudden, John stopped and dropped his head, unable to continue. Fighting back his tears, he took a deep breath, regained control, and looked up at Daniel and Alea.

"Well, I'm sure you're both wondering how we finally ended up here at Miracle Island? This will be the hardest part for me to talk about, Daniel.

"One man was assigned to my boat every day. His name was Curtis Cambridge, a native of St. Thomas, with a beautiful wife and infant son. Twice a week, he and I were assigned a night watch for the boats along the docks and shoreline, from 6:00 pm to midnight. Our job was to make sure they were properly tied up, secure, and unmanned. If we saw anything out of line, we were ordered to notify one of the armed guards that were stationed about every 500 feet. They stayed put and we did the walking until the next shift came on from midnight to six a.m.

"He was devastated when his infant son died in September from a severe upper respiratory infection and pneumonia. There was no medication. It took his little body three days to die, struggling desperately to breathe. They forced Curtis to fish with me the day his son was thrown in the Pit. I'll never forget the look on his face.

"When we pulled back in that evening, he immediately went to comfort his anguished wife, but she wasn't at their allotted space. When he searched for her, a couple of guards snickered and told him she would be quite busy that night, in Rutledge's bed. He liked it rough and if a woman cried out in pain, well, he'd make sure the screaming didn't end for hours. It was common knowledge that when Rutledge was finished with a woman, he handed her over to his goons. Beauty was only a curse for the women of St. Thomas.

"Her bruised and torn body was found two days later. With thinly disguised smiles, they told him she had thrown herself off the cliff in front of Rutledge's hilltop house. Curtis never said a word and fished everyday as usual. Only I could see his anguished pain, the simmering anger, his complete disbelief in their story. He covered it well for the guards. I tried my best to comfort him, but he would just look at me and thank me for my kind heart. He believed his wife and son were with God and he would see them again someday, but I knew it was only a matter of time before he lost control. It was terrifying to imagine being in his shoes, but it might easily be my turn next.

"One day, Curtis located me at the common latrines. He had a plan, he said, and clasped my hand warmly. His family was dead, but he wanted to honor their memory by helping my family to live. That night was our watch together. If I could get Josey and the boys down to the docks after sunset, he knew of a place to hide them. Around 11:00 pm we would all meet at Barefootin'. The guards were posted several hundred feet to either side in sheltered stations. Under cover of darkness, I was to slip everyone onboard and untie the lines. Curtis would push us into the bay, then create a loud distraction to allow us to drift away from the dock, unnoticed, on the outgoing tide. I begged him to come with us, but he simply looked at me with a macabre joy and shook his head. His time for vengeance had come.

"Now I'm just a general practitioner, not James Bond, but I somehow smuggled my family down to the bushes near the dock. Curtis was waiting. He had previously scouted a deep depression in a rock wall behind a thick bramble of bushes only twenty feet from Barefootin'. Josey steeled herself, knelt down, and crawled in first, with the boy's right behind her, disappearing completely into the dark, even with the bushes held apart. With instructions not to make a sound until they heard my voice, Curtis and I casually walked away and continued our usual rounds. After completing several passes, which were over a mile in each direction, we stopped in front of the hidden cave and Barefootin'.

"The wind was a strong offshore, the tide was starting to go out, the half-moon and the night stars were our only source of light. There would never be a better time.

"I called softly for Josey. She crawled out, stiff and sore, with Noah and Sam at her heels. Curtis checked to the right and left. The guards were barely visible. One man appeared to be dozing and the other was fast asleep. We quickly slipped over to Barefootin' and tiptoed aboard. I began to untie the tangle of ropes, my hands shaking, until the lines finally released. The boat was free! Curtis gripped my arm firmly, and I, his. No words needed to be spoken. It would be goodbye forever. He jumped back on shore, pushed us away from the dock with all his might, and watched as we drifted slowly into the bay, his form getting smaller as the wind and tide bore us silently away from hell."

John leaned forward towards the fire, hands clasped, dark shadows flickering across his weary face. "But I did witness the vengeance he carried out for his family."

"We heard a loud war cry as he ran up the hill and away from the dock. Our loyal friend had begun his distraction to save us and he shouted out his defiance. He scorned the new regime and the filthy pig Rutledge. His machete sliced through the air to meet the neck of a startled guard that ran too close too fast, bright red blood spurting in rhythmic bursts from his half-severed neck. Another guard snuck up from behind, and as Curtis whipped around in a circle like a ninja warrior, the arc of the machete slit the guard's throat. A third guard took aim with his rifle as Curtis bore down on him, his face contorted with rage. The rifle fired, hitting him straight in the heart. But he refused to fall, and with nothing but sheer willpower, kept running forward until his avenging machete crashed down and split the man's head in half. Two lives for two lives. And one for his own.

"Josey, Noah, and Sam wept uncontrollably at my feet. I whispered a final good-bye as we drifted into the night.

"I truly believe that as he lay dying, he must have smiled with great joy, as his beautiful and loving wife, with his baby son clutched close to her bosom, ran towards him to welcome him home."

****

"We kept sailing north, with no plan or destination in mind, anchoring at night on uninhabited islands or on shallow reefs at sea. I wanted to get my family far away from that evil place. Rutledge was obviously insane, waiting for an opportunity to become some kind of post-apocalyptic king. The EMP allowed him to assume quick control, under the veil of his position as the island's police commissioner and there were whispers he had executed any official that he perceived as a threat.

"After that terrible experience, I certainly did not want to try landing on another known populated island. It was difficult to decide on a course or to know where to go. I'd heard so many rumors about living conditions being the same or worse on other islands in the Caribbean, and that the U.S. itself was in upheaval, with millions dead and anarchy the rule. Rutledge had a working shortwave radio and his people would taunt us with bits and pieces of information, trying to get us to believe we were the fortunate and that our lives were so much better. I couldn't leave my dear family there and I weep for the others forced to remain.

"We had no water except rain catch from tarps on deck. I tried to catch fish every day, but we had to eat them raw. We were slowly starving. Josey was getting weaker and the kids were not doing well either. I was the only one with strength left to sail the boat. Sorry, Alea, you know I don't cry easily, but I've been an emotional mess for months now.

"Daniel, I thought I was seeing a mirage when I spotted your tender! I didn't remember an inhabited island in this area and at that point there was nothing more to lose. So, I said a prayer and turned the wheel to see who you were, hoping beyond hope that Curtis' sacrifice had not been in vain. And here I am, sitting at a warm campfire, eating delicious fresh food, my family recovering, with a wonderful friend that I know and trust. And with her new husband, a man I will always thank for saving our lives."

John stared sadly into the flickering campfire. "My only regret is that Curtis and his family couldn't be here too."

Chapter 22 Birth

Six-year old Sammy raced along the beach, clutching his little sharpened wooden spear and screaming at the top of his lungs. "Haayah!" as he heaved a mighty toss into the shallow water along the shore. "Mom, I almost speared that fish!"

He was a mini-me of his dad, with light brown hair and hazel eyes. A little rascal that chattered all day long, he entertained everyone with his well-considered opinions and feats of great strength and cunning.

Josey looked up and waved from her padded deck chair, positioned well into the shade of the beach hut, and grinned at Alea sitting next to her. "That one is a wild man. This island is perfect for him."

Alea nodded in agreement. "The boys are so different from each other, but they are a real team. Noah watches out for Sam in a quietly protective way. Sam pushes Noah to do things he might not attempt on his own."

The ladies were enjoying an hour of siesta in the warmest part of the day after preparing lunch for the men, who ate quickly and vanished. Off to do manly things, Josey drowsily thought. Just as well, I need a nap.

She was rapidly gaining weight under Alea's gentle care and attention, her naturally curvy figure taking shape again and her long blonde hair clean, brushed, and gleaming from the moisturizing coconut oil Alea gave her to rub in. The horrors of St. Thomas no longer reflected in her smiling blue eyes, and the sight of her two sons playing happily on a warm beach made her bask in contentment. Her belly was huge with her unborn child, due any day, but she did not know which sex to expect.

Alea was still concerned about the health of the baby. The second half of Josey's pregnancy had been spent hungry and dehydrated. Since she arrived on Miracle Island, the others all conspired to save her the choicest fillets, the smaller and more tender lobster tails, the freshest fruits and vegetables. As for herself, Alea had no concerns. At three months, she was barely showing and in robust health and condition.

The two women had re-bonded immediately, reminiscing about pleasant times spent together. Alea didn't realize how much she'd been missing the companionship of another woman. Her friendship with Josey was meeting a social need she was grateful to have again.

In the safety of Miracle Island, Josey shared memories of her harrowing months on St. Thomas, some quietly whispered only to Alea, the rest re-lived during group story time in the evenings. Even Sam and Noah told tales that made everyone cry, a few their parents were hearing for the first time. Alea shivered when she learned of the atrocities and suffering. Several nights of bad dreams woke her, tearful and wet with perspiration. Only Daniel's loving arms and soft murmurings would allow sleep again. If only she'd been able to help Curtis' baby... and so many others.

Daniel, John, and ten-year old Noah would probably not re-appear until late afternoon, Alea guessed, having rowed out in the tender to the Atlantic for a dive. Noah was very intelligent, a quiet, reserved, and serious boy. He did not often volunteer conversation but was unfailingly pleasant and responsive if approached. He often appeared to be in deep thought and would startle slightly if questioned, pulling himself back from his reflections. He observed the world around him intently and suggested several improvements to the building of the recently expanded treehouse that Daniel considered quite helpful. His rare and wry smile was a victory for whoever succeeded to inspire it, and if he decided to play a practical joke on someone, the unwitting victim never knew it was coming. But he'd laugh as hard as everyone else when the prank was over.

With a shock of short, bright blonde hair and dark blue eyes, he loved being in the ocean as much as Daniel and paid close attention to his teachings. But he occasionally strayed from accepted protocol. On one Atlantic dive, Noah discovered a thriving sponge bed three hundred feet straight out from the entry cove, a distance and solitary swim not sanctioned by his father, but that he decided to try on his own anyway. Rinsed in fresh water and dried in the sun, the sponges were a luxury not only for bathing, but for the many cleaning jobs on both boats. He was forgiven after a lengthy lecture from John and Daniel on water safety, team communication, common sense, and following instructions. But his mother pulled him aside privately and gave him a thankful hug.

Sammy also became a hero one afternoon. He was trailing along with Alea on one of her forays into the bush for greens and herbs. She had cut him a digging stick like her own, smaller and better suited for his height and little hands. He wanted to learn how she found all the good stuff they ate, and she was always patient with his constant questions.

She located a sprawling bed of a vine that resembled ivy and tasted like mint. She loved to crush up the small leaves and sprinkle them on top of her green salads for flavor. She was on her knees, busy trimming off long sections, when Sammy ran up behind her.

"What's this, Auntie Alea?"

She turned to see what he was holding and dropped her knife to the ground in excitement. "Let me see that, Sammy," taking the large tuber from him and brushing away the clinging soil. "No, it can't be!" she exclaimed. She turned to Sam and ruffled his hair in happy approval.

"How would you like French fries for dinner?" He had found a large bed of cassava root!

Cassava was the potato of the Bahamas. Originating in South America, the tuber migrated to the islands a thousand years ago with the Arawak, then with the Carib Indians, a war-like cannibal tribe who attacked the Arawak people at every opportunity to take their lands and women. She and Daniel often conjectured how some of the vegetation and fruits they found might have reached Miracle Island and she reminded herself to ask Daniel to explain his thoughts on that matter to the newcomers.

Cassava was poisonous if eaten raw and cooking the orange-brown root was the only way it could be safely used. Alea was sorely missing bread, sweets, and starches. She immediately pictured the tasty treats she could cook, and a grilled flatbread was high on her list of recipes.

She and Sam dug up twelve good-sized cassava and packed them in her carry sack. The reveal at campsite would be one to remember. Alea was particularly pleased that Sam was the one to find the delectable potato that would help nourish his new brother or sister before birth.

That afternoon, as the experimental flatbreads baked on the open hearth, Alea brought up the question again, for the benefit of the group gathered around the campfire.

"Daniel, why do you think Miracle Island was uninhabited and how did so many plant species that need roots or cuttings to grow even get here?"

Daniel had given this question much thought during the last six months. Even with 700 islands making up the Bahamas proper, less than eight percent were inhabited. The remainder were small islands with one common feature. No available freshwater. The other negatives included lack of safe moorage, flat sea level terrain that put them at high risk for storm surge, and no access to electrical power.

"Well, here's my theory, guys. I do think ancient Indians visited this island by canoe, searching for safe and fertile land, and carrying plants and animals to begin a new life. They may have been attacked and driven from their original homeland by their enemy, the Caribs. Not sure, but the history books do record that terrible conflict. As they sailed the Caribbean and once they finally located this island, they would have entered through Hidden Pass and found Osprey Bay. Perhaps there were more streams of water, like ours, that encouraged them to establish a village. They probably tried to grow trees and plants that were not native to Miracle Island from starts, cuttings, and seeds they brought along with them, but without enough water to drink, as well as care for their crops, the tribe just gave up and sailed away. No one ever discovered the Black Hole, thankfully, or this island would have a McDonald's right here at Casuarina Cove," he chuckled.

"But the starts and seeds they left behind must have taken hold during the wet seasons. That may be why we are finding non-native plants such as avocado, banana, mango, papaya, sour orange, and cassava root."

He pushed a stick into the fire to make it throw sparks. "All just my silly theory."

A buzz of conversation lit the group as they bantered ideas and opinions about Daniel's theory, each adding their own interpretation, hands flying, eyes flashing, and excited voices echoing off the trees.

He studied each person sitting in the circle around the fire, light flickering over their faces as they talked and gestured. He felt a deep love for each one, the honor and responsibility to guide and care for them sealed in his heart.

"I know those ancient people were called the Arawak. What shall we name our little Tribe?" he joked.

Before anyone could answer, Josey gave a surprised squeak and clutched her belly.

"I don't know what to name our Tribe, but one more Indian is about to make an appearance. My water just broke!"

****

"Breathe in! Breathe out! Josey, we're here for you. You're doing great! Not your first time, sweetheart," John reassured her confidently, as he held her hand tightly. He hadn't assisted in a birth since his internship, but he remembered what to do quite well.

Josey panted, trying to relax as another contraction caused beads of sweat to break out on her forehead. She recalled that primitive women sometimes squatted between two supports to allow gravity to help push the baby out and asked John to let her attempt the birth that way. The men set-up two solid chairs and she struggled to position herself. Even with their help, it wasn't possible. The deprivations on St. Thomas had weakened her more than she realized. She would give birth the same way she had done twice before.

After her water broke, they swiftly transported her to Mystic and onto the queen bed in one of the guest cabins, the bed first draped with a plastic tarp and the sheet put back on. The sky was darkening rapidly and both John and Alea knew they would need light as the birth progressed. She asked Daniel to turn on the rarely used special connection.

Daniel bypassed the original electronic circuit controls and enabled a direct wire connection that would allow one of the 24-volt batteries to power the cabin lights. He prayed there was still enough charge to get through the night. They did not use this lighting feature very often, with no solar panels to re-charge the batteries, but today was definitely an emergency. It was a wonderful bonus the Flare could not destroy.

Josey labored for two more hours. Alea manually confirmed the baby was positioned correctly with its head at the opening of the birth canal. Piece of cake, she thought, this is her third child. Hopefully I won't have to stitch her closed. But she prepared a homemade birthing kit, just in case, with boiled and triple strained saltwater and sours juice to sterilize the sewing kit needle. Regular thread would just have to do, and she really hoped it would not be needed.

Alea was fascinated by the process of this birth. She would be undergoing the same event in six months and was mentally recording every moan, grunt, curse, and contraction. It was messy, it was noisy, but oh my, a new life would be joining the world! What a world to be born into, she mused, but life itself was such a precious gift.

Sam and Noah were given permission to camp onshore by themselves in the beach hut, a decision by their father that left them speechless with delight. They were worried about their mom but the idea of a night on the island, by themselves, was too enticing. Alea smiled at their enthusiasm. She knew they would be quite safe while all the adults were on Mystic and there'd be plenty of time to meet their new sibling later. Both boys were skilled in the care and handling of the campfire and were now in the process of planning secret night missions they would discuss with no one. Alea chuckled to herself. She'd be able to see them from the deck anyway.

Daniel felt helpless and sat out on the deck watching the sun drop behind the trees while John and Alea stayed with Josey. He disliked hearing her cries of pain and worried about Alea, when it would be her time. After a while, he went to the master cabin. I could use a fresh t-shirt, he thought, and rummaged in the dresser drawer. His hand bumped a small square object. A box? He pulled it out. It was attractively wrapped in gold paper and a silver bow and ribbon, with a card from Ben and his entire family. They hadn't opened any of their wedding gifts while on their honeymoon and he must have tucked Ben's present away in the drawer for safekeeping. He opened the envelope, suddenly missing Ben tremendously, and began to read the message with tears in his eyes.

Daniel, my friend, here is the Key for the surprise I created for you. As I've always taught you boys, never assume and always think ahead. In a pinch, the contents may come in handy. Enjoy your honeymoon with your beautiful wife. I left something special for her too. Let the treasure hunt begin!
Love, Ben, Vernita, Gil and Will

The memory returned. Ben had prepped Into The Mystic for the wedding right after Matt and Ronny brought her down to Spanish Wells and told Daniel something very special had been created on the boat that he might later appreciate. But their conversation was completely forgotten in the flurry of preparations for the wedding and the honeymoon cruise, and certainly in the aftermath of the Flare. He must have stashed the small box in his drawer, thinking he would open Ben's gift another day. His curiosity was peaked, but he decided to leave it until morning, after the baby was born.

"No, oh my God, no!"

Daniel raced to the guest cabin and burst in the door. John was holding the limp body of Josey in his arms and Alea was cradling a tiny blue form in her hands.

"Alea, what is going on?" he cried out.

"Her heart stopped just as the baby was coming out. Daniel, go to John and get him started on CPR. I think he's in shock. I'm dealing with this baby. It's not breathing!"

Daniel bolted to the bed and gripped John's shoulder firmly. No response. He shook his shoulder harder.

"John... John, Josey needs you, man. Alea wants you to start CPR, NOW!"

He shouted to get the stunned man's attention. It worked. John's glazed eyes cleared, and he looked down at his listless wife. She'd already been through hell. He'd never let her go like this. He laid her back down on the mattress.

"Dan, get me something firm to put under her!" He dropped his mouth to Josey's and blew a deep breath into her lungs, watching as her chest rose. He immediately placed the heel of one hand at the base of her sternum, covered it with his other hand, and began compressions as he counted. He then blew another deep breath into her mouth.

Daniel ran out, returning quickly with one of his surfboards. He detached the three fins and held it up for John's approval. Without stopping his compressions, John nodded agreement. The board had a slight curve, but it would just have to do. Before he blew the next breath, he rolled Josey onto her side as Daniel shoved it underneath her. John rolled her back onto the board, blew another breath into her mouth, and resumed his compressions. He had regained his composure and was fighting for the life of his wife. Neither John or Daniel were aware of Alea and the baby.

Alea pulled the baby out of the birth canal once the head was visible. Blue and still, the child was not breathing. She cut the umbilical cord with a knife even as she fervently prayed for help. Wrapping the limp form in a warm towel, Alea gently pushed her pinkie into the gaping mouth and found what she expected. She extracted a trailing and congealed mass of blood and mucus from between the tiny lips and tossed it in disgust to the floor. Without a second thought, she placed her own lips over the small blue mouth and puffed. She saw the miniscule little chest rise and proceeded to compress with two fingers on the soft sternum. One more puff of air. More compressions. The room faded around her. She and this precious little being floated alone in the endless universe; they were as one. Time stood still as she blew the breath of life into the tiny body.

As she fought for the child, she gradually became aware of a soft fragrant warmth brushing past her, as if the wings of a bird were lightly fanning overhead. Alea instantly sensed she was not alone.

What she would never see was the radiant loving smile and the gentle wave of an unseen hand over the bloody scene.

The baby suddenly gasped. A small taste of air and the little chest rose, fell, and rose again on its own. The child was alive! Life had been gifted, had been allowed. Alea's eyes closed as a joy she had never known overwhelmed her, and she suddenly understood, the message undeniably clear.

She was the instrument, but the ultimate decision would never be hers.

John lifted his head from her mouth as Josey's eyes fluttered open. Daniel dropped to his knees at the side of the bed, lost in amazement, as he saw life instantly flow back into the wife of his friend. John held Josey in his arms and neither man tried to stop his tears from falling.

After ensuring that Josey was stable, resting, and had taken some fluids, Alea tenderly passed the tiny little baby girl to her father and watched as he lovingly lowered her to her mother's breast. Josey struggled to speak, and they all leaned in closer to hear.

"I want to name her... Angel."

Alea collapsed against Daniel and fainted in his arms.

Chapter 23   The Tribe

Josey lay comfortably reclined on pillows and covered with a warm blanket, not at all embarrassed that the entire Tribe was standing around the bed, locked on to the scenario before them. Angel sucked greedily on a nipple, unaware that she was center stage, the entertainment of the afternoon for the cooing and smiling island family surrounding her. Damp tufts of white-blonde hair covered her head and her eyes were closed in contentment, hiding their color for now. Her soft skin was a healthy rose-white and her arms waved around outside of the wrappings that enveloped her tiny form.

"She is so beautiful," Alea whispered. She and Daniel stood together, arms wrapped around each other, gazing down at the tender scene.

John kneeled next to the bed, his joyful smile still beaming since the resurrection of his wife and child the day before. He silently thanked Curtis again for his brave sacrifice, his heart still in pain for him. He earnestly wished his friend and his family could have been here today, rejoicing over the miracle of Angel's birth.

In his honor, John built a wooden cross and set it into a pile of heavy rocks high on a clifftop overlooking the Atlantic. He occasionally went alone to pray. He brought Sam and Noah with him once and re-told the story of Curtis' brave sacrifice. The walk home was quiet. They remembered the nightmare too, and both boys, as young as they were, understood they owed their very lives to this selfless man.

The boys were happy to have a little sister, but when would she be able to catch a coconut football or spear a fish? Until then, they decided she was useless. Maybe now, though, Mom would let them camp and explore more often by themselves. But the grip of her impossibly small fingers around an offered thumb made each of them melt inside. Not that either would ever confess to that weakness. With their father's permission, they leaped into the tender and headed to the beach.

Daniel was relieved that Angel's birth ultimately ended so well. He had been fully prepared for a much sadder outcome, but with both Josey and Angel healthy and happy, he could re-apply his energies to enlarging the treehouse. He recruited more support trees to expand the original floorplan, adding a spacious roomy addition for John's family. The boys were pleading with him to build another smaller treehouse, much higher of course, for their private and exclusive use.

Christmas was only two days away. Daniel wanted to make this a memorable time for everyone and Alea came up with a generous and thoughtful idea. They hadn't opened even one wedding gift since leaving on their honeymoon cruise before the Flare. Packages were stacked high in the closets of all three sleeping cabins, along the walls, and in other storage areas around the boat. They decided that Christmas Eve would be the best time to gather the gifts together in the lounge and distribute them equally to each person. After unwrapping, exchanges and trades could be bartered, if the item was not something the person wanted or could use.

The week before, Daniel, Sam, and Noah picked a casuarina tree close to the beach hut to serve as their Christmas tree. The Tribe walked the beach and collected dozens of colorful shells to use as ornaments. Alea pierced each one with a small hole or used a natural opening in the shell, looped a bit of Daniel's clear fishing line through the hole, and tied a knot. The simple ornaments were hung as high as they could reach, the delicate pastel colors shining brightly in the sunlight, and the brisk ocean breeze making them dance and sway. Blooming white beach lilies and pink hibiscus flowers were also tucked into the boughs. John found a dried red starfish to serve as the Star, the perfect finishing touch to honor the Christ Child, the real reason for Christmas in the first place.

The pair of osprey were often seen perched on the tree's branches, gazing curiously around the camp and pecking at the shell ornaments. Their presence was strangely comforting and on the days they did not appear, everyone missed them.

Josey was the first to create intricate hanging shell designs, stringing individual shells on long lengths of fishing line, then tying each section to a top crosspiece of two gnarled sticks. Everyone attempted a design of their own, a gallery of creative configurations soon surrounding the entire camp.

Large pieces of driftwood were readily available along the shoreline to serve as tables and seats and were sometimes positioned around the campsite just for their unique beauty. It burned too quickly to be used as dependable firewood, but a small piece was helpful to start a fire. A larger log was often tossed into the flames simply to watch the glowing chunks of charcoal drop off into the pit, with the enjoyable smell of the salty wood smoke permeating the air.

Daniel was starting to miss surfing. His attention had been so driven by survival needs that he almost forgot the pure joy of riding a big wave. He'd often noticed an enticing wave that popped up occasionally on an outside reef when he dove the Atlantic but dismissed it out of sheer necessity. He decided to watch and determine the conditions that caused it to break. He could row out with his board on the tender, tie up at the buoy, and paddle out. His only mistake was in mentioning his plan to Noah and Sam, who pestered him mercilessly until they'd extracted a promise from Uncle Daniel to teach them to surf. He agreed, with the stipulation that he surf the wave first to assess the currents and other safety hazards. The whoops and hollering made everyone pause whatever they were doing and chuckle. Daniel smiled. Weren't we all that young once?

The boys took to island life and the ocean like a pair of young dolphins. School...they were living in the schoolroom of the real world. Texting...replaced by meaningful conversations with people they could look straight in the eye. Daily life was their internet. The wilderness and cliffs of Miracle Island were better than any video game, the boats and surfboards more exciting than any fancy car. They explored the far reaches of the island daily, going off for hours at a time. The only rules were to tell their parents the direction they planned to go and to make sure they were back well before sunset. Hunger usually brought them home early. They were both growing fast, strong and agile, and were living a young boy's dream come true.

Josey, however, who had been a grammar schoolteacher in Boston, came up with an idea. The boys didn't like her idea at first, but she knew their future depended on it. Now that Angel was born, she began an island school for her brood. The hour or two was flexible, but each day she arranged for them to meet with one member of the Tribe and learn from a selection of subjects, each person becoming one of their teachers in a topic of their choice: math, writing, history, medicine, biology, agriculture, mechanics, engineering, building, languages, art, cooking, fishing techniques, ocean wildlife, stellar navigation, course plotting, shared personal stories, ethics, and studying the family Bibles, as well as other books on board the boats.

There were no actual textbooks, no paper, no pens, but the adults on Miracle Island offered a lifetime of experiences and education to share with her sons, passing their knowledge down either by word of mouth or by example. It was all Josey could give them since the world they knew was gone, but much more valuable under their present circumstances than most of the required, mind-numbing, and impractical curriculum of the disrupted modern age. She envisioned them as strong men who chose their own paths and beliefs, and she prayed they would be guided to the good. Josey had seen enough evil to know that it would take more than what man alone could do to defeat it.

✳✳✳✳✳✳✳✳✳✳✳✳

It was Christmas Eve and Daniel chanced that the batteries on Mystic would keep the main lounge lights on until their celebration was over. Silver and gold-wrapped wedding gifts were piled in a corner, lovely reminders that this was the last time they'd ever see such gilded trimmings again. But nothing could dampen the high spirits in the room.

Little Angel enjoyed her dinner, suckling her mother's milk with vigor. She was thriving, despite her difficult birth, but her frame was small. Alea and John attributed her size to the deprivations Josey had endured on St. Thomas. She cried very little and was happily accommodating enough to sleep each night away peacefully, without disturbing anyone.

Daytime temperatures cooled to a pleasant level with the onset of winter. A long-sleeved t-shirt or windbreaker was the only outer covering needed in the evening. Mosquitos all but disappeared, thanks to their usual seasonal decline, and their absence was greatly appreciated.

John, Daniel, and Noah dove in the morning for lobster and brought back at least fourteen good-sized bugs. Sam was still too young to be permitted to dive the Atlantic or use a pole spear or spear gun. He practiced his swimming, diving, and breath control daily in Osprey Bay, hoping to be allowed the privilege soon. John was supervising his handling of the spears until they felt he was ready.

While the men cracked, cleaned, seasoned, and prepared the succulent lobster tails and the meat-packed legs for grilling, the women laid out their offerings for the feast. Alea put together one of her fresh salads, made of greens, papaya, and herbs that were seasonal and available. She made a dressing of sea salt crystals, crushed mango, and sour orange juice, with sprinkles of shaved coconut as a topping.

After many failures, she taught herself to make a delicious cassava flatbread, baked in minutes on the grill top. Crispy on the outside but soft and bread-like on the inside, the flatbread was created with no butter or oil. She loved to make hearty sandwiches by wrapping up chunks of fish or lobster with a heaping handful of greens. Other cassava roots were washed, pressed with sea salt and herbs, and baked whole on the outer edge of the fire. For lunches, she often thinly sliced chunks of cassava before toasting the pieces on the grill, the resultant crispy chips a favorite snack for Sam and Noah.

Josey turned out to be skilled in conch cleaning and prep, and with a coating of pre-boiled, crushed, and herbed cassava paste, she grilled battered bits of conch in a pan over the fire. She loved the lemongrass tea she first tasted on the island and boiled a large pot of water the day before Christmas, steeping cut sections of lemongrass overnight. By the next morning, the tea was ready for Christmas Eve and could be served cold or re-heated.

Dessert was usually simple and consisted of whatever fruits were in season at the time. But tonight, Alea blended bananas and shredded coconut, crushed together until soft and mushy. Forming the mixture into round fritters, she rolled them in cassava paste, and grilled them. Not quite as sweet as modern appetites would have required, but delicious to the Tribe. She had a hard time keeping up with the demand of the many darting fingers and kept forming and grilling the delicious bite-size bits until everyone was satisfied.

After banking the fire and packing up the leftovers, they rowed the tenders over to Mystic. The long-awaited Christmas Eve celebration and gift opening was about to begin, with the entire Tribe to sleep on the boat that night.

Daniel looked around the lounge thoughtfully. Eager faces smiled back at him as everyone settled in on a couch or chair, eating the last morsel of a favorite food or sipping water and tea. Angel chortled contentedly against her father's chest. He couldn't help but remember John's nightmare experiences on St. Thomas. What a tremendous difference it made when men and women cared about each other, respected one another, and worked together for the good of each person! Yes, there would always be differences of opinion and daily obstacles to overcome. Even the Tribe had those problems. But if people would hold to the goodness that he believed God had placed in mankind since the beginning, the new post-Flare world had the potential to be so much better than before. The opposing tendency to evil, also ingrained for some mysterious reason Daniel didn't think he'd ever comprehend, could be overcome, the battle won.

Earth could be a Miracle Island for all.

But every man had to choose his path, his ultimate destiny then determined. He reverently bowed his head in worship. Daniel had already made his choice.

****

The sounds of wrapping paper tearing and ooh's and aah's echoed in the lounge as the wedding gifts, no, the Christmas presents, were torn open and the contents examined.

"Uncle Daniel, you haven't even opened one yet!" Sam poked him in the leg with a finger.

Daniel grinned and picked up a package, then suddenly stopped himself. "Hey, why don't you crack this one, Sammy, I just remembered something," and tossed the box over. He got up and went to the master cabin. Sliding open the dresser drawer, he pulled out the box from Ben and walked back out to the group.

"My friend Ben on Spanish Wells gave this to Alea and I for our wedding. Honey, will you do the honors?" He handed the box to Alea. She tore off the paper and opened the cardboard lid. A solitary silver key lay in a bed of white cotton.

She looked up at Daniel, puzzled. "What is this?"

"Ben wants us to go on a treasure hunt."

Leaving John's family talking and examining their gifts, he and Alea began a search of Mystic. They searched each cabin, the heads, the galley, the pantry, every closet, and the storage lockers. The key fit nothing. After completing the main level, they checked the flybridge. Again, nothing.

"Well, I was hoping not to have to go below in the dark, but we should look," he said.

"Can you get the lights to go on down there so we can see?"

"Hopefully the batteries will hold their juice, but yes." Daniel enabled the direct connection and they headed below. The lower deck contained the engine compartment, equipment lockers, the battery bank, and the many mechanical systems that ran Mystic. Daniel believed he was already quite familiar with this area and was ready to give up when Alea tugged on his arm.

"What's back there?" she queried, pointing to an open area near the battery racks. It looked like an expanse of solid white wall except for a small round metal disk. Daniel strained in the dim light. It did look as if a lock barrel was set into the wall. He knelt down to see more clearly, then reached forward, inserted the key into the barrel, and turned.

The lock clicked open. It was then he noticed a molded recessed door pull next to the key.

"It works!" he exclaimed. Inserting the fingers of both hands into the door pull, he yanked. An almost invisibly edged hatch door pulled away from the wall.

Chapter 24   The Gift

Daniel's eyes widened. Ben. Ben did this for him before the Flare even happened! It was just too much of a coincidence. But at this point, Daniel was a firm believer that nothing in his life had ever been coincidence.

A stainless-steel hatch covered a cavern of empty space left available during the building of Mystic. The hatch was bonded with white molded plastic to make it look like part of the wall. But it was what was behind the hatch that took Daniel's breath away. A security locker had been configured and built-in to fit the space, made entirely of stainless steel. It was essentially a Faraday cage and was filled with objects he might never have appreciated prior to the Flare.

"What in the world are you looking at, Daniel?" Alea could contain herself no longer when she saw his startled reaction. She bent down to peer inside, but he was blocking her view.

"Alea, you won't believe what Ben left for us, protected from the EMP!" He reached in and pulled out a box, carefully prying open one end. "A shortwave radio with antenna and battery connectors! And a printed sheet of call signs for other users, including Ben's."

"Really? Wasn't that the way the military communicated in World War II? We can talk to others if they have one too! But it won't do us much good unless we can power it, right?"

Daniel smirked as he reached in deeper and began pulling out the next items. "How about two 300-watt solar panels and all the wiring to attach to a 12 or 24-volt battery?"

"No way!" She grabbed the priceless rectangular solar panel he handed her, examined it, and laid it carefully to one side. "This is unbelievable!" Rechargeable power capability was a real game-changer.

Daniel started to laugh wildly as he climbed part of the way into the locker. Alea could hear the sound of something heavy being dragged to the opening. "No!" He popped his head out and looked at Alea in amazement.

"Do you remember I told you that Mystic's diesel engines have electronically-controlled fuel injectors and because their control units were fried by the EMP, they weren't getting any fuel? And that's why the engines wouldn't run?"

"Yes, I do remember, but I'm no expert about engines."

"Benjamin Knowles, my wonderful friend, has gifted us with a 1970's Evinrude 15 hp outboard that has a standard ignition system. No electronics at all in those older motors! And it's in mint condition!"

"And for us that means..?"

"It means we have a working outboard for our boat! Not for Mystic, of course, but it'll power the tender. Maybe John and I can rig this motor to propel Barefootin' if we need to. At the very least, we could tow her safely out to the Atlantic."

As he dug deeper into the locker, Daniel was excited to find multiple boxes that contained items Ben must have decided were essential for their survival, in case anything happened to Mystic on their month-long honeymoon.

Brand-new 2 and 5-gallon gas cans, bottles of fuel stabilizer and 2-stroke oil, a set of four rechargeable walkie-talkies, four rechargeable flashlights, a solar charging unit, six firelighter sticks, a flint and steel manual firelighter kit, a magnifying glass, two military grade canteens, two sharpening stones, two new machetes, six 100-foot coils of ½ inch rope, a multi-pack of zip-ties, and a magnetic compass.

There was a large box with Dr. Alea Devereaux's name on the front. She was overjoyed to find sterile suture kits, gauze pads and roll wraps, paper tape, elastic bandages, band-aids, peroxide, alcohol preps, topical antibiotic creams, scissors, an old-style mercury thermometer, a manual blood pressure cuff and stethoscope, two tubes of prescription poisonwood cream, aspirin, and a variety of oral antibiotics. She had no idea how Ben had acquired four bottles of prescription pain pills, but she was thankful, nonetheless. Not one person in the Tribe was taking required medication of any kind and Alea knew just how rare and fortunate that was.

They looked at each other, instantly recognizing the value of Ben's gift, which might have drawn a quizzical look before the EMP. But today? It was manna from heaven. Daniel couldn't wait to tell the others. He and John were going to be kept very busy for the next few days. What a Christmas!

The next morning, John and Daniel began the test run of the small motor. The twin 4-stroke 100 hp engines on Barefootin' would never run again, but the ample containers of unmixed gas that ran them were useable for the 15 hp outboard. All they had to do was create the proper mix with some of the two-stroke oil in one of the new gas cans. They mounted the motor to the transom of Daniel's tender. Two pulls of the cord and it easily zoomed to life, accompanied by the pumping fists and loud cheers of the boys jumping up and down on the beach. The tender roared off into Osprey Bay, the wind whipping past their faces. They circled the bay once and roared out through Hidden Pass. Daniel's excitement grew.

We can explore the perimeter of the island! He was already envisioning the preliminary expedition to the surrounding shores of Miracle Island. So far, he hadn't spotted any other beach or entry from his vantage points on land, but he wanted to see for himself firsthand from the water. It also occurred to him they'd no longer have to row against strong winds when venturing into the Atlantic. A run out using the new engine would set them up quickly for a dive. He planned to be very conservative with Barefootin's limited supply of gasoline. Regrettably, Mystic's fuel was diesel and not suitable for the new outboard, but she carried several cans of unmixed gas for the tender, which was now available for Ben's motor.

With John taking the tiller, they ran back to Casuarina Cove, where the boys were attempting to start a fire in the firepit using the magnifying glass. The small tuft of dry tinder was starting to smoke as the magnifying glass focused the rays of the sun, creating a searing beam of light. Just as the men walked up, the tuft burst into flame. Noah quickly added more brush and before long a solid fire burned bright. John praised his sons and asked them to keep the fire going for the rest of the day. He'd also allow them to sleep onshore again and try to keep the fire banked all night, a good survival experience for both of them.

With the addition of the two new machetes, Daniel issued one right away to John. Sam and Noah would have to earn the use of one after instruction in safety and care. Alea never let hers leave her side and had fabricated a belt and sheath that enabled her to wear it safely.

Daniel treasured the coils of ½ inch rope. He could replace the homemade vine ropes that secured the floor supports of the treehouse with the sturdy rope from Ben. 600-feet of rope might sound like a lot, he knew, but real rope was island gold and he'd be selective in how it was used.

The walkie-talkies were a major relief to have and invaluable for safety and communication. Individuals or groups traveling into the bush or on a water run would carry one. Josey was given a unit right away and Daniel wore his on his belt. Each device could be recharged daily with the small solar charging unit.

Daniel began installation of the two solar panels after lunch, deciding to mount one of them on top of Mystic's flybridge. Daniel and John hauled one heavy battery to the helm and connected the panel to begin charging. He would've preferred to place both panels in a location where the entire battery bank, two at a time, could be re-charged. But his most urgent priority today was setting up the shortwave radio.

It was time to call Ben.

Daniel was very anxious to hear how Ben and his family were doing and how the island of Spanish Wells was faring in the post-Flare world. But he was afraid of what he might find out as well. He needed to know if his parents, the Gabrielle's, and Ronny's family were still there. There was no guarantee that friends and loved ones were even alive.

John's nightmare experiences as a prisoner on St. Thomas had cautioned him considerably regarding interaction with other people, and he decided not to reveal the location of Miracle Island to anyone. Daniel was almost positive he could pinpoint Miracle Island's exact location by sextant. The use of GPS and satellites to plot a course was gone and navigation by the stars was practically a lost art. He was extremely grateful that his father, grandfather, and their friend Ben, had made sure that stellar navigation was taught and passed down not only to Daniel, but to Ronny, Matt, and Ben's sons Gil, and Will. Travel by sea would now completely depend on a sailor's knowledge, skills, and courage, just as it had for thousands of years before. He planned to begin teaching stellar navigation to John, Noah, and Sam. Alea had already proven herself an apt student and he was confident she'd soon be able to guide a boat by herself.

That evening after dinner, the entire Tribe gathered on the flybridge in great anticipation, but also with quiet reservation. Daniel was about to try the shortwave radio. If it worked, the news might not be what they wanted to hear. Alea and Josey sat together on a padded bench seat with Angel held close in Josey's arms. Noah and Sam sprawled on the floor. Daniel and John stood at the helm where the radio was positioned.

With a silent prayer, Daniel turned the radio on. Yes! Static crackled through the speaker. He adjusted the dial to Ben's call frequency and picked up the microphone.

"This is Daniel Devereaux calling Benjamin Knowles. Do you copy? Over."

Silence. He tried again.

"This is Daniel Devereaux calling Ben Knowles on Spanish Wells, Eleuthera. Do you copy? Over."

The only sound in the room was Angel. She gave a hiccup and a squeak and reached for her mother's chin. Suddenly, the radio crackled again, and clicked on.

"Copy that! This Ben Knowles. Daniel, my God, you're alive! Over."

The room erupted in shouts of joy. The boys leaped off the floor, Alea ran to Daniel's side. He waved his hand to shush everyone as he raised the microphone back to his mouth. He could barely control the tears threatening to spill down his cheeks and his voice cracked with emotion.

"Ben! It's Daniel! Alea is here with me and we survived the Flare. We are on a small island south of San Salvador. There is another family with us. How are you, Ben? Over."

"Daniel, my dear boy, my sons and their families are alive and well. However, we did have a death." Ben's voice dropped low and Daniel braced himself. "Vernita died three months ago. There was no insulin left anywhere. Over."

Daniel was speechless. Vernita and Ben had been married for thirty-five years and her joyous free spirit made Ben, the more reserved of the two, laugh and enjoy life just a little bit more. She adored her two sons and her eight grandchildren and was the beating heart and soul of the large and boisterous Knowles family. She was a diabetic, but well-controlled with insulin. Without shipments of the life-giving medication to the islands, she could not survive.

"Ben, Alea and I are so sorry. You know how much I cared for Vernita, my friend. I can't imagine how you felt. Over."

"I miss her every minute, son. The family keeps me going though, Danny, my grandkids. They will be the future. But you and I have stories to tell and now that we are talking by radio, I am assuming you opened my present, eh? Over."

"Ben, you have my gratitude forever! What a life-saving gift! Thanks to you, I'm powered up and we're waiting to hear your story first. Is this a good time for you to talk? Over."

"Danny, never thought I'd ever see times like these in all my born days...Over."

Chapter 25   Ben's Story

"You know, Danny, I was born here on Spanish Wells the same year your dad was born in New Bedford. My pa worked long days on the lobster boats, but they see he was best to fix the engines, dings, and holes, so the boss set him up on shore with a repair shop. He paid all that start money back in time and the business was transferred to his name. Pa taught me everything about the boats, and as you know, he bought more waterfront land along the harbor and started the marina, boat storage, and rental business, too.

"You were only one when your family first sailed Red Cloud down to Spanish Wells. They ended up buying the big house that year and came back every winter after that. Jimmy, your dad, we got to be good friends, just like you did with Will and Gil. Friends to this day, and people sure need friends in this time of sorrow. To help Alea and your people get a feel for what's goin' on here now, I want to tell them about the old days of Spanish Wells, the Spanish Wells you and I remember and love.

"The whole island is really named St. George's Cay, after the King of England at the time. The English first came over to the island back in 1647 after getting shipwrecked off the Devil's Backbone Reef and living for a while in Preachers Cave on the north Eleuthera mainland. Not sure why they deserted the big island to come over to Spanish Wells. I think it was because freshwater was tough to find and they wanted to be left alone, to worship the way they chose. And they did find water, ponds of it, and even more in the reservoir when they dug the wells. Plenty of safe moorage too. With the constant wars between the English and Spanish, it's a wonder they allowed their ships to dock and refill before sailing home. I bet they charged them a pretty penny. But ever since then, the main settlement on this island has been called Spanish Wells.

"More English folks came over to lick their wounds after the American Revolution. They left the colonies to settle here with solid loyal-to-the-Crown Brits. They refused to allow anyone with slaves on this island. Sure, there were plenty of slaves on other Bahamian islands, even on Eleuthera, but no sir, none on Spanish Wells! The English eventually banned slavery long before Lincoln and many people risked their lives coming to the Bahamas for freedom. Nuff said and here we are today. Hasn't always been an easy road for me and Vernita since we got married, she bein' white. But times do change, just like it has again.

"Well, the people of Spanish Wells have always been close knit, along with our neighbors on Russell Island. The short bridge connects us. Our folks work together, play together, families be tight. We made sure not to lose who we were as a community. Tourists come and go. Take us or leave us. If you want luxury, go to Harbour Island, a carbon copy of a fancy U.S. hotel row with a pretty pink beach. Mind you, everything there has to be shipped in. Water. Food. Not so fancy today after the EMP, I can tell you. I'll say more about that later.

"Daniel, I know you have your own tale about the solar flare and how you and Alea managed to survive. But I'm sure you're anxious to hear about your families. Let me assure you that James and your mother are doing well and living at the Bonefish Bay house. Alea's parents are there too, and they have been godsends to the people here, being a doctor and a nurse. Alea's brother, Dr. Roger Gabrielle, met a Spanish Wells girl, Lorena Sweeting, and they're living at her cottage. She's a teacher at the Samuel Guy Pinder All-Age School. The school is staying open half days. Ronny, Pearl, and their kids are living at Bonefish Bay, too.

Matt Kennedy up and flew home the day after the wedding. Surprised everyone when he said he just had to leave, with no explanation. His parents and sisters were worried about him, so they decided to go too. Haven't heard from them since, even though I've tried to bring up the Devereaux Fishing shortwave frequency. I'll keep trying, but other folks I've talked to in the Bahamas and in the states tell me the situation is very bad, deadly serious, and still degenerating. Not many shortwaves operational out there, but I'm getting enough information to piece together what's going on. I try to broadcast every day at dusk so other survivors will take hope that life is still possible. That's when I heard your voice, praise God!

"Okay, here's the nit and grit. The entire planet went down. Every country is on its own. Forget invasions for power and control, it's all about survival. The U.S. military that has any capability can barely maintain order and only in a few isolated pockets. Haven't heard a peep about your president or any big governments around the world.

"The Bahama Islands are also on their own. The government we did have has disappeared. Nassau is a deathtrap, Abaco and Grand Bahama not far behind. Foreign tourists who were stranded on any of the islands were the first to die. Not always of natural causes, if you get my drift. Then the battle began in earnest between Bahamian people themselves for whatever resources were left, because the importing of foreign goods was suddenly impossible. No diesel, no gas, no electric power, no shipping of goods from any port.

"Disease from raw sewage, garbage, and rats spread quickly. Dengue fever from mosquitos broke out in large areas. People were dying for lack of medicine, their bodies stacked high in the graveyards. Existing sources of water were used up until drained or polluted. Some good friends of mine in Freeport were murdered for the well on their property. The hurricane and the other summer storms that followed the solar flare salted down existing crops and many homes were damaged. Starvation killed the most. Still is.

"Harbour Island really suffered. Hundreds of tourists with no water, no food, no place to live. Many were jumping into Bottom Harbor and trying to swim across to Three Island dock on North Eleuthera, only to drown in the inter-island current. Schools of sharks, never seen before, were spotted feasting on floating corpses. Bodies were washing ashore around the bay and many swept out to sea through Whale Point Cut. The stink and the flies, I'm told, were terrible. The swimmers that did make it, well, better they drowned. On shore, bad people were waiting. The survivors were robbed of their belongings and left stranded with no shelter or food. No one wanted tourists to use up any of the rapidly decreasing food sources. Credit cards did not help those poor folks.

"We use shortwave radio for land to sea communication for my charter business and on the lobster and fishing boats, all outfitted with solar power back-up. It didn't take long before confirmation came in from operators on other islands and in Miami/Ft Lauderdale that the solar flare had pounded us with a major electromagnetic pulse, stopping the modern age dead in its tracks. Electricity was gone, except for anything that could run off batteries or hadn't been damaged by the EMP. Newer shortwave radios didn't make it. The older tube style, like mine and the sentimental relics that many Spanish Wells residents hung on to over the years, were able to continue to function without Faraday shielding.

"As you know, we handle things different on this island. We treat each other like family and decided to pull together. Mr. Edward Curry, our local administrator, called an island-wide meeting at the big church near the Food Fair grocery two days after the solar flare terrified the community.

"He's a short man, good-looking, in his 40's, slight of build with dark curly hair and dark skin. He spent ten years in the Bahamian police force on mainland Eleuthera before realizing he preferred administration and government. He's been our Spanish Wells Commissioner for goin' on five years, has been to social events at our homes, and personally knows every man, woman, and child here by name. He's not married and many an island girl has flashed him an interested eye. Didn't take the bait. An honest decent man. We trust Mr. Curry and he acted fast, for our island's protection.

"He sent bicycle messengers to every home on Spanish Wells and Russell Island and set the meet date for two days off. He ordered the Food Fair and other groceries to lock down until after the meet and posted guards at their doors. None of us wanted any violence and we had enough food to get by, for the time being.

"On the day of the meet the church was packed with people, fanning themselves in the heat. Faces were full of fear and worry, children crying. I sat up front with Vernita so we could hear real good. Mr. Curry stood at the pulpit, Pastor Higgs sitting right behind, and he began to speak. Could've heard a fishbone drop it was so quiet. Here's what he said."

"My friends, I greet you today with a heavy heart. By now you have all heard that the sun, that has embraced our beloved Bahamas with its warm and radiant light since the dawn of time, has rendered us a severe and painful blow. A blow we can do nothing but accept as part of the Divine Will. A blow that may have been sent to define our humanity. But why, you may still ask? Why has this happened?

"Are we to judge The Almighty and His mysterious plan and ways? I, for one, will not. However, I do believe that He pre-determined that my place was here to serve you, my people, my island family, the best I am able. Let us strive to show that despite the odds against us, we can be the best of human, that we can have compassion for one another, that each of us can grow the love seeded deep within us, like yeast in a loaf, to expand and ultimately feed each other in peace and safety.

"I will now ask you a very important question, a question that each one of you, alone, must answer for yourself. And your answer will determine the direction of our future."

He surveyed the room slowly before proceeding.

"Do you, the people of Spanish Wells and Russell Island, accept me as your leader? Will you abide by the decisions I will have to make, and any actions I may have to take, that I promise will be for the good of each one of you and for our community as a whole? Decisions and actions that I will keep you well-aware of and only pursue with the consent of the majority? If no, then I will relinquish the floor to whomever would choose to put him or herself forward as a leader."

"Daniel, his words were so moving, and more than one eye was moist, more than one hand found its way to a loved one sitting near. I couldn't help myself. I jumped up and turned to the crowd."

"I say it's Mr. Curry for us!"

"The entire room erupted in applause, with raised hands and shouts of agreement. Renewed hope flowed over the faces of the men and women, black and white, who just a short time earlier had been mired in despair. The pastor rose to stand next to Mr. Curry and shook his hand. The vote was in. We had chosen a leader for our apocalypse. Edward Curry raised his hands for quiet."

"God bless the islands of the Bahamas!"

"Then, with an expression that somehow combined humility and enthusiasm, he began to tell us his plan for the survival of Spanish Wells. And I can tell you, Daniel, his ideas have saved lives and are keeping our people afloat.

"He had obviously been thinking about his plan during the two days before the meet. His first order of business was to set-up a registration station. Every family and its members would give their names, ages, and living location to Mr. Curry's assistant, Harold Pinder, and be assigned a personal number. Their name and number would identify them and allow them immediate access to the emergency central food bank that Mr. Curry was in the process of developing, with registration to start right after the meet.

"The locked-down Food Fair and other grocery stores were to be re-opened. Mr. Curry gave the owners the responsibility of taking a complete inventory of their stock and dividing it into as many parts as the number of people registered, with the food and supplies to be equally distributed in two days to each person with a number. It was a short-term temporary fix. New food sources would have to be found.

"The last of the controlled medications would be issued to whoever held prescriptions with the Food Fair pharmacy. Our two pharmacists, Donald and Geoffrey, would hold the non-prescription stock for protection and use as they saw fit. They were each practically a doctor in the eyes of the settlement anyway, offering competent medical information and helpful advice freely to anyone with questions. But they could only offer medications that were already on the pharmacy shelves. No supply shipments would be coming in again. People were going to die for lack of life-saving drugs. They accepted and mourned this fact privately, and they both attended every funeral held on Spanish Wells since the EMP, hearts breaking quietly each time. I know...they were right there with me when I buried my Vernita." Ben's voice went silent.

"Daniel, of the 2000 folks that lived here before what you called the Flare, only 1100 people are alive and registered today. So many good friends gone..." He needed to clear his throat before resuming.

"Our water wells have provided for many years, but without electric pumps to pull the water up from the underground reservoir, something had to be done quickly. The numerous city and private wells are manned with daily bucket brigades to draw water and distribute to containers brought for filling. Even the children follow their parents, bearing a small bucket or bottle to fill. The recent rains helped replenish the reservoir and cisterns. We are praying that water stays plentiful. Believe me, no waste is allowed, and we comply willingly. Water is the most valuable resource we have in this powerless age and we mean to protect it.

"Each home is required to dig a pit for waste, use an existing limestone hole, or open their septic tank and create a toilet. The doctors insisted on that, as they are real concerned about diseases. With no working commodes in the houses, everyone was mighty happy to do whatever was needed!

"Food? Well, lad, we do live in the middle of the ocean! I bet you're eating plenty seafood, eh? Same here. Mr. Curry talked with the owners of every sailboat and rowboat on the island. They agreed to go out daily, except Sunday, to fish and dive, weather permitting. The boats tie-up in the harbor or dock along the channel shoreline. Mr. Curry arranged a schedule for the boats and crews of two days on, three days off. Many men and women volunteered to work the boats. The catch is gathered and distributed to families with an assigned number at the seafood market at the dock.

"Anyone with even a small amount of yard space is growing a garden. We harvested seeds from vegetables and fruits, pooled our seed packets, and took roots and cuttings from trees. Russell Island has lots of undeveloped land and we're in the process of cultivating as many plants as possible. We eat seasonal food, of course, but some staples are year-round, like potatoes and cassava. Got pineapple growing too!

"Each family contributes a portion of their garden produce to the general food bank at the Food Fair grocery. No one goes hungry, even if portions are small and folks have lost weight. With people starving to death elsewhere, we count ourselves blessed. Many people kept goats and pigs before the Flare, and the roosters and chickens provide meat and eggs.

"Geoffrey, the pharmacist, is an excellent sharpshooter with his rifle and leads a group of hunters that sail over to Current Island occasionally to shoot wild pig and boar. Now that's a real lip-smackin' treat, roasted whole over an open fire!

"The useless powerboats were floated on the tides to both the east and west entries to the harbor and partially sunk as a blockade, leaving a thirty-foot opening to allow the sailboats to leave and return. At night, the openings are chained off and guarded. Why? Security. Mr. Curry doesn't want people we don't know coming here for questionable purposes. The folks who live in waterfront homes are responsible to report any vessel approaching the shoreline to one of the newly assigned roving deputies, who will then notify Mr. Curry. He has vowed to protect us from harm.

"Dozens of power boats at Harbour Island sat abandoned after the Flare. It didn't take long for the locals and tourists with sailboats to leave. Quite a few sailed over here to Spanish Wells, seeking safety. Before being allowed access, Mr. Curry or one of the deputies personally speak with the captains of each sailboat right out at the new security cuts. If they and their crew agree to support the community, to work, fish, or farm, they are allowed to stay. He even lets them live in one of the many shuttered homes that belong to part-year resident snowbirds, who are probably gone for good.

"The only boat turned away so far was a large catamaran that showed Nassau as home port. It was overloaded with thirty men, looking scruffy, angry, and brandishing machetes and military-style guns. Their leader called himself Leon the Lion, a giant muscular man with long dreadlocks, his skin almost completely covered in tattoos of skulls, weapons, and women. Mr. Curry spoke with him briefly, refused to drop the chains, and ordered them to move on. Four of the guards that day were police officers and they had to display their weapons as a show of force. A dozen or more Spanish Wells men backed them up with their own hunting rifles and pistols, threatening to sink their boat with gunfire if they didn't leave. They finally sailed away, cursing and flaunting obscene hand gestures. We will never allow thugs and criminals to land on Spanish Wells.

"Another meet was called the next day and we voted in a new rule. If anyone committed a crime, caused repetitive trouble, or refused to work, they'd be taken into custody, sailed over to mainland Eleuthera, and released with whatever possessions they could carry. They would never be allowed to return to Spanish Wells. That may sound harsh but, needless to say, we have no crime. We walk our streets unafraid and free and will fight to keep it that way.

"Well, son, I'm sure you want to speak with your parents and friends. Alea too. But I need to recharge. I have some of those handy solar panels myself. Can we agree on tomorrow at dusk to talk again? I'll make sure everyone is right here by the radio and I want Mr. Curry to know that we've spoken. He'll be very interested to hear how you have survived."

"No problem, Ben," Daniel said. "We'll be ready and waiting for your hail."

"There is one problem I still need to tell you about, Daniel, but it will have to wait until tomorrow. So, for tonight, this is Ben Knowles signing off. God be with you. Over and out."

Chapter 26   Reunion

The flybridge of Mystic was wrapped in silent darkness as Daniel shut down the radio for the night. While Ben was speaking, Alea got up to sit next to Daniel, her hand clasping his tightly. John was deep in thought, holding Josey close as they both looked down at the sweetly sleeping Angel in her arms. Sam was asleep on the floor, but Noah was awake and alert, still thinking about what he had heard.

The boy vividly remembered the misery, hardships, danger, and midnight escape from St. Thomas. There were obvious glaring differences between the way St. Thomas and Spanish Wells were governed. Spanish Wells sounded safe, and it did seem that the people were making good progress since the Flare, but Noah was not ready to trust. If he were given a choice, he'd take Miracle Island any day. He loved his life here and did not want to leave. He hoped his parents were feeling the same way.

Daniel shifted to face the quiet group. Ben had given them much to ponder and he wanted to hear everyone's opinion, but they were exhausted. He knew they'd be talking to Ben every night, giving everyone plenty of time to digest the flood of new information before any decisions were made.

"I, for one, need a break," he announced. "Tomorrow after breakfast, why don't we sit down and hear each other out." He didn't think he'd get any argument.

****

"I imagine each island is dealing in their own way with the Flare," John said thoughtfully, as he sipped a steaming cup of lemongrass tea. The sun was starting to rise above the eastern cliff and the lounge of Mystic was filled with golden light.

"There doesn't seem to be any organized government. An island can choose to be the hell of St. Thomas or the heaven of Spanish Wells, depending on the moral integrity of the leader. There's no way to find out until after you dock."

"I agree with John." Josey draped herself politely from view with a piece of white sheet and lifted Angel to her breast. "If we landed on an island intending to harm us for the boat and our belongings, like St. Thomas, we wouldn't know until it was too late. I refuse to risk my children by leaving Miracle Island, where we've been safe. Spanish Wells sounds stable, but Ben did infer there was some problem he hasn't told us about yet. I will personally need to hear more," she ended emphatically. As a grammar schoolteacher, Josey was gratified when Ben told them that Spanish Wells was keeping their school open half-days and the children were able to continue their studies. Books were suddenly important and valuable all over again, with the internet wiped out.

Daniel turned to Noah and Sam. "What do you guys think?"

Sam's hand shot quickly into the air and he waved it around as if asking permission to speak in class. The adults chuckled, trying to hide their smiles, loving his enthusiasm and vibrant optimism.

"Go ahead, Sammy, we're listening."

He jumped up and planted his feet firmly, hands on his hips, and looked Daniel fiercely in the eye, a cowlick of hair pointing straight up.

"I won't go!" he declared. And sat back down.

The room burst into laughter. As usual, Sam expressed what the whole group was silently thinking. The actual possibility of leaving Miracle Island had been remote, at best, for each of them. Noah just smiled and high-fived his brother.

Wiping her eyes dry, Alea raised an arm in the air and waved it around. Everyone choked on another bout of laughter, with Daniel finally regaining control of himself first.

"Go ahead, Alea, we're listening."

She grinned playfully. "Okay, it's my turn? Well, first of all, Daniel's parents, my parents, my brother, and Ronny and his family are alive and safe! It's such a relief. I can't wait to talk to them tonight! And with my dad and Roger being doctors and my mom a nurse, they'll have plenty to keep them busy on Spanish Wells. It's great for the island, as I believe they did not have a permanent full-time doctor. Vernita told me their two visiting doctors came over a couple of times a week from Nassau. Now that my family is living there and have nowhere else to go, the people will have as much daily medical care as can be offered."

Alea deliberately chose to exclude Matt from her comments or mention his unexpected departure right after the wedding. That was a situation she hoped she'd never have to share with Daniel. She knew it had to happen sooner or later, but since the Flare, it was something of a moot point. It could wait.

John nodded in complete understanding. As a physician and general practitioner, he felt disturbed after listening to Ben. Should he have been pushing to go to Spanish Wells and serve their community? But Alea needed him to be here when the time came time for her to give birth. He felt less pressured to leave once he found out there were two physicians and several nurses living on Spanish Wells and his assistance would not be as necessary. He loved Miracle Island, as did his entire family, and the grim maelstrom of the states was no longer a viable option.

Alea turned to Daniel with a gentle smile. "Your parents, Daniel. I'm thinking that they might want to come here and live with us. I understand that your father is a boatman and sailor and is important in the organization of the fishing fleet there, but so many others on Spanish Wells already have the experience to do that. They must miss you terribly. You might want to find out what they would prefer to do."

Daniel looked down in awe at the woman he loved. She was willing to take on the extra care, attention, and responsibility of his older parents for his sake. He knew she loved them but living on Miracle Island took constant hard work every day. And she was pregnant. Both James and Dolores adored Alea and he knew his mother would never forgive him if she missed the birth of her first grandchild. How could he refuse?

"Honey, I will most definitely ask them. If we have to sail Barefootin' to Spanish Wells to pick them up, we'll do it." He hesitated for a long moment, looking at each person one at a time, with a serious expression.

"The coordinates of Miracle Island can never be divulged to anyone except if we are all in agreement. I cannot emphasize how important this is for our safety, maybe for our lives. Sailboats from other islands might be combing the Caribbean, looking to rob people of their life-saving food and goods. They may even kill for it. They may have, uh, other needs too. I'll do anything to protect us. Anything."

Alea took his hand and solemnly agreed, as did the others.

"Finally," she said, "I've been thinking about Ronny, Pearl, and the twins. They'll never return to Boston, and after what we've heard, why would they even want to?" She shuddered. "Can we invite them to come here too? Ronny is your friend, and a great diver and fisherman. He'd be extra hands for you, Daniel, more help for you and John. And if Noah and Sammy are any indication, the children will really enjoy it here!"

"Alea, my love, I believe our little Tribe is going to grow!"

****

The call to Ben was highly anticipated. At the agreed time, Daniel hailed Ben and received an immediate reply.

"Daniel, my friend, good evening! How is your lovely wife and all your party tonight? Over."

"It's so good to hear you again, Ben! You gave us much to think about last night, and to consider. But first, are both my parents with you? Over."

The emotional exclamations and tears took time to subside. James was barely able to speak at first, breaking down in unabashed tears at hearing his son's voice. His mother was weeping and chattering at the same time, her love for Daniel and Alea unable to be contained.

They were living at Bonefish Bay with Alea's parents and Ronny's family. Everyone worked a daily volunteer job, there was enough food to satisfy, and they were safe. James and Ben were indeed instrumental in organizing the daily fish and dive sailboats that prowled the blue waters surrounding Spanish Wells, the catch providing the primary proteins so desperately needed by the hard-working community.

Dolores helped care for the younger children at a make-shift daycare at The Gospel Church. With a large recreation hall and nearby beach access, the building was perfect for the children to play, eat, and nap while their parents worked.

Armand, Nadia, and Roger were relieved and elated to hear Alea's voice. The four wept at the same time, microphones at both ends damp with tears of happiness. When she revealed her pregnancy, their joy was palpable and loud. Their first grandchild! James, Dolores, Armand, and Nadia celebrated with a group hug that never seemed to end.

Resigned to the reality of their situation, her parents were reveling in their new life on Spanish Wells. Although Armand would never again perform intricate and complicated heart surgeries, he compassionately treated the varied ailments of the townspeople in the clinic he and Nadia were given to use. Unable to continue his practice in neurosurgery, Roger was the first responder to any emergency, his blue bicycle with saddle packs full of medical supplies a welcome sight to the injured or ill. They worked closely with Donald and Geoffrey, who were well-aware of the patient histories and peccadillos of every man, woman, and child on Spanish Wells. Together, they made a caring healthcare team that inspired confidence, despite obvious limitations and supply shortages.

Alea's serious and quiet brother had fallen in love. Loreen Sweeting, one of the island schoolteachers, had twisted her ankle badly and Roger was sent to treat her at her small beach cottage. Her sun-streaked long blonde hair, green eyes, full figure, and vivacious manner captivated him immediately, but he waited a few weeks before inviting her to accompany him to Mr. Curry's birthday social. Inseparable since that day, he moved into her cottage a month later, the expectation of a wedding not far off.

It took over two hours for the families to finish talking before Daniel could ask for Ronny. His wife Pearl and their twins, Robbie and Rhonda, had flown in to join Ronny for the wedding and chose to stay on for a lengthy vacation. Daniel was certain destiny had been kind in making sure they were still there when the solar flare erupted. If not, who knew if they would even be alive? Attempts to contact Matt in the states were so far unsuccessful.

"Is Ronny there, Ben? Can you put him on? Over."

"Daniel! Dude! It's Ron, man. I thought you were dead and gone. Couldn't believe it when Ben told us he was in contact with you and Alea! And she's pregnant? Congratulations! Talk to me. Oh yeah... Over."

"It's me, buddy! Ronny, you're really there! How are you doing? Is the family alright? I still can't believe it! Over."

"I know, Danny. The whole scene was incredible with that flare. It was like the 4th of July times a million! Pearl didn't stop crying for a month. The twins, though, they love it. Half-day school and an island to play with. Well, when you're only eight years old... hey, you remember how we were. Over."

"Oh, I remember very well. Those years are what helped me to survive the last six months. We're on an island you could only dream about, Ronny. It still amazes me that in all our years sailing we never saw or heard of this place. We call it Miracle Island and I'll be telling our story tomorrow. Sorry, I can't share our location. Can't risk anyone finding us. Over."

"Got it. But let me confess something. Wait, hang on. Over."

"Okay, I'm back. I asked the others to give me some privacy for a few minutes. To be honest, life is good here, I'm not complaining. Pearl and the kids are settling in, got food, water, and we're safe. But you know me, Daniel. I need to move around. I'm feeling cramped, caged. I do fish and it feels great to do something worthwhile for the island. Maybe I'm spoiled. Yeah, I'm spoiled. But I miss being on the ocean and just sailing on toward the horizon, taking what comes. I loved those days with you and Matt. Don't want anyone to think I'm ungrateful, but I wish I was with you. Over."

"Well, my friend, guess what's coming out of my mouth next? Over."

"No way! How would we get there? Daniel, do you mean it? Wow, I mean, Over."

"Ronny, I want to bring my parents to Miracle Island, and I want to make the same offer to you, Pearl, and the kids. This island is phenomenal, but I would feel better with more people living with us, people we know and trust. You'd really love John, Josey, Noah, Sam, and baby Angel. We can sail his 45-foot catamaran over to Spanish Wells to pick everyone up and maybe trade for supplies. We can't come over right away with Angel just being born, but Alea still has time 'till she's due and she wants to come along. Can we keep this between us for now? I haven't spoken with my parents and I don't want to upset your applecart there. Over."

"Daniel, my lips are sealed. Not even Pearl will hear about this until you say so. Can't wait, can't wait! Over."

"Let's talk again soon. Hey, put Ben back on. He wanted to tell me something. And you know what? I miss you. Over."

"I miss you too, Danny. Love you, man. Over."

****

"Ben here. Daniel, I sent everyone home so I can tell you about the problem I mentioned last night, the problem Mr. Curry is most worried about. Maybe you'll have some advice to share that might help.

"If you recall, I told you about that sailboat from Nassau that showed up with thirty men, headed by the big guy they called Leon. Well, we drove them away from Spanish Wells alright, but that very night we saw fires right across the channel at Gun Point on mainland Eleuthera. Those criminals sailed over there, anchored up, and set fire to some of the homes near Mr. Thompson's house at the tip. God only knows what they were doing, but we heard screams and gun shots from across the water. Women screaming, Daniel. Didn't get quiet again until dawn and it's been like that every night since. Mr. Curry has doubled the guards on the eastside blockade.

"A week later, one of Thompson's sons, Bernard, washed up outside the blockade, barely clinging to a piece of driftwood, dehydrated and confused. Our guards pulled him out of the water and carried him to the clinic. Made my boys lose their lunch, it did. He'd been beaten and lashed, one eye blinded and, oh Lord, one hand chopped off and the stump burned closed. Dr. Gabrielle had just enough sedative to calm him down. He and Nadia treated him best they could, but it took several days before he was coherent enough for Mr. Curry to finally talk to him.

"We got big trouble comin', Daniel. Leon and his gang call themselves the Barracudas. They stole a boat and fled Nassau when it got too rough even for them. They been stoppin' at settlements for one, two days at a time, killing survivors for whatever food was left, raping the women, and burning the buildings. They're heavily armed, don't care who they kill or injure, take what they want, and move on to the next victim. Bernard heard them say they're tired of traveling and want to take over an area that looks like it can support them long-term. And they got their eye on Spanish Wells.

"He told us Leon was furious that we drove em' off. He's hunkering down at Gun Point and it looks like he might be planning a move on us. They heard about our freshwater wells and growing fields. They only got the one sailboat and they're eyeing our boats over here. We're set-up better than mainland 'Lutra because most folks in Spanish Wells keep a good-size sailboat. That's a lot of sail on one island! And that means a lot of fish and lobster. Not many sailboats in Bogue, Bluff, Hatchet Bay, Governors Harbor, Tarpum Bay, or Rock Sound, especially in hurricane season, and boats that don't use power are highly valuable since the Flare.

"God help us, Bernard said they beheaded the old men and infants the first day. No need for them... The younger men are kept as slaves to work the fields near James Bay. They do it because their women and the children who are still alive are locked-up in a house in the village. Let's them out to cook and work during the day, then locks them back up at night. Well, the lucky ones get locked back up. Bernard's young wife, Thomasina, wasn't so lucky. He tried to stand-up to them, so they made him watch while they raped her, one at a time. They kept him tied to a tree in the center of the village and chopped off a little piece of his body every night after they finished with her, making him the terrible example of what would happen to anyone who resisted.

"He got away when Thomasina somehow snuck out of the locked house late at night and got past the guard. She used an old rusty machete to cut the ropes around his feet and arms. They made it to the shore of the east channel when another guard spotted them and started to shout. Without a moment's hesitation, she kissed him goodbye and pushed him into the water before she ran shrieking down the beach, leading them away from where he lay in the shallows, only his eyes and the top of his head showing. He knew they wouldn't see him in the dark and began to swim towards our island, so weak and in so much pain he was sure he'd drown in the current. He thanked God when a floating chunk of driftwood bumped him, and he was able to hang on.

"He doesn't know what happened to Thomasina after that. Her shrieks went silent as he drifted away from Gun Point. That man wants vengeance and he wants his wife back. I pray to God they'll be together again someday.

"So, Daniel, share this with whoever you trust. I want you to stay on guard, day and night, for people who might approach your island. The sharks are hungry and circling. I don't want your family to be their next meal. Over."

Chapter 27   Decisions

For the next week Daniel slept restlessly, with disturbing dreams. He frequently faded away from a conversation briefly or sat gazing out over the bay lost in thought. Alea wisely chose not to pursue him with questions. He would share when he was ready.

Her belly had started to round as the child within her grew. This baby was born of the love between her and Daniel and she was unable to contain her happiness. She would lay awake in the quiet night, marveling at the mystery and miracle of life, overcome by an avalanche of powerful emotions for the child she had yet to meet. Daniel often fell asleep with his head on her lap, his hand protectively resting over the small beating heart.

She peppered Josey with questions and pondered every bite of food before it entered her mouth. Was it good for the baby? She laughed at herself, a physician, behaving like every other mother since the dawn of time. But her medical education only made her more aware of the many complications that could occur during pregnancy and birth.

John checked on her progress daily. As her attending doctor, he wanted to stay aware of her condition, watching closely for any negative symptoms or problems that might present. He was content that she was doing quite well.

Angel was growing every day, healthy and happy. Her daily bath in Osprey Bay was a highlight for the vivacious child as she splashed fearlessly in the cool winter water. Small passing baitfish, as fast as they were, could not escape her grasp. But she released them gently and unharmed, with a radiant smile that made Josey not even question why she had chosen her particular name. Sea life seemed to gravitate to her, circling and darting close without concern, as if they sought to be near, wanting to be touched by her soft tiny hands. Angel cooed and screamed joyfully, crying as soon as she was lifted out of her beloved water. But it wasn't long before she chose to entertain herself with the next unwary individual she could waylay, in order to relentlessly probe ears, eyes, noses, mouths, and hair. The object of her detailed examinations patiently waited until her curiosity was satisfied and her attentions turned to a new and willing victim.

The Tribe was happily thriving. Daniel, John, and the boys completed the Treehouse, and during the relatively bugless winter season of January through April, they chose to sleep onshore. The Treehouse had a central common area with private rooms on the perimeter for Daniel and Alea, John and Josey, and one for Noah and Sam. More rooms could be added later, or separate dwellings built in the future, as they were needed. But for now, they enjoyed the secure feeling of being close and together.

Every so often, Daniel and Alea slipped away at dusk for a night alone on Mystic. On other nights, they volunteered to babysit for John and Josey so they too could have their own private time on Barefootin'.

This is how it was supposed to be, Daniel reflected, resting on his favorite tree stump overlooking the bay. His search for an Eden of safety for Alea had ended with Miracle Island. He'd never settle for less. He would not, could not, allow anything or anyone to destroy the good life that they, and their friends, were working so hard to build for themselves and for their children.

The cruelties of St. Thomas and the risk on Eleuthera preyed on him heavily night after night. Could he leave his parents, Alea's family, and Ronny any longer in a place that might be destroyed by greedy, vicious, and sadistic men? What about all the other families on Spanish Wells? On Eleuthera? Were the islands to be constantly threatened by evil at a time when men should be helping each other? Learning new ways to live in the powerless world and bequeathing a peaceful heritage to their children? Had it ever really been done?

Why couldn't it be done now? Daniel asked himself. If the imminent threat to Spanish Wells and Eleuthera from the Barracudas was decisively dealt with, the two islands would have time to prepare for potential dangers from outside their borders. They would also have the opportunity to demonstrate and teach their successful methods of living without electricity to the survivors on Eleuthera, with the power of love and hope creating a better world than ever before. The other suffering islands of the Bahamas would need that hope too.

He knew that the Bahamian islands were better equipped to survive than any large nation in the western hemisphere. The bountiful ocean surrounding them was their special gift, their lifeline to the future. It protected them as well, standing as a vast buffer to separate them from the tribulation, crime, and anarchy on the densely populated and starving U.S. continent. Not only did he love the islands, but they had now become his only home. And for his wife, child, and Tribe. For the rest of their lives.

He stood up from his well-worn tree stump and gazed out over Osprey Bay. He knew exactly what he had to do.

****

"Dad, I have an important question for you and Mom. Over."

"We're both here, Daniel. Go ahead. Over."

"I want you and Mom to leave Spanish Wells and come live with us on Miracle Island. Alea wants this too. Do you want to stay there, or would you consider coming with us? Over."

The radio fell silent. When it came back on, his father's voice cracked with emotion.

"Son, I really believe Spanish Wells is about the best a larger community can get in these post-Flare times. Instead of giving in to hopelessness and selfishness, these people joined hands with care and respect, and are working very hard to make sure everyone has the best possible chance for survival. We love them and have a role to play here. That being said, and I'm speaking for your mother too, we miss you both and would be honored to share the life you and Alea are building. And your mother says to tell you she lives to see her first grandchild. So, our answer is yes! Over."

"That's great Dad! Mom, we can't wait! Dad, can you grab a pencil? There are a few things I need you to take care of before we get there. Yes, we are going to come and get you! But not before you finish the list for me. Shouldn't take too long and once completed, let me know. Over."

An hour later, the wheels of change had been set in motion. Alea's parents decided to stay where they were most needed; to provide medical care on both Spanish Wells and Russell Island. Roger Gabrielle decided to remain as well. He planned on marrying Loreen and she chose not to leave her work, her family, and her friends of many years.

Ronny, Pearl, Robbie, and Rhonda were coming to Miracle Island! The twins had heard so much about Sam and Noah and were excited to live on a "deserted island" like pirates. Pearl just wanted to be with her man and her children and became good friends with Alea after she met Daniel. Ronny was as contented as a purring cat and couldn't wait to leave. Spanish Wells was wonderful, but he longed for adventure and the open seas again.

Ben, Gil, and Will declined to leave their community. Ben wanted to be with his grandchildren. Will was commanding the volunteer security forces and spearheading the training of Spanish Wells residents in self-defense and use of weapons. Gil was supervising the fishing and dive boats. Their families were well-established, and they were adamant the Flare would never destroy their island or their people. Daniel understood and extended an open invitation for them to someday visit Miracle Island.

James immediately began to work on accruing Daniel's list of requests. He sought out individuals he knew that owned sailing catamarans in the 40 to 45-foot range and negotiated an even trade for his 60-foot sailboat Red Cloud. Dances with Wind was a sleek 45-foot sailcat, small enough to pass safely through Hidden Pass and into Osprey Bay.

The entire family began searching for the rest of the items on Daniel's list, trading for the desired goods with food, tools, or furniture from the Bonefish Bay house. His mother offered to baby-sit for busy parents. James agreed to repair homes and boats, or substitute for a guard shift. Armand, Roger, and Nadia did not receive a salary for the medical services they provided, but let it be known to satisfied patients that extra seeds, cuttings, soap, clothing, and other sundries would be greatly appreciated.

Roger was particularly pleased to have worked out a deal for a young male and female pig and a rooster and two hens to make the trip home with Daniel. This would enable the Tribe to breed the animals and enjoy fresh eggs as well.

Ronny was beside himself with excitement the next time he spoke with Daniel on the radio. The search of an unoccupied snowbird's house revealed a garage packed full of solar panels and hardware. Ronny quickly squirrelled six panels away for Daniel, three for the Bonefish Bay house, and three for Ben. He gave away the rest of the panels to friends and neighbors, who were pleased to have a renewable source of power derived from the same sun that had devastated their planet. Most people owned batteries, but only a few could recharge them.

Ben's contribution was another shortwave radio he found in one of the marina's storage closets, protected from the Flare, and he was quietly in discussion with friends for two more. He wanted Daniel to install a radio on each of his three boats, in addition to having one onshore in the Treehouse.

It took almost a month, but every item on Daniel's list was finally tucked away at Bonefish Bay or contentedly grazing in the small backyard fenced enclosure, ready for the voyage to their faraway destination.

Daniel made it very clear that the location of Miracle Island was a secret. Once the new Tribe members arrived on the island, however, he would reveal the coordinates figured by sextant and star. With two sailing vessels at their disposal, one boat could make the trip to Spanish Wells at least once a year for supplies, and Nadia and Armand wanted to meet their first grandchild at some point.

Daniel and Ben alternated calling each other every evening. Their conversations were sometimes short, of necessity, and other nights they spoke for several hours. No communication from Matt was ever received and repeated efforts to reach him at the New Bedford or Boston Devereaux Fishing frequencies were always met with silence. Daniel began to believe they'd never hear from Matt again.

So far, the Barracudas had not made any aggressive move toward Spanish Wells, but Ben was certain it was just a matter of time. It was highly likely that resources were drying up on the mainland and the Barracudas would be on the hunt for sources to re-supply. The marauders now moored two more catamarans alongside their original boat. Ben was afraid to imagine how those boats had been acquired and how many people died in the process. The nightly screams continued, and it was all they could do to keep the vengeful Bernard from jumping back into the current to swim over with his machete. Mr. Curry posted him over to the west end of Russell Island to prevent him from listening to the sounds of torment and pain that rang out from Gun Point and the adjacent village. It was time to end the barbaric inhumanity.

Mr. Curry was considering a bold move he was not yet ready to discuss with anyone but Ben and Will. It had been a tough enough job to steady frightened Spanish Wells after the Flare, but despite shortages and lack of medicine, the death rate was decreasing, and the settlement was thriving. The Barracudas were now his primary focus.

He presided over a weekly meeting that allowed residents with concerns, squabbles, demands, or other issues to present their complaints. Mr. Curry and a panel of selected men and women deliberated and made an agreeable recommendation for resolution. In most cases, both parties were satisfied, and peace restored. It was rare the panel needed to enforce a decision. If only this civilized tactic could be used to resolve the pressing matter of the Barracudas.

He knew that Spanish Wells had two special resources that would prove a major temptation for any post-Flare invader. First, Spanish Wells was home to sailboats of many sizes, in harbor and private moorage even before the Flare, and they were the main reason the people were eating so well. The daily fishing and dive trips were saving the lives of every soul on the island by providing a dependable source of protein. Almost every man and woman was skilled in at least one of the many methods of providing seafood for themselves from the ocean. A boat, whether skiff or trawler, was part of daily life even before the Flare, as Spanish Wells had been a major hub for the lobster and tourist charter boat industries for decades.

On the Eleuthera mainland, people could handline and dive off miles of rock and beaches, but the numbers of fish caught would be limited. Without volume, shoreline catch would not be near enough to feed the higher population numbers of up to 11,000 people pre-Flare. That number was most certainly decimated due to starvation, disease, and lack of fresh water, but still higher than Spanish Wells. Sailboats were invaluable to reach the schools of fish that briefly moved inshore for seasonal breeding but ultimately moved back out into deeper water. A good day's catch was practically ensured with access to the many offshore reefs close to Spanish Wells, and the sailboats often ventured to productive fishing grounds much further out, sometimes overnighting for days at a time.

The second tempting resource were the ancient water wells. Numerous wells were scattered across the island and clean water had been drawn from the massive underground granite reservoir for centuries, regularly replenished by the summer rains and hurricanes. Since the Flare, these wells were more desired than gold.

On the mainland, there were no deep reservoirs. The shallow public limestone cisterns that supplied Eleuthera often dried up during the winter, as did private property rain catch systems. The majority of Eleutherans had depended for years on expensive seawater desalinization first introduced by the U.S. Navy in 1960, and on the technique of reverse osmosis for filtering bottled water. Without electricity to power these two processes, freshwater was scarce and unsafe to drink. The resulting death count from this alone was catastrophic.

From his earliest days in government service, Mr. Curry never sought power or recognition for himself. He was a humble Christian man, not just in word, completely devoted to the Bahamas. Because of his solid moral standards, he was often passed over for advancement. But the repeated slights did not affect his intense desire to help his people. He refused to accept a dollar other than his allotted paycheck, and this made him suspect to the ranks of the powerful and greedy. He continued to earn the trust of the people he worked for and spoke with every day, who would have gladly voted for him as Prime Minister, if he were so inclined.

He mourned the conditions on Eleuthera and the plight of its suffering people. Shortwave transmissions coming in from nearby islands told him that each one was recovering slowly, despite devastating losses. Some, like Nassau, were ravaged by violence and starvation. Other islands were trying to adapt, some succeeding, some struggling, all suffering with a myriad of problems still to overcome.

Ben finally introduced Mr. Curry and Daniel by radio two weeks before Daniel planned to sail from Miracle Island. They immediately felt comfortable with one another and spent several hours speaking privately. Daniel revealed his thoughts regarding the Barracudas, and they discovered they were in complete accord. The Barracudas would not be the only threat to peace the islands might have to face someday. As they discussed the security needs of Spanish Wells and Eleuthera, Daniel impressed Mr. Curry with his sincerity and offer of assistance when he arrived. They both held the strong belief that a different but simpler way of life, without reliance on electric power, could and should be demonstrated not only to Eleuthera, but to all the struggling Bahamian islands. He was quite pleased to have Daniel's support and was anxious to meet him face to face.

Using the successful survival of Spanish Wells as his vision for the future, he turned his sights to the plight of Gun Point. The evil of the Barracudas could no longer be endured. It was time to deal with the threat, and with the solid support of Ben, Daniel, Will, and Gil, he began to plan.

Chapter 28   Into the Darkness

Deja Vue. Alea's long dark hair rippled in the wind as Daniel tacked Barefootin' north towards Spanish Wells. Standing at the bow, she felt the rush of the wind on her face. It feels like our honeymoon cruise, she thought wistfully, except we've already lived two lifetimes since our wedding. How different she felt compared to that uninitiated and innocently clueless woman who envisioned a Bahamas vacation as tiki bars, ATV rides on a sandy beach, 5-star restaurants, and a deliciously cold Yellow Bird cocktail.

Alea's survival skills now rivaled those of an experienced prepper. Under Daniel's tutelage, she'd learned how to spear fish and lobster and was quite competent with her machete. He was giving her regular shooting lessons with the Glock and he complemented her marksmanship and safe handling of the weapon. Despite plenty of ammunition, she vowed to use as little as possible and made every shot count. Aside from the fact that the very thought of taking a human life was abhorrent to her, she accepted the grim reality that she might someday need to protect her child, the Tribe, or even Daniel.

He affectionately called her his Wonder Woman. Her lean physique was toned and firm, with well-defined muscles that visibly flexed when she moved. The baby was clearly showing at almost five months. She gleamed with a golden tan and her hair was streaked with shimmering highlights.

Daniel was more heavily muscled than ever before, despite his past habit of regular gym workouts. The work of surviving had developed strength and a sculptured form that often caught Alea's desirous attention. His skin was a ruddy tone and his dark brown hair had lightened perceptibly from sun and salt exposure.

Alea wisely learned to take cover from the blazing sun, since she was constantly exposed, and wore loose knee-length cargo shorts, a tank top, and a light beach cover. Her newly woven hat with an extra-wide brim was firmly tied under her chin. She tried to encourage Daniel to wear one too, but when he put on her first design, Noah and Sam laughed uproariously and told him he looked like a dork. Back to the drawing board she went. An acceptable sun hat was eventually created that met with the boy's approval.

Lack of soap was a real problem since the supply on Mystic ran out long ago. She never felt completely clean after a beach sand scrubbing, saltwater bath, and freshwater rinse. But the very oils that stubbornly refused to wash away only served to keep her hair soft and her skin protected from wrinkling. She would often steam a pot of herbs, flowers, aloe, and crushed almonds to use as a sweet-smelling body rinse. No deodorant, no problem, as they usually jumped into the bay to swim and cool down after any sweaty task.

She and Josey were at somewhat of a loss over what to do for their monthly feminine needs. Pregnancy ended that problem for Alea, but they came up with a comfortable and non-itchy blend of soft dry grasses, moss, and leaves that were absorbent and easily replaceable. She found there was always something in nature to replace the old world's manufactured offerings, although not exactly the same or quite as refined. As long as it served its purpose, it was enough.

Daniel stood at the helm, scanning the calm seas ahead. He'd plotted a course he believed would take him near well-known waters, and once he had his bearings, he was sure he could locate Spanish Wells. Alea's arm encircled his waist as she joined him at the wheel.

They were impossibly beautiful as they stood together, tall, golden brown, strong, and in love. Facing an uncertain future and on the move again... into the mystic.

****

The first night out, Daniel anchored along a stretch of white sand on the leeward side of a small uninhabited island, close to the beach and shallow enough to wade to shore easily. He preferred not to sail at night, especially with Alea pregnant.

He sat back on a deck chair to rest. It was still several hours until sunset, time enough to dive up some dinner. But he was in no hurry. Alea walked out from the cabin, dressed in a filmy white nightgown that hid nothing. She was silhouetted against the deep blue sky as she stood on deck, facing him. Her pink nipples and swollen breasts were outlined against the sheer fabric. Her belly was round, the dark patch between her sleek loins enticing.

"You're beautiful," he whispered, as he felt himself getting aroused.

She smiled alluringly. "And which of the five senses would you like to try this evening?"

His eyes blazed and a half-smile curved his lips.

"All of them."

The light evening breeze molded the translucent gown to her body as she walked towards him and sank down to her knees between his thighs. "Why don't you lay your chair back and relax," she suggested softly, as she slipped his trunks down and off his legs. He did as she requested, the backrest of the chair reclining, the sky a brilliant sapphire blue above him.

Her hair tumbled around his thighs as she ran her hands up to his chest, stroking and massaging lightly as Daniel moaned in anticipation. Her hands circled his groin, her fingers gently combing through the dark, tightly curled hair surrounding his hardening member. She continued to caress his firm muscled body everywhere, except for his throbbing organ, making him groan with desire.

She lowered her head to his lap, exhaling hot breath into his dark curls. His hips jerked in response and she blew warmth again on the tip of his pulsing organ, still not touching him with her mouth. He reached for her hair to pull her down.

Suddenly, she captured his head completely with her full, wet lips. He cried out as she swirled her tongue over the smooth skin, tasting his essence, feeling him throb and harden even more. Slowly, she pulled him into her mouth, then back up to the tip, over and over, deeper and deeper into her throat until she could take no more. He writhed with pleasure as her tongue teased him mercilessly with each leisurely stroke, and he knew he was ready.

"Alea!"

She stood up, the loss of her wet warmth devastating. But her thighs spread as she straddled his hips and slowly lowered her moist mound until she was fully impaled on his rock-hard erection. Their hands clasped as she began to ride him, slowly at first, then pistoning harder and faster until he shouted once and exploded inside her.

Still impaled, she fell forward onto his damp chest as they lay together gasping for breath. He enfolded her in his arms as the evening breeze cooled their skin. She raised her head to look at him, her eyes smiling.

"Did I get all five?"

****

Lighthouse Point, at the south end of Eleuthera, appeared on the third day, late in the morning. They had entered Exuma Sound, the deep channel running well offshore along the west side of Eleuthera.

When he passed the next major point, Cape Eleuthera, his curiosity caused him to veer right, into the shallower waters of the Bight along the west coast shoreline. He hoped to see what effect the Flare was having on the island communities they'd visited on their honeymoon. Daniel's excitement began to grow as he recognized terrain, landmarks, and waterways he'd become quite familiar with over the years.

He was troubled to see smoke rising at intervals along the shoreline, the source unable to be determined. He hoped it was for good purpose, but his gut told him otherwise.

With the binoculars he could see Rock Sound, a small town and the southernmost bay on the island. The area seemed quiet and he could see a few boats with masts in the distant harbor. As they steadily cruised along the coastline, he spotted Governors Harbor, the capitol of Eleuthera. He grimaced as he noticed most of the buildings were burned.

They continued north. James Cistern, Rainbow Bay, and Gregory Town looked deserted but there was no smoke and the buildings appeared intact. He veered Barefootin' to the northwest to pass through the Current Cut, a wide channel of water that ran between North Eleuthera and Current Island, the most direct route to Spanish Wells from their position. No smoke was evident on Current Island, and if any boats were there, he knew they'd be anchored near local moorage. As they sailed through the Cut, it was sobering to see the Current Pride ferry half-sunken in the small cove where the boat usually docked when not in service.

The sun was almost touching the horizon when he spotted Spanish Wells in the distance, their journey almost complete and without serious incident. They would enter the harbor from the west side. He called Alea over to take the helm and turned on the shortwave radio to contact Ben.

"This is Daniel Devereaux on the sailcat Barefootin' calling Ben Knowles. We're almost there, Ben! No more than thirty minutes out. Can you let the boys know to drop the chains at the west entrance? Over."

There was no immediate response as the static crackled. A muted voice finally spoke.

"Danny, this is Will. The blockade gate will open when we see you. Anchor up at any free spot near the old gift shop and bring your tender in. I'll meet you down at the dock. Over."

"Hey Will, I told you we'd make it over here soon, didn't I? Can I talk to Ben real quick? Got a question I know he can answer before we arrive. Over."

The radio came back on. But this time, Will's quavering voice could not restrain his emotions.

"Daniel, my father is dead."

Chapter 29   The Sacrifice

Benjamin Knowles woke up to a beautiful balmy morning with the winds at 10 knots out of the northeast. A perfect day to take the kids out for a sail on the east bay! He had planned on teaching his young grandchildren how to sail after Spanish Wells stabilized after the Flare and today seemed like a good day to do just that. He decided to run two boats.

Sailfish was a 22-foot day sailer, with Ben and his old friend Joseph taking out Kayla and Billy, his son Will's eight and ten-year old children. Albacore was a 28-foot sailcat, manned by Gil and his buddy Lawrence, taking out Gil's boys, Bruno, Gordie, and Harry, ages seven, nine, and ten. Will remained on duty at the radio in Ben's office.

The children were beside themselves with excitement! Gil and Will walked them to the docks, where boxes with lunches and bottles of water were loaded onto the boats. Ben insisted that each child wear a flotation vest for safety, even though they were all strong swimmers. Gil and Lawrence escorted the three boys to the catamaran and Ben helped Kayla and Billy board Sailfish. The kids were instructed to pay close attention to every action being taken by the crew and only to observe unless specifically asked to do a task. It would be the first of many such voyages to help them practice and ingrain sailing skills over time.

The east blockade was opened by Will's security guards and many hands waved in greeting as the two boats slipped out into the bay, where the wind and calm seas would make for a spectacular day of sailing. The boats stayed in close proximity as Ben and Joseph began to show the two children how to raise the sails, how to tack with the wind, and how to steer. Ben supported Kayla as she stood tall and took the helm, turning the boat at his direction, but not before planting a happy kiss on her grandpa's cheek. Joseph took

Billy in hand to show him how to furl and unfurl a sail. The children's eyes sparkled with the thrill of the boat slicing through the waves as wind filled the sails. Excited shouts echoed across the water from Albacore as the boys egged their father to pass Sailfish in an unofficial race.

Ben was content. His family had been spared death, except when he lost his beloved Vernita. Their home was secure and prospering. These children were now the future of his family, and of the world. He was committed to making sure they would benefit from all the knowledge and skills his sixty-two years could give them. Their excited faces, enthusiasm, and joy made him burst out in a laugh that rose from his soul, the cool breeze rushing past his face and his body warmed by the morning sun. God was so good!

He was helping Kayla tack when he caught movement out over the water and his head whipped around. Ben's breath caught. One of the three large catamarans moored by the Barracudas was pulling away from the dock at Gun Point. He saw at least ten men visible on board, the metallic flash of machetes in their hands. And the boat was heading straight towards them, minutes away. Before today, they had not been aggressive, but Ben knew what they wanted.

He whistled to get Joseph's attention. His old friend, white of hair and with dark weathered skin, looked over knowingly at the approaching boat, his face solemn. Joseph called the children to his side as Ben steered Sailfish closer to Albacore. Hailing Gil, he pointed at the Barracudas. Gil held his father's eyes, the grim unspoken message clear to both. He then waved Sailfish to move in even closer and headed to the radio.

Ben threw his arms around Kayla and Billy and hugged them tight, his eyes closing in pain and heartache. But he smiled as he gently released them.

"I love you both so much. But Grandpa needs you to go for a swim with Uncle Joe right now. Can you jump in the water and swim with him over to Uncle Gil's boat?"

Kayla began to cry. "Grandpa, why? I want to stay with you! Please don't make me go!"

Billy stood close to Ben and placed one hand on his shoulder. "It's okay, grandpa, you're the captain, right? You told us to always obey our captain. I'll take good care of Kayla." The boy glanced over at the Barracuda's boat, a tear glistening in the corner of his eye as he looked back at his grandfather. "See you later?"

"Yes, my boy, I will see you later," he said sadly. "I love you."

He turned to Joseph, whose eyes were brimming with tears. They grasped each other's hands firmly, eyes locked.

"This is goodbye, my old friend. Please get my grandchildren back to their parents. Tell everyone I loved them. Blessed be the name of The Lord."

****

Leon was angry and bored. He sat up in bed and glared around the room. Shit, this place was no better than Nassau. The drugs were gone, with no replacements anywhere. He had the shakes and his nerves were on the edge of a knife. He needed a line and a thick steak. After that, a hard fuck with a big-breasted hottie. A bottle of rum and some ice would be the capper. Was that too much to ask for?

Instead, he got skinny, dirty bitches who had to be beaten, sometimes cut, before doing what he wanted. And he was sick of the screaming and crying. Especially from the little girls. He smirked. Well, he sorta liked that.

He pushed the two naked sleeping teens off the bed and got up, long dirty dreadlocks falling haphazardly on his tattooed chest. Scratching under one arm, he walked to the bayside window and peered out at Spanish Wells. Assholes. They had water, and plenty of it. And fields of food. Untouched women. His men were getting mighty tired of his leftovers.

His initial plan to take over the nearby town of Bluff had been a disaster. Someone got to them first and warned them. He suspected it was Bernard's wife, Thomasina. Damn, she was hot! Long legs, big boobs. Leon was reluctantly forced to finish with her before turning his drooling boys loose, making her and Bernard an example to the rest of their people of what defiance would get them. She escaped the same night Bernard disappeared, slipping right past his men and vanishing into the darkness. Donny, the lead guard at the women's shack, took quite a lashing for that fuck-up. Leon had wanted to take him out, but knew he needed all his men. He was quite sure, however, that the idiot got the message.

Leon and twenty-five of his men moved against Bluff early one morning, believing the town was weak and defenseless. They were completely surprised when seventy determined men and women, brandishing machetes and even a few guns, jumped them outside the village border before they could even draw their weapons. His men were physically attacked and overcome by sheer numbers and some of their weapons were confiscated. Leon was pushed back decisively, losing three men in the battle. His plan to raid inland settlements for food was not going well, and he was hoping to recruit disillusioned hungry men as he went from town to town, to grow the ranks of his fighters. Unfortunately, the out-islanders were close-knit and family-oriented. No one was volunteering to join his little army. No matter. They'd eventually come around. He'd see to that.

As he stood at the window, he noticed two boats emerging from the blockade across the bay. One of them was a good-sized catamaran. Leon knew that without their boats, Spanish Wells was weak and vulnerable. Fishing was their mainstay for food. It came to him that by capturing their boats, one at a time, their downfall would be inevitable. And they all seemed rather passive, doing nothing to interfere with him at Gun Point over the last couple of months, easy pickings for he and his heavily armed men to take over. If they wanted to eat, they would comply and obey. Or he'd start burning boats. His eyes narrowed and his mouth twisted in a savage grin.

It was time to lay siege to the castle.

****

Ben watched anxiously as Joseph and the two children swam over to Albacore and were hauled aboard. Gil raised his hand in farewell to his father, tears streaming down his cheeks. Albacore then veered away. They would be safely back to Spanish Wells in fifteen minutes. Guards flooded the blockade opening and retrieved the chain, armed with several shotguns and a few semi-automatic pistols. Geoffrey was an expert marksman with a bolt-action Winchester rifle. He dropped into position on the blockade, the Barracuda catamaran in his sites, but the boat was still too far away.

Ben took a deep breath and turned Sailfish in the direction of the Barracuda's path. I must keep them from reaching Albacore, he determined. They will never touch my family!

The other boat saw him coming and swerved to avoid him. Ben altered his heading to continue to drive them off-course, repeating the diversionary tactic several times. And it was working! The angry thugs on deck threatened with machetes and guns, screaming out foul curses, most lost to the wind. But they'd been ordered not to fire. Leon was in the mood to play just a bit longer.

The Barracudas broke out and attempted another fast run towards the real prize, the larger catamaran Albacore. Gil and the children had not yet reached the blockade and were still in danger of being taken. Ben knew there was only one thing left to do and there was no time to lose. With the wind in his favor, he turned the wheel and aimed straight at his target. His eyes closed as he prayed for courage, the bow of Sailfish crashing and splintering into the Barracuda's hull at a 45-degree angle. The sudden impact stopped them both dead in the water, men toppling as the force of the strike pushed Sailfish up into the air, the keel then slamming down hard on the Barracuda's deck. The chase was over.

But not for Ben.

With both boats entangled and free-floating in the current, Leon's men began to climb towards him, machetes drawn. He gripped his own machete with a strong hand. This was for his grandchildren! With a shout, he leaped off the deck of Sailfish, swinging his sharpened blade through the air. As he landed, the head of one of the thugs rolled across the deck.

For a stunned moment, no one moved. Ben was crouched and catching his breath when multiple arms grabbed him, crushing him into the deck, the blood-stained weapon torn from his hand. A laugh sounded as Leon emerged from the main cabin door, casually sauntering over to where Ben lay, held down by four men.

"Well, well, what have we here?" he sneered. "And we were having such a fun game of cat and mouse. Not only have you damaged my boat, but you seem to be the only reason I'm not the new owner of a very nice catamaran, old man. Someone has to pay. Guess that'll be you."

The men yanked Ben roughly to his feet and held his arms. He stood tall and unyielding and looked straight into Leon's mocking eyes.

"Your days are numbered, fool. The righteous Lord sees your evil. There is no escape from God's wrath."

Leon smirked and lunged forward, driving his fist brutally into Ben's gut. Ben grunted and doubled over, coughing and choking, but refused to cry out.

"Well, no escape for you today, that's for sure. I got your sailboat, but I'll be wantin' more than that if I'll be living on Spanish Wells from now on. Saw that sweet young thing with you too. Um-um, that's gonna taste real good. More like that back home? Got your solar panels. Got your shortwave radio. I'll need those. But there's one thing I won't be needin'."

Leon gestured to one of his men. "And that would be you."

The machete swiftly descended from behind in a deadly arc that struck Ben on the side of his neck. Blood began to spurt like a fountain, spraying Leon in warm red fluid. He rubbed the droplets of Ben's dripping blood into his skin and hair, laughing wildly.

"Tie his hands. Let's troll for shark."

Chapter 30　　　　The Plan

Daniel wept unashamed on Will's shaking shoulder, both men wracked with sobs. The children cried in the comforting circle of Alea's arms. Gil sat stone-faced, unable to cope, as the rest of Ben's family filed slowly into the crowded church.

Ben was dead. Grandpa was gone. A hero had been born.

Daniel had raced Barefootin' into Spanish Wells where Will met him at the dock, barely able to speak, still in shock from the cruelty witnessed the day before. Daniel guided him to Ben's office and shut the door behind them.

"What happened, Will? Why is Ben dead? I spoke with him not even two days ago."

Will shook his head, still in disbelief. It would be hard to tell his blood brother and friend what happened to his father. His jaw clenched. The rage boiling inside him must be kept under control... but beware the fury of a patient man.

Gil had radioed Will immediately about the assault by the Barracudas. It happened so fast Will did not have time to launch a counterattack. He had no choice but to helplessly watch his father's murder from a distance with binoculars.

Sailfish was pushed off the Barracuda's boat and several thugs boarded her to sail back to Gun Point. After his father was viciously struck with the machete, the cowards tied his hands together, attached a rope, and threw him over the side, still alive. They began sailing towards open water, trolling Ben behind on the rope like bait, blood streaming from his neck wound. The men were laughing and joking as Ben struggled in the wake, finally going still.

It was then that the sharks arrived.

The water erupted with bloody foam as the sharks attacked, ragged flesh impaled on white teeth in open, red-stained jaws. Suddenly, as he watched in horror, Will saw his father was not yet dead, eyes white with fear and legs kicking helplessly.

He did not last long.

The sharks fed for over an hour. No trace of Ben's body was ever recovered.

****

Mr. Curry asked to meet with Gil, Daniel, and Will the day after Ben's memorial service. The mood was somber, the men vibrating with angry energy, as was all of Spanish Wells. Mr. Curry was actually grateful to feel that energy. He had a plan and he needed these men. For Ben's sake. For the future of the people of Eleuthera. For the future of all the islands.

"Ben was our friend. And is now our inspiration. We can no longer sit back and believe that defense is our only option. Our children are at great risk, our island in jeopardy. There are also men and women in grave danger on the mainland and we are finally stable and in a stronger position to help. Can we as God's people do otherwise?"

Will looked at him, eyes blazing. He would never forget the violence he had silently viewed in his binoculars, forever burned into his soul, until the end of his life.

"I'm ready. I want those bastards down. When the evil few can torment the many, there is no justice, no balance."

"I'm in."

He turned to Gil. Will knew what his brother would say. He knew what everyone on Spanish Wells would say.

"I want them gone," Gil barked. "No human being should treat another the way they did. I loved my father." He looked at each man in the room, one at a time. "And my children were out there."

"I'm in."

All heads turned to Daniel. His eyes were still rimmed with red and his handsome face looked haggard and weary.

"You know how much I loved Ben. He was my second father. He would have gladly died for any of us. And he did." Daniel stopped and choked back his tears.

"These monsters must be stopped. Our islands have suffered enough. Can we let this go on? It is our duty to do whatever is necessary to protect our families from these horrors. Each one of those men had a lifetime to hear the way of good and put away evil. They made their choice and must now pay for their despicable crimes. Even before the Flare, these actions would have been harshly punished. We will do the same."

"I'm in."

****

"I have to come with you, Daniel! Once the people of Gun Point village have been freed, they will need medical care. Roger, Donald, and I want to be there. We have to help them!" Alea earnestly pled her case to a stone-faced Daniel, his arms folded across his broad chest.

"No! Again, our baby would also be in danger if anything happened to you. Afterwards, I'll bring your whole team over myself and can provide protection as you work. This won't be pretty, Alea. It's just too risky."

"We can stay at the boats until you send someone to tell us it's safe. Minutes may be very important. What if Gil or Will are injured? Geoffrey? How many more names do I have to bring up? Our care might make the difference between a man returning to his family or his death."

Daniel pondered her suggestion. She made sense. If he left four armed men at the boats with them and if the plan was successful, a runner could tell them to come to the village.

Or, at the very least, have them sail back to Spanish Wells for safety. He knew first-hand she was relentless when it came to her medical vows. He sighed and pulled her rounded softness into his chest, enjoying the light scent of coconut in her hair.

"Alright Alea. You must stay with the boats and four guards until you hear from us. If we have stopped them, you can come to the village and establish your hospital. But if you sense any problem at all, leave at once and return to the harbor. Is this a deal? Do you promise?"

"I do, Daniel. Thank-you. And I speak for all of us. It would be hard to live with ourselves if anyone from Spanish Wells was lost unnecessarily."

"Okay, here's the way Curry, Will, and I want to run this. We have 150 men who have volunteered, and we'll establish two fronts. First, at 3:00 a.m. tomorrow morning, I will lead eight boats with eighty fighters, and your medical team, out of the west blockade. We'll sail along the north side of Spanish Wells over to Salt Kettle Bay on Eleuthera. It's a small bay further east from Gun Point village, but far enough away they won't see us or hear us land. We'll have to walk in from there and wait for first light at dawn. Geoffrey will be our long-range sharpshooter. Bernard will be our point, as he knows the area well. Never saw a man so ready.

"By dawn, Gil and Ronny will sail seven boats with seventy fighters into position surrounding the Thompson house where Leon is based, right at the tip of Gun Point. He won't be able to slip away on the water without being caught. This diversion will hopefully keep his attention long enough to allow the rest of us to come in from behind. Not sure how many men he has stationed in the village, but Bernard told us he usually kept 2-4 armed men guarding the slave shacks at night. This will be guerilla warfare. We must incapacitate them quietly and keep working our way toward Leon. We aren't planning to kill if we don't have to and may have to take on prisoners. But we will kill if we must, Alea, even though I'd prefer to see Leon held responsible for his actions, as well as the members of his gang. The people of Eleuthera need to see lawful judgements being made. It will be the only way to re-establish confidence, peace, and order."

Alea was grave as Daniel spoke. She understood what they needed to do and with all her heart wished people would not treat each other with such cruelty. Why? she wondered. Was brutality and aggression so indelibly ingrained in mankind it was impossible to overcome? Perhaps someday God would allow her to know the answer. But for today, her main concern was not only the fighters of Spanish Wells, but the health of the men, women, and children of Gun Point. She didn't want to think about the atrocities she might have to deal with but steeled herself. No one would die on her watch, if she could help it.

****

It was midnight, dark and moonless. Bernard sat in his small house on Russell Island with his two friends, Gordon and Francois Symonette. Each harbored a serious grievance with the Barracudas. The brothers lived in Gun Point and were out fishing on their rowboat the day the village was attacked. They escaped to Spanish Wells, where safe haven was offered, but were tormented by the knowledge that their families were still held captive. The three men were the first to volunteer for the ground assault team, departing in three hours.

No words were spoken. Bernard led the men outside to a blazing fire where they squatted down in a circle around the flames. His empty left eye socket was covered with a black patch, his maimed left forearm healed at the stump where a hand used to be. Lash marks were raised in long scars across his back, legs, chest, and arms. His good right eye gleamed in the firelight with fervent purpose.

Singing the ancient warriors chant, Francois raised a knife to the heavens, then pushed the blade into the fire. The three men's eyes met, and each offered an arm. Francois slid the hot knife across their right forearms, one at a time, a line of red blood instantly oozing from the cuts. They stood and slapped the wounds together, their blood blending and dripping into the sputtering flames. The vow was uttered. The blood pact was sealed.

Bernard bared his left stump as Francois held the handle of a machete against his inner forearm. Gordon pulled out a roll of duct tape and began to secure the handle of the weapon to Bernard's arm. The machete became a part of him, a super-sharpened hand of death. He slashed the air, testing the blade. Laughing with satisfaction, he lifted a second machete in his good right hand.

"Yes, Leon, The Scorpion is coming. I'm coming for you."

Chapter 31   The Taking of Gun Point

The fleet of eight attack catamarans glided noiselessly into Salt Kettle Bay at 4:00 am, the hulls quietly shushing up onto the sandy beach, one next to the other. The fighters jumped into the wet sand, tied the dock lines off to the nearest trees, and gathered around Daniel at an old picnic table.

Teams of ten had been pre-arranged and the leader of each team carried a rechargeable battery flashlight to help guide them in the dark. The 80 volunteer fighters would be pitted against Leon's 26 remaining heavily armed men. The Spanish Wells fighters more than outnumbered the Barracudas, but their personal hunting rifles, shotguns, and pistols were far less deadly than the military-style automatic weapons their enemy possessed. Surprise and stealth would be their strength and advantage. Bernard's team was taking point, as most of his men were familiar with the roads, terrain, and the village layout. Curious flashlights zeroed in on the one-eyed man they now called The Scorpion. His razor-sharp left machete arm had caused quite a stir back at the docks. Daniel simply put his hand on Bernard's shoulder and nodded once.

"I would have done the same, my friend. Good hunting."

The plan was not complicated, and if it worked, there should be minimal injuries and hopefully no innocent deaths. Alea, Roger, Donald, and the nurses were to remain stationed at the boats with four guards. Once informed by the runner that the battle was over and was a success, they could move into the village and establish a field hospital for the injured and sick. They sincerely hoped not to be ordered to flee back to Spanish Wells instead.

The teams would begin moving out just before dawn, with Bernard's team leading the way, the other teams fanning out to follow, taking down any Barracudas encountered as quietly as possible. The objective... to free the suffering men, women, and children held captive in the slave shacks, in any manner it took. If a thug surrendered, he'd be arrested and detained for later prosecution. If not... well, Daniel left that decision to each of his fighters.

The job of the diversionary catamarans surrounding the tip of Gun Point was to agitate and distract Leon and his men while the teams made their way through the village and on to the Thompson house, where Leon was based. Daniel hoped to apprehend him alive, to be held publicly accountable for his crimes, and as a graphic example of what would never again be tolerated on their islands.

As light began to filter into the eastern sky, Alea clung to Daniel. She had waited for him for so long and the thought of losing him was unbearable. Unable to speak, her bowed head nestled against his chest, her heart in turmoil.

"Alea, my love. I promise you I will return. I will hold our precious child when born. I will never leave you while I have breath and I will love you forever, my wife."

He raised her chin and kissed her deeply.

"I have to go, dearest. Wait for me. I'll send word."

He turned and disappeared into the morning mist.

****

Bernard saw the first house through the trees. There was no sound in the sleeping village other than the cackle of a hen and the distant crowing of a rooster. The morning breeze lightly rustled the leaves in the trees. The once-vibrant settlement might have been deserted, for all he could tell.

But it was the smell that re-ignited his anger. The smell of death, blood, rotting human flesh, raw sewage. Flies buzzed his face, landing on his hair, his ears, his lips. This is what he last remembered. This was why he was here. The dual blades of his machetes trembled, reflecting rays from the rising sun. Patience. The end was in sight.

He motioned his team forward with his machete arm. They stopped when they saw the first guard standing at the second house from the town border. The man was heavily armed with an AR-15 automatic rifle slung over his shoulder, a 45-caliber handgun in a holster, and a machete sheathed at his waist. He ambled around to the front of the shack he was guarding, pausing at the door to light a cigarette. He appeared bored, inhaling the smoke deeply and blowing out as he looked up into the trees. After crushing the butt under his heel in the dirt, he turned to face the building, unzipped his pants, and began to urinate on the wall. He never got to finish.

Two gleaming blades swept through his neck, one after the other. The head rolled off into the weeds and the body fell, the silence unbroken. The Scorpion smiled. The rest of the team checked on all sides of the shack but saw no other guard. Leon was slipping.

Bernard peered into a window. Piles of women and children were asleep on the floor and he chose not to awaken them. They were not even close to being done. They cautiously made their way further into the village until another armed guard was spotted pacing in front of a larger shack. This time, a second guard joined him. They bantered back and forth, laughing, oblivious to the watchful eyes surrounding them. In the meantime, a second team moved in from behind. Daniel crept up next to Bernard and took out his Glock with silencer, the question clear on his face. Bernard held up one machete as a sign for his men to hold in place. Daniel took aim.

Two shots dead on to the head. The men dropped. Daniel ran to the window and looked in. Several dozen men lay sleeping on the rough wood floor. It was time to wake them up. Daniel motioned for one of Bernard's team members to approach the door. The blades of the vengeful Scorpion would only frighten the sleeping men. The villagers probably thought Bernard was already dead and his appearance might alarm them.

"What's your name, man, sorry, I don't recall?"

"Gordon Symonette. I used to live here."

"Yes, Gordon. Thank-you for doing this with us. Can you go in and wake up someone you know? Tell them what's going on but keep everyone quiet until this is over. We've got more bad dudes to catch and we need silence."

"No problem. I still want to bloody my beak, but these are my people. They'll know who I am, and I'll take care of them," Gordon assured him. Daniel smiled. He could appreciate that kind of commitment.

The teams moved silently forward towards the west end of the village, where they finally converged around Daniel.

"I see everyone is here, so I'm assuming all targets in the village are down?"

"We counted bodies and thirteen worthless scumbags have been righteously killed," Will reported, wiping his machete off on his pants leg. "I can confirm that four of them were on the boat the day my father was murdered. I made sure they knew exactly who I was before they died. Hoo-rah."

"Copy that, Will. Good job! That leaves about ten more plus Leon. They must be hunkered down at the Thompson house and may have women with them. I'll bet the boat blockade has them a bit concerned, and they may be sending guys back to the village for reinforcements, thinking it's cool. Let's make sure it's not."

Daniel looked the group over and came to a decision.

"Geoffrey, still got that awesome rifle?"

"Got it, Daniel. What can I do?"

"Make yourself a cozy, well-hidden sniper nest within your range of the Thompson house. I want two men protecting you. If you see Leon or any of his goons attacking or threatening anyone, please take the opportunity to practice your already excellent marksmanship. You'll save lives by taking them out early, if possible. I'd sure like to take Leon to trial, but if he's a danger, he's done."

"My pleasure, Daniel!" Geoffrey pointed at two of his friends and they disappeared into the bush.

****

"Hey, Boss! You need to see this!"

Leon was incensed. It was barely daylight and this moron was waking him up? He kicked the young girl at his feet in anger and she cried out in pain.

"What you talkin' about, Wolf? Better be somethin' good."

He rolled off the bed and lazily stretched before walking over to the anxious guard standing at the window. His eyes popped open. Seven boats were anchored up surrounding the Point. His own four boats were nowhere to be seen. He could see men standing on the decks with firearms, and every gun was aiming at him.

"Shit! Call the guys!"

"Boss, I been tryin'. There's only Snake, Lost Boy, Maniac, Stinger, and me in the house. Nobody else around."

Suddenly, the staccato of gunfire erupted outside, shouting and cries of pain filling the air. Leon cursed. Damn it, the gig was up. But there was always one last play.

"Get those women up here!"

Wolf opened the closet door in the hall and gagged. Damn, he should've remembered to cover his nose with a towel. No showers or toilets permitted for five days after that reddish-haired bitch bit Leon, down there... Wolf still couldn't believe he let her live. Must've liked somethin' about her.

The three women and two girls rolled out of the cramped closet and pleaded with Wolf for water. Disgusted, he shoved them away and yelled for them to follow. They reeked of feces, urine, sweat, and bad breath, their hair matted and filthy. His nose wrinkled at the smell of blood as well. What did Leon want with these skanks? Time for replacements.

The women stumbled into Leon's bedroom and fell to the floor. He walked over and grabbed one of the young girls by the hair, dragging her out on the deck in full view of the armed flotilla, his remaining five men lining up behind him.

"I want a boat and safe passage in exchange for the life of this little ho," he shouted, gesturing a slice across her throat. "You've got one hour to produce, or she dies. And another girl an hour after that!"

"I don't think they can hear you, jackass." Will's sarcastic voice taunted him.

After approaching the perimeter of the house, Daniel and Bernard's teams surprised and took down five of Leon's gang in a deadly exchange of gunfire. Two of his own men had been injured and transported quickly away from the scene, but Daniel, Will, and Bernard maneuvered silently to the rocks in front of the deck and took cover. The Scorpions blades were covered in blood and he shook with anger as soon as he saw Leon, the man responsible for so much agony and death. He wanted his blood to be the last of the many taken that day.

Leon screamed in fear and defiance and held the terrified young girl in front of him for cover.

"She dies unless you let me go!"

****

Geoffrey sat up in his hastily constructed sniper's nest and re-adjusted his sites. I'll be darned, how did I get so lucky?

Leon himself had appeared on the deck, flying dreads and all, standing right there in front of God and, well, Geoffrey. And clutching a battered and screaming girl? Oh, bloody hell, this was rich... The guy was like a rabid dog.

He casually and deliberately cocked his rifle and settled in comfortably to take aim. Deciding he would pay attention to Daniel's instructions, he waited. So far, the nutjob was only yelling and holding the child, with no obvious weapon in hand. It had already been a good pig hunt, so to speak, and he could afford to bide his time. But maybe not too long...

✳✳✳✳✳✳✳✳✳✳✳✳

"Let's be reasonable, Leon," Daniel said calmly. "The rest of your men are dead, and you're completely surrounded. You know you'll have to answer for your crimes. I promise you a fair trial, and if the judgement goes against you, a merciful end. Or should we hand you over to Bernard for final justice? I'm sure you remember him and his wife Thomasina? What'll it be, Leon? Your call."

"Boss, let's just take the man's deal here!" Wolf's panicked face mirrored the faces of the other four wide-eyed men. "We can always try to escape later, but if we're dead, we're dead."

Still holding the girl, Leon swung around, pulled out the gun he always wore at his waist, and aimed. The rest of his men jumped back as Wolf's body hit the deck.

"You can stop worryin', Wolf, cause' now, you are dead!" he snarled sarcastically. "Any of you other boys wanna give in to this fuckin' jerk?" He turned back toward Daniel's voice as he put the gun to the girl's head.

"You got the balls to stand up and promise me my boat and my freedom, man? I'm countin' to three. One..."

Daniel looked at Bernard even as he and Will were shaking their heads, No!

"Two..."

Putting his weapon down, Daniel started to rise.

A sharp crack sounded in the distance. Leon flew sideways, his head shattered in a mass of blood and brains, the girl falling to the deck crying in fear.

Geoffrey blew out a breath and lowered his rifle. No doubt about it. Sometimes you just had to take down a rabid dog.

Chapter 32   Salvation

The naked and crying women in the bedroom were hastily covered in sheets and given bottles of water to drink, with the instruction to sip slowly and regularly. The women begged to be allowed to wash off the crust of filth on their bodies at the beach in front of the house. Once they were bathed and clean, team members lifted and carried each one back to the small house in the village designated as the hospital.

Alea and Roger chose two rooms for medical examinations, with Donald and the nurses assisting. They had brought over large containers of whatever medical supplies were available, as well as food and bottles of water, which the fighters were distributing to the villagers. One at a time, each person was examined and treated to the best of their ability.

Alea fought back her tears as she treated the horrific injuries inflicted on many villagers. But it was the children that broke her heart. Worked to the point of exhaustion, with ribs clearly visible from starvation, many of the little boys were beaten, cut, and whipped, some sexually abused. The girls, my God, none had been spared from that torture, and their devastating injuries were particularly hard to take.

But there was joy despite the misery. The men and women of the village were brought together in the yard outside the hospital and families were reuniting. This time the tears being shed were of happiness, and cries were not of pain but of relief to again see loved ones who survived.

The day grew hot. Once everyone was fed, no longer thirsty, and with their safety assured, many walked to their homes to see the damage. It would take time to re-group. They had just been hit by the Flare, the town leaders only starting to figure out how to survive, when the Barracudas landed at

Gun Point and took control. Now, in such a weakened condition, with so many dead, they needed help.

Mr. Curry came over at midday with his team of helpers. After praising and congratulating the fighters, Daniel and Will disappeared with him into one of the houses for well over an hour to make a full report. The last four of Leon's gang on the deck surrendered after he was shot and were being held in custody for a trial whenever Gun Point was ready to proceed. The others had all been killed in skirmishes, the bodies hastily buried under piles of rock in the bush, without ceremony.

It was over.

After report, Mr. Curry requested a designated spokesman for the village join them to discuss the future and a possible alliance. Spanish Wells was prepared to assist the village with food, water, seeds, and manpower to help build a new town; smaller, efficient, with guaranteed protection. If a consistent local source of fresh water could not be located, water would be shipped over. When they were ready, the trading of goods, skills, and boats would help the two settlements grow and prosper. In a new way. In the new age. With violence not permitted. With respect for each other as human beings and people of individual value. The vision was becoming reality.

The spokesman, Bruno Sands, was pleased. His town would survive, the torment ended. He and his wife had lost their 12-year old son. A month before, one of the thug's gave a casual machete chop to Bobbie's foot as a reprimand for playing with a basketball he and his friend found while working in the fields. Infection developed quickly. Bobbie was in severe pain for days, with red streaks rapidly traveling up to his thigh. No treatment was offered. His father was unable to prevent what he knew was coming next.

Leon ordered the weeping child taken into the bush. He was never seen again.

Bruno had time to mourn, but his wife had only learned of the boy's death that morning, having been kept separate from the men for months. She was in agony, with relatives caring for her in their home. Others were also being consoled, as they mourned their terrible losses.

The men had leaned heavily on Bruno during their captivity. His quiet strength and ability to control his anger calmed them, even if it earned him many a beating. The death of his captors was welcome, and he was more than ready to help lead his friends and neighbors into a better future.

Daniel emerged from the meeting, the bright sunlight of early afternoon temporarily blinding him. He hadn't seen Alea since early morning and immediately headed to the hospital house. Before he could even enter, she flung open the front door and leaped, throwing her legs around his waist, the unborn baby pressed between them, smothering his face with kisses, over and over. He laughed as he fended off her loving attack, holding her chin in his hand, his eyes blazing into hers. He dropped his head and crushed her lips in a passionate embrace. She moaned as he softened the kiss, in no hurry as he enjoyed her warm and eager mouth. They stayed locked together until Will's voice drawled behind them.

"Whatever. Get a room."

****

The Scorpion was rather disappointed. Leon was dead. But his death did not result from two razor sharp machete blades gradually slicing off important and treasured body parts. His personal vengeance unfulfilled, Bernard decided to accept the outcome as it was. The scum was dead and buried.

The Scorpion could rest.

He took his knife and cut off the tape that held the bloody machete to his left forearm. It had served him well. He took the two blades to the beach and washed them off in the clear turquoise water. When dry, he inserted them into the leather sheaths he wore on his belt and headed into the village. It was time to find out what happened to Thomasina.

Bernard reached the hospital and spotted his friend Gordon sitting with a group of animated men under the shade of a poinciana tree. Gordon leaped up to greet him, grinning at Bernard's weaponless left forearm.

"Man, it's good to see you! We heard what you did," as he clasped his hand firmly.

"Gordon, yeah, you ok?"

"We all good now. Just catchin' up with the boys. It's sad, Bernard, just damn sad. Gordon looked at him closely. "He's gone, right?"

"Leon's dead. It's over and done." He cracked a small smile and patted his machete. "No more Scorpion."

"The Scorpion stung many. Good for you."

"I need to know about my wife, Thomasina. Anyone know what happened to her?"

A tall, thin man he knew stood up, Franklin, and walked over to Bernard.

"I'm pretty sure she's okay. She saved the town of Bluff."

****

"We could only listen, you know. They never told us things outright. We'd overhear bits and pieces through the walls at night when the guards talked. We saw the hell they put you through, but you know there was nothin' we could do. And you wasn't alone, Bernard. They chopped up Dennis pretty good after he spit on one of em'... but he didn't make it. Anyway, one morning the ropes were hangin' empty at the tree you was tied to. We heard shouts in the night and figured they took you to the bush, one more of us dead.

"A week later, somethin' big happened. They locked us up with only one guard and left town. A few hours later they came back real angry and we overheard a lot of loud talkin'. Seems they tried to take over Bluff cause' they were running low on food. Then they started cursing Thomasina.

"She must have got away and made it to Bluff! She warned them about Leon and they was ready. They posted scouts to warn the town if Leon was comin'. The guard said there was about 60 or more, both men and women, and they stopped them at the north edge of town. The Cudas could not break through, even though they shot a couple of folks. Came back empty-handed. So, my guess is that your woman is in Bluff. I bet they took real good care of her after that."

****

Bernard told them the story of his escape and his belief that Thomasina had been re-captured or murdered. He gratefully shook the hand of each man and started the four mile walk south along the bay to the town of Bluff.

The sun was touching the horizon when he neared the small waterfront town. About a quarter mile out, two men emerged silently from the bush on the side of the road and ordered him to stop, brandishing M-16 rifles and machetes. They looked at him closely before lowering their weapons.

"Lord Almighty, it's Bernard! You remember him, Calvin. Bernard Thompson from Gun Point? Thomasina's husband? Thought you was dead. That girl gonna be awful happy!"

Bernard relaxed and shook their enthusiastically offered hands. He knew Calvin and Stuart from way back. His hopes soared. She was alive! As the men walked to town, Bernard informed them that Leon was dead and told them briefly about the battle at Gun Point. He promised to meet with all the townspeople of Bluff to tell the whole story. After repeated assurances to the relieved men that Leon and the Barracudas were no longer a threat, they took him to the white steepled church overlooking the Caribbean. Reverend Johnson came out to meet them on the porch, pausing for a moment in shock before greeting Bernard joyfully.

A cry came from inside the church and a woman ran out the door, the back of her hand to her lips as she slid to a stop.

"Bernard!"

Thomasina flew into his arms, babbling incoherently against his lips. Bernard was speechless. She was here! His woman was unharmed! His beautiful wife who had saved his life. He buried his face in her neck and sobbed. "I love you, Sina, I love you," he repeated over and over.

The men watched shyly, touched by the tender reunion. The pastor enclosed them both in a warm bear hug until the three slowly parted. Bernard's eyes widened.

Thomasina was round with child. He looked at her and she knew immediately what he wanted to know.

"I never got the chance to tell you. They separated us right away. I was waiting for your birthday and was already two months pregnant. Couldn't see the baby yet."

She took his hand and pulled it to her lips, her eyes pleading but her head high.

"I can't help what they did to me, my husband, but this child is ours."

Bernard captured her hand and kissed it tenderly, all his love in his eyes. Thomasina was forever back in his arms. It would not have mattered.

Chapter 33   The Vision of Unity

"I guess you are all wondering what I want to do from here on out."

Mr. Curry called a town meeting the next day. The people of Spanish Wells overflowed the pews and aisles of The Gospel Church, relieved that the threat was over, and their island was no longer in danger. The hard-working community was ready to get back to daily life.

For the present time, their minimal electrical power needs for the shortwave radios, low-voltage lighting, and battery charging were being adequately supported by the solar panels. But they clearly understood these luxuries were doomed to ultimate failure. Creative methods of producing and storing energy would have to be found if they wanted to keep using any of the disappearing conveniences of the pre-Flare world, while they lasted. But if not, they would live as human beings had lived for millennia and learn to be content.

Daniel, Will, Gil, Bernard, and a handful of other men were aware of what Mr. Curry was about to present. Daniel was in complete agreement with his idea and was curious what the population of Spanish Wells would have to say.

"Our beloved Bahama Islands have been more fortunate than many other countries. We already lived a simple life and close to nature for hundreds of years. Yes, it was hard to resist the tantalizing lure of the internet, computers, television, and I-phones, but these devices did not essentially change who we were.

"The sea has been our Mother and The Lord, our Father. He has provided us with ample food right outside our door, the harvest left in our hands. We were blessed with many boats that needed no power. And we have survived. And we will continue to survive, perhaps exploring the use of wind and water for new sources of energy, for a different way of living.

"But we do not know how our brothers and sisters on the mainland are faring. Gun Point and Bluff have joined us in our quest for peace and unity. I am now asking your permission and help to seek out survivors on the rest of Eleuthera and come to their aide.

"I know you toil for what we have, and we are prospering, praise God. But please, try to imagine the suffering in Upper and Lower Bogue, Gregory Town, Governors Harbor, Rock Sound, and even further south down to Cape Eleuthera. What about Royal Island and the other Family islands surrounding us? Can we leave them afflicted, alone and afraid?

"Here is my proposal. I would like to establish volunteer Care Teams to explore the settlements of Eleuthera and see first-hand what is happening, who has survived, and how they are doing it. To offer the hand of friendship, assistance, and support to those who will work as tirelessly as we do to build a new life in this electrically powerless world. To establish fair trade for goods and skills. The central government in Nassau we once depended on has disappeared. We must be our own masters now. We will choose our leaders from among the people we live with, who we know and trust, who have the best interests of the people of Eleuthera in their hearts. The rest of the world is in chaos and may never recover if they refuse to accept what the Flare has done to our planet and release the past. Change is inevitable. Let the people of Spanish Wells and Eleuthera lead the way and show mankind we can survive; in peace, unity, and harmony, caring and respecting one another as individuals, each contributing willingly to the growth of a life, a world, no longer based on electrical gadgets and toys.

"Once Eleuthera and our nearby islands are safe, secure, and prospering, we can branch out to our brothers and sisters on the other Bahamian islands to offer help and hope."

He paused, his face lit with strong emotion, as his gaze swept the crowd. "We may be powerless, but we can be powerful," he cried out.

"We can be Eleuthera United!"

The church pews erupted with enthusiastic applause and shouts. The people of Spanish Wells and Russell Island had spoken. Help was on the way for the survivors on Eleuthera, and ultimately, for all the Bahamian islands.

Chapter 34   Time to Go

Alea rested on a shaded wooden bench at the dock as Ronny and Daniel rowed the heavily-laden tender out to Barefootin's mooring, carrying the last load of supplies to take home. Her abdomen was noticeably rounded in her eighth month of pregnancy and her back ached. How she wished she knew if the baby was a boy or a girl! She had been gifted with used baby clothes and toys for either sex at the shower hosted by her mother at the church. It would most likely be next year before they returned to Spanish Wells to visit. Armand and Nadia were impatient to see their first grandchild and didn't want them to leave, but she reminded them that Roger and Loreen were planning to start their own family soon.

They were married in early May, a month after the siege on Gun Point, with a touching ceremony at the public beach park, graced by a spectacular pale orange sunset. As soon as their vows were spoken, the barbecue reception began. The entire island attended, with each family contributing a dish for the wedding supper. An open invitation was made to anyone who wanted to come, and dozens were ferried by sailboat to the event from Gun Point and Bluff.

Several goats and a half dozen pigs were roasted whole over fragrant wood logs and served along with platters of steamed lobster, grilled tuna and hogfish, conch salad, loaves of potato and cassava bread, vegetable salads, and fruits. In place of the traditional tiered wedding cake, the women baked two dozen different cakes, all made with an improvised blend of flour from potatoes and cassava, and laid out on a long table with a palm frond archway and congratulatory banner. The delicious smells of pineapple upside-down cake, guava duff, mango and banana cakes, cookies, and sweet pumpkin bread wafted in the breeze. The outdoor stone and brick ovens recently built next to the Food Fair grocery for community use were proving quite useful.

Excited children climbed down ropes hanging off the short connecting bridge to Russell Island and dropped, screaming and laughing, into the warm water of the west canal. A band of musicians with acoustic guitars, bongo drums, and rake n' scrape played as the bride and groom led the first dance and tiki torches lit the night. Many people even relinquished a few treasured bottles of rum and red wine, pouring a taste from the old days for anyone who wished.

Mr. Curry shocked everyone when he arrived with a date, her slender arm protectively enfolded in his own. Flora Russell was a beauty from Bluff, with wavy black hair, dark flashing eyes, and cafe au' lait skin. They had just been introduced the month before, but Edward was feeling quite hopeful she was the one. The ladies of Spanish Wells put their heads together and murmured hopefully. Another wedding soon?

It had been a wonderful day, which also served as an event to bring the three communities together. Relatives who hadn't seen each other in months met in tearful reunions, friendships were re-established, new relationships begun.

As Alea waited for Daniel and Ronny to return, she thought about the last three months spent on Spanish Wells.

Her brother and his new wife were so in love. Alea sighed, remembering her own amazing surprise wedding. Had it only been last July? It seemed a lifetime ago, but her love for Daniel was unshakable in her heart and her commitment to making this uncertain world safe and happy for their unborn child, for all children, was strong.

John, Josey, Noah, Sam, and Angel were waiting for them on Miracle Island. They had remained in Spanish Wells much longer than planned and she missed them terribly.

Their only shortwave radio had been needed for the journey and there was no way to find out how the five were faring.

Daniel's leadership and skills were essential in the aftermath of the battle and he was a great help to Mr. Curry and Will in establishing the new alliances, training community guards, consolidating town borders to more manageable sizes, and locating renewable water sources for Gun Point and Bluff. Alea was kept very busy seeing patients at the two new clinic sites she established, one in each town. But despite their busy pursuits, she was feeling homesick.

The rope tugging in her hands pulled her out of her wistful reflections and she looked down. Two round soulful brown eyes stared back at her and a small tail wagged as the puppy sat back on his haunches. Bear barked out a yip and his tongue lolled out. Was he actually laughing at her? The Rottweiler pup nuzzled her leg for much needed attention and Alea instantly melted, bending down to scratch behind his tiny ears. He panted with gusto, his eyes closing as he enjoyed the touch of her warm and loving hand.

A grateful patient in Gun Point brought her to the puppy, born in the bush to a litter of four. The woman found the newborns, protected them, and even fed portions of her own meager food allotment to the mother. She camouflaged the den and made sure the Barracudas never found them. The dogs would have been savage entertainment for the goons. After Alea set and treated the woman's arm, broken during a beating several days before the final raid, the woman offered her the choice of a pup.

She knew Noah and Sam would love a dog and accepted the offer, following her to the location of the mother's den. Of the four tiny pups, one little brown male pulled away from his mother's teat, looked Alea straight in the eye, and hobbled over to drop against her foot. She felt as if the puppy had chosen her and picked him up. He nuzzled her cheek and cuddled close. It was love at first sight for them both.

The rope in her other hand tugged and a wet nose nudged her leg. Ah yes, Brandy's feeling left out, she thought, and stretched out her hand to deliver the expected petting. With orange-red fur, light brown eyes, and a long furry tail, the little female was an island potcake of mixed heritage. Alea guessed there'd been an Irish Setter ancestor somewhere in the pup's questionable lineage.

Brandy was discovered by a surprised Daniel, sleeping alone and curled up on the back deck of Bonefish Bay one morning after Alea left with Roger for work at the new Gun Point clinic. He cupped the soft ball of fur in his hands and lifted her up to look more closely. She scrambling to nestle into the warm curve of his neck, whimpering and trembling. Angel would love her, he thought, as he stroked her delicate little head. Alea wouldn't mind a dog, he reasoned.

Would she?

That evening when Alea returned home, Daniel thought she looked somewhat nervous. Maybe she was just tired. He knew he felt nervous. A dog? Was he asking too much for her to care for a dog as well as a newborn? Even with his help?

"Daniel, I need to show you something," she said, standing in the doorway.

"Okay, honey, but I'd like to ask you a question."

"Hey, give me a second and then we'll talk."

She ran back outside to the front porch and brought in a covered basket. Placing it gently on the floor, she turned to Daniel and smiled.

"You go first."

He brought his hands around from behind and held out a small reddish ball of fur.

"I got us a dog."

Alea laughed and lifted the lid off the basket.
"So did I."

****

With the last of their supplies loaded, Daniel and Ronny returned to the dock where Alea and the dogs were waiting. Barefootin' and their new sailcat, Dances With Wind, were ready to go the next morning. Ronny, his son Robbie, James, and Dolores would crew Dances With Wind. Daniel, Alea, Pearl, and Rhonda would sail Barefootin' as she took the lead returning to Miracle Island. Both renovated catamarans now boasted multiple solar panels to re-charge their batteries, as well as shortwave radios.

The three walked back to Bonefish Bay together. As they arrived at the front porch, Nadia ran out in great excitement. Mr. Curry had sent a gift, she told them, in thanks for their noble efforts during the crisis.

A pair of male and female goats were tethered in the yard and Alea was surprised and pleased. The Tribe would benefit tremendously from the fresh milk and the goat cheese she knew how to make, and she could breed the animals too. It was a fantastic gift from Mr. Curry!

He had privately met with them a few days after the battle and thanked Daniel profusely for his leadership and bravery. Many people were alive because of Daniel's decisive and self-sacrificing actions, and recruitment for a full-time defensive militia was already in progress. And because of Alea's medical skills and compassion, many who might have died from illnesses or suffered needlessly from their abusive injuries were doing well. The two clinics she established, staffed by Armand, Roger, Nadia, Donald, Geoffrey, and several local nurses, were serving the medical needs of Gun

Point, Bluff, and Spanish Wells. Mr. Curry was very appreciative. It was a wonderful start!

They all wished Ben could have seen it too.

Eleuthera United was rapidly becoming more than a vision. Care Teams were contacting survivors from Lower Bogue on the north end to Bannerman Town and Cape Eleuthera in the south. The suffering population was a mere fraction of what it had once been, but hope was being restored.

Eleuthera would survive. Eleuthera would be re-built. He knew the ultimate goal of re-building all the islands of the Bahamas was not far behind.

****

The family gathered that evening to say goodbye. Friends filtered in and out, leaving small gifts and tokens of affection. Alea clung to her mother. She understood that her parents felt needed on Spanish Wells and had grown close to many people. She and Daniel would eventually come back to see them with the baby and Daniel promised Will and Mr. Curry he'd return if called upon in the future. But Miracle Island was where Alea wanted her baby born.

"Mom, a year can go by so quickly. When we come to visit next May, you'll be holding your first grandchild."

"Alea, my daughter, I am so proud of you and what you have accomplished! You are an excellent surgeon, but every one of us is adapting to a different way of life since the Flare. Your Tribe could not wish for a more loving and devoted woman to care for them. We both love you and Daniel very much and we happily leave you in his hands." Nadia began to cry. "Please radio as soon as the baby is born. I can't wait to hear if Armand and I have a grandson or a granddaughter."

After a late dinner with the family, Roger and Loreen said their final tearful farewells, and the doors of the Bonefish Bay house closed for the night.

Daniel took Alea's hand, leading her carefully up the stairs to the cozy bedroom that faced the bay. A cool salty breeze lifted the edge of the silky blue curtains and the only sound in the night was the repetitive whisper of gentle waves breaking on the beach.

They stepped outside to their private deck and dropped into the wicker chairs with a sigh, hands still tightly clutched. Alea pulled Daniel's hand over to feel the baby kicking vigorously inside her. Even in the darkness she could see the love in his expression, feel his awe and wonder.

It was time to go home.

Chapter 35 Shark Jumper

Daniel tacked Barefootin' west and away from Spanish Wells before veering south, as Dances With Wind copied his course, tailing a few hundred feet behind the lead boat. Ronny was beaming and wearing a happy grin as he stood at the helm. Robbie ran up to the bow to wave to his sister, sitting mournfully on the dive platform of Barefootin', clutching her knees to her chest, lost in thought. The twins hated being apart during the day, but Ronny felt that for the purposes of this trip, the kids would be able to pay more attention to learning about sailing and attending to their assigned chores than if they distracted each other in constant play. They had celebrated their 9th birthday two weeks earlier. Uncle Daniel, as they called him, was sure their real names should have been Rowdy and Raucous, much more fitting for the ever curious and adventurous brother and sister.

Their mother Pearl was a beautiful Portuguese-Northern Italian girl who displayed the patience of a Vatican saint when dealing with her children. Her curly black hair brushed her shoulders, with her colorful signature scarf draped artfully around her neck. Her eyes were sparkling green and her olive skin was flawless. She was almost thirty, but looked much younger, with the voluptuous bosom and slender hourglass figure of her teens undiminished.

Pearl Ferraro turned twenty-one the same day she started bartending part-time her senior year at Cambridge College, heedless of her protective father's displeasure. It was the same night she first caught Ronny Robello's attention, despite the delicate porcelain blonde hanging on his arm.

Exotically beautiful was merely the tip of iceberg to describe the real Pearl. Her feisty but good-natured humor, coupled with quiet strength, managed to charm the darkly handsome, tempestuous thrill-junky who could never stay in one place for long. He wanted her from the first moment he saw her behind the crowded bar, unceremoniously handing his bewildered blonde date over to a friend to take home and pursued the intriguing beauty from that night on. She agreed to marry him two months later.

Her Italian father ensured the courtship remained rigidly old-fashioned, but Ronny didn't care. He would wait as long as it took. He didn't discover his bride was a virgin until their wedding night. Pearl wanted to surprise him, and he'd never asked. They announced her pregnancy soon after, happy, in love, and inseparable ever since.

The twins inherited a throw-back of their mother's Northern Italian heritage, with light brown hair that streaked gold in the sun and saltwater, and pale olive skin that tanned easily. Their eyes were replicas of Pearl's brilliant green and they flashed with constant mischief and mayhem from morning until their heads protestingly dropped to the soft pillows of their beds at night.

Roberto Robello, Robbie, would regularly suggest wily and hilarious plots and practical jokes to his sister, who eagerly agreed to help inflict their innocent ploys on the unwary and unsuspecting. They were usually successful, with only a few justifiable spankings. The twins rolled in laughter as they recounted many a Joke-Gone-Well, safe from adult incursion in their homemade tent fort in the family living room.

Rhonda Robello wanted desperately to change her name. Why did her parents pick something that just didn't suit her at all? But the name Gypsy, she was sure, would be so much more romantic! Her sun-kissed waves of silky light brown hair flowed down her back, almost to her waist, and her intelligent green eyes missed nothing. As much as Rhonda adored her mother, she secretly longed to be like Alea. She wanted to wear a sharp machete and knife on a belt, dive and spear fish, swim like a mermaid. She was Ariel! She was Aquawoman! And she wanted a hot guy like Uncle Daniel by her side someday, too.

As she watched the wake of Barefootin' splitting the ocean water neatly behind the boat, Rhonda again wondered about Miracle Island and what exciting adventures might lay ahead. She was fixed and determined to change her name once they arrived. Gypsy she was and Gypsy she would be!

She bided her time. They were almost there.

****

The catamarans sailed past Lighthouse Point at the southern tip of Eleuthera by mid-afternoon. The sea was calm, and they were making good progress. As long as the winds remained favorable and his calculations were accurate, Daniel estimated a timetable of only two more full days of sailing to reach Miracle Island. Once there, he'd sail around to the east shore and find the entry cove and Hidden Pass. If it took another day or two of sailing, so be it. There was no clock on their journey and the weather was good.

The bleat of a goat turned his head. There was good reason he wanted this trip over as soon as possible. Shaded under the stern canopy, a chicken wire pen corralled the restless male and female goats, soon to inhabit their new home on Miracle Island. A tarp had been spread out on the deck, the wire pen on top, with a thick layer of dry grasses and brush to absorb waste. Mercifully, the wind was blowing from bow to stern and the pungent odor was kept somewhat in check.

A smaller but similar wire pen was nearby, the red-combed rooster and his two hens unhappily clucking and prancing in the contained space. Rhonda was put in charge of feeding the animals and cleaning the pens, a job she protested at first but now curiously seemed to be enjoying. She gave each animal a name, insisting that personal names proclaimed them as unique and special, and spent a good portion of their first day at sea petting the goats and attempting to calm the terrified chickens. The pigs were penned on Dances With Wind, with Robbie delegated to their daily care, but he was not enjoying his designated task quite as much as Rhonda.

His thoughts turned to John and his family. No contact for three months, as he and Alea had taken the only shortwave radio with them, but he smiled as he thought of the three new radios and solar panels that were stowed and ready for use. Daniel was confident in John and the boys to protect and feed their family. They had become good divers, fishermen, and skilled in the ways of the Bahamian bush. With plenty of food, water, and shelter, and with Mystic as a back-up protective haven, he was certain they were safe and sound.

He wondered about baby Angel and his thoughts turned to his own soon-to-be born child. The mystery of creating human life... at least that pleasant endeavor required no electricity! He fervently hoped Alea's delivery would go smoothly.

They anchored a few hours before sundown on the leeward side of an uninhabited island. Daniel and Ronny jumped in for a dive as the entire group gathered on Barefootin' to prepare dinner. Ronny bagged four good-sized lobster and Daniel speared the largest hogfish he'd ever caught, a lunker that weighed 20 pounds. They could conserve their cargo and live off the sea for the duration of the voyage.

He lifted the lid off the old charcoal grill, a welcome gift from Roger, and laid chunks of dry casuarina and buttonwood to fire. The hogfish fillets were sprinkled with salt and pepper, topped with slices of raw onion, and loosely wrapped in the last of the precious aluminum foil to steam and bake in their own tasty juices.

Daniel chose to lay the lobster tails directly on the hot grill with only salt and pepper as spicing, allowing the wood smoke to permeate the meat. Potatoes were laid around the sides to cook through. The meal was simple, but fresh and rich in flavors. No leftovers remained as the sun dropped out of sight and the stars took its place. Daniel shut the grill down to cool, the coals still useable for the next meal.

Bear happily devoured a hogfish fillet and was sleeping in Alea's arms, nestled on top of her warm belly. Brandy was nuzzling Robbie's neck, searching for a warm nook to curl into and go to sleep. Both puppies were too small to wander the decks unsupervised and someone always carried a pup around for safety. Each one wore a rope collar and leash that allowed them to do their urgent doggie business safely on the dive platform, which was rinsed after each mess.

Tired yawns signaled an end to the first night of the journey. They would set sail again at dawn and everyone returned to their boat for the night. Pearl and Rhonda hugged Daniel and Alea with warm affection before disappearing into the cabin they shared, and Daniel sat down for a brief respite.

Alea walked over to the siderail, holding Bear, and gazed up into the night sky. The uncountable stars that clustered the path of the Milky Way were thick and bright, a river of light with no beginning and no end. They flowed as ancient and glimmering guardians over an earth billions of years old, over the race of humans that had been born and existed in only a fraction of that unfathomable time. She was humbled as she stood beneath those stars, her hand unconsciously seeking her child. She silently breathed a prayer of no words, her soul touching and recognizing the familiar power she felt starting to surround them.

As Daniel watched her, his soul also awakened to the unseen presence enveloping them. Alea turned, as if in a dream, and sought him, her face alight with pure glowing love. All of a sudden, Daniel's heart was overwhelmed with a simple and joyful knowing that the Lord God, of great and immeasurable power, was right there with them at that very moment.

A blessing had been given, and they both understood, their spirits trusting and at peace. Tomorrow they would again be traveling, into the mystic.

But they would never be alone.

****

The next morning dawned clear and bright, with a favorable northwest wind starting to strengthen. Daniel opened his eyes and stretched, anxious to resume their journey. Alea was still asleep. He kissed her cheek softly and closed his eyes, smiling. Feeling reassured, he rolled quietly out of bed, dressed, and went out to the galley.

An enticing aroma caught his immediate attention. "Good morning, Pearl. No! Really? Is that what I think I smell?"

Pearl tossed her head of curls and laughed. She carried over a steaming pot and a cup.

"I think I remember how to brew a cup of COFFEE, Daniel, even on a charcoal grill! Ronny wanted to surprise you after we reached Miracle Island, but I think we all need this today. I know I certainly do. Ronny and your parents will probably swim over here naked when they smell it." They laughed as she poured Daniel a cup, then walked out on deck, waving the pot enticingly in the morning breeze.

Coffee was the new currency. The small amounts remaining were hoarded and only brewed for very special occasions. It was invaluable as trade. Until someone figured out how to obtain and propagate coffee bean trees, offering a pot of coffee was the most appreciated gift imaginable.

Daniel held the precious cup of hot black liquid to his nose and inhaled deeply. It was the one smell he preferred to any other, except for Alea's fragrant hair. Pearl walked back in to announce the imminent arrival of the rest of the crew and set more cups out on the table.

"Where's my coffee?"

Ronny appeared in the doorway, dripping with seawater as Pearl predicted, but thankfully dressed in his swim trunks. Robbie came in next, just as wet. A few minutes later, James and Dolores arrived, dry from the row over to Barefootin'. Alea and Rhonda emerged from her cabin, arm in arm, to join the smiling group. Of all the things not to have anymore, Rhonda thought, I miss soft drinks the most. She disliked coffee but accepted half a cup to wake up.

Bear and Brandy waddled freely around the room, greeting legs or hands with cold wet noses and the swipe of a warm tongue. These people were their pack and each one must be properly identified and marked. This attention often resulted in the offer of food as well. It was good to be a dog!

"Alright, Captain D, what's our plan for today?" James asked his son as they entered the lounge. Dolores gave Daniel a hug and a mom-kiss on the top of his head before filling cups for herself and James.

"Morning, Dad! Love you, Mom! Well, we need to get going as soon as we eat. Got a full day's sail ahead before we pick an anchorage for tonight. We keep going south and east and I'll figure it out as we go. The island is southwest of San Salvador. I re-checked our position with the sextant last night and will again tonight. We're basically on course."

The day was uneventful, and they made excellent headway. A brisk wind continued to blow from the northwest, allowing Daniel to maintain a direct southeast course without needing to tack. Both boats sped over the water and by late afternoon he spotted a shallow, barely exposed island where they could anchor for the night. Daniel was glad to see the island was more rock than sand. This usually guaranteed lobster, and he enjoyed searching rock crevices and holes for grouper. There were still several hours of daylight, perfect for he and Ronny to spear some dinner.

Barefootin' and Dances with Wind double-anchored side by side. Both crews again gathered on Barefootin' to prepare the evening meal, settle the fretful farm animals, and wait for whatever feast the men brought up from the ocean. It was always exciting to see the divers swim to the boat and reveal their catch to the waiting crowd.

Daniel dropped off the dive platform, with Ronny following right behind. It was best to hunt with a trusted partner in unknown waters. They would watch each other's back and be ready to add a second spear, if needed, to land a difficult fish.

Alea sat on the stern deck in a comfortable chair with Bear and Brandy on their rope leashes. She wanted to help, but with her large belly in the way, she asked Rhonda to keep her company and to assist the divers. As soon as Daniel or Ronny began heading back to the boat, Rhonda jumped down to the platform with a 5-gallon bucket and held it firmly near the water. Using the bucket edge to hold the captive in place, the spear was yanked out, and the diver was then free to resume the hunt.

The sun was touching the horizon as Ronny brought in his final catch and climbed up the ladder, having speared six lobster and a grouper. The grouper had bled copiously from a hit near the gills and he tried to hold the spear tip up and out of the water as quickly as possible before returning to the boat. Blood in the water was never good.

Daniel was tiring, but the dive site was unusually beautiful. The coral reefs were spectacular and untouched, with hazy clouds of small baitfish, large black and yellow striped Sargent Majors, and Blue Tangs. He speared a good-sized hogfish on a grassy flat and a mutton-snapper near a rock pillar. He was dogged constantly by a sinister barracuda at least six feet long, the sharp-toothed predator never approaching him closer than twenty feet. But Daniel was always alert and brought his catch up into the air as fast as he could. Barracuda in an unfished area like this were unpredictable and not used to divers. His body size and spear had been enough to keep the creature wary.

Daniel was swimming back to the boat and Alea saw a large grouper struggling at the top of his spear. She stood up and walked to the stern above the dive platform, holding a hand over her eyes to block the blinding sun. Rhonda was in place, waiting for his arrival with her fish bucket. He was fifteen feet away from the boat.

She stopped breathing, the leashes falling from her hand.

"SHARK!" she screamed. Her heart sank. There was no way he could hear her. The ominous dark shape had slowly risen from below and was moving towards Daniel's fins. The beast appeared to be about ten feet long, an aggressive bull shark, tail swishing side to side in a leisurely and confident manner, as the shark zeroed in on its anticipated meal.

Rhonda startled and fell backwards, the bucket dropping. The splash drew Daniel's attention as he reached the platform and raised his head out of the water. He yanked off his mask and was met with Alea's stricken face and the fear in Rhonda's eyes. He quickly guessed the reason and spun around.

Alea heard a commotion behind her as the lounge door burst open and the four adults frantically piled out. She was frozen in place, her worst nightmare about to be realized. A moving flash out of the corner of her eye released her from her inertia and she turned her head.

"Aaaayaaaaaaaaah!"

With a running leap, Robbie cannonballed off the stern and flew into the air, his little body in a tight tuck, landing like a bomb exploding on the back of the shark's head. The stunned shark was hammered hard, abruptly stopping the attack and dropping deeper underwater as Robbie rolled off to one side. The creature shook its head angrily, then veered off and swam away from the unexpected assault.

Daniel pushed the hogfish off his spear and grabbed Robbie by the arm, protectively pulling him close into his body. They were both still in the water, hanging on to the ladder, when another cry rang out.

"It's coming back!" Alea dropped to her knees in horror as Ronny rushed past her with his own spear and jumped down to the dive platform. He was not fast enough.

With a tremendous heave, Daniel threw Robbie up onto the boat and turned, spear ready. The bull shark was agitated and moving in fast, straight at Daniel. He held the spear tight in both hands and waited.

The shark rushed in, jaws open to bite, with razor-like teeth gleaming. Daniel saw his only opportunity and re-positioned quickly. His spear thrust into a rolling eye, blood spurting out into the water, the forward momentum of the shark sealing its own doom. The beast began to thrash wildly and dove down, taking the spear with it, still impaled.

The attack was over in seconds.

****

"I really liked that spear," Daniel joked. He was sitting on a couch in the lounge, wrapped in a blanket, a cup of hot tea in his hand. He could not convince Alea he was uninjured. She refused to release him; his arm, his hand, his leg, wrapping herself around him and not letting go. He hoped this would continue after the baby was born.

Both families crowded around him, finding a place to sit on the floor or chairs near Daniel. They finally finished plates of lobster and fish. Dinner had been much later than usual, but after what happened, they simply wanted to be together, relieved beyond measure that Robbie and Daniel were safe and unharmed.

"Did I hear something about your spear?" Ronny walked in from the stern deck with his arms behind his back and stood proudly. "Could it be this spear?" He swung one arm in front, holding a familiar long slender pole.

Daniel's mouth dropped open. "What the...? How did you get that back? Last time I saw it, the shark was swimming off into the sunset, my spear sticking out of its eye."

"Hey man, guess what bumped into the hull ten minutes ago, dead as a doornail? Well, most of it, anyway. I just took back what was yours."

Daniel removed the blanket from his shoulders and gently disentangled himself from Alea's arms. Standing up, he shook Ronny's hand. "Well, I did save your son."

"Come on, Uncle Daniel, I think it was me who saved you!" Robbie leaped up from the floor, hands on his hips, and glared playfully at Daniel.

No one disagreed. Especially not Daniel. The boy had risked his own life tremendously by performing the now legendary cannonball that threw the shark off its initial attack. If Robbie hadn't reacted so quickly with his extremely unique, from-the-gut diversionary maneuver, Daniel probably would have been killed or seriously maimed. The boy demonstrated courageous responses and self-sacrificing instincts and showed no fear.

Life on Miracle Island was about to become very interesting.

Robbie had already been the recipient of unending hugs and kisses from Alea, proud pats on the back from his father and James and fended-off repeated expressions of affection and pride from his sister and Dolores. His mother, after her initial fury at his reckless action, broke down in tears and held him until she recovered. Extra portions of lobster somehow found their way onto his plate as well.

"Yes, oh Great Shark Jumper! We honor you," Daniel teased.

Then, in a serious tone, he extended his hand. "Thank-you, son. You saved my life. Alea and I will never forget that." He lifted the boy and held him close. "I love you, Robbie."

Robbie looked at the man he admired as much as he did his father. "I love you too, Uncle Daniel."

The day had been too much, even for Robbie. He threw his arms around Daniel's neck and sobbed.

He was still just a nine-year old boy.

Chapter 36   Finally Home

Daniel raised the binoculars and scanned the turquoise-blue waters to the east. It was the fourth day of their journey and they'd been sailing since dawn. The sun was now high in the sky overhead and he was pushing to keep going with no more stops. He wanted to get Alea home.

After tossing and turning all night, she commented about a severe ache in her low back. After breakfast, she returned to the cabin, quiet and drawn. Daniel was worried. The shock of the bull shark attack had worn her out both emotionally and physically. She was more than eight months pregnant and he wanted her in familiar surroundings and feeling safe. If only John was available to consult. Daniel knew next to nothing about pregnant women. He checked on her frequently, letting Rhonda take the wheel when he did.

Rhonda's face lit with excitement each time he invited her to take the helm. In her mind she became a pirate queen, sailing the Seven Seas, searching for buried treasure. Her hair blew back wildly in the wind and she tied one of her mother's colorful scarves around her forehead to keep the tawny mass out of her eyes. If only I were grown-up, she bemoaned, I'd have me own ship! I am Gypsy. The Gypsy Queen!

Gypsy raised the binoculars to search the Caribbean waters for ships bearing precious cargo, for flags bearing the pirate skull and crossbones to appear on the horizon, for drawn swords flashing sunlight off gleaming metal blades! What Gypsy did see made her eyes grow wide.

"Uncle Daniel, Uncle Daniel, I see an island!" Her excited cry brought Daniel and Pearl racing to the helm. He slammed the binoculars up and focused.

"It's Miracle Island! Thank God we're almost home!" Pulling Rhonda over, he happily kissed her blushing cheek.

The three of them hugged and Pearl raced inside to radio the exciting news to Ronny. Moments later, James, Dolores, and Robbie appeared on the deck of Dances With Wind, arms waving and pointing at the approaching island. Passing the helm over to Rhonda, Daniel went to the cabin where Alea lay sleeping to tell her they were home. She drowsily woke up long enough to smile weakly at his news and fell back to sleep.

It took another hour to approach the west shore. Ronny kept his boat in close tandem with Daniel as the wind cooperated, speeding them towards their goal. They rounded the southern tip of the island and turned north along the rougher Atlantic side. Daniel was watching for Hidden Pass. Memories of the first time he drifted this route with Alea hit him hard and he searched the sky for his favorite osprey. The welcoming and widespread wings of the soaring bird would certainly tell him when they were near the pass.

The current was again helping to sweep the boats along the cliff. Daniel searched the rock formations ahead for familiar dive spots and after some time, the buoy appeared, bobbing up and down with the ocean swell. Daniel closed his eyes in thanks and instructed Pearl to radio Ronny to tie his boat to the buoy and wait.

Daniel was taking Barefootin' straight into Osprey Bay.

****

He reefed the sail of the catamaran and turned into Hidden Pass, expertly and confidently guiding Barefootin' through the channel until it emerged into Osprey Bay, sunlight streaming down on the sparkling turquoise-blue water.

Pearl and Rhonda stood at the bow, transfixed by the beauty that bombarded them on every side. This was now home. They were amazed by the protective bank of rock cliffs, the long arc of golden sandy beach, the casuarina tree groves waving in the soft breeze, and the clean white lines of Into The Mystic lazily rolling on the calm bay waters. Pearl put her arm around her daughter's shoulders. This was not what she had planned for her children, but in this uncertain and angry world she could sense how right this place was for her family.

She saw a tender pulled up on the sand near a cove indenting the beach. Suddenly, a small group of people ran out from the trees and began to wave and shout.

"Daniel, is that John and his family?" Pearl asked.

"Yes, those are the folks I told you about; Dr. John Garner, Josey, their sons Noah and Sam, and baby daughter Angel." Daniel beamed with relief and happiness. "I know everyone will get along great, Pearl. You'll love them as much as we do."

Daniel and Pearl glanced about, searching for Rhonda, but she was nowhere in sight. Pearl was turning to find her when the lounge door opened, and Rhonda stepped out. Her sandy hair was tied in a ponytail that hung to the small of her back, with a long colorful scarf wrapped around her forehead, the ends whipping in the breeze. She marched over to her mother and Daniel and lasered them with her gaze, hands on her hips and feet firmly planted.

"I am now an island girl, and my name is Gypsy."

****

The entire Garner clan packed into the tender and sped out to Barefootin', scrambling aboard in a tumble of bodies and excited cries of greeting. Daniel, John, and the boys hugged and slapped each other on the back.

330

"John, man, good to see you! Alea and I thought about you guys every day. You know we didn't plan on being away this long and I'm really sorry. But wait 'til you hear why!"

"I did start to get a bit concerned after one month. Without Barefootin' we'd really be marooned here. Not that Noah and Sam would mind, of course. But Josey kept telling me not to worry. And we did fine! Got some new things to show you that the boys and I worked on."

"I talked about bringing our families and some friends back with us but not everyone was ready to leave Spanish Wells. Let me start the introductions with our brave new settlers." Daniel motioned for Pearl to come over and put his arm around her shoulders.

"This is my friend Ronny's wife, Pearl Robello. Pearl, this is Dr. John Garner and his lovely wife Josey. The beautiful little girl in her arms is their daughter Angel. This tall young man is Noah and this rascal here is Sam."

Pearl extended her hand to shake but Josey pulled her in for a warm hug. "No formalities on this island, Pearl. Welcome to our Tribe!" With that, everyone moved in close to greet and welcome Pearl, awed by her exotic dark beauty and piercing green eyes.

Daniel knew there was one more new face to introduce. He spotted her standing off to one side, trying not to stare at Noah and Sam. Daniel walked over, took her hand firmly in his own, and brought her over to the group.

"I'd like you all to meet Pearl and Ronny's daughter, Gypsy."

****

"Where's Alea?" Josey asked.

"She's still asleep in the cabin, Josey, since last night. She hasn't been feeling well and I don't want to wake her up until

I've brought in Dances With Wind. Yes, we brought a second catamaran! They're tied up at the buoy and I need to get them into the bay."

"Is there anything I can do, Daniel? She's over eight months pregnant. What are her symptoms?" John queried. He would never forget Josey's difficult birth and how he almost lost both her and Angel.

"Low energy and back pain. She's been through a lot in the last few months, believe me. Once I get Dances With Wind in here, I'll wake her up to see everyone and you can examine her." He turned to the others. "Do you mind staying here while John and I take the tender?"

While the group noisily settled in to get better acquainted, Daniel and John motored out through Hidden Pass, where Dances With Wind was tied up at the buoy. Daniel decided to use the tender to pull the catamaran into Osprey Bay. The rising tide would help push the boat through the channel and he climbed onboard to tell Ronny his plan.

With the sea-tow gear bridled, John detached from the buoy. The tandem ropes gradually tightened, and the boat began to move forward as Daniel slowly ran the tender into Hidden Pass. With Ronny at the wheel, his parents and Robbie stood at various locations on deck with poles to repel the hull away from the sharp rock cliffs.

Dances With Wind glided through the narrow channel with no hull damage and emerged into the sunny bay. The crew was stunned. What an island! Robbie's jaw dropped. Ronny was rendered speechless. Each one wondered what life would be like, living in a beautiful place like this. James and Dolores smiled at each other and held hands tightly. They realized they would call this home for the rest of their days, content that their twilight years would be spent with their only son Daniel and with Alea.

After anchoring close to the other boats, they jumped in the tender and ran over to Barefootin', where an animated group was immersed in conversation. Ronny stepped into the noisy lounge unnoticed, with Robbie at his side.

"Hey, guys, I'm Ronny Robello and this is my son Roberto."

Robbie glanced up at his father, frowning. "Dad, it's, uh, Robbie?"

Ronny grinned sheepishly and chuckled. "Oops, I meant to say my son... Robbie." Everyone laughed and shook hands, but neither escaped a warm hug from Josey.

Daniel introduced his parents and more warm hugs ensued. His mother gravitated immediately to Angel and asked Josey's permission to hold her. Within minutes, the ladies were deep in discussion about diapers, diarrhea, and formula. With the introductions made, they settled down to cook a meal, the first to be shared together as a growing Tribe. The afternoon was off to a good start.

Robbie, Noah, and Sam were already thick as thieves by the time dinner was ready, with ideas, plots, and adventures to pursue together. Gypsy hovered near her mother, feeling lonely and left out. Her brother had found new friends and seemed to have forgotten all about her. But she watched and studied them. She would know the right time to reveal the Gypsy Queen. Besides, Noah was cute, and she was feeling uncharacteristically shy.

Bear and Brandy ran from person to person, dashing about the lounge in excitement, tails wagging, noses in action. More members of the pack! A delighted Noah and Sam could not stop playing with Bear, a spirited tug-of-war with a dish towel taking center stage. Brandy was lifted to Josey's lap, where the sweet little pup and Angel beheld each other for the first time. Angel squealed with joy as soon as her hand touched Brandy's soft red fur and tugged on the puppy's ears and tail. Patiently accepting her playful invasion, Brandy sniffed her nose, licked her chubby cheek, and snuggled close. They were fast friends from that moment on.

Daniel stood watching his people laughing and talking. He was exhausted from his efforts to bring the boats to safety, but he was satisfied. They were finally home! Perhaps it was time to awaken Alea to share these special moments. She'd been sleeping soundly all day and he hoped the rest would do her good. She must be hungry, too.

Her cabin door swung open abruptly and Alea stumbled out, gripping her swollen belly with one hand and supporting herself on the doorframe with the other. Her face was ashen, and she panted for air. She did not even notice the crowd of shocked faces in the lounge.

"Daniel, my water just broke. The baby is coming early." She slipped down to the floor before he could reach her.

"Take me to Mystic."

Chapter 37　　The Power of Love

Daniel carefully laid Alea on the big bed in Mystic's master cabin as John and Josey prepared her for what John believed might be a very long birth. This was Alea's first child and he knew the odds were high this baby would be taking its time.

Ronny ferried the rest of the Tribe over to Mystic, where they gathered in the lounge to re-group. Pearl took charge of Angel, who did not complain when her mother passed her over. She intently studied the kind face holding her, then settled down contentedly against Pearl's warm bosom for a nap. James set-up one of the boxed shortwave radios on a corner table and connected it to the lower helm battery. Dolores prepared a buffet table of fruits, bread, nuts, and juices for anyone who was hungry, and Noah and Sam settled down on a couch with a plate of food. The Tribe would wait all night, if need be, for news of Alea and the baby.

****

"What do you mean your name is Gypsy?" Robbie rolled his eyes, challenging his sister when she pulled him away to talk in the galley. It was silly. Girls were silly.

"I want Gypsy to be my name here. You know I never liked the name Rhonda. I don't ever want to hear it again. Please, Robbie? Please?"

Her brother considered her carefully. He sort of understood. He too was feeling strongly that coming to this island was the beginning of something extraordinary and life-changing for everyone. He was chaffing at the bit to start exploring and thought Noah and Sam were awesome. Robbie couldn't wait to see the cave they found. Hadn't even told their parents yet. And big enough to drive a truck inside!

"Okay... Gypsy. Let's go eat. Hey, wait 'til you hear about the cave!" He roughed up the stray curls on top of her head and grinned. He loved his sister, but he could never tell her that. It just wasn't cool.

****

The pain was unlike anything Alea had ever experienced. Knife-like agonizing contractions that gradually backed off, only to grip and bite again, over and over. Josey was holding one hand tightly, murmuring words of encouragement as Daniel held her other hand, his facial expression strong and comforting until uncontrolled flashes of bewilderment and anxiety betrayed his real feelings. John was monitoring the baby's progress, checking periodically for its position, timing the contractions, and taking her vital signs.

Alea had no clue how ancient women could even conceive of squatting between two rocks to give birth, letting gravity help push the baby into the world. She longed for a clean white hospital bed and pain meds, lots of pain meds. But if this is what she needed to go through to bring their baby into the world, she would endure anything to make that happen. Even squatting between rocks. A contraction clutched her abdomen and there was nothing she could do to stop herself.

Her scream made Daniel's jaw clench down hard. It was going to be a tough night.

****

All activity in the lounge stopped cold as Alea's muffled scream echoed off the walls. James held his wife as they sat helplessly on the couch, recalling when Dolores gave birth to Daniel and her own painful labor. She prayed quietly, to the only One able to help her daughter-in-law in her ordeal.

****

Ronny sat down next to his wife, who was gently rocking a peacefully sleeping Angel. He suffered for his best friend, who had been through such hurtful agony in his first marriage. Alea was his dream, lovingly resurrecting Daniel in every way. Even though Ronny knew that childbirth was no picnic, he looked at his own two children who were alive and well. Women had given birth like this since the beginning of time. Alea would too, right? He pulled Pearl closer and kissed her tenderly.

****

Robbie pulled his sister over to Noah and Sam when they left the galley. "Hey guys, tell Gypsy about the cave you found!"

Noah looked at Gypsy, then over to Sam, whose mouth was twisted with doubts. "Is she cool, Robbie? She won't blab?"

"No way, she'd never do that. And she can probably outrun, outswim, and outclimb both you guys."

"I'm standing right here, lamebrains! You got something to say, say it to me!" Gypsy shouldered past her brother to face Noah and glared. A surprised smile curled Noah's lips and he stepped back, as he took in her wild streaked brown hair and flashing green eyes.

"Okay, Gypsy, I'll tell you about the cave. But if I do, you got to promise not to say a word. We're working on something big, something that'll help a lot in a hurricane. It's not ready, but if you want, you can work with us too."

Gypsy gave Noah a wide grin. His heart seemed to stop for several beats. And he knew he was lost.

****

The night sky was filled with stars and the roar of the ocean echoed over the cliff into the bay. Other than the deep rumble of crashing waves, silence covered Mystic like a blanket.

Alea was drenched in sweat and breathing in shallow gasps. She fell asleep briefly and Josey was glad to see it. She gently wiped her face with a cool wet towel and Daniel fanned her with a piece of cardboard. It was after midnight and John was asleep, sprawled in a chair across the room.

Josey chose to remain awake at Alea's side. She remembered very little of the difficult birth of Angel. But what she would never forget for the rest of her life was the powerful summons that had pulled her back, that had spoken to her soul in a voice she still heard in her dreams. It was a voice of incredible love, reassuring her of the final joy to come someday, but also of the many joys yet to be. She felt that joy and love overflow when she first saw her baby daughter, and she so wanted the same for her friend.

Daniel refused to release Alea's hand and remained with her constantly. He hadn't slept since dawn the previous day, but it didn't matter. He was determined to birth this baby right along with her. His child. Created by his spirit joining with the essence of Alea to bring forth another human being. It was a mysterious wonder and he honored his woman, all women, who endured such terrible pain to bring forth life. He couldn't wait to meet this young and innocent soul destined to enter a world so different from the one both parents had grown up knowing. Daniel committed himself once again to ensuring that every life that had joined them in building a better world on Miracle Island would never suffer harm. He dropped his head to Alea's hand and prayed.

****

Gypsy was the first to succumb, falling asleep on the floor with pillows and a blanket, both puppies curled around her. Ronny made sure she was tucked in and comfortable before returning to Pearl and Angel.

James and Dolores finally headed to their cabin, exhausted and no longer able to stay awake. They suggested that Ronny and Pearl get some rest too, but they both decided to stay in the lounge, in case they were needed.

The three boys were still wide awake, thrilled to be up past midnight and taking full advantage of the many board games stocked on Mystic. With a bowl of fresh fruit and a loaf of cassava bread, they saw no need to interrupt a perfectly good night of gaming with sleep.

A loud splash suddenly sounded outside the open windows of the lounge. The boys leaped up.

"What was that?" Robbie yelled.

"Robbie, pipe down!" Ronny exclaimed. "People are trying to sleep."

"Sorry Dad. But can we go outside to look?" Robbie pleaded. Sam and Noah stood quietly, waiting politely for Ronny's permission. Looking at their expectant faces, he couldn't say no. He was also curious and grabbed a flashlight.

"What the heck, guys, let's go!" He held the door open with a grin and the boys raced out to the deck. Ronny walked along the rail, shining the light into the water, the boys following close behind. The splash sounded again, right where they were standing, and Ronny quickly aimed the flashlight down.

"Oh wow, check this out!" Noah exclaimed.

Three reef sharks were tearing into a school of medium-size mullet off the starboard side of the boat. Blood and bits of fish floated on the water, the backs of the sharks rising and hitting the surface as they slashed and bit.

Sammy jumped up on the rail and hung over the top for a better view, causing Ronny to grab the boy's shirt. Not a good time to go swimming. The three boys gaped with mouths open as the water swirled and splashed, frantic mullet jumping to avoid hungry jaws. They watched, mesmerized, until the school of fish and the sharks moved away, the water gradually smoothing out as the feeding frenzy ended.

"That was the coolest ever!" Sam exclaimed.

Ronny chuckled and herded the thrilled boys back towards the lounge, giving Robbie a knowing wink.

"Well, I guess it's time to tell you guys the story of "Shark Jumper.""

****

The eastern sky was still dark when Alea startled awake. Where am I? she questioned, confused and foggy. Turning her head, she could see Daniel was asleep, kneeling on the floor next to the bed, his head laying on their clasped hands. Josey was curled up in a chair behind him, her eyes closed.

Alea was parched. She needed water desperately but was too weak to speak. She tried to move her numbed hand out from under Daniel's head; her arms felt leaden. She lifted her head slightly; it fell back heavily on the pillow. But she could see her abdomen remained swollen. My baby! Still not born! A sharp contraction began to build, and her face twisted in pain, but all she could do was moan. Daniel's head popped up and he saw she was awake.

"Alea, my darling! What can I do, what do you need?"

"Water," she said weakly. He immediately raised a bottle to her lips and carefully held up her head. As she drank, her fogged mind began to clear rapidly.

"How long?"

"It's been almost twelve hours."

"You need to get me up."

"Oh, sweetheart, let me have John check you over first." He walked over to the chair where John was sleeping and shook his shoulder. He popped awake and rubbed his eyes.

"She wants to get up, John. I don't know..."

"Let me get her blood pressure and we'll see. Often, the mother instinctively knows what she needs to do." He greeted Alea gently, applied the cuff, and inflated.

"She's a bit low, but not too bad, Daniel." He turned back to her. "You want to get up, dear? Why?"

"I need to do this the old-fashioned way, John. Can you put two heavy chairs together? I'm going to kneel between them and let gravity help me."

John and Daniel looked at each other, and John nodded.

"Let's try it your way, little mother."

****

Ronny awoke with a start and sat straight up on the couch. Was I dreaming? But he heard the sharp crackle again. The radio? Was someone signaling on the shortwave? Yep, sure enough. Who was this, in the middle of the night? He walked over and picked up the handset.

****

"Push, Alea, push!"

Daniel stood behind her, supporting under her arms, with Alea's elbows resting on the seats of the chairs as she lowered

341

herself between them. She wore nothing but an old white t-shirt of Daniel's, her hair piled haphazardly on top of her head and tied with a ribbon. Daniel thought she had never looked so beautiful. Josey laid a pile of towels on the floor to protect the baby, and John positioned himself in front as coach and doctor, ready to assist.

"Aaaaaaaaaah!" she screamed, as the contractions began to pace closer together. "Aaaaaaaaaah!"

"You're doing great, Alea!" John encouraged. "I can see the crown! It won't be much longer. Push, dear, push!"

Daniel suffered with every contraction, each stab of pain. He was in awe of his wife and had never felt so much love.

John's hands suddenly dove down beneath her. "Good! Good! Alea, your baby is coming!"

****

Ronny woke up Pearl immediately, then raced to the guest cabin to get James and Dolores. He anxiously paced until they were all gathered in the lounge.

"Jim, you won't believe this! Will just radioed from Spanish Wells." He stopped to take a deep breath.

"Matt is alive! He's in Boston. And he said it's hell on earth."

****

Alea was spent. After Josey washed her, Daniel lifted her in his arms, carried her to the cleaned bed, and laid her down. Stretching out alongside, he enfolded her gently in his arms. They lay face to face, Daniel's eyes shining with love. She was exhausted but kissed his cheek tenderly. He dropped his head and wept, tears of relief streaking his stubbled cheeks.

"Where is our baby?" she softly whispered.

Josey walked over to the bed with a blanket in her arms and laid the tiny bundle on Alea's bosom. Daniel looked at her first and she smiled. He reached over and unfolded the blanket.

****

Alea's cries of pain no longer echoed in the lounge. Everyone was wide awake and awaiting news. Was Alea alright? Was the baby born? What was happening?

It seemed an eternity, but the cabin door finally opened, and Daniel emerged, carrying a small bundle carefully in his arms. The Tribe crowded close around him to catch a first glimpse of their newest member, so far unknown.

Daniel surveyed the faces of his people, the family he would love and protect for the rest of his life. They were his Tribe, and the power of the love they shared would sustain them, nurture them, heal them, and protect them no matter what the future might bring.

But Daniel also knew in his heart and soul there was another love, an unimaginable Power of Love and Hope surrounding them again, at that very moment, a Power that would never leave them.

A tiny hand emerged from the protection of the blanket and grasped Daniel's little finger. He smiled with tender pride as a pale wrinkled face with a tuft of dark brown hair appeared.

"I'd like to introduce all of you to my firstborn son."

"Adam Benjamin Devereaux."

Outside the cabin window, a plaintive cry rang out. Startled, they turned towards the sound. Although the night sky was still dark, the osprey was perched on the rail of Mystic, staring intently into the cabin. The bird tilted its head questioningly, as piercing black eyes held Daniel's gaze.

Daniel nodded, lifting his newborn son for the bird to see.

The osprey screeched joyously, majestic wings of white and grey spreading wide, and as it lifted to the stars, Daniel was sure he saw a wing dip in greeting.

Amal Guevin

"For I know the plans I have for you," declares The Lord. "Plans to prosper you and not to harm you. Plans to give you a future and a hope."

Jeremiah 29:11

Acknowledgements

It would be simple to list the names of the people who contributed helpful insights, tireless beta reading, and a shoulder to cry on as your book progressed. But you already know who you are, and you have my heartfelt thanks for your help and support!

It's not quite as simple to describe how writing this book was very personal for me, the story revealing itself day by day, with a gentle nudge at the appointed time by God to put it all to paper. When the Lord is your co-author, you cannot refuse. Thank-you, Lord Jesus, for your inspiration and guidance!

I've been enjoying the Bahamas and the Caribbean since 1980, and with my fish/dive/boat/surfing husband Dennis since 1995. Many of the situations in the book are based on actual experiences in our lives, the events enhanced or altered, of course, to create a fictional story for your enjoyment.

Watch for the sequel coming out in 2021! Daniel, Alea, Adam, and the Tribe's adventure will continue!

To my wonderful readers...

Your opinion matters to me! Please consider leaving your review on Amazon. It would be greatly appreciated, and I'd love to answer any questions you may have on my Facebook site as well.

Direct link for review: https://www.amazon.com/dp/1077047029
Scroll down to Customer Reviews. Forward arrow to Write A Review option

The Power of Love can change the world, one heart at a time!

Amal Guevin

About The Author

Born in Chicago, Amal Guevin dreamt of writing a book for many years while
working as a physiotherapist. She and her husband Dennis have traveled the
Bahamas and the Caribbean for 25 years, diving, surfing, fishing, and boating.
Now a full-time author, Into The Mystic is her first novel.
Facebook.com/Amal Guevin

Amal Guevin

Made in the USA
Middletown, DE
09 July 2020